'An... ... supposed to go... ... ...ed heatedly, her temper rising. 'It takes time to relocate.'

'You'll have at least a month to find somewhere else.' Cristo fielded her questions without perceptible sympathy while he watched the breeze push the soft clinging cotton of her top against her breasts. He clenched his teeth together, willing back his arousal.

'That's not very long. Five children take up a lot of space…they're your brothers and sisters too, so you should *care* about what happens to them!' Belle launched back at him in furious condemnation.

'Which is why I'm here to suggest that we get married and *make* a home for them together,' Cristo countered.

'*Married?*' Belle repeated, aghast, wondering if she'd missed a line or two in the conversation. 'What on earth are you talking about?'

'You said that you wanted your siblings to enjoy the Ravelli name and lifestyle. I can only make that happen by marrying you and adopting them.'

A stray shard of sunlight broke through the clouds to slant across his lean, strong face. All over again Belle studied him in .... he had the smoulderin... ... ... angel. His brilliant ... ... f stunning below the ... ... suddenly she felt bre...

THE LEGACIES OF POWERFUL MEN

*Three tenets to live by:
money, power and the ruthless pursuit of passion!*

Cristo Ravelli, Nik Christakis and Zarif Al Rastani
know better than most the double-edged sword of their
inheritance. Watching their father move from one wife
to another, leaving their mothers devastated
in his wake, has hardened each of these men
against the lure of love.

But, despite their best efforts to live by the principles
of money, power and passion, they find themselves
entangled with three women who challenge the one
thing they've protected all these years…

Their hearts!

Read Cristo's story in:
RAVELLI'S DEFIANT BRIDE
June 2014

Read Nik's story in:
CHRISTAKIS'S REBELLIOUS WIFE
July 2014

Read Zarif's story in:
ZARIF'S CONVENIENT QUEEN
August 2014

RAVELLI'S
DEFIANT BRIDE

BY
LYNNE GRAHAM

Published in Great Britain 2014
by Mills & Boon, an imprint of Harlequin (UK) Limited,
Eton House, 18-24 Paradise Road, Richmond, Surrey, TW9 1SR

© 2014 Lynne Graham

ISBN: 978 0 263 246469

ROM
Pbk

Harlequin (UK) Limited's policy is to use papers tha
renewable and recyclable products and made from w
sustainable forests. The logging and manufacturing p
to the legal environmental regulations of the country of origin.

Printed and bound in Spain
by Blackprint CPI, Barcelona

Lynne Graham was born in Northern Ireland and has been a keen Mills & Boon® reader since her teens. She is very happily married, with an understanding husband who has learned to cook since she started to write! Her five children keep her on her toes. She has a very large dog, which knocks everything over, a very small terrier, which barks a lot, and two cats. When time allows, Lynne is a keen gardener.

Recent titles by the same author:

THE DIMITRAKOS PROPOSITION
CHALLENGING DANTE *(A Bride for a Billionaire)*
THE BILLIONAIRE'S TROPHY
  (A Bride for a Billionaire)
THE SHEIKH'S PRIZE *(A Bride for a Billionaire)*

For Michael and thirty-five happy years.

CHAPTER ONE

CRISTO RAVELLI SURVEYED the family lawyer in disbelief. 'Is this an April fool joke falling out of season?' he enquired with a frown.

Robert Ludlow, senior partner of Ludlow and Ludlow, did not react with amusement. Cristo, a leading investment banker specialising in venture capital, and richer than Croesus, was not a man to be teased. Indeed, if he had a sense of humour Robert had yet to see it. Cristo, unlike his late and most probably unlamented father, Gaetano Ravelli, took life very seriously.

'I'm afraid it's not a joke,' Robert confirmed. 'Your father had five children with a woman in Ireland—'

Cristo was stunned by the concept. 'You mean, all those years he went on his fishing trips to his Irish estate—?'

'I'm afraid so. I believe the eldest child is fifteen years old—'

'*Fifteen?* But that means…' Cristo compressed his wide sensual mouth, dark eyes flaring with anger, before he could make an indiscreet comment unsuited to the ears of anyone but his brothers. He wondered why he was even surprised by yet another revelation of his father's notorious womanising. After all, throughout his irresponsible life Gaetano had left a trail of distraught and angry ex-wives and three legitimate sons in his wake, so why shouldn't there have been a less regular relationship also embellished with children?

Cristo, of course, could not answer that question because he would never ever have risked having an illegitimate child and was shaken that his father could have done so five times over. Particularly when he had never bothered to take the slightest interest in the sons he already had. Cristo's adult brothers, Nik and Zarif, would be equally astonished and appalled, but Cristo knew that the problem would fall heaviest on his own shoulders. Nik's marriage breakdown had hit him hard and his own part in that debacle still gave Cristo sleepless nights. As for their youngest sibling, as the new ruler of a country in the Middle East Zarif scarcely deserved the huge public scandal that Gaetano's immoral doings could unleash if the easily shocked media there got hold of the story.

'Fifteen years old,' Cristo mused, reflecting that Zarif's mother had evidently been betrayed throughout her entire marriage to his father without even being aware of the fact. That was not a reality that Zarif would want put out on public parade. 'I apologise for my reaction, Robert. This development comes as a considerable shock. The mother of the children—what do you know about her?'

Robert raised a greying brow. 'I contacted Daniel Petrie, the land agent of the Irish estate, and made enquiries. He said that as far as the village is concerned the woman, Mary Brophy, has long been seen as something of a disgrace and an embarrassment,' he framed almost apologetically.

'But if she was the local whore she would've been right down Gaetano's street,' Cristo breathed before he could bite back that injudicious opinion, his lean, darkly handsome face grim, but it was no secret to Gaetano's family that he had infinitely preferred bold and promiscuous women to clean-living ones. 'What provision did my father make for this horde of children?'

'That's why I decided to finally bring this matter to your attention.' Robert cleared his throat awkwardly. 'As you will be aware, Gaetano made no mention of either the woman or the children in his will.'

'Are you telling me that my father made *no* provision for these dependants?' Cristo prompted incredulously. 'He had five children with this…this woman over the course of many years and yet he settled no money on them?'

'Not so much as a penny piece on any of them… *ever*,' Robert confirmed uncomfortably. 'I thought he might have made some private arrangement to take care of them but apparently not as I have received an enquiry concerning school fees from the woman. As you know, your father always thought in terms of the present, not the future, and I imagine he assumed that he would be alive well into his eighties.'

'Instead of which he died at sixty-two years old, as foolish as ever, and tipped this mess into *my* lap,' Cristo ground out, losing all patience the more he learned of the situation. 'I'll have to look into this matter personally. I don't want the newspapers getting hold of the story—'

'Naturally not,' Robert agreed. 'It's a given that
the media enjoy telling tales about men with multiple
wives and mistresses.'

Well aware of that fact, Cristo clenched his even
white teeth, dark eyes flaming pure gold with rage at
the prospect. His father had been enough of an embarrassment while alive. He was infuriated by the idea
that Gaetano might prove even more of an embarrassment after his death.

'It will be my hope that the children can be put up
for adoption and this whole distasteful business quietly buried,' Cristo confided smooth as glass.

For some reason, he noted that Robert looked a little disconcerted by that idea and then the older man
swiftly composed his face into blandness. 'You think
the mother will agree to that?'

'If she's the usual type of woman my father fa-
voured, she'll be glad to do as I ask for the right…
compensation.' Cristo selected the word with sugges-
tive cool.

Robert understood his meaning and tried and failed
to imagine a scenario in which for the right price a
woman would be willing to surrender her children for
adoption. He had no doubt that Cristo had cause to
know exactly what he was talking about and he was
suddenly grateful not to be living a life that had made
him that cynical about human nature and greed. But
then, having handled Gaetano's financial dealings for
years, he knew that Cristo came from a dysfunctional
background and would be challenged to recognise the
depth of love and loyalty that many adults cherished
for their offspring.

Cristo, already stressed from his recent business

trip to Switzerland, squared his broad shoulders and lifted his phone to tell his PA, Emily, to book him on a flight to Dublin. He would get this repugnant business sorted out straight away and then get straight back to work.

'I *hate* them!' Belle vented in a helpless outburst, her lovely face full of angry passion. 'I hate every Ravelli alive!'

'Then you would also have to hate your own brothers and sisters,' her grandmother reminded her wryly. 'And you know that's not how you feel—'

With difficulty, Belle mastered her hot temper and studied her grandmother apologetically. Isa was a small supple woman with iron-grey hair and level green eyes the same shade as Belle's. 'That wretched lawyer hasn't even replied to Mum's letter about the school fees yet. I hate the whole lot of them for making us beg for what should be the children's by right!'

'It's unpleasant,' Isa Kelly conceded ruefully. 'But what we have to remember is that the person responsible for this whole horrible situation is Gaetano Ravelli—'

'I'm never going to forget that!' her granddaughter swore vehemently, leaping upright in frustration to pace over to the window that overlooked the tiny back garden.

And that was certainly the truth. Belle had been remorselessly bullied at school because of her mother's relationship with Gaetano Ravelli and the children she had had with him. A lot of people had taken exception to the spectacle of a woman carrying on a long-running, *fertile* affair with a married man. Her mother, Mary, had been labelled a slut and, as a sensitive adolescent, Belle had been forced to carry the shadow of that humiliating label alongside her parent.

'He's gone now,' Isa reminded her unnecessarily. 'And so, more sadly, is your mother.'

A familiar ache stirred below Belle's breastbone for the loss of that warm, loving presence in her family home and her angry face softened in expression. It was only a month since her mother had died from a heart attack and Belle was still not over the shock of her sudden passing. Mary had been a smiling, laughing woman in her early forties, who had rarely been ill. Yet she'd had a weak heart, and had apparently been warned by the doctor not to risk another pregnancy after the twins' difficult birth. But when had Mary Brophy ever listened to common sense? Belle asked herself painfully. Mary had gone her own sweet way regardless of the costs, choosing passion over commitment and the birth of a sixth child triumphing over what might have been years of quiet cautious living.

Whatever anyone had said about Mary Brophy—and there had been all too many local people with a moral axe to grind about her long-term affair with Gaetano—Mary had been a hardworking, kind person, who had never had a bad word to say about anyone and had always been the first to offer help when a neighbour was in trouble. Over the years some of her mother's most vociferous critics had ended up becoming her friends when they finally appreciated her gentle nature. But Belle had never been like the mother she had seen as oppressed: she had loved her mother and hated Gaetano Ravelli for his lying, manipulative selfishness and tight-fisted ways.

As if sensing the tension in the air, Tag whined at her feet and she stretched down a hand to soothe the family dog, a small black and white Jack Russell whose big brown adoring eyes were pinned to her. Straightening again, her colourful hair spilling across her slim shoulders, Belle pushed a straying corkscrew curl from her Titian mane out of her strained eyes and wondered when she would find the time to get it trimmed and how on earth she would ever pay for it when money was required for far more basic necessities.

At least the Lodge at the foot of the drive winding up to Mayhill House was theirs, signed over by Gaetano years earlier to give her mother a false sense of security. But how much use was a roof over their heads when Belle still couldn't pay the bills? Even so, homelessness would have been far worse, she acknowledged ruefully, her generous mouth softening. In any case, in all likelihood she would have to sell the Lodge and find them somewhere cheaper and smaller to live. Unfortunately she was going to have to fight and fight hard for the children to receive what was rightfully theirs. Illegitimate or not, her siblings had a legal claim to a share of their late father's estate and it was her job to take on that battle for them.

'You *must* let me take charge of the children now,' Isa told her eldest granddaughter firmly. 'Mary was my daughter and she made mistakes. I don't want to stand by watching you pay the price for them—'

'The kids would be too much for you,' Belle protested, for her grandmother might be hale and hearty but she was seventy years old and Belle thought it would be very wrong to allow her to take on such a burden.

'You attended a university miles from here to escape the situation your mother had created and you planned to go to London to work as soon as you graduated,' Isa reminded her stubbornly.

'That's the thing about life…it changes without warning you,' Belle fielded wryly. 'The children have lost both parents in the space of two months and they're very insecure. The last thing they need right now is for me to vanish as well.'

'Bruno and Donetta both go to boarding school, so they're out of the equation aside of holiday time,' the older woman reasoned, reluctant to cede the argument. 'The twins are at primary school. Only Franco is at home and he's two so he'll soon be off to school as well—'

Shortly after her mother's death, Belle had thought much along the same lines and had felt horribly guilty to admit, even to herself, that she felt trapped by the existence of her little brothers and sisters and their need for constant loving care. Her grandmother, Isa, had made her generous offer and Belle had kept it in reserve in the back of her mind, believing that it could be a real possibility. But that was before she got into the daily grind of seeing to her siblings' needs and finally appreciated the amount of sheer hard graft required and that any prospect of her grandmother taking charge was a selfish fantasy. It would be too big a burden for Isa to take on when some days it was even too much for Belle at the age of twenty-three.

Someone rapped loudly on the back door, making both women jump in surprise. Frowning, Belle opened the door and then relaxed when she saw an old friend waiting on the step. Mark Petrie and Belle had gone to school together where Mark had been one of her few true friends.

'Come in,' she invited the slimly built dark-haired man clad in casual jeans. 'Have a seat. Coffee?'

'Thanks.'

'How are you doing, Mark?' Isa asked with a welcoming smile.

'I'm doing great. It's Belle I'm worried about,' Mark admitted heavily, throwing Isa's granddaughter a look of unvarnished male admiration. 'Look, I'll just spit it right out. I heard my father talking on the phone this morning and he must've been talking to someone from Gaetano Ravelli's family. I think it was the oldest one, Cristo—'

Tensing at the sound of that familiar name, Belle settled a mug of coffee down on the table for Mark. 'Why do you think that?'

'Cristo is the executor of Gaetano's estate and my father was being asked about your mother and, of course, he doesn't even know Mary's dead yet. Nobody's bothered to tell him that she passed while he and Mum were staying with my uncle in Australia—'

'Well, your father and my mother weren't exactly bosom pals,' Belle reminded Mark bluntly. There had been a lot of bad blood over the years between the land agent, Daniel Petrie, and Mayhill's housekeeper, Mary Brophy. 'So why would anyone mention it to him?'

Cristo Ravelli, Belle was thinking resentfully. The stuffed-shirt banker and outrageously good-looking eldest son, who never ever smiled. Over the years she had often researched Gaetano's tangled love life on

the Internet, initially out of curiosity but then more
often to learn the answers to the questions that her
poor trusting mother had never dared to ask. She knew
about the wives, the sons and the scandalous affairs
and had soon recognised that Gaetano was a deceit-
ful, destructive Svengali with the female sex, who left
nothing but wreckage and regrets in his wake. Furthermore, as Gaetano had only ever married *rich* women,
her poor misguided mother had never had a prayer of
getting him to the altar.

'The point is, evidently Ravelli's family have decided they want Gaetano's children with Mary to be
adopted—'

'Adopted?' Belle interrupted, openly astonished by
that suggestion coming at her out of nowhere.

'Obviously the man's family want the whole affair
hushed up,' Mark opined with a grimace. 'And what
better way to stage a cover-up? It would keep the story
out of the papers and tidy up all the loose ends—'

'But they're *not* loose ends—they're children with
a family and a home!' Belle argued in dismay. 'For
goodness' sake, they belong together!'

Uncomfortable in receipt of that emotional outburst,
Mark cleared his throat. 'Are you the children's legal
guardian?'

'Well, who else is there?' Belle asked defensively.

'But it's not down legally on paper anywhere that
you're their guardian, is it?' Mark prompted ruefully
as her clear green eyes lifted to his in sudden dismay.
'I didn't think so. You should go and see a solicitor
about your situation as soon as you can and get your
claim to the children recognised with all the red tape
available…otherwise you might discover that Gaeta-

no's family have more legal say on the subject of what happens to them than you do.'

'But that would be ridiculous!' Belle objected. 'Gaetano had nothing to do with the kids even when he was here.'

'Not according to the law. He paid the older children's school fees, signed the Lodge over to your mother,' Mark reminded her with all the devotion to detail inherent in his law-student studies. 'He may have been a lousy father in the flesh but he did take care of the necessities, which could conceivably give Gaetano's sons a bigger say than you have in what happens to the children now.'

'But Gaetano left all five of them *out* of his will,' Belle pointed out, tilting her chin in challenge.

'That doesn't matter. The law is the law,' Mark fielded. 'Nobody can take their birthright away from them.'

'Adoption…' Eyes still stunned by that proposition, Belle sank heavily back down into her chair. 'That's a crazy idea. They couldn't have tried this nonsense on if my mother were still alive!' she exclaimed bitterly. 'Nobody could have said their mother didn't have the right to say what should happen to them.'

'If only Mary had lived long enough to deal with all this,' Isa sighed in pained agreement. 'But maybe, as the children's granny, I'll have a say?'

'I doubt it,' Mark interposed. 'Until you moved in here after Mary's death, the children had never lived with you.'

'I could pretend to be Mum…' Belle breathed abruptly.

'*Pretend*?' Isa's head swivelled round to the younger woman in disbelief. 'Don't be silly, Belle.'

'How am I being silly? Cristo Ravelli doesn't know Mum is dead and if he thinks she's still alive, he's very unlikely to try and interfere in their living arrangements.' Belle lifted her head high, convinced she was correct on that score.

'There's no way you could pretend to be a woman in her forties!' Mark protested with an embarrassed laugh at the idea.

Belle was thinking hard. 'But I don't need to look like I'm in my forties…I only need to look old enough to have a fifteen-year-old son and, at the age women are having children these days, I could easily only be in my early thirties,' she reasoned.

'It would be insane to try and pull off a deception like that,' her grandmother told her quellingly. 'Cristo Ravelli would be sure to find out the truth.'

'*How?* Who's going to tell him? He's a Ravelli—he's not going to be wandering round asking the locals nosy questions. He would have no reason to question my identity. I'll put my hair up, use a lot of make-up… that'll help—'

'Belle…I know you're game for anything but it would be a massive deception to try and pull off,' Mark said drily. 'Think about what you're saying.'

The kitchen door opened and a thumb-sucking toddler with a mop of black curls stumbled in. He steadied himself against Belle's denim-clad thigh and then clambered up clumsily into his sister's lap, taking his welcome for granted. 'Sleepy,' he told her, the words slurring. 'Hug…'

Belle cradled her youngest half-sibling gently.

Franco was very affectionate and he was quick to curve his warm, solid little body into hers. 'I'll take him upstairs for a nap,' she whispered, rising upright again with difficulty because he was a heavy child.

Belle tucked Franco into his cot beside her bed and for a moment stood looking out of the rear window, which provided a picturesque view of Mayhill House, a gracious grey Georgian mansion set in acres of parkland against the backdrop of the ancient oak woods. Her mother had been a widow and Belle only eight years old when Mary had first started work as Gaetano Ravelli's housekeeper.

Belle's own father had been a violent drunk, renowned for his foul-mouthed harangues and propensity for getting into fights. One night he had stepped out in front of a car when under the influence and few had mourned his demise, least of all Belle, who had been terrified of her father's vicious temper and brutal fists. Mother and daughter had believed they were embarking on a new and promising life when Mary became the Mayhill housekeeper. Sadly, however, Mary had fallen madly in love with her new boss and her reputation had been destroyed from the instant Belle's eldest half-sibling, Bruno, had been born.

Someone like Cristo Ravelli, Belle reflected bitterly, could have absolutely no grasp of how other less fortunate mortals lived. Cristo was handsome, brilliant and obscenely successful. He had grown up in a golden cocoon of cash, the son of a very wealthy Italian princess who was renowned as a leading society hostess. His stepfather was a Hungarian banker, his home a Venetian palace and he had attended an exclusive school from which he had emerged literally weighed down with academic and athletic honours. It was hardly surprising that Cristo was a dazzling star of success in every corner of his life. After all, *he* didn't know what it was to be humiliated, ignored or mocked and she'd bet he had never had to apologise for his parentage.

On the other hand Bruno had only been thirteen when Gaetano first accused his son of being gay because that was the only way Gaetano could interpret Bruno's burning desire to be an artist. Belle's little brother had been devastated by that destructive indictment from a father whom he had long been desperate to impress. His growing unhappiness at school where he was being bullied had resulted in a suicide attempt. Belle still got the shivers recalling it, having come so terrifyingly close to losing her little brother for ever. Bruno *needed* his family for support. Bruno, just like his siblings, needed love and commitment to grow into a contented, well-adjusted adult. There was nothing Belle would not have done to ensure that her siblings remained happy and together.

Having delivered his warning, Mark was taking his leave when she returned downstairs.

'I'll get supper on,' Belle's grandmother declared.

'You're not serious about trying to pretend to be Mary, are you?' Mark pressed on the doorstep.

Belle straightened her slight shoulders. 'If that's what it takes to keep the family together, I'd do it in a heartbeat!'

The evening light was fast fading when Cristo's car finally turned up the long driveway to Mayhill.

He had never visited Gaetano's Irish bolt hole before because Gaetano had never invited any of his relatives to visit him there or, indeed, anywhere else. His father had never bothered to maintain relationships and the minute he was bored he had headed for pastures new and wiped the slate clean of past associations.

A woman with a little dog running at her heels was walking across the sweeping front lawn. Cristo frowned; he didn't like trespassers. But a split second later he was staring, watching that cloud of colourful curls float back from a stunning heart-shaped face, noting the way her loose top blew back to frame her lush full breasts and a sliver of pale flat stomach, exposing the denim shorts that hugged her derriere and accentuated her long, long shapely legs. She took his breath away and the pulse at his groin reacted with rampant enthusiasm. He gritted his teeth, trying to recall when he had last been with a woman, and when he couldn't blamed that oversight for his sudden arousal. In reality, Cristo always chose work over sex for work challenged and energised him while he regarded sex as a purely stress-relieving exercise.

He unlocked the massive wooden front door and stepped over the top of a pile of untouched post into a large black-and-white-tiled hall. His protection team composed of Rafe and John moved past him. 'We'll check the house.'

A fine layer of dust coated the furniture within view and Cristo was not surprised when Rafe confirmed that the house was vacant. But then, what exactly had he expected? Mary Brophy and her five children occupying the property? Yes, that was *exactly* what he had expected and why he had used his keys to emphasise the fact that he had the right of entry. He strode through the silent rooms, eventually ending up in the kitchen with its empty fridge standing wide open, backed by the sound of a dripping tap. His handsome mouth curved down as he noted the phone on the wall. One of the buttons was labelled 'house-keeping'. Lifting the phone, he stabbed the button with exasperated force.

'Yes?' a disembodied female voice responded when he had almost given up hope of his call being answered.

'It's Cristo Ravelli. I'm at the house. Why hasn't it been prepared for my arrival?' he demanded imperiously.

At the other end of the phone, Belle went on all systems alert at the vibrating tone of impatience in that dark, deep accented drawl and her green eyes suddenly glinted as dangerously as emeralds in firelight. 'Do you think maybe that could be because the housekeeper's wages were stopped the same day Mr Ravelli crashed his helicopter?'

Cristo was not accustomed to smart-mouthed replies and his wide sensual mouth hardened. 'I didn't make that instruction.'

'Well, it doesn't really matter now, does it? Regrettably nobody works for free,' Belle told him drily.

Cristo bit back a curse. He was tired and hungry and in no mood for a war of words. 'I gather you're the housekeeper?'

It was the moment of truth, Belle registered, and for a split second she hesitated. An image of her siblings rehomed in an orphanage on the slippery slope to a

foster home gripped her tummy and provoked nausea.
'Er…yes,' she pronounced tightly.

'Then get yourself up to the house and do your job.
I can assure you that you will be well paid for your
time,' Cristo informed her grittily. 'I need food and
bedding—'

'There's several shops in the village. You must've
driven past them to get to the house,' Belle protested.

'I'm happy to pay you to take care of those tasks
for me,' Cristo fielded smoothly before returning the
phone to the wall and wondering if it had been wise
to recall an insolent housekeeper to her former du-
ties. Reminding himself that he only planned to stay
a couple of days before arranging to have the house
sold, he dismissed the matter from mind. The housekeeper, he reflected, would be a useful source of local
knowledge to have on hand.

Following that call, Belle was in an infinitely more
excitable state. After all, it was now or never. She
couldn't introduce herself as Mary's daughter and
then change her mind. Either she pretended to be
her mother or she went up to Mayhill and told Cristo
Ravelli that his father's former housekeeper/lover was
dead. But when she thought of the influence she could
potentially wield for the children's benefit by acting
as their mother, her doubts fell away and she hurried
upstairs, frantically wondering how she could best
make herself look more mature.

The first thing she did was take off her shorts and
top. Rustling through her wardrobe, she found a short
stretchy skirt and a long-sleeved tee. Her mother had
never ever worn flat heels or jeans and Belle owned
only one skirt. Clinging to those Mary Brophy hab-

its as if they might prove to be a good-luck talisman,
Belle pulled out a pair of high heels and hurriedly got
dressed. That achieved, she went into the bathroom,
pushed her hair back from her face and grimaced at
her porcelain-pale complexion, which she had often
suspected made her look even younger than her years.
Surely if she put her hair up and went heavy on the
make-up it would make her look older? Brows pleating, she recalled the smoky eye treatment that a friend
had persuaded her to try on a night out and she dug
deep into her make-up bag for the necessary tools.

She stroked on the different shadows with a liberal
hand, blurred the edges with an anxious fingertip and
added heaps of eyeliner. Well, she certainly looked
different, she acknowledged uneasily, layering on the
mascara before adding blush to her cheeks and outlin-
ing her mouth with bright pink gloss.

'I was about to call you down for supper...' Isa
Kelly froze in the tiny hall to watch her granddaughter come downstairs. 'Where on earth are you going
got up like that?'

Belle stiffened. 'Why? Do I look odd?'

'Well, if you bent over you could probably treat me
to a view of your underwear,' Isa commented disapprovingly.

An awkward silence fell, interrupted within seconds by the noisy sound of the back door opening
and closing. Children's voices raised in shrill argument broke the silence and a dark-haired boy and girl
of eight years of age hurtled into the hall still engaged
in hurling insults.

'If you don't stop fighting, it will be early to bed
tonight,' Belle warned the twins, Pietro and Lucia.

The twins closed their mouths, ducked their tousled heads and surged up the stairs past their eldest sister.

'You can tell me now why you're wearing a skirt,' Isa pressed Belle.

'Cristo Ravelli phoned…in need of a housekeeper.' Belle quickly explained what had transpired on the phone. 'I need to look at least ten years older.'

As Belle spoke, Isa studied the younger woman in consternation. 'You can't possibly pretend to be Mary… It's an insane idea. You'll never get away with it.'

Belle lifted her chin. 'But it's worth a try if it means that Cristo Ravelli has to listen to what I have to say. He obviously knows nothing about Mum. I don't think he even realises that she was his father's housekeeper.'

'I doubt if he's that ignorant,' Isa opined thoughtfully. 'It could be a shrewd move. Naturally he's going to want to meet the children's mother as soon as possible. But I don't want you going up there to run after the man, doing his shopping and cooking and making up his bed, especially dressed like that!'

'What's wrong with the way I'm dressed?'

'It might give the man the wrong idea.'

'I seriously doubt that,' Belle responded, smoothing her stretchy skirt carefully down over her slim hips. 'As far as I'm aware he's not sex-mad like his father.'

Isa compressed her lips. 'That kind of comment is *so* disrespectful, Belle.'

'It's a fact, not a nasty rumour.'

'Gaetano was the children's father. He may not have been much of a father but you still shouldn't talk about him like that where you could be overheard,' her grandmother rebuked her firmly.

Aware that the older woman was making a fair point, Belle reddened with discomfiture. 'May I borrow your car, Gran?'

'Yes, of course.' Belatedly aware that Belle had successfully sidetracked her concern about the deception she was preparing to spring on Cristo Ravelli, Isa planted a staying hand on the front door before Belle could open it. 'Think about what you're about to do, Belle. Once you try to deceive this man, there's no going back and he'll have every right to be very angry with us all when he discovers the truth…as eventually he must,' she reasoned anxiously.

'Cristo is a Ravelli, Gran…shrewd, tricky and unscrupulous. I need an advantage to deal with him and the only way I can get that advantage is by pretending to be Mum.'

CHAPTER TWO

BELLE DROVE DOWN to the garage shop in the village to stock up on basic necessities for the Mayhill kitchen and was taken aback by the cost of the exercise.

Cristo Ravelli was expecting her to cook but she couldn't cook, at least not anything that required more than a microwave and a tin opener. She pondered her dilemma and decided on an omelette, salad and garlic bread. Surely even she could manage a meal that basic? She had often watched her mother and her grandmother making omelettes. Bruno was also a dab hand in the kitchen. They always ate well when he was home at weekends.

Tense as a steel girder, she drove round to the back of the house, noting that the lights weren't on. The back door was still locked and with a groan she lugged her carrier bags round to the front, mounted the steps and pressed the doorbell.

Cristo was on the phone when the bell echoed through the hall. Brows drawing together, he went to answer the door, stepping back in surprise when a slender redhead in sky-high heels tramped in past him. The housekeeper? Not his idea of a housekeeper, he conceded, swiftly concluding his call, his brilliant

dark eyes flaring over one of the shapeliest bodies he
had ever seen and very probably the best ever legs.
Legs that put him in mind of the girl he had seen
walking across the lawn, his gaze rising to the woman's face to note the huge anxious green eyes lost in
the heavy make-up and the ripe full mouth. She was
not his type, no way was she his type, too obvious,
too loud, hair too red. Indeed Cristo knew to his cost
that he was most attracted to tiny ice-cool blondes
with big blue eyes. His conscience sliced through that
thought instantaneously, reminding him that that particular image was forbidden for very good reasons.
Lush black lashes shielding his grim and guilty gaze,
he rested his attention quite deliberately on the redhead's remarkable breasts. Now, those were truly a
work of art like her legs, he conceded abstractedly.

Sadly accustomed to the effect her full bosom
tended to have on the male sex, Belle studied Cristo
Ravelli at her leisure. By any estimate, he was drop-
dead gorgeous. He had luxuriant black hair closely
cropped to his arrogant head, spectacular bone structure and quite stunning dark-as-charcoal eyes enhanced by absurdly long sooty lashes. A light shadow
of stubble roughened his olive-skinned jaw line, adding to an already overpoweringly masculine presence.

Her pupils dilated, her heart began hammering
an upbeat tempo and her tummy performed acrobat-
ics. It was nerves, she told herself, nerves and adrenalin reacting to the challenge of the deception she
was embarking on. It didn't help that Cristo was also
extremely tall, actually tall enough to make her feel
small even though she was an easy five feet eight
inches in height and stood even higher in heels. His

shoulders were broad below the tailored jacket of his no doubt expensive business suit, his chest wide, his lean hips tapering down to legs that were very long and powerful.

'I'll take these down to the kitchen and start cooking,' Belle told him, raising her arms to display the bulging carrier bags.

Her rounded breasts shimmied below the fine jersey top and Cristo's mouth ran dry. 'You're my father's housekeeper?' he prompted because she was not at all what he had expected, having dimly imagined some feisty but sensible countrywoman of indeterminate age.

Abandoning her attempt to walk right by him, Belle set the bags on the floor at her feet and lifted her head high. 'I'm Mary Brophy,' she announced, thrusting up her chin in challenge.

Both disconcertion and disbelief assailed Cristo and his dark deep-set eyes narrowed to increase their searching intensity as he scrutinised her. 'You were my father's…mistress?' he asked.

Nausea stirred in her tummy at that label but she could think of no more accurate description for the compromising position her late mother had occupied in Gaetano's life and colour fired her cheeks. 'Yes.'

A split second earlier, Cristo had been mentally undressing her and that awareness now revolted him as the ultimate in inappropriate activities now that he knew who she was. This was the woman who had occupied his father's bed for at least fifteen years, earning a longevity that no other women had contrived to match in Gaetano's easily bored existence. And looking at her, suddenly Cristo was not surprised by that fact because self-evidently this woman worked at her appearance. Even after giving birth to five children she still had the slender waist of a young girl and, below the make-up she seemed to trowel on as thick as paste, her fine pale skin was unlined and still taut. She was too young, way too young-looking though to match the woman he had expected to meet, he decided, his ebony brows pleating in perplexity.

'You were also Gaetano's housekeeper?' Cristo questioned.

'Yes.' With determination, Belle bent down to lift the bags again. 'Omelette and salad all right for you?' she asked, heading for the kitchen at speed.

A very decorative housekeeper, Cristo thought numbly, still quite unable to picture her as the mother of five children. *Five!*

'You must have been very young when you met my father,' Cristo commented from the kitchen doorway.

Belle stiffened as she piled the perishable food into the fridge. 'Not that young,' she fielded, wanting to tell him to mind his own business but reluctant to cause offence. After all, she needed his support to secure a decent future for her siblings. Although what realistic chance did she have of gaining it? At worst, Cristo Ravelli might despise and resent his father's illegitimate children, and at best, he might be simply indifferent to them. Adoption, for goodness' sake, she reflected in lingering disbelief. How many people would even *dare* to suggest such an option?

'I assumed you would be living here in the house,' Cristo remarked, his attention clinging of its own volition to the amount of slender thigh on view as she crouched down to pack the fridge.

'I only…er…lived in when Gaetano was here,' Belle said awkwardly.

'And the rest of the time?' Cristo enquired, because as far as he knew his father had only come to Ireland three or four times a year and had never stayed for longer than a couple of weeks at most.

'I live in the lodge at the gates,' Belle admitted grudgingly, straightening to set out lettuce and eggs on the granite work counter.

Cristo gritted his teeth at the news because she and her children would have to vacate the lodge house before he could put Mayhill on the market. Of course he would have to pay her for the inconvenience of finding another home. Her hair shone bright as a beacon below the lights, displaying varying shades of gold, auburn and copper, tiny curls of hair adorning the nape of her long, elegant neck. She had very curly hair, the sort of hair he had once seen on a rag doll, he mused absently, irritated by the random nature of the thought. He studied the smooth line of her jaw and the full lush softness of her bold red-painted mouth with a persistent sense of incredulity. She had to be a lot older than she looked to be the parent of a teenager, although perhaps he was being naïve. It was perfectly possible that Mary Brophy looked so amazingly youthful because his father had paid for her to have plastic surgery.

Belle unwrapped the garlic bread and shoved it on an oven tray to cook. She wished he would go away. Standing there, all looming six feet four inches or so of him, he made her feel nervous and clumsy. She had to search through cupboards to find the utensils she wanted because she had rarely visited Mayhill

since childhood. Indeed she had avoided it on principle whenever Gaetano was in residence. Her green
eyes darkened as she recalled the way she and her
ever-growing band of siblings would go and stay with
her grandmother in the village even before Gaetano
arrived, leaving her mother free to make her prepa-
rations for his arrival. Mary had always, *always* put
Gaetano Ravelli first.

Belle remembered her mother's excitement when
Gaetano was due to arrive, the frantic exercising, hair
appointments and shopping trips to ensure that Mary
could look her very best for her lover. Belle had long
since decided that she would rather die than want to
please any man to that extent. Certainly Mary's rather
pathetic loyalty and devotion had not won her any
prizes.

Belle prepared the salad quickly, heaping it into a
bowl and then making up her mother's favourite salad
dressing as best she could because she couldn't quite
recall the proportions of the different ingredients. That
achieved, she embarked on the omelette. Cristo had
vanished by then and she heaved a sigh of relief as she
walked through to set the table in the spacious dining
room across the hall.

He had accepted that she was Mary Brophy without protest and why shouldn't he? It meant nothing to
him that her poor mother was gone. Mark's father, the
land agent Daniel Petrie, would eventually catch up
on the local gossip and learn that the woman he had
long despised was dead and buried. But Belle thought
it was unlikely that Daniel would bother making an
announcement of that fact to Cristo Ravelli as, not
only would he feel foolish about having misinformed

his employer, but he would also most likely assume that Cristo had already found out the truth. Soothing herself with such reflections, Belle returned to her cooking and struggled to control the gas burners because she was accustomed to cooking with electric.

Cristo surveyed his meal with an appetite that very quickly vanished. He prodded the omelette with a fork. It had the solid consistency of a rubber mattress but lacked the bounce. The salad had been drowned in a vat of oil. Even the garlic bread was charred although valiant attempts had been made to cut away the most burnt bits. He swallowed hard and pushed the plate away. She couldn't cook, but presumably she and his father had dined out. Distaste suddenly filled Cristo and he stood up in a lithe movement, his lean strong face hard and taut. He didn't want to be in Ireland. He didn't want to deal with the wretched woman and the consequences of her sordid long-term affair with his father. But he knew that he didn't have a choice. Mary Brophy and her children were not a problem he could afford to ignore. In any case, there was no one else to deal with the situation.

Belle was digging into the linen cupboard on the upper landing when she heard a noise behind her and whirled round to stare in dismay at the tall square-featured young man leaning back against the bannister. He was built like a solid brick wall.

'So this is where the bedding is hidden,' he remarked.

'Who are you?' Belle demanded nervously.

'Rafe is one of my two bodyguards,' Cristo interposed, strolling up onto the landing. 'Rafe and John are staying here with me.'

'John and I need bedding. We can take care of ourselves though,' Rafe declared, stepping past her to peruse the tidy, labelled shelves just as she emerged clutching the linen she required for the master bedroom. Conscious of Cristo Ravelli's stare, and feeling somewhat harassed, Belle walked stiffly down the corridor. Damn the man! Why was he watching her like that? Did she have two heads all of a sudden? And why hadn't he told her he had companions? She hadn't bought enough food and that thought reminded her that she had to get him to settle up with her for the shopping she had done on his behalf. Dropping the linen on the bed, she dug into her pocket for the till receipt and turned to offer it to him.

'This is what you owe me,' she told him.

Cristo dug out his wallet and extended a banknote while still engaged in frowning at the gilded furniture and mirrors and the fantastically draped red king-size bed. 'Is this my father's room?'

'Yes.'

'I'll sleep somewhere else. The Victorian brothel design doesn't appeal to me,' he informed her curtly.

The décor was dark, fussy and horrible, Belle was willing to concede. She lifted the linen again and trudged across the corridor to one of the few guest rooms that enjoyed an en suite. Mayhill was badly in need of updating.

'When I said that about the decoration, I didn't intend to insult you,' Cristo remarked, standing poised by the window, thinking that at this early stage it would be most unwise to offend her. He swore to himself that he would make no cheap cracks about her role as his father's mistress, not least because it was becoming clear that it had not been a profitable position, he reflected wryly, which was hardly surprising when Gaetano had been renowned for his stinginess. Indeed in every one of his three divorces Gaetano had made money off his ex-wives in spite of the fact that in each case the women had been the injured parties. That Gaetano's secret mistress had still been working as his housekeeper and wore cheap off-the-peg clothing should really not come as a surprise. For that reason he found it hard to believe that Gaetano had stumped up for plastic surgery to keep his mistress looking young but, of course, he reminded himself, it was perfectly possible that there had been no cosmetic enhancement. Mary Brophy could simply be, and probably was, a very lucky woman who looked much younger than her years.

'I'm not offended. I wasn't involved in choosing the furnishings here. About ten years ago, Gaetano hired an interior decorator,' Belle explained, recalling how very hurt her mother had been not to be trusted with that responsibility by her lover. But then good taste had not been her mother's strong point either. The Lodge rejoiced in every shade of pink known to man, pink having been Mary's favourite colour.

Cristo watched Belle crush the pillows into pillow slips, her slender figure twisting this way and that, allowing him to notice her ripe, pouting curves at breast and hip from every angle. His wide sensual mouth slowly settled into a harder and harder line as he studied her delicate flushed profile, scanning her fine brows, her subtle little nose and full pink mouth.

And his body reacted accordingly, stirring with forbidden interest until he angrily turned his back on her, castigating himself for viewing his father's mistress as if she were some kind of sex object. But then he reminded himself that she was dressed to attract in an outfit and shoes that accentuated her long legs and shapely figure, and, when all was said and done, he was still a man with all that entailed and almost guaranteed to look.

Belle shot a sidewise glance at Cristo from below her lashes. His detachment, his air of command and superiority reminded her of his father, who had barely acknowledged Belle's existence on the rare occasions when he had seen her. Suddenly she regretted agreeing to play housekeeper because no doubt as intended it made her feel inferior. Her soft mouth tightened as she shook out the duvet with unnecessary violence and then carried the towels into the bathroom. Unfortunately she carried the image of Cristo Ravelli with her, those penetrating eyes dark as sin, that sleek bred-in-the-bone sexiness that lent him such charismatic appeal. She could feel her nipples pushing hard against the scratchy surface of her lace bra, a tightening, sliding sensation of warmth between her thighs and she was deeply disturbed by her reaction. But there was no denying it: *he* appealed to her; *he* attracted her on the most basic level. Did that mean that at heart she was as foolish as her mother had once been about Gaetano?

'I'd appreciate the opportunity to have a private word with you here tomorrow morning,' Cristo murmured smoothly as she emerged again. 'Shall we say at ten?'

Belle nodded agreement. 'When will you want to meet the children?' she prompted.

Cristo froze, his facial bones locking tight. 'I *don't*...wish to meet them, that is,' he extended unapologetically, dark eyes cold as black ice.

Belle paled, uncertain of how to take that statement. Was his lack of interest good or bad news for her siblings? Did that mean that the adoption idea was just a silly rumour? She scrutinised his lean, handsome features with frowning green eyes, unnerved by his icy reserve and lack of humanity. Did he think nothing of the blood tie? A lot of people would just have agreed to meet the children for the sake of it, even if they weren't particularly interested in them, but Cristo Ravelli had chosen to spurn even that polite pretence.

In acknowledging that, Belle felt sheer loathing suddenly leap through her in a fierce wave of antagonism because she was gutted on her siblings' behalf by his detachment. Was he refusing to accept that the children were part of the Ravelli family? *Obviously.* Clearly, Mary Brophy's children were not good enough to make the grade, just as Mary had never been good enough for Gaetano to marry. Bile scoured Belle's throat as she sped downstairs to clean up the kitchen and go home. She hoped he wasn't expecting her to come up and cook breakfast when she found the meal she had cooked thrown in its entirety into the bin. Her face burned but her chin came up. So, it hadn't been one of her best efforts but in her opinion it had been as much as he deserved!

After spending half the summer with Mary over twenty years earlier, Gaetano had confided that he was unhappily unmarried and Mary's hopes of a happy ending for her romance had risen high. But Gaetano had not asked his Arabic wife for a divorce or even a separation. Over the years the media had published several stories about his extramarital affairs. Her mother had refused to believe the stories, even after Belle had shown her revealing pictures on the Internet. Mary had always been very quick to make excuses in Gaetano's defence.

'He feels trapped and lonely in his marriage. It's only a business arrangement. She was a friend for years before he married her and he doesn't love her. He needed a hostess to entertain his business colleagues and she comes from an old-fashioned country where a woman needs a husband if she wants any freedom,' Mary had reasoned. 'I can't hold his marriage against him, Belle. I'm not even an educated woman. I couldn't do what his princess can do for him.'

Mary Brophy had been hopelessly infatuated with Gaetano Ravelli from the moment she first met him and she had allowed nothing to interfere with her rosy view of their relationship. Her grief in the wake of the helicopter crash that had taken Gaetano's life had been all-consuming.

'I know you don't understand,' she had said to Belle, 'but Gaetano was the love of my life. I know he wasn't interested in marrying me but nothing's perfect. I wasn't his match in money or background and I can't blame him for that. When you love someone, Belle, you accept their flaws and he was too much of a snob to want to marry an ordinary woman like me.'

A woman like me, Belle recalled painfully. It was little wonder that Mary had suffered from low self-esteem. She had travelled from a shotgun wedding at the age of seventeen straight into an abusive marriage and had finally ended up as a married man's mistress. Life had always been tough for her mother, but then, as Isa was prone to reminding Belle, Mary had *always* made the wrong choices when it came to the men in her life.

Isa was waiting up for Belle when she got back to the Lodge.

'Well?' her grandmother pressed. 'Did he actually credit the idea that you were a woman in her forties?'

'No, he assumed I must have got involved with his father when I was very young,' Belle advanced with a dismissive toss of her head. 'He did do a lot of staring, though. He's invited me up to the house to talk to him tomorrow at ten, so presumably the kids' future will be discussed then.'

The older woman released a heavy sigh. 'I don't like the way you're going about this, Belle. Honesty is always the best policy.'

'But I won't be dealing with a nice, honest guy.'

'You hated Gaetano. Don't take it out on his son.'

Belle folded her lips at that unwelcome advice. 'He doesn't even want to meet the kids.'

Her grandmother shook her greying head, her unhappiness at that news palpable. 'If only your mother had thought about what she was doing and how much the children would be resented by the rest of Gaetano's family.'

Cristo had a troubled night of sleep. He dreamt that he was pursuing a woman with the longest legs possible across a misty landscape. Every time he got close she pulled away and laughed and her resistance made him want her more than ever, lust pounding through his veins like an explosive charge. But when he finally caught up with her, she was a different woman, pale blonde hair falling back from her piquant face to highlight big blue enquiring eyes and instantaneous recoil wakened him. He had broken out in a cold sweat, angry frustration and guilt slicing through him for the one woman he couldn't enjoy having even in his dreams…Betsy, his brother Nik's estranged wife. His jawline rigid, Cristo sprang out of bed and went for a shower.

His eyes closed tight shut below the refreshing blast of the power shower. He hadn't meant to wreck his brother's marriage. There had been no intent on his part to inflict damage, he reasoned painfully. Betsy had come to him for support, devastated by what she had learned from Zarif. But, unhappily, it had been Cristo who first gave Zarif the destructive news that had ruined Nik's relationship with his wife. Cristo had broken his brother's confidence and spoken out of turn, but he had never ever at any stage planned to harm Nik or hoped to steal Betsy from him.

For his own benefit, however, he listed the sins he had committed. He *had* thought that Nik didn't deserve a woman like Betsy. He *had* stood by watching while his brother took his wife for granted and he had *not* warned him of what he was doing. With the basest disloyalty, he *had* cherished feelings for his brother's wife. That was why Gaetano's mess in Ireland was *his* mess to clean up, Cristo reflected grimly. Nik already had enough on his plate to deal with and Zarif was still suffering the fallout from the loose-tongued confession that had wrecked Nik's marriage because ever since then the three brothers had barely spoken to each other.

'Very mumsy,' Isa pronounced the next morning with a raised brow when she saw what Belle was wearing. 'Did that skirt belong to your mother?'

Belle paled. 'Yes, I kept a couple of things just to remember Mum by. It's a little big but it looks all right with the belt.'

'Which is more than you can say about that flapping cardigan and the beads round your neck with that fussy blouse,' Isa groaned disapprovingly. 'You look like a young woman trying to look older.'

'Yes but that's because you know the truth. It's daylight now and I need to make a better impression than I did last night,' Belle pointed out anxiously.

'Even daylight couldn't penetrate the amount of make-up you've got on,' her grandmother said drily. 'But you're right—it does age you.'

'Look, I accept that Cristo is eventually going to find out the truth but I want that adoption idea off the table first,' Belle told her.

'Even at the cost of infuriating him?' Isa asked. 'Gaetano had a very low threshold for provocation.'

'Whatever happens, I'll deal with it.'

'I can't see how,' Isa said bluntly. 'You're pretty much powerless up against his wealth and intellect.'

Belle trudged up the drive in her high heels, striving not to feel like someone got up in fancy dress. She was *not* powerless. Money wasn't everything, nor was intellect. She was not stupid. She had a first-class degree in business and economics and she had the power of the unexpected on her side. He thought she was who she had said she was and, whether he knew it or not, that meant he would be fighting with one hand tied behind his back. Where her mother would have rolled over on command for a Ravelli and said thank you very much for the attention, Belle was programmed to fight dirty.

Cristo watched her approach from the window in the drawing room. No miniskirt in evidence today, but high-heeled court shoes with pointy toes embellished those award-winning legs. He gritted his even white teeth together, stamping out that inappropriate thought. So, she was an attractive woman. It was par for the course: his father's lovers had always been beauties even while his wives were more of the plain variety. Gaetano had always rated wealth and class above looks. Cristo wondered how much money it would take to persuade the older woman into his way of thinking. He was a skilled negotiator and envisaged few problems because Mary Brophy had not been enriched in any way by her relationship with his father and was currently penniless. Furthermore she couldn't be the brightest star in the firmament when she had given the wily older man five children he could never have wanted and kept on slogging away for him as a humble housekeeper.

Surprisingly a rare shard of pity stabbed Cristo at that acknowledgement, making him register that where Mary Brophy was concerned he didn't want to use a sledgehammer to crack a nut. He didn't want to threaten or intimidate her into doing his bidding; he simply wanted a neat and tidy solution to a very messy and potentially embarrassing problem for *all* their sakes.

CHAPTER THREE

'MR RAVELLI IS in the drawing room,' Rafe informed her.

Breathing in deeply and slowly to maintain her calm front, Belle walked into the over-furnished room where the ornate drapes and blinds cut out much of the daylight. Cristo swung round to study her and instantly her every sense went on high alert, her backbone stiffening, her slim legs bracing, her soft pink lips parting as she dragged in a sudden extra shot of oxygen.

Cristo scanned her appearance, his nostrils flaring with sudden impatience. She was dressed in a frumpy skirt and cardigan that a maiden aunt might have worn and she had inexplicably teamed that look with the kind of bold make-up a streetwalker might have flaunted like a signpost. And he realised then that there was something he wasn't seeing, something he wasn't grasping about this woman, because so far her long-term affair with his father wasn't adding up at all. Whatever else might have been said about Gaetano, he had been a connoisseur of women and a sophisticate and there was no way his father had returned again and again to Ireland in order to take advantage of the charms of the woman currently standing in front of him.

'Mr Ravelli…' she said breathily and she turned her head away to glance out of the window, her hair a sunburst of colour, her fine profile delineated against the light, soft, glossy mouth full and pouting peach pink, long lashes fluttering up on big eyes as green and verdant as Irish grass.

And Cristo ground his perfect white teeth together on the smoulderingly sexual pull of her in that instant, recognising that she had buckets of that inexpressible quality that reduced the male mind to mush and turned a man on hard and fast. For a split second, he wanted to snatch her up into his arms and crush every line of the remarkable body concealed by the unattractive clothing to his own while he discovered if that voluptuous mouth of hers tasted as impossibly good as it looked. His hands closed into fists of restraint while he fought off the erection threatening, struggling to think of something, *anything*, that would take his thoughts off her mouth and her breasts and her legs and, even worse, what lay between them. That she could be affecting him on such a level outraged his every principle.

Trying to avoid direct contact with those spectacular dark-as-night eyes of his, Belle could feel her colour heightening, awareness of him leaping and pounding through her in an uncontrollable surge. She stared at him, breathless, frozen like someone cornered by a wild animal, and all the time she was noticing things about him: the way his sleek ebony brows defined his eyes, the way the faint line of colour accentuated the hard masculine angle of his high cheekbones, the way the pared-down hollows below enhanced his wide, sensual mouth. Very, very good-looking but, yes, she had noticed that before, certainly didn't need to keep *on* noticing it. The atmosphere thickened and the silence screamed at her nerves as every muscle in her body tightened defensively. It was as if there were nobody else in the world but them and what she was feeling: the insidious warmth blossoming in her pelvis, the sudden tightening discomfort of her nipples.

Lean, strong face rigid, Cristo expelled his breath in a sudden hiss and took a measured step back from her and away from such treacherous ruminations as to what she might *taste* like, what her skin would *feel* and smell like. He was appalled that she could drag such a strong physical reaction from him against his will, but even more annoyed that she could somehow cloud his usual crystal-clear clarity of thought.

'Miss Brophy.'

'It's Mrs actually.'

Cristo frowned. 'You're married?'

'I've been a widow for many years,' Belle replied tightly, straying over to the window, partially turning her back to him while she fought to regain her mental focus. The deception she had entered on demanded her whole concentration. She was Mary Brophy, Gaetano's former mistress and the mother of five of his children, she reminded herself doggedly.

'I invited you here today to discuss your future and your children's,' Cristo delivered smoothly.

Lifted by that solid assurance, Belle's spirits perked up. 'Yes…Gaetano has left us in a pretty awkward position.'

'Naturally, you're referring to your financial situation. My father was most remiss in not making provision for you in the event of his death.'

'Yes...but he *did* sign the house over to me,' Belle pointed out, keen to sound like a loyal woman in Gaetano's defence because she could not afford to let an ounce of her loathing for the man betray her true identity in his son's presence.

Cristo went very still, allowing her to take in the faultless cut of the dark business suit he wore teamed with a bland white shirt and blue silk tie. His brows drew together in a frown. 'Which house?'

'The Lodge...he signed it over to me years ago to ensure that we would always have a home.' Belle's voice faltered slightly because he seemed so taken aback by the news, yet surely he should've known that already as the executor of the estate. 'But bearing in mind the running costs and the children's current needs I'll probably be selling it now.'

'Excuse me for a moment,' Cristo urged, striding out of the room into the one next door and pulling out his phone to call his father's lawyer, Robert Ludlow. If she owned part of the property, he should've been informed of the fact.

Robert's initial disconcertion over Cristo's query trailed away as he trawled through Gaetano's files and then emerged with the facts of a minor legal agreement drawn up about fifteen years earlier, which Robert's elder brother had apparently handled shortly before his retirement. Robert was volubly apologetic for the oversight. Brought up to date, Cristo was triumphantly aware that he knew something Mary Brophy did not appear to know. Under no circumstances would she be selling the Lodge.

Conscious that Cristo Ravelli clearly had not known about the ownership of the Lodge, Belle paced and wondered anxiously why he had not been aware of the fact. She was trying not to recall the fact that the solicitor who had dealt with her mother's estate had found no paperwork confirming the older woman's ownership. He had brushed off the matter and said he would look into it, and at the time Belle had had so many other things on her plate that she hadn't pursued it.

Cristo strolled back into the drawing room with the lithe, unconscious grace of a male who was confident that he was in the strongest position. 'I'm afraid you don't own the Lodge,' he spelt out softly, his Italian accent edging his vowel sounds.

'That's not possible,' Belle countered, her chin rising in challenge. 'Your father told me it was mine—'

'But for your lifetime only, after which it reverts back to the Mayhill estate,' Cristo qualified smoothly.

Suddenly Belle felt as if the ground below her feet had opened to swallow her up. 'That's not what Gaetano led me to believe.'

'My father had a way with words and may have wished you to believe that you *owned* the Lodge but, in fact, you only have the *use* of it.'

A shot of rage flamed through Belle like a lightning strike. That hateful, manipulative man whom her wretched mother had loved! How could he have misled her like that over something so important? Hot colour sprang into her cheeks as she parted her dry lips. 'And this right to live there while…er I am alive, does it devolve to the children after my…er death?' she prompted sickly.

'I'm afraid not.' Cristo Ravelli gave her a specious

smile of sympathy, which wouldn't have fooled her in any mood, least of all the one she was in. 'But to all intents and purposes, the Lodge does belong to you for the present. You can't, of course, sell it, use it as security for a loan or indeed make any extensive alterations to it, but you do have the right to live there for as long as you wish.'

Belle had lost every scrap of her angry colour by the time he had finished speaking. It was appalling news, the very worst she could have heard. Her mother was dead and the right to live in the Lodge had died with her, which meant that Belle and her siblings were illegally occupying the house. Indeed, her pretence that she was her mother could be seen by some people as an attempt to defraud. She had taken their ability to live at the Lodge for granted, she registered, stricken. Now she was being punished for it because, in reality, they were about to be made homeless.

'My father was very…astute with regard to money and property,' Cristo murmured softly, watching her standing there, white with shock below the garish make-up, eyes wide and stunned by what he had revealed. 'But I'm willing to find you another property and put it into your name.'

With difficulty, Belle struggled to concentrate. 'And why would you be willing to do that?'

'It will be easier to sell this estate without what would be…in effect…a sitting tenant in the Lodge,' Cristo admitted.

'That…' Belle made a valiant attempt to swallow the massive surge of fury heating her to boiling point and utterly failed to hold it in. 'That…bastard! How could he do that to his own children?' she gasped.

'My father wasn't a sentimental man,' Cristo said drily. 'And he has left a mess in his wake. I have a proposition to put to you which *could* solve all your problems…'

Belle was rigid, furious that she had cursed Gaetano to Cristo's face but unable to overcome the bitter resentment threatening to consume her like a living flame. He was so calm, so assured, so very much in control that she hated him with every fibre in her straining body.

Cristo watched her snatch in another audible breath, eyes green as emeralds in sunlight and literally alight with fury. She was highly volatile, a woman with strong emotions she couldn't hide and everything he had always avoided in her sex. But she looked magnificent and the seductive shimmy of her lush rounded breasts below the silky blouse every time she moved was incredibly attention-grabbing.

'Pro-proposition?' Belle framed shakily, fighting like mad to maintain control over her temper. So, she'd had bad news and she was going to have to deal with it. She stared stonily back at Cristo, clashing with stunning dark eyes nailed to her with unsettling intensity. In the rushing silence that had fallen, her throat closed over and her mouth ran dry.

'I want to ask you to consider the idea of having your children adopted,' Cristo suggested quietly. 'It would surely be best for them to leave their troubled and questionable parentage behind them and have the opportunity to live a normal life.'

'I can't believe you just said that to my face,' Belle confided between gritted teeth of restraint.

'I would make the sacrifice very well worth your

while,' Cristo continued evenly as if what he was suggesting were perfectly normal and acceptable. 'My father should have ensured that you have a home and an income but since he hasn't done it, I will take care of it instead.'

'No decent mother would surrender her children for financial gain,' Belle declared in a raw undertone while shooting him a look of scorn that he could even suggest otherwise. 'What sort of women are you used to dealing with?'

'That's not your affair. I am not my father and I have no children,' Cristo replied with cold dignity.

'And don't deserve any either!' Belle lashed back at him. 'For goodness' sake, those children you're talking about are your own brothers and sisters!'

'I do not, and *will* not, acknowledge them as such,' Cristo retorted with icy hauteur.

'Why? Aren't they good enough to be Ravellis?' Belle shot back at him resentfully. 'The housekeeper's kids…not very posh, is it? Not quite the right background, am I right? Well, let me tell you something—'

'No. I don't want you to tell me anything while your temper is out of control,' Cristo cut in with the cutting edge of an icy scalpel.

'And you pride yourself on being an iceberg, don't you?' Belle launched back fearlessly, her generous mouth curling with contempt. 'Well, I'm not ashamed to be an emotional person and ready to do what's right no matter how unwelcome or difficult it is!'

'Does your ranting ever get you to the point?' Cristo enquired witheringly.

Belle's slender hands coiled into tight fists. She had never wanted to hit another living person before and she was shocked by the fact that she would very much have liked to slap him. How dared he stand there looking down on her and her siblings as if they were so much lesser than him? How dared he suggest that her brothers and sisters be torn away from the people they loved and settled in another home with adoptive parents? Couldn't he appreciate that the children were living, breathing people with emotions and attachments and a desperate need for security after the losses they had already sustained? And couldn't he accept that while Mary Brophy might have had her flaws when it came to picking reliable men, she had also been a wonderful loving mother every day of Belle and her siblings' lives?

'The point is...' Belle breathed in a voice that literally shook with the force of her feelings. 'My mother may only have been a housekeeper and she may have been your father's mistress for years, but she was also a very special, kind and caring person and, having lost her, her children deserve the very best that I can give them.'

'Your...*mother*?' Cristo repeated flatly. 'Mary Brophy was your mother?'

And Belle froze there, her skin slowly turning cold and clammy with shock as she realised what she had revealed in her passionate attempt to bring Cristo round to her point of view. For a moment, she had totally forgotten that she was pretending to be her mother in her desperate need to defend the older woman's memory.

'So, if you're not Mary Brophy...where is she? And who are you?' Cristo framed doggedly, incensed that she had dared to try and fool him.

'I'm Belle Brophy. My mother died about a month after your father. She had a heart attack,' Belle admitted with pained green eyes, accepting that she could no longer continue the pretence and that her own unruly temper had betrayed her when she could least afford for it to do so. Unfortunately Cristo Ravelli's unfeeling detachment and innate air of command and superiority were like vinegar poured on an already raw wound.

'You had no intention of telling me that your mother was dead… You lied to keep the Lodge,' Cristo condemned without hesitation.

Dismay assailed Belle at how quickly he had leapt to that unsavoury conclusion and had assumed she had had a criminal motivation for her masquerade. 'It was nothing to do with the Lodge. Until I came here today I believed my mother owned it and that as her children it became ours after her death,' she reminded him. 'But I didn't think you'd listen to what I want for the children if you knew I was only their sister and not their mother.'

Cristo had a very low tolerance threshold for people who lied to him and tried to deceive him. He was remembering the long-legged redhead crossing the lawn the evening before and guessing that that had been Belle Brophy all along. Outrage swept through his big powerful body, sparking his rarely roused temper. Anger fired his dark eyes gold and he took a sudden livid step towards her. 'You pretended to be your mother… Are you crazy? Or simply downright stupid?'

Her heart suddenly thumping very fast at the dark masculine fury etched in his lean, strong face, Belle sidestepped him and raced for the door. She never hung around long when a man got mad in her vicinity; her childhood had taught her that rage often tumbled over the edge into physical violence.

Cristo closed a hand round her slender forearm as she opened the door. 'You're not going anywhere yet.'

'Let go of my arm!' Belle slung up at him furiously, feeling intimidated by the sheer size of him standing that close. 'I made a mistake but that doesn't give you the right to manhandle me!'

'I'm not manhandling you!' Cristo riposted in disgust. 'But you do owe me an explanation for your peculiar behaviour!'

Her green eyes flared with anger and she yanked her arm violently free of his hold. 'You're a Ravelli! The day I owe you anything there'll be two blue moons in the sky!'

For a split second, Cristo watched her stalk across the hall, stiletto heels tap-tapping, slender spine rigid, red corkscrew curls beginning to untidily descend from her inexpertly arranged chignon. 'Come back here!' he roared at her, out of all patience.

Belle spun round angrily, watching him move towards her, and then she spun out a hand and grabbed up a heavy vase from the table beside her and brandished it like a weapon. 'Don't you dare come any closer!' she warned him.

'Is it normal for you to act like a madwoman?' Cristo asked softly, mastering his fury and his exasperation with the greatest of difficulty.

'I'm going to take you to court, *force* you to recognise the children!' Belle spat back at him in passionate challenge. 'They have legal rights to a share of your father's estate and you can't prevent them from receiving it. And I am not a madwoman.'

An inner chill gripped Cristo at the threat of a court case in which every piece of Gaetano's dirty linen would be aired with the media standing by happy to scoop up and publicise every sordid detail. 'Calm down,' he advised tersely. 'And we'll talk.'

'I don't trust you!' Belle hurled back. 'Let me leave or I'll throw this at you!'

An instant later, Cristo could not comprehend that he had walked forward in the face of that warning instead of just letting her go, particularly when it was clear that he wouldn't be able to get a sane word out of her until she had calmed down.

Belle flung the vase at him and fled, cringing from the sound of breaking porcelain hitting the tiled floor as she hauled open the front door and raced down the front steps.

'Technically that was an attempt to assault you,' his bodyguard, Rafe, remarked from the stairs as Cristo brushed flakes of porcelain from his suit, his handsome mouth compressed and lean, dark face a grim mask.

'She couldn't hit a barn door at ten paces. Next time, I won't jump out of the way,' Cristo breathed from the steps as he watched her stalk down the driveway, her head held high like an offended queen. She was mad, completely and utterly mad, nutty as a fruitcake. How was he supposed to negotiate with a woman like that? But he *had* to deal with her or face a very public and embarrassing court case.

'There'll *be* a next time?' Rafe could not help responding in surprise.

Cristo's smile was as cold and threatening as a hungry polar bear's. 'Oh, there'll be a next time all right.'

CHAPTER FOUR

'It's all out in the open now, which is much better,' Isa told Belle comfortably. 'Now we all know where we stand.'

Belle dashed a stray curl from her hot brow with a forearm, finished wiping the work surface and dried her hands. She had indulged in an orgy of cleaning since returning to the Lodge. She had needed a physical outlet to work off her excess energy. Her grandmother always reacted to stressful situations with calm and acceptance and when Belle had mentioned worst-case scenarios in the homeless field, Isa had quietly reminded her that it would be a few weeks before Bruno and Donetta returned home for the summer and that that was ample time in which to find somewhere to rent. Belle had had to swallow back the thorny question of how she would *pay* rent because she didn't have the money and Isa didn't either.

Tag began to bark noisily a split second before the doorbell went. Belle walked out to the hall with Tag bouncing excitably at her heels.

Cristo Ravelli stood on the step, six feet four inches tall at the very least and Belle had no heels on, so he towered over her, radiating raw energy and power. His lean, darkly beautiful face was hard and forbidding. 'Miss Brophy?'

'Belle,' she corrected curtly.

Cristo looked his fill from the mane of colourful curls tumbling round her shoulders to the porcelain-pale delicate features that provided the perfect frame for grass-green eyes and a full pink mouth. Out of disguise and bare of the tacky make-up she was absolutely breathtaking.

Belle flushed and parted her lips to ask what he wanted and her grip on the door loosened, allowing Tag to take advantage and dart outside to spring an attack on the visitor.

Cristo got off the step fast as the little dog snarled and attacked his ankles. Belle squatted down, saying not very effectively, 'No, Tag, no!'

Cristo received the impression that the dog was welcome to eat him alive if he chose to do so.

'Grab Tag!' an older woman snapped from the hall.

Belle gathered the frantic little dog into her arms. 'I'm sorry. He's suspicious of men.'

'Come in, Mr Ravelli,' Isa Kelly invited politely over her granddaughter's crouching figure.

Belle's head came up fast, green eyes stormy. 'I wasn't going to ask—'

'Mr Ravelli is a guest,' her grandmother decreed. 'He will visit and you will talk like civilised people.'

Tag growled at Cristo from the security of Belle's arms. 'Your father kicked him…so did mine,' she confided grudgingly. 'That's why he doesn't like men. He's too old now to change his ways.'

The older woman studied Cristo, hostility creeping into her voice, despite the civility of her words.

Cristo strolled into a hideous lounge with pink walls, hot-pink sofas and embellished with so many pink frills and ostentatious fake-flower arrangements that it was as if his worst nightmare had come to life. 'I've never liked dogs,' he confided.

A curly-haired toddler clamped both arms round his leg before he could sit down.

'No, Franco,' Belle scolded.

'Or kids,' Cristo added unapologetically.

Franco looked up at him. He had Gaetano's eyes and Cristo found that sight so unnerving that he sat down with the kid still clamped awkwardly to one leg.

'Man,' Franco pronounced with an air of discovery and satisfaction.

'He's a wee bit starved of male attention,' Belle breathed, setting down the dog to grab the toddler in his place and convey him struggling and loudly protesting into the kitchen with her.

'Cristo drinks black coffee,' her grandmother told her from the doorway.

Belle gritted her teeth but she knew that the older woman was talking sense; she *did* have to talk to Cristo and, having set out her expectations, at least he already knew her plans.

Cristo ignored the dog snarling at him from below the coffee table. It was little and grey around the muzzle and should have known better in his opinion than to embark on a battle it couldn't possibly win. Cristo never wasted his time on lost causes or thankless challenges but Belle would, no doubt, have been pleased to learn that her threat had focused his powerful intellect as nothing else could have done.

The instant the tray of coffee and biscuits arrived,

Cristo rose back upright, feeling suffocated amidst all that horrible pinkness. 'I don't want you to take the question of the children's parentage into court.'

'Tough,' Belle said succinctly, not one whit perturbed by his statement because she could hardly have expected him to be supportive on that score. 'My brothers and sisters have been ignored and passed over far too many times. I want them to have what they're entitled to.'

'A few years ago, Gaetano sold up most of his assets and he salted away the proceeds in overseas trusts, which no Irish court will be able to access,' Cristo volunteered. 'With the exception of the sale of the Mayhill estate there is very little cash for you to demand a share of on behalf of your siblings.'

'I'm not looking for a fortune for them.'

'I have a better idea,' Cristo told her.

'I imagine that you *always* have a better idea,' Belle quipped helplessly, leaning back against the kitchen door with defensively folded arms while she wondered how any man could look so fit and vital clad in a tailored business suit that belonged in a boardroom.

She was slim as a whip in her tight faded jeans and an off-the-shoulder black tee that revealed an entrancing glimpse of a narrow white shoulder bisected by a black strap that Cristo savoured, glorying in the fact that he was now free to appreciate her glowing beauty while he speculated as to whether or not she was that pale all over, her skin in vibrant contrast to her bright hair and eyes. The instant he developed an erection, he regretted that evocative thought.

'I will make a settlement on your siblings in compensation for their not pursuing their rights through the courts,' Cristo delivered, half turning away from her to look out of the window overlooking the drive.

'We don't want Ravelli charity,' Belle traded, lifting her chin.

'But it wouldn't be charity. As you said, they're my father's children and I should make good on that for all our sakes. My family would find a court case embarrassing,' Cristo admitted tight-mouthed.

Belle didn't shift an inch. 'Why should I care about that?'

'Publicity is a double-edged sword,' Cristo warned her. 'The media loves sleaze. Your mother won't emerge well from the story. At least three of the children were born while Gaetano was still married.'

At that blunt reminder, a veil of colour burned up below Belle's fair complexion. 'That can't be helped and Mum can't be hurt now. I have to consider the children's future. I want them to have the right to use the Ravelli name.'

'No court that I know of has the ability to bestow that right when no marriage took place between the parents,' Cristo countered, exasperated by her pigheadedness. 'You're being unreasonable. If you keep this out of court and allow me to handle things discreetly, I will be generous. It's the best offer you're going to get.'

'Forgive me for my lack of trust. As I learned today with regard to the ownership of this house, your father was a good teacher.'

'I will not allow you to take this sordid mess into a public courtroom,' Cristo spelt out harshly. 'If you do that I will fight you every step of the way and I warn you—you don't want me as an enemy.'

'Fight me all you like…it's still going to court,' Belle replied thinly. 'We have nothing to lose and everything to gain.'

'What would it take for you to drop this idea?' Cristo growled, almost shuddering at the threat of how much damage a media smear campaign could do to his brother. Zarif's standing in Vashir was delicate, his having only recently ascended the throne. The last thing Zarif needed right now was a great big horrible scandal that would give all too many people the impression that he was from a sleazy family background and was far from being the right ruler for a very conservative country. Zarif, Cristo reminded himself grimly, had already taken the fall for revealing Nik's biggest secret to Nik's estranged wife, Betsy, when the first careless spilling of that secret was entirely Cristo's fault.

'I'd probably be asking for the impossible,' Belle admitted ruefully, 'but I want my siblings to have the lifestyle they would have enjoyed had Gaetano married my mother. It's very unfair that they should have to pay the price for the fact that he didn't marry her.'

'You're being irrational,' Cristo condemned, impatiently, moving out of the room. 'You can't change the past.'

'I don't want to change the past. I simply want to right the wrongs that have been done to my siblings.'

'Leave the past behind you and move on.'

'Easy for you to say,' Belle quipped. 'Not so easy in practice. And I'm not irrational—'

In the hall, Cristo swung round, surprisingly light on his feet for so large and powerfully built a man. 'You're the most irrational woman I've ever met.'

Belle collided with his stunning dark eyes and for a timeless moment the world stopped turning and she stopped breathing.

'And for some reason I find it incredibly sexy,' Cristo purred the admission, his accent roughening his dark deep drawl as he flicked her tee shirt back up over her exposed shoulder with a long careless forefinger.

'You can't get round me. I'm not as naïve as my mother was,' Belle told him tartly.

'Wake up and smell the roses, *cara*. You're a child trying to play with the grown-ups,' Cristo told her thickly, his intimate intonation vibrating down her taut spinal cord.

Suddenly, Belle was short of breath and she stared up at him, her eyes very wide and scornful. 'A child? Is that the best you can do on the insult front?'

'I wasn't trying to insult you.' Up that close his dark eyes had tiny gold flecks like stars. His hand curved to her shoulder and the scent of clean, warm male overlaid with a faint hint of cologne ignited a burst of heat low in Belle's tummy. Just as suddenly she was locked into his eyes and it was as though her feet were encased in concrete and she literally *couldn't* move. He lowered his handsome dark head and took her parted lips with a scorching urgency that sent something frighteningly wild and alive flying through her like an explosive charge. It was a fiery kiss and like no other she had experienced. The minute his tongue plunged into the tender interior of her mouth, it sent a wave of violent response crashing through her, and she was lost. Her hands roamed from his broad shoulders up into his luxuriant dark hair while she rejoiced in the

taste of him, the unique sexual flavour of a dominant
and surprisingly passionate male. His arms tightened
round her, long fingers smoothing down her spine to
pin her into uncompromising awareness of his erection. She gasped beneath the thrust of his tongue, mind
flying free to picture a much more sexual joining and
craving that completion with a strength that started an
ache between her thighs.

The sheer intensity of what she was feeling totally
spooked Belle. With a startled sound of rejection, she
pushed him back from her. 'No, we're not doing this!'
she told him furiously.

Dark eyes veiled, Cristo stepped back and drew in
a long, deep, steadying breath. *Maledizione!* He was
too aroused to be comfortable with the sensation or
the woman who had got him into that condition. 'I
seem to recall that I was trying to persuade you not
to take private family business into a court of law,'
he murmured flatly.

Belle shot him a disconcerted glance, unable to
credit that he could act as frozen as ever in the wake
of that passionate kiss. Passion, it seemed, didn't control Cristo Ravelli. All in the space of a moment she
resented his assurance, was insulted by his cool indif-
ference and furious that she hadn't fought him off. But,
my goodness, he could kiss. That mortifying thought
crept through her mind no matter how hard she tried
to kill it dead.

Belle had done a lot of kissing and not much else as
a student, very much hoping to experience a volcanic
reaction that would signal that all-important spark of
true, overwhelming physical attraction. Now fate was
having the last laugh by finally serving up that long-

awaited, miraculously special kiss and it was happening with the *wrong* man. She had no doubt that Cristo Ravelli was wrong in every way for her. He was stuffy and cold and unfeeling and she was a warm, emotional and impulsive individual.

'I'm sorry. I'm going to do what's best for my siblings and take this matter to court to get it sorted out,' Belle told him curtly.

'You can't,' Cristo countered with chilling bite. 'It will damage other people. You and your siblings are not the only individuals likely to be affected by this.'

'I don't care about anyone else,' Belle admitted truthfully. 'I want my brothers and sisters to be able to hold their heads high and know who they are without shame.'

'You want the impossible,' Cristo derided, turning on his heel.

'No, I want justice.'

Justice! Cristo reflected contemptuously, a deep sense of frustration ruling him, for Cristo never backed down and never failed to find solutions to problems. Damage limitation was his speciality. How could it be justice that Zarif's throne would be rocked by the extent of Gaetano's infidelity and the revelation of his secret family in Ireland? Like father, like son, Zarif's critics would sneer. Mary Brophy had made her choices when she chose to get involved with a married man and have his children. Her daughter, Belle, had too much pride and her resentment of the Ravelli family, or, more specifically, his father, had persuaded her that she could somehow rewrite history. But washing the family dirty linen in public was *not* going to make those children feel that they could raise their heads high. No, it was much more likely to shame them by depicting their parents in ways they would never forget. No child of Gaetano's had *ever* been proud of him or his name. Gaetano had been a cruelly selfish and uninterested parent.

Ironically, Cristo had always believed growing up that he would be a better man than his father and now he wondered what had happened to that dream and at what point cynicism had killed that honourable goal stone dead. He knew that he had not once considered the plight of Mary Brophy's children from any viewpoint other than his own. He was a pragmatic man and he knew he was selfish. But even *he* recognised that Belle Brophy was too young and her grandmother too old to take on full responsibility for Gaetano's children. Cristo was suddenly very conscious that those kids, right down to the little one with his father's eyes, were his flesh and blood too, even though he didn't want to recognise that unwelcome fact.

And then the answer to the problem came to him in a sudden shocking moment of truth. He recoiled from the prospect at first, but as he filtered through the list of challenges he currently faced and that solution ticked every box he began to mull it over as a genuine possibility. It was not as though he were ever likely to fall in love again. Indeed it was a wonder it had happened even once to a male as detached from emotion as he was, he reasoned grimly. Gaetano and Mary's affair could be decently buried and the children's antecedents concealed from the media. As for Belle, in the role he envisaged, which was frankly Belle reclining wearing only a winsome smile on his bed in London, well, she would be perfect there, he reflected with the very first flicker of enthusiasm for the challenge of sacrificing his freedom for the greater good.

Belle suffered a restless night of sleep. She relived the kiss again and again and got hot and bothered while tossing and turning in guilty discomfiture. Cristo was a Ravelli just like Gaetano and the very last man alive she should enjoy kissing. In the morning, she made breakfast for the children on automatic pilot because her brain felt fuzzy and slow. There had been too much agonising over whether or not going to court was the right thing to do for the children, she decided irritably. She did not have a choice. There had never been a choice and there was no way on earth that she planned to trust in any promises made by Cristo Ravelli, who would undoubtedly be every bit as slippery in such delicate negotiations as his late father had proved to be. Exasperated by the constant parade of anxious thoughts weighing her down, Belle saw the twins off to school and then told her grandmother that she was taking Franco down to the beach.

When he reached the beach, Cristo had the pleasure of seeing Belle looking relaxed for the first time. Her wild mane of curls was blowing back from her face in the breeze that plastered her jeans and her blue tee to her lithe, shapely body. She was engaged in throwing a stone into the sea while the leg-clinging toddler bounced up and down in excitement and the dog circled them both barking noisily. Espying Cristo first, the Jack Russell raced across the sand to attack.

'*No!*' Cristo thundered as he strode across the sand.

Tag cringed and rolled over and stuck his four little legs up in the air, beady eyes telegraphing terror.

'You didn't need to shout at him,' Belle criticised, rushing over to crouch down and pet the little animal. 'Look how frightened he is! He's very sensitive.'

'I'm a little sensitive to being bitten,' Cristo murmured drily.

'Man!' the toddler exclaimed and immediately went for Cristo's left leg. Cristo froze, wondering if he could *do* it—actually take on the whole bunch of them and survive with his dignity and sanity intact. He wasn't a family man, he hadn't a clue how a normal family functioned and didn't really want to find out.

Belle was looking up at him, her lovely face flushed and self-conscious, clear green eyes wide above her dainty freckled nose, and her vibrant beauty in that instant scoured his mind clean of all such thoughts. She made him think about sex, lots and lots and lots of sex, and on one level that unnerved him and on another it turned him so hard it literally hurt.

Belle stood up. Tag, the terrified dog, was clasped to her bosom, and now giving Cristo a rather smug look. 'Did Isa tell you where I was?'

'I could be down here for a walk.'

Belle raised a fine auburn brow, scanning his lean, powerful body with assessing eyes. It amazed her that a man who spent so much time in a business suit could be so well built but there he was: broad of shoulder and chest, lean of hip and long of leg with not even the hint of jowls or a paunch. Clearly, he kept fit. And although she had long thought business suits were boring Cristo's dark, perfectly tailored designer suit screamed class and sophistication and was cut close to his powerful thighs and lean hips, directing her attention to areas she didn't normally appraise on men. Her colour heightening, she tore her attention from the prominent bulge at his crotch and dropped it down to his highly polished shoes, which were caked with sand, and she wondered why he couldn't just admit that he had come looking for her.

'You didn't come down here for a walk dressed like that.'

'Sand brushes off,' he fielded carelessly as she settled the dog down on the beach and he scampered off.

In silence, Belle studied Cristo's lean, extravagantly handsome features, heat blossoming in her pelvis and butterflies flying free in her tummy. She felt as clumsy and ill at ease as a schoolgirl in the presence of her idol. But then was it any wonder that she was embarrassed? She had looked at his body and positively delighted in the strikingly strong muscular definition inherent in his build. She could not recall ever doing that to a man before. But the need to look at Cristo felt as necessary as the need to breathe. In reaction to that humiliating truth she flushed to the roots of her hair, mortified by her failure to control her reaction to his looks and dark, charismatic appeal.

Cristo reached down to detach the toddler's painful grip from his leg. *Starved of male attention*, he recalled, thinking that he could certainly understand that. Neither in childhood nor adulthood had Gaetano ever touched him or, indeed, enquired after his wellbeing. 'We have to talk,' he said succinctly.

'There's nothing more to talk about. We said it all last night,' Belle tossed over a slim shoulder as she started down the beach again and extended her hand. 'Franco, come here!'

'No!' the toddler said stubbornly and, deprived of Cristo's leg, grasped a handful of his trousers instead, making it difficult for Cristo to walk.

Cristo expelled his breath in a slow measured hiss. 'I placed the Mayhill estate on the market this morning,' he fired at her rudely turned back.

Belle came to a dead halt, her narrow spine suddenly rigid as panic leapt inside her at the prospect of losing the roof over their heads. There was certainly no room for them all to squeeze into Isa's one-bedroom apartment in the village. She stared out to sea but the soothing sound of the surf washing the sand smooth failed to work its usual magic. She turned her bright head, green eyes glittering. 'Couldn't that have waited for a few weeks?'

Cristo took his time crossing the sand to join her, her little brother clinging to whatever part of Cristo he could reach and finally stretching up to grip the corner of his suit jacket with sandy fingers. 'No. I want the property sold as soon as possible. I want Gaetano's life here to remain a secret.'

'And what about us? Where are we supposed to go?' Belle demanded heatedly, her temper rising. 'It takes time to relocate.'

'You'll have at least a month to find somewhere else,' Cristo fielded without perceptible sympathy while he watched the breeze push the soft, clinging cotton of her top against her breasts, defining the full rounded swells and her pointed nipples. The heavy pulse at his groin went crazy and he clenched his teeth together, willing back his arousal.

'That's not very long. Bruno and Donetta will be home from school for the summer soon. Five children take up a lot of space… They're your brothers and sisters too, so you should *care* about what happens to them!' Belle launched back at him in furious condemnation.

'Which is why I'm here to suggest that we get married and *make* a home for them together,' Cristo countered with harsh emphasis as he wondered for possibly the very first time in his life whether he really did know what he was doing.

'Married?' Belle repeated aghast, wondering if she'd missed a line or two in the conversation. 'What on earth are you talking about?'

'You said that you wanted your siblings to enjoy the Ravelli name and lifestyle. I can only make that happen by marrying you and adopting them.'

Frowning in confusion, Belle fell back a step, in too much shock to immediately respond. 'Is this a joke?' she asked when she had finally found her voice again.

'Why would I joke about something so serious?'

Belle shrugged. 'How would I know? You thought it was acceptable to suggest to their mother that she give them up to be adopted,' she reminded him helplessly.

'I'm not joking,' Cristo replied levelly, a stray shard of sunlight breaking through the clouds to slant across his lean, strong face.

All over again, Belle studied him in wonder because he had the smouldering dark beauty of a fallen angel. His brilliant dark eyes were nothing short of stunning below the thick screen of his lashes and suddenly she felt as breathless as though someone were standing on her lungs.

'I'm a practical man and I'm suggesting a practical marriage which would fulfil *all* our needs,' Cristo continued smoothly. 'You're aware that I don't want a court case. I also want to prevent the squalid story of Gaetano and his housekeeper leaking into the public domain. You would have to agree not to discuss the children's parentage with anyone but nobody need tell any lies either. As far as anyone need know, the children are simply your orphaned brothers and sisters.'

Belle breathed in deep and slow but it still didn't clear her head. 'I can't believe you're suggesting this.'

'You didn't give me a choice, did you? The threat of a court case piled on the pressure. *Are* you prepared to settle this out of court?' Cristo studied her enquiringly.

Belle didn't hesitate. 'No.'

Cristo raised a sleek ebony brow. 'Then what's your answer?'

'It's not that simple,' Belle protested.

'Isn't it? I'm offering you everything you said you wanted.'

Her lashes flickered above her strained eyes. She felt cornered and trapped. 'Well, yes, but...*marriage*? I could hardly be expecting that development!'

Annoyance lanced through Cristo. It was his very first proposal of marriage and he had never before even considered proposing to a woman. Without a shade of vanity he knew he was rich, good-looking and very eligible and yet she was hesitating and he was grimly amused by his irritation.

'Look, I'll think it over until tonight,' Belle muttered uncomfortably.

'*Di niente*...no problem,' Cristo fielded, his wide,

sensual mouth compressed. 'By the way…I mean a *real* marriage.'

'Real…?' Belle spluttered to a halt, the tip of her tongue stealing out to wet her dry lower lip. His intent dark gaze flashed pure naked gold to that tiny movement. Heated colour swept her face as she grasped his meaning in growing disbelief. 'You'd expect me to *sleep* with you?'

'Of course,' Cristo murmured with an indolent assurance that suggested that that idea was entirely normal and acceptable. 'I have no plans to emulate my father and entertain mistresses while I'm married. And I don't want a wife who plays around behind my back either. That kind of lifestyle would not provide a stable home for the children.'

Belle got his point, she really did, but she flushed scarlet at the thought of sharing a bed with him, suddenly very conscious of her own lack of sexual experience. Growing up, she'd had to combat the expectations of the local boys who saw her mother as free and easy in that department and she had had to prove over and over again that she was different. Saying no had been a matter of pride and self-preservation, but as she got older that conditioning along with other needs and insecurities had influenced her and *trusting* a man enough to drop her guard and make love had proved to be even more of a challenge for Belle.

Cristo settled a business card into her limp hand and she stared down at it blankly.

'My private cell number. Let me know by seven

this evening, *bellezza mia*,' he instructed with unblemished cool. 'That way I can make an immediate start on the arrangements.'

CHAPTER FIVE

'DON'T DO THIS...don't do this...' Isa's constant refrain was still sounding like a death knell in Belle's ears as she climbed out of the car Cristo had sent to collect her and mounted the steps that led up into the chapel of St Jude's. She was wearing an elegant but rather plain vintage dress with a boat-shaped lace neckline. It was her late mother's wedding gown.

The symbolism of that gesture had appealed to her and in the three weeks that had passed since she last saw Cristo she'd had the dress lengthened to suit her greater height. Mary might never have got her Ravelli to the altar but her daughter was succeeding where she had failed, Belle could not help reflecting with guilty satisfaction. She knew it wasn't right to feel that way because Cristo was not Gaetano and he had not committed his father's sins but she couldn't help it. She was the talk of the neighbourhood, for nobody was quite sure how she had hooked a husband who had only set foot in Ireland for the first time less than a month ago. Indeed there was a crowd of well-wishers waiting outside the old church, quietly ignoring Cristo's request that the wedding be regarded as a private affair.

Of course, Cristo definitely knew how to garner

support and respect in the locals, Belle conceded ruefully. He had decided not to sell Mayhill but to instead
gift the historic house to the village as a community
centre and endow it for the future. Money talked,
money certainly talked *very* loudly in an area where
incomes were low and jobs were few. Mayhill would
put the village on the map by becoming a tourist attraction and its maintenance and the business prospects it would provide would offer many employment
opportunities. And naturally, it was tacitly and silently
understood by the recipients of Cristo's extraordinary
largesse that his father's affair with Mary Brophy and
the birth of their children were matters to be buried
in the darkest, deepest closet never to see the light of
day again.

Her sisters, thirteen-year-old Donetta and eight-
year-old Lucia, were beaming at her from a front pew.
Her brothers Bruno, Pietro and little Franco were beside them. Bruno was frowning, too intelligent to be
fooled by the surface show and still suspicious of what
was happening to his family.

'Do you really *want* to marry Gaetano's son?'
Bruno had demanded the night before when he had
returned from school with Donetta, both teenagers
granted special leave for the occasion of their sister's
wedding.

'It was love at first sight,' Belle had lied, determined to remove the lines of concern from his brow
and the too anxious look from his sensitive gaze. 'And
how can you ask me that?'

'I'm not saying I don't believe you…but it seems
very convenient in the circumstances. I mean, here
we are, broke, virtually homeless and sinking fast and

along comes Cristo Ravelli *in* the rescue boat and suddenly our every dream is coming true,' Bruno had recited thinly. 'It doesn't *feel* real to me—it's too good to be true. How did you finally bury the hatchet?'

'What hatchet?'

'You grew up hating the Ravelli family and now all of a sudden you're *marrying* one of them?'

'He's your brother,' Belle had reminded the teenager stubbornly.

'He's a super-rich banker and as sharp as a whip. It's you I'm concerned about. What do you know about being married to a guy like that?' Bruno had asked worriedly. 'He lives in a different world.'

But right now, Cristo was in Belle's world, she savoured helplessly, finally allowing herself to look at the tall, well-built male waiting for her at the altar. Not an iota of the traditional bridegroom's nervous tension showed on his lean, darkly handsome features. In fact he might just have been an attendant at someone else's wedding for all the awareness he was showing. Unconsciously, Belle's chin lifted as if she had been challenged; her heart was pounding fast as a hammer blow behind her ribs and her spine was rigid with all the tension he lacked. After all, she had barely slept since texting him a single word, 'Yes', on the day he had proposed to her on the beach.

Accepting had taken a massive amount of courage and she had garnered that courage only by focusing on the advantages of marrying Cristo Ravelli and suppressing all awareness of the downsides. Her family would finally be safe, absolutely *safe and secure* and that was the bottom line and the only important thing she should concentrate on. What it cost her personally wasn't important and couldn't be weighed on the scale of such things.

After all, she had never been in love and was even more certain that she didn't want to fall in love with anyone. Her memories of her mother's unhappiness during Gaetano's long absences were still fresh as a daisy. Mary had only really come alive when Gaetano was around. Every time he departed it had broken Mary's heart afresh and he would leave her pining and lifeless with only the occasional brief phone call to anticipate while she counted the weeks and days until his next visit. Belle had kept one of those painstakingly numbered calendars as a reminder of what such unstinting, unhesitating love, loyalty and devotion could do to wreck a woman's life. Mary had *lived* for Gaetano. Belle only wanted to live for her family and ensure that they enjoyed a much happier and more stable childhood than she had received.

Isa was staying on in the Lodge for the summer and had insisted that Bruno, Donetta and the twins stay on there with her, leaving only Franco to stay with Belle because her little brother was too attached to her to be separated from her for weeks on end. 'You get your marriage sorted out before you uproot the kids to London and new schools and all the rest of it,' her grandmother had told her bluntly. 'You know I don't approve of what you're doing and if there's a risk that this marriage will only last as long as it takes you to come to your senses, you shouldn't drag the children into it with you.'

Belle had argued until she was finally forced to acknowledge that the older woman was talking good sense. Of course there was a chance that she and Cristo wouldn't make a go of their 'practical' marriage. She would have to make a success of their relationship before she could risk disrupting the children's lives and bringing them to London to live on a permanent basis. That was a pretty tall order when she had, more or less, agreed to marry a complete stranger.

Thinking along those lines, Belle decided she had to have been insane to say yes with so little thought. It was not that she had not thought about things, simply that she had avoided considering the negative aspects. Going to bed with Cristo had to be one of the more intimidating negative aspects, she conceded, turning hot and cold at the very thought of it, but just *living* with Cristo, indeed with *any* man, would surely be the ultimate challenge.

Wintry dark eyes slashed with gold by the sunlight piercing the stained-glass window behind him, Cristo watched his bride approach. She looked absolutely amazing in white, red gold curls tumbling round her narrow shoulders, her bright head crowned by a simple seed-pearl coronet. Lust engulfed Cristo in a drowning wave and his wide, sensual mouth compressed hard. *Maledizione!* He was convinced that he had never wanted a woman as much before yet he was equally convinced that she would ultimately prove as disappointing as her predecessors. Of course she would, he reflected impatiently, being no fan of optimism or fairy stories. But at least he already knew the worst of her, which was that she was a virtual blackmailer, a gold-digger and a social climber. Better the devil you know than the one you don't, he conceded sardonically and he was exceptionally well versed on the habits and needs of mercenary women.

Her hand trembled in his when he slid on the wedding ring. A nice touch, he thought cynically, a bridal display of nerves and modesty and utterly wasted on Cristo, who was the last man alive likely to be impressed or taken in by such pretences. He was gaining a very beautiful and desirable wife, he reminded himself doggedly, and putting a lid on the threat of an unsavoury scandal. Even his brothers didn't know what he was doing, for the last thing he would have risked was bringing either of them to the scene of Gaetano's reckless shenanigans in this little Irish village.

Cristo pretty much ignored Belle on the short drive back to the Lodge, where a small catered buffet and drinks had been laid on for the family and the few friends invited. It had not escaped Belle's notice that Cristo had not invited a single person and it bothered her, making her wonder if he was ashamed of her and her humble background and lack of designer polish.

Bruno walked up to Cristo in the hall. 'Could we have a word?' he asked, youthful face taut and pale.

Bruno was the living image of Zarif as a teenager and that likeness had unsettled Cristo at their first brief and awkward meeting the evening before. It seemed that Gaetano had stamped the Ravelli genes very firmly on all his offspring.

'Is there a problem?' Cristo enquired, a fine ebony brow lifting.

The teenager backed into the small space at the foot of the stairs and said gruffly, 'If you hurt my sister like your father hurt my mother, I swear I'll kill you.'

Cristo almost laughed but a stray shard of compassion squashed his amusement when he recalled his own turbulent teenaged years. In any case the warning had all the hallmarks of a prepared speech and, having delivered it, Bruno was backing off fast, troubled brown eyes nervously pinned to Cristo as though he was expecting an immediate physical attack. Before the boy could leave, Christo called him back.

'We're family now and I'm not like my father in any way,' Cristo responded very quietly to the teenager. 'I have no desire to hurt any woman.'

From a tactful distance, Belle absorbed that little interplay. Although she hadn't heard the conversation, she suspected that Bruno had probably been very rude in his outspoken need to protect her and she recognised with a sense of unfamiliar warmth that Cristo had handled her kid brother with surprising sympathy. *Their* kid brother, she mentally corrected, yet there it was—Cristo might not be ready yet to acknowledge that blood tie, but he had restrained both his cutting tongue and his temper when he dealt with Bruno and she was grateful for his kindness.

As Bruno moved hurriedly away, his goal evidently accomplished, Cristo studied the slim dark man whose eyes were welded to Belle's vibrant face as she talked to her grandmother's friends. Cristo stiffened, aggression powering through him as he recognised the son of the land agent, Petrie. Petrie's son, Mark, was attracted to his wife. *His* wife. The shock of that designation ricocheted through Cristo as well and he suppressed his awareness of both strange reactions. He concentrated on Belle instead and watched when she fell still the instant she saw him looking at her, enabling him to clearly see her sudden tension and insecurity.

The golden power of Cristo's gaze was almost mesmeric in its intensity and Belle gulped down the rest of the wine in her glass.

'Eat something,' Isa instructed. 'You didn't have any breakfast.'

Belle accepted the sandwich extended for the sake of peace, for although her tummy felt hollow it had nothing to do with hunger. 'I'll go and get changed,' she said uneasily, ruffling Franco's curly head where he stood by her side.

Cristo was still in the hall, detached from the small crowd by a barrier of reserve that chilled her.

'He's not very friendly, is he?' her sister Donetta whispered in her ear.

Belle forced a smile, cursing Cristo's detachment and his clear reluctance to use the opportunity to get to know his younger siblings. 'He's just shy.'

'Shy?' Donetta gasped in surprise.

'*Very* shy,' Belle lied, wanting to lay the teenager's concerns to rest. 'It'll be different when he gets to know all of you properly.'

And the burden of ensuring that it would be different was on *her* shoulders, Belle acknowledged apprehensively, registering what a challenge she had set herself. Cristo had been raised an only child and a family the size of hers had to be a shock to his reticent nature. Franco was tugging at his jacket, looking up at Cristo with adoring brown eyes, and Cristo was at least tolerating the child, she reasoned ruefully, wondering if that was the most she could hope for from him when it came to the children. And her? Would he only be *tolerating* her as well? A shiver of distaste at that image ran down her back until she was warmed by the recollection of his considered response to Bruno.

'Where are you going?' Cristo enquired when she brushed past him to head for the stairs.

'I'm getting changed...for the flight you mentioned,' she extended awkwardly, lashes screening her strained green eyes.

He was her husband, for goodness' sake, and he had decreed that they would be flying out of Ireland within hours of the ceremony. She had thought about arguing but then had seen no point in trying to put off the inevitable. She had given up her life to enter his and leaving home was the first step in that process.

'No. I like the dress. Don't take it off.'

Thoroughly taken aback by the command, Belle glanced up at him in astonishment at the request. 'I can't trudge through an airport dressed like this.'

'I have a private jet and we won't be trudging anywhere. Don't take the dress off, *bellezza mia,*' Cristo instructed sibilantly, a strong dark forefinger curling below her chin to lift it so that she collided with smouldering golden eyes. '*I* want to be the one who takes it off.'

Face burning, breath coming in tortured bursts, Belle fled upstairs, barely able to credit that he had said that to her. She had read about male fantasies and he had just told her his with a lack of embarrassment that made her all the more conscious of her own ignorance. He was already fantasising about removing her bridal gown. It was a useful message as to what went on in Cristo's arrogant head. While she was worrying about him getting to know and like their brothers and sisters *he* was thinking about sex. Was that all their marriage meant to him? Sex and the threat of a big scandal removed?

And if it was, what on earth could she do about it? All her gran's warnings and dire predictions came crashing down on her at once. What if he was cruel? Unfaithful? Belle swallowed hard, mastering her tumultuous emotions. You made your bed, now you have to lie on it...*literally*, she told herself sternly as she checked that she had packed the most essential things for herself and Franco.

Franco cried and begged to get out of his car seat all the way to the airport. Aware of the irritation Cristo couldn't hide and with her own spirits low at having left home and everything and almost everyone familiar behind her for goodness knew how long, Belle tried to distract the child.

'Why did your mother have so many children with my father?' Cristo asked suddenly.

'She always wanted a big family and I think the kids were her compensation for not seeing much of your father,' Belle opined and then, hesitating, added, 'Gaetano wanted nothing to do with them though. When he was here they went to stay with Isa and maybe only saw him once for about ten minutes and it would be very strained. He just wasn't interested.'

'He was the same with me and my brothers.'

'I *hated* him!' Belle admitted in a driven undertone. 'I felt guilty about that when he was killed in the crash.'

'You shouldn't, *cara*,' Cristo parried. 'He was a very selfish man, who lived only for his pleasure and his profit. Nothing else mattered to him.'

Belle settled into her seat on Cristo's opulent private jet. Franco was in the sleeping compartment and,

once she had settled her little brother down for his nap,
Cristo had informed her that he had hired a nanny for
the child, who would be waiting when they reached
their destination.

'Which…*is*?'

'Italy. I'm taking you to my home in Italy.'

'Venice…we're going to Venice?' Belle carolled in
sudden excitement.

'No, that is where my mother and stepfather live.
I inherited a house in Umbria, which has belonged
to my mother's family for generations. Sorry, it's not
Venice,' Cristo quipped.

'Won't your mother be upset that she wasn't at your
wedding?' Belle prompted, shooting him a look of
wide-eyed curiosity.

'I doubt it. Anything that reminds Giulia of Gaetano
puts her in a very bad mood,' Cristo admitted, compressing his lips. 'She never recovered from what he
put her through. You couldn't be in her company for
five minutes before she told you that he stole the best
years of her life, robbed her blind and slept with—
among others—her best friend and her maid.'

'Good grief…' Belle breathed, reeling from that
blunt admission.

During the flight, even with his laptop open in front
of him, Cristo found his attention continually straying
from the financial report he was checking. He studied
Belle's delicate profile from below his dense lashes,
marvelling at the display of innocence and vulnerability that she continued to exude. Was he supposed to be
impressed? Did he strike her as that stupid? After all,
Mary Brophy's daughter was considerably shrewder
than her mother had ever been because she had not

hesitated to use Gaetano's children as a weapon to enrich herself. But his awareness of that aspect of her less than stellar character faded whenever Cristo looked at her, appreciating the vibrancy of her Titian curls against her porcelain-pale skin, the clarity of her beautiful green eyes, the feminine elegance of the fingers and unpainted nails adorning the slim hands that held a magazine. She always looked so amazingly natural, he registered, black brows drawing together in a bemused frown as he questioned the depth of his fascination and hurriedly returned to his financial report, trying and singularly failing to rustle up an immediate image of Betsy's face.

The nanny, Teresa, a middle-aged woman with a warm smile, greeted them at the airport and gathered up Franco with enough appreciation to persuade Belle that her little brother would enjoy the best of attention. Though quite what Cristo expected her to do with her time while someone else looked after Franco, she had no idea. After driving through miles of extensively cultivated agricultural land the sun was going down fast when the limousine began to climb mountain roads with hairpin bends that soon slowed the speed of their passage.

'It feels as if we're travelling to the end of the world,' Belle commented.

'As far as my mother was concerned, the Palazzo Maddalena, named for one of her ancestors, might as well have been. It was never her style.'

And as the car travelled slowly towards to the massive stone building presiding over the hill tops, Belle knew it wasn't her style either and her heart and her courage sank to their lowest ever level. For the first time it really hit her exactly what marrying Cristo entailed and the little girl whose earliest home had been a tiny house was ready to surface again because the adult woman was overpowered by the sheer size and grandeur of the property confronting her. Ancient mellowed stone encased the three-storeys-tall palazzo, which had graceful wings spreading to either side. Elaborate terraced gardens in an ornamental pattern spread down the hill in front of it and behind the solid bulk of the building loomed the imposing snow-capped tops of the Sibillini mountain range.

As pale as a newly created ghost, Belle climbed out of the car, her lovely face frozen and expressionless, her wedding gown glimmering eerily in the twilight. Cristo surveyed her with a level of satisfaction that disconcerted him. *His* wife, *his* home where he was free to be himself. *Her* tension, though, was not a surprise because Cristo was convinced he knew precisely why Belle would have preferred Venice. What was the point of marrying a billionaire if she couldn't enjoy the expected rich advantages that came with the wedding ring? In Venice she could have partied with his mother's wealthy and famous friends and shopped in expensive boutiques and jewellery stores. An ancestral palazzo in the mountains was no fair exchange.

'It's a great place for a honeymoon,' Cristo informed her with something that just might have been amusement glimmering in his keen gaze.

A honeymoon? Well, she *was* married. But why was he laughing at her? Did he also see the ludicrous gulf between a boy raised in a gilded Venetian palace and the housekeeper's daughter? How could he fail to? A tide of self-conscious colour washed Belle's complexion as they entered the enormous palazzo. She knew time was running out. They had dined on the plane, so not even the need to eat could be stretched out to lengthen the evening ahead. For goodness' sake, she urged herself, lighten up, *wise* up. This was the deal; this was the agreement that would ensure her siblings received everything that should have been theirs from birth. They would grow up secure and safe as Ravellis and nobody would have an excuse to mock them or sneer at them. They would have the best of educations and opportunities to equip them to enter adult life. They would never have to worry about where their next meal was coming from. As she listed the countless benefits of having married Cristo Ravelli, Belle's breathing slowly steadied and she steeled her spine.

Franco clutched at her dress as they mounted the stairs and the manservant who had let them in showed them first to a nursery suite where the nanny tried to detach Franco from Belle. But Franco didn't like strange places and he started to sob and clutch at his sister and it took Cristo to detach him from her.

'Kiss-do,' Franco warbled mid sob, ready to smile until Cristo handed him over to the nanny, and then in desperation stretching his arms out to Belle instead.

Belle moved forward to go to Franco but Cristo forestalled her with a hand on her arm. 'It's our wedding night,' he reminded her drily and the very dryness of his tone disturbed her.

In her opinion only people who loved each other had wedding nights, but that wasn't what she had signed up for, she reminded herself squarely as Cristo led the way along the corridor and cast open a door across yet another landing into a huge bedroom. In spite of her nervousness, the thrill of desire began to build within her.

Belle's attention centred on the giant gilded four-poster bed topped with a gilded coronet and stayed there as if a padlock had snapped her into place. Suddenly she was regretting the innate shyness and mistrust that had kept her out of other men's beds. A little sexual experience would have felt better at that moment when ignorance felt more like a threat.

Cristo closed his arms round her rigid figure from behind and the scent of him engulfed her. He smelled so good, a citrusy mix of designer cologne and aromatic male that did something strange to her senses. Her heartbeat kicked up pace as he tugged her hair back from her shoulders and bent his mouth to her nape. His chest was against her spine and as solid as rock, and lower down against her bottom she was suddenly startlingly aware that he was aroused and that had the oddest effect on her. Even as her nervous tension heightened, she couldn't help being pleased that she could have that much influence over a male who tended to reveal very little on the surface, and who had stood at the altar in the chapel as though he were an innocent bystander on the brink of boredom.

'I love you in that dress, *gattina mia,*' he growled against her skin, and buried his mouth there in a place she hadn't even known could be sensitive. Every cell in her body pulled taut with anticipation as he laved her flesh with the tip of his tongue and grazed her with the edges of his teeth in an incredibly erotic approach she had certainly not expected from Cristo Ravelli. She was already trembling, her nipples tingling, a sliding sensation of warmth rising between her thighs. A slice of cooler air feathered her spine and her wedding gown slid down her arms without any warning. A gasp of surprise was wrenched from her but ten seconds later the dress was pooled round her feet and he was lifting her out of it.

He spun her round, swiftly engulfing her hands in his before she could make any move to cover the lacy bra, knickers and hold-up stockings she wore beneath. Shimmering eyes, dark as Hades, flared naked gold as they scanned the full curves of her breasts cupped in the bra, sliding down to her narrow waist and the flare of her hips before seguing down the long, shapely length of her legs.

'You were definitely worth waiting for,' Cristo told her with hungry conviction lacing every syllable. 'You're gorgeous, *cara*.'

Belle sucked in a shaken drag of oxygen and then he kissed her with a heat and strength that consumed her. He caressed the seam of her lips, parted them, delved deep and sent a shudder of excitement racing through her that startled her. Yes, as she had noted before, Cristo knew how to kiss and his mouth on hers was deeply addictive and intoxicating. He teased her with his tongue and she shivered and dimly recognised that she was being very efficiently seduced by a man she had once written off as a stuffy banker. Her fingers laced into the thick black hair at the back of his neck and an appreciative growl escaped low in his throat. Just as quickly she became airborne when he scooped her up and settled her down on the bed.

Green eyes dazed, Belle stared back at him, nerves beginning to rise again as he undressed, shedding his tie, his jacket and shoes with a careless haste that flat-

tered her. With his scorching golden eyes pinned to
her as intently as though she were Helen of Troy, she
realised that he truly did appear to find her very attractive, and when he shed his shirt to reveal six-pack
abs and a torso straight out of a male centrefold Belle's
mouth ran dry because for the first time ever *she* was
appreciating the male body. With his every movement
sleek muscles flexed below smooth golden skin. A
thin furrow of dark hair ran from below his navel
and disappeared beneath his waistband and then just
as quickly he was skimming off the trousers as well,
displaying tight buttocks and a...and a massive bulge
in the front of his boxers.

At that point, all of Belle's virginal concerns surged
to the forefront of her mind. Was he supposed to be
that big? Was that normal? She could hardly ask.

Cristo wondered why she was blushing as red as a
tomato. He had never seen anything more beautiful
or more innately satisfying than the sight of her on
top of his bed, clad only in delicate lace lingerie. He
tugged off his boxers and left them in a heap, on fire
for the climax his body craved.

The full-frontal effect caused Belle to edge back
up towards the headboard. He didn't seem to have a
single inhibition in his entire body. Her lashes lowered to screen her expression, heat and what she didn't
immediately recognise as hunger snaking through the
secret places of her body.

'You're very quiet,' Cristo remarked, tugging her
back into the shelter of his arms and reaching behind
her to unhook her bra.

'And you're very...single-minded.' Belle selected

the word shakily because she thought he had a lot in common with a bullet aimed at a target.

'I've had three weeks to think about this moment,' Cristo growled low in his throat. 'Three weeks too long…I wanted you the first moment I saw you.'

'When you thought I was my mother?' she parried incredulously.

'You were crossing the lawn with the dog in tow and looking exactly like yourself,' Cristo contradicted, raising almost reverent hands to the spill of pale breasts he had unveiled, long fingers tracing the underside of the full round swells. 'You are totally magnificent, *cara mia*.'

Her breath was feathering in and out of her lungs in insufficient drags while he played with her straining nipples, teasing and plucking the tender crowns and sending trickles of fire flaming down into her pelvis. He smoothed his hands down over her quivering frame.

'Are you cold?' he asked in surprise.

'Just a bit nervous,' she gasped, her voice strangled at source as he rested his palm on her inner thigh and then hooked a finger below the lace edge of her knickers and stroked so that a current of pure tingling warmth ran through her veins.

He tipped up her face with his other hand and burning golden eyes assailed hers. 'Why would you be nervous?'

'I haven't done this before.'

'With me,' he filled in.

'With anyone!'

Cristo froze in the midst of trailing off her last garment. 'Are you trying to tell me you're a virgin?'

The heat of mortification flushed her fair skin like a flaming tide and she couldn't find her voice and was forced to nod affirmation with a jerk of her head.

'And this is not a tease?' Cristo prompted. 'Not a stupid idea to give me what you think could be a wedding-night fantasy?'

Belle focused on him with disconcerted eyes, striving to imagine how he could even suspect such a thing.

Cristo collided with those clear green eyes and discarded his plans of a wedding-night sex marathon. She wouldn't be able to handle that. A virgin. He was good at reading people. He was convinced she wasn't lying and he was shell-shocked because it was not at all what he had expected from her and he did not know whether he liked the idea or not.

'No, not a tease, *cara*,' Cristo said for himself.

'You're disappointed, aren't you?' Belle guessed.

'No, I'm not. You're my wife,' Cristo pointed out with a sudden sense of satisfaction that she would never be able to compare him to another man in bed, never know anything other than what he showed her. A possessive vibe he didn't know he had pulsed through him at that awareness.

'I don't see what difference that makes. I'm not what you expected,' Belle protested.

Still taut with arousal, Cristo was tired of talking. He kissed along her delicate jaw bone and then crushed her generous mouth urgently beneath his, shifting over her to lower his mouth to her generous breasts and then string a line of kisses down over her straining midriff to the very heart of her. He eased a finger into her tight channel and she bucked up her hips and he smiled, loving her responsiveness, parting her thighs for a more intimate caress.

'No...no,' she began, trying to move away.

Glancing up to meet dismayed green eyes, Cristo made a soothing sound he was sure he had never had to make in the bedroom before. 'Trust me...I'll take care of you.'

Belle rested her head back against the pillows and closed her eyes tight, trembling with a crazy mix of mortification laced with tingling sexual awareness and anticipation. He touched her and she gasped out loud because she was so sensitive there and the more he licked and nibbled and tormented her, the more frantically excited she became, all control wrested from her, her body moving in a new feverish rhythm like an instrument being strummed by an expert. Incomprehensible moans and sounds fell from her lips as she writhed and the unbearable ache at her core rose to a crescendo and her whole being was straining towards a climax.

And that was when Cristo lifted over her and eased slowly into the slick, wet welcome of her body. Her eyes flew wide at that shock of sensation, of sudden fullness and stretching inside her.

'This could hurt,' he told her gently.

'I know...' she said breathlessly. 'I'm not a baby.'

For the first time in his life Cristo was more concerned about his partner than himself, which felt strangely alien to him. 'You're so tight,' he bit out, flexing his hips, tipping her up to him for a deeper connection and then sliding home to the very heart of her, causing a stinging, fleeting pain that made her grimace.

'Not too bad,' she told him shakily. 'Just do it.'

Just do it? Cristo laughed out loud and grinned down at her preoccupied face. She looked up at him, rocked by the dark beauty of him at that moment wearing that flashing brilliant smile she had never seen before. And then he moved again, sliding back and delving into her again until he was seated to the hilt and strong sensation was exploding like fireworks inside her. The delicious friction as his hips pounded against hers and the speed of his breathtaking thrusts consumed her with wild excitement. It was electrifyingly intense and passionate and so was he, she registered as her body stiffened and clamped tight around him, and wave after wave of pleasure cascaded through her in a climax so powerful she felt utterly drained in the aftermath but decidedly floaty and full of well-being.

'Well, that was definitely worth getting married for, *bellezza mia,*' Cristo groaned hoarsely in her ear. 'You might be a blackmailer, a gold-digger and a social climber but you're fabulous in bed.'

Belle's eyes flew wide in shock and suddenly she was pushing against those brown muscular shoulders and levering out from underneath him in a rage of disbelief at what he had dared to say to her.

She slid out of the bed like an electrified eel and raced into the bathroom in search of a weapon of mass destruction but there was no club, no gun, no whip, nothing with which to thump him good and hard as pride demanded she must. In desperation she filled a glass by the sink with water and stalked back into the bedroom and slung the contents of the glass at him.

Astonished, Cristo sat up dripping in the tumbled

bedding, looking extraordinarily and quite irresistibly handsome with his golden skin and bright eyes and tousled black hair and her awareness of the fact only inflamed her more. 'What the hell?' he demanded, wiping away the water dripping from his face.

'Don't you dare speak to me like that, you pig!' his bride screeched at him like a harpy from his worst nightmares.

'Speak to you...?' For a split second, Cristo frowned. 'Oh...didn't you like me being honest?'

'I am not a blackmailer, a gold-digger or a social climber!' Belle fired at him furiously. 'How dare you accuse me of those things?'

Cristo shot her a derisive look. 'I hate drama queens.'

'You think I care about that? You think I'm ever going to get into that bed again with you after what you called me and the way you spoke to me?' Belle screamed across the depth of the bedroom, so outraged she could barely frame the words.

Cristo lounged back against the banked pillows looking remarkably unconcerned by that threat. 'I think you will because if you *don't*, I'll be asking for a divorce,' he spelt out without hesitation.

'Right then...I want a divorce!' Belle spat at him before flouncing back into the bathroom and locking shut the door with a loud click.

Well, didn't you handle that well? Cristo reflected, very much in shock himself at what he had divulged to her of his opinions. After all, it wasn't as though such frankness came naturally to him. In fact, Cristo, a man of few words, invariably kept his convictions to himself, but somehow something about that fantas-

tic sex had clashed with his opinion of her inside his
head and he had found himself delivering judgement
there and then. Had he *wanted* her to know what he
thought of her? he queried with a bemused frown. Had
he wanted her to prove him wrong or endeavour to develop her character into something more acceptable to
him? And why was he even thinking along such lines?
He had meant every word he said and he wasn't taking
it back or apologising for telling the truth as he saw it.

CHAPTER SIX

ALMOST TWO HOURS later, Cristo scrutinised the empty four-poster bed as if further attention might magically conjure Belle up from below the tossed bedding. His even white teeth clenched so hard his jaw ached. He had gone for a shower in another room, giving her time to settle down, but Belle being Belle, both impulsive and tempestuous, had evidently emerged from the sit-in in the bathroom to take off instead. But to where? It was eleven at night and the palazzo lay several kilometres from the main road.

Cristo expelled his breath with an audible hiss. He had screwed up, screwed up spectacularly and for a reserved and clever male, who rarely ever miscalculated with women, that was a bitter and maddening acknowledgement. Why had he told her what he thought of her and in such terms? That he couldn't answer his own question only made him more angry and unsettled by the experience. It was their wedding night and his bride had run away, not what anyone would call a promising start and for Cristo, who was an irretrievable perfectionist, it was a slap in the face and an unwelcome reminder that he was only human and that humans made mistakes.

At the bottom of the terraced gardens, Belle swung her legs up on her stone bench, striving for a comfort that was unattainable on such an unyielding surface. Unfortunately she could not think of anywhere else to go, certainly not back to the grand building on the top of the hill with its vast and intimidating heavily furnished rooms where she felt like an old-style kitchen maid roaming illicitly from her proper place in the servant's quarters. Oh, Gran, why *didn't* I listen to you? Belle was thinking with feverish regret and an intense sense of self-loathing.

She had married a man who clearly despised her. And worst of all, she had *slept* with him, which just then felt like the biggest self-betrayal of all. Tears dripped silently down Belle's quivering cheeks because she had never felt so alone and out of her depth in her life, at least not since the teenaged years when she had been horrendously bullied. Now she felt trapped, trapped by the marriage, trapped by the promises she had made to her siblings about the wonderful new life ahead of them all. She couldn't just walk away; it wasn't that simple. Telling him she wanted a divorce had been sheer bravado and he had probably recognised it as such.

Cristo Ravelli. He got to her as no other man ever had, rousing feelings and thoughts and reactions she couldn't control. She had become infatuated with him, she decided, mentally and physically infatuated and, as a result, she had acted every bit as foolishly with him as her late mother had once behaved with Gaetano, unable to keep her distance and failing to count the costs of the relationship. How was she supposed to handle Cristo? He was streets ahead of her in the sophistication stakes. He was a Ravelli, taught from birth that he was a superior being. She hugged her knees, rocking her hips against the hard stone beneath her in an unconscious self-soothing motion, her fingers clenching convulsively together as she fiercely blinked back tears.

Well, the infatuation was dead now. He had *killed* it stone dead. She hated him, absolutely hated him for what he had said within moments of using her body for his pleasure. All right, she reasoned guiltily with herself, it had been *her* pleasure as well. She couldn't pretend to have been an unwilling partner in what had transpired, but then she had not been prepared for that level of passion or pleasure. She had dimly imagined that something much less exciting awaited them in the bedroom.

Mercifully it was a clear night, Cristo conceded grudgingly, tramping down the multitude of steps that featured in the gardens. He was in a filthy mood. Telling Umberto, who ran the palazzo, that his bride was missing had embarrassed him and very little, if anything, embarrassed Cristo. But if he couldn't find Belle, he knew that calling the police in would be considerably *more* embarrassing. He didn't know what he was going to say to her if he *did* find her either. Was he supposed to lie and pretend he hadn't meant his indictment? Apologise for speaking the truth? He was damned if he was going to apologise when she was forcing him to tramp all over his extensive property in search of her in the middle of the night. *Dio mio!* Obviously he was worried about her. Suppose she had come down here in the dark and she had fallen? Hitched a lift out on the country road from some cruising rapist or pervert? Her temper might make her do something self-destructive or dangerous, he reasoned

grimly. Cristo's imagination was suddenly travelling
in colourful directions it had never gone in before.

And then he heard a noise, the human noise of feet
shifting across gravel. *'Belle?'* he called.

Dismay gripping her at the sound of Cristo's voice,
Belle returned to her stone bench, having stretched and
glued her lips together, but he kept on calling and her
silence began to feel childish and selfish and eventually she parted her lips to shout back. 'Go away!'

Relief assailed Cristo. She was safe, would no doubt
live to fight many another day with him, a reflection
that sent a wash of something oddly like satisfaction
through his tall, well-built frame. He followed the voice
to its most likely source: the garden pavilion at the very
foot of the garden, sited beside a craggy seventeenth-
century-built rushing stream and waterfall. Rounding
a corner on one of the many paths, he saw her there
sitting in darkness, long legs extended in front of her
along a stone bench, eyes reflecting the moonlight.

'I was worried about you,' Cristo declared, coming to a halt a couple of feet from the pavilion steps,
intimidatingly tall, outrageously assured. 'You didn't
answer your cell phone.'

'I don't have it with me and I'm sure you weren't
that worried about my welfare,' Belle remarked curtly
while quietly noting that he looked more amazing than
ever when clad in faded jeans and a casual tee, bare
brown feet thrust into leather sandals. 'Not after the
way you spoke to me.'

'It was the wrong place, wrong time,' Cristo admitted, mounting the steps to lift the lighter from its
hook on the wall and ignite the fat pillar candle in the
centre of the stone table.

Not even slightly soothed by that comeback, Belle tilted her chin as the candle flame illuminated his darkly handsome features while he looked down at her from the opposite side of the table. 'But it was obviously what you thought...*blackmail*?'

'I did tell you that other people could be seriously embarrassed by you taking such a story to court on your siblings' behalf,' Cristo reminded her stubbornly. 'You told me you didn't care.'

Your siblings, not his as well, she noted in exasperation, since he was clearly still set on denying that blood tie. 'Why should I have? Neither you nor your brothers care about them.'

'Neither Nik nor Zarif even know of your siblings' existence as yet,' Cristo pointed out. 'Nik's not into children though. For Zarif, however, the news that throughout the whole of his parents' marriage Gaetano was sleeping with another woman and having a tribe of children with her would be deeply destructive and damaging. He's the new King of Vashir.'

Belle rolled her eyes, unimpressed or, at least, *trying* to seem unimpressed. 'I know that.'

'Vashir is a very devout and conservative society and Gaetano's behaviour would cause a huge scandal there, which would engulf Zarif's image in Gaetano's sleaze. Every ruler has opponents and it would be used against him to remind people that his father was a foreigner with a sordid irreligious lifestyle. He doesn't deserve that. Like all of us, he paid the price of having Gaetano as a father while he was still a child,' Cristo informed her grimly. 'I offered to marry you and adopt those children to prevent that from happening.'

'But you didn't tell me that, so you can hardly

expect me to be sympathetic now,' Belle told him roundly. 'It's not only a little late in the day to start calling me a blackmailer, it's also darned unfair when you never gave me those facts in the first place!'

At that spirited retort, Cristo gritted his teeth again in smouldering silence.

'I did *not* blackmail you!' Belle exclaimed, sliding off the bench to stand up and walk down the steps before turning back to face him while his attention lingered on her slender leggy proportions in the denim shorts and camisole she wore. 'Evidently my plans to go to court on the children's behalf put you between a rock and a hard place but *you* made the decision to propose marriage!'

Lean, strong features set in forbidding lines in the shadowy candlelight, Cristo stared broodingly back at her. 'I did but even now I know that your plans to have your day in court would have damaged those children more than you can possibly appreciate.'

'You don't know what you're talking about!'

'I know *exactly* what I'm talking about—in fact nobody knows better!' Cristo parried with unexpected rawness, his dark eyes glittering like stars. 'Gaetano trailed my mother through court in a supposed attempt to gain custody of me when I was a child. Of course what he really wanted was a bigger payoff from the divorce. He didn't want me; he never wanted me. All the dirty secrets of my parents' marriage were trailed out in court and made headlines across Europe and you can *still* read about it online if you know where to look. Do you really think those children would thank you either now or years from now for seeing their parents' less than stellar private life splashed across the tabloids and the net?'

That angle hadn't occurred to Belle and she gulped. 'Naturally I didn't want your charity when the children were legally entitled to a share in their own name.'

'It wouldn't have been charity.'

'No, but you would've been buying my silence and theirs!' she lashed back at him angrily. 'I watched what you did with Mayhill—all aboard the Ravelli gravy train to keep everyone quiet about Gaetano, Mary and their kids.'

'Didn't you climb aboard the same train with a wedding ring?' Cristo taunted with sizzling derision.

'No, I darned well didn't!' Belle hurled back, temper leaping up in a surge of inner flame. 'Because no matter what you think I'm *not* a gold-digger or a social climber! I married you for the sake of my brothers and sisters, so that they would never have to go through what Bruno and I went through!'

'What did you go through?' Cristo demanded with galling impatience.

'When Mum started the affair with Gaetano and then later when she gave birth to Bruno, I think people were inclined to turn a blind eye to it all because everybody knew she'd had a rough time with my father until he died.' Belle breathed in deep, angry pain and mortification coursing through her slender length. 'Back then the locals felt sorry for her—my father was an abusive drunk.'

'And then?' Cristo's attention was locked to her beautiful face and the glistening lucidity of her wide green eyes.

'And then it went sour for all of us because Mum

continued the affair with Gaetano and went on having children. Everyone knew Gaetano had a wife abroad. They decided Mum was shameless and bold and stopped talking to her, wouldn't even serve her in some village shops,' Belle recounted unhappily. 'But she lived in the Lodge outside the village and shopped elsewhere so the hostility didn't really touch her...but I went to local schools with the children of those judgemental parents...'

Her voice momentarily ran out of steam and then picked up again as she shared a memory, a haunted look on her face as if she had drifted mental miles away, and in a way she had because she was back there, walking into a classroom as a vulnerable adolescent, being called a slut by a bunch of girls because everyone knew her mother was a woman who had just given birth to two more children by her married lover. Nobody had intervened when she was bullied because it was widely known and accepted that Mary Brophy was a wicked woman raising her children in a degenerate home where the most basic rules of morality and decency were being broken on a regular basis.

'I never had any friends apart from Mark,' she admitted curtly. 'The other mothers wouldn't let their daughters mix with me or come to my house. It got worse as I got older because then I had the boys calling me names as well and making approaches...well, you can imagine the approaches.'

Cristo, raised from an early age in a city that bred anonymity, was genuinely taken aback by what she was telling him. He'd had no suspicion of the moral rectitude in a small rural community where those who dared to defy public opinion and break the rules could be punished by exclusion and enmity.

'I didn't want my sisters or my brothers to go through that.'

'Obviously not, *cara*,' Cristo murmured ruefully, suddenly grasping one very good reason why his bride had been inexperienced because she had naturally been denied that outlet as a teenager and young woman when to give way to the desire to experiment could have surely seen her labelled as having followed in her mother's footsteps. 'And Bruno?'

'I'll tell you about that some other time but he was bullied as well. That's why he and Donetta were sent to boarding school in the first place.'

'Are you coming back up to the house?' Cristo enquired in the dragging silence that had fallen. 'It *is* two o'clock in the morning.'

Belle prayed for calm and restraint as she walked away from the pavilion. 'You were very offensive and insulting...and disrespectful too.'

'*Sì, bellezza mia*, but it is possible that complete honesty could be the best way forward in a marriage such as ours,' Cristo stated thoughtfully.

Belle mulled that concept over while she mounted yet another endless flight of steps. All the emotion and activity of the day were suddenly hitting her in one go and exhaustion was weighing her down. 'I haven't forgiven you, though,' she was quick to tell him, lest he be assuming that the slate had been wiped clean when it wasn't.

Having watched her pace flag, Cristo closed an arm round her slender spine to guide her up the steep incline. 'That's okay.'

Cristo felt surprisingly buoyant as he urged her

back upstairs to their bedroom. In the light he could see the marks of tearstains on her face and his conscience pierced his tough hide. She was so much more emotional than he was and that unnerved him. He would never forget the wounded expression on her face when she had told him about the bullying she had endured at school. To his way of thinking, her mother had been every bit as selfish in her own way as his father, he reflected grimly, but he knew better than to share that thought.

At the same time, he could only be impressed by how very protective Belle was of her brothers and sisters. He had never known that family intimacy, never appreciated that love could bond a family so tightly together, and he could not help wondering how different he might have been had he shared a similar experience. In spite of the misfortunes Gaetano had caused Mary Brophy's children, they remained a very closely connected unit.

'I'm not getting back into the same bed,' Belle announced one step inside the bedroom door.

Payback time, Cristo acknowledged. 'I'm not that insensitive. I wasn't about to make a move on you.'

Her eyes were prickling with the sudden heat of tears and she held them wide to hold the tears back. 'I know, but I still need my own space for a while,' she said tightly.

Cristo searched the pale, unhappy tightness of her lovely face and compressed his stubborn mouth, knowing without even thinking about it that he didn't want her away from him and, even worse, had a disturbing desire to keep her close. 'I'd prefer you to stay with me.'

Mere minutes later, having won that last battle, Belle settled heavy as a stone into the comfortable bed in the room next door and lowered her lashes on her damp eyes. She had wanted to be with him but had angrily denied herself that choice because common sense had told her it would be wrong. Wrong to let Cristo think he could do and say as he liked without consequences, wrong to let him hurt her and then put a brave face on it to the extent that he would think he might as well do it again. *Blackmailer, gold-digger, social climber?* Was it even possible for her to disprove such suspicions? And should she even want to? Did it really matter? After all, theirs was a marriage of convenience and she simply had to learn to keep a better hold on her emotions and stop looking for responses she was unlikely to receive. She couldn't afford to start caring about a male who didn't care about her but, regardless of every other factor, she was utterly determined that, at the very least, Cristo would give her respect.

Cristo lay sleepless in bed and expelled a groan. He knew Belle was treating him just as she treated Franco with the 'no means no' approach and the withdrawal of privileges until better behaviour was established. In the darkness he suddenly surprised himself when amusement surged over him and he laughed out loud. She had thrown him a challenge. No woman had ever done that to Cristo before and it bothered him to appreciate that he actually admired her nerve.

The next morning, Cristo wakened when something bounced hard on the bed and his eyes flew wide on the dawn light piercing the curtains.

'Kiss-do!' Franco carolled from below his mop of black curls and looked down expectantly at him. *'Belle?'*

'Belle's asleep,' Cristo responded, anchoring the sheet more firmly round his naked length as Franco threw his small solid body at him. 'Bekfast?' Franco asked hopefully, leaning over him with wide eyes.

Wondering where the nanny was, Cristo promised breakfast and Franco beamed. Indeed, Cristo was startled when his little brother wound his arms round his neck and bestowed a soggy kiss on him. The toddler accompanied him into the en suite, chattering endlessly but using few recognisable words. Cristo showered and shaved while Franco played with the contents of the drawers and cupboards and made an unholy mess. While he got dressed, Franco played under the bed with, 'Bekfast, Kiss-do?' a constant refrain to the activity.

Franco closed his hand into Cristo's as they left the bedroom and the flustered nanny appeared several doors further down the corridor.

'I'm so sorry, Mr Ravelli. I've been looking everywhere for him. He disappeared while I was in the bathroom,' Teresa confided.

'Relax, I'll ensure he gets breakfast.'

'Bekfast,' Franco repeated urgently, swinging on Cristo's hand and skipping with excitement. There was a definite charm to the child's open-hearted affection and liveliness, Cristo conceded reluctantly.

In the dining room, Umberto provided an ancient wooden high chair for Franco's use and Cristo advised the manservant to see that a new one was purchased with a safety harness because he was already aware that Franco was an escape artist and guilty of frequently climbing out of his cot. Whatever Cristo ate, Franco wanted to eat and Cristo was quietly appalled at the mess the child made. When he threw a piece of tomato, Cristo told him off and Franco burst into floods of tears, which had to be the exact moment when Belle entered the room.

'Oh, my goodness, I didn't know he was with you!' Belle gasped in dismay.

'He's a very determined little character,' Cristo remarked above the racket Franco was making. 'I told him off for throwing food.'

'No hug, then,' Belle ruled as Franco held out his arms to be comforted. 'You know you're not allowed to throw food.'

Franco sulked when his complaints were ignored and finally started eating again.

Belle grinned across the table at Cristo. 'Thanks for looking after him.'

The natural glory of her smile took his breath away and his dark eyes narrowed appreciatively. It was first thing in the morning and as far as he could tell she wasn't wearing much make-up but she still looked amazing, her translucent china skin flushed and freckled, green eyes bright, her mane of hair coiling round her slim shoulders with a life all of its own in every bouncy corkscrew curl of auburn. 'He's my brother as well,' Cristo murmured wryly. 'And quite a handful.'

'Yes, he is…far too much for Isa to cope with at this age.' Pleased by that long-awaited concession that Franco was *his* brother too, Belle stared at Cristo, trying to stop herself from doing it but quite unable to resist the temptation. Her gaze traced the line of his high-cut cheekbones, perfectly straight nose and wide shapely mouth. The perfect features of a dark fallen angel, which got to her every time. A rush of heat tightened her nip-

ples and surged low in her pelvis in a betrayal she could
not squash. She still found him irresistibly attractive,
she conceded ruefully.

The thwack-thwack of noisy helicopter rotor blades
somewhere nearby made Cristo frown and spring upright to stride over to the window. Still munching her
toast, Belle followed suit. 'What is it?'

'I think you're about to make the acquaintance of
one of my brothers,' Cristo murmured tautly. 'Nik.
Make allowances for him if he's short with you. He's
going through a tough divorce and it's unsettled him.'

'I'll just make myself scarce while you catch up
with him,' Belle offered, hastily lifting Franco out of
the elderly high chair.

'No, he should meet you now that he's here, *gioia
mia,*' Cristo overruled without hesitation. 'You're my
wife. I'm not ashamed of you, nor am I going to hide
you.'

CHAPTER SEVEN

CRISTO STRODE OUTSIDE to greet his brother, Nik. The two men stopped on the terrace to talk. Belle hovered, hearing an animated exchange between the men in a foreign language. It didn't sound like Italian and she wondered if it could be Greek. When she heard the other man expostulate loudly several times she guessed that Cristo was telling him about her mother and the children and she winced uncomfortably, feeling agonisingly self-conscious.

Nik Christakis was a big man, even taller than her bridegroom, but he did bear a strong resemblance to Cristo. Nik frowned across the room at her and his frown only darkened more when he saw the young child standing by her side.

'My wife, Belle, and our youngest little brother, Franco,' Cristo imparted in calm explanation in response to his brother's interrogative look. 'My brother, Nik.'

'*Our?*' Nik queried straight away. 'The child's nothing to do with me. Five of them? You would have to be crazy to take that on, Cristo! Gaetano's dead and buried. What does it matter what comes out about him now?'

'It would matter to Zarif,' Cristo countered squarely.

'Like I care about that!' Nik quipped darkly, digging into an inside pocket on his jacket to extract a document, which he extended to his brother. 'Read it and weep. Learn what happens when you get married without a pre-nup.'

'We didn't have a pre-nup,' Belle remarked awkwardly, uneasy with the tension flowing around them, and Nik's reluctance to even acknowledge her, never mind make polite conversation.

Cristo raised his dark gaze slowly from the document to say, 'I have to admit that I'm surprised.'

'Are you? Are you still that naïve? Obviously Betsy married me for my money and now she's trying to steal half of everything I own!' Nik declared with raw, unconcealed bitterness.

'She *didn't* marry you for your money,' Cristo contradicted with quiet assurance. 'She fell in love with you.'

'Don't be naïve. I give you and your wife and her little bunch of Ravelli by-blows two years at most before she walks out and tries to take the shirt off your back!' Nik vented with ringing derision.

Belle flushed and lifted her chin. 'I wouldn't do that. Look, I'll leave you two to talk in private,' she completed, anchoring Franco's hand in her own.

As she left she heard Nik Christakis cursing, something that was instantly recognisable in many languages. She realised that she was very grateful not to be married to a man like that. Nik's hard-featured face, cold eyes, not to mention the smouldering bitterness that escaped every time he mentioned his estranged wife, Betsy, chilled Belle to the marrow. Nik was clearly tough, obstinate, furiously hostile and, she suspected, the sort of man who would make an implacable enemy, a man who saw only the worst in anyone who crossed him.

Cristo, she reasoned, was more reasonable, more civilised...wasn't he? She respected him for speaking up in defence of his sister-in-law. Furthermore the night before she had been surprised and reluctantly impressed when Cristo had suggested that complete honesty between them might well be the way to make their marriage work. That was a rational and mature attitude to take, she acknowledged thoughtfully. She liked and respected honesty, hated the lies and persuasive pretences that Gaetano had shamelessly employed to keep her mother content and make his own life smoother.

Two hours later, after Nik had finally departed and a second helicopter had flown in and deposited its colourful cargo, Cristo went off in search of Belle and found her sitting in the shade of a tree clutching a book. 'You own a massive library of books,' she complained as she heard his approach and lifted her head, auburn hair gleaming rich as silk in the shadowy light below the overhanging foliage, 'but I could only find a couple written in English.'

Cristo swiped the hardback from between her fingers and studied the spine. It was a heavy-duty tome on the history of his mother's family, written by one of his ancestors and translated by a more recent one. 'I'll order some English books for you. I'd suggest that you start learning Italian but it would hardly be worth your while.'

Her bone structure tightened, tension leaping

through her as she absorbed that reminder that their relationship was of a strictly temporary nature. Images of his passionate lovemaking the night before swam up through her mind and killed every sensible thought stone dead, making concentration impossible while sending a wave of unwelcome heat travelling through her slender length. Her face hot, she studied the book fixedly as he returned it to her with an elegant gesture of one long-fingered hand. Last night those hands had touched her with breathtakingly erotic expertise and had extracted more pleasure from her weak body than she had known it was capable of experiencing. His complete poise in the aftermath of their passionate argument the night before, however, set her teeth firmly on edge. Evidently, as far as he was concerned, everything was done and dusted but Belle still felt as though her reactions, emotions and even her thoughts were whirling around in a maelstrom and out of her control.

'Were you looking for me?' she asked curiously.

'Yes, *cara*. It's time for you to enjoy your wedding present.'

'Wedding present?' Belle parroted as she rose slowly to her feet in discomfiture. 'What on earth are you talking about?'

'Wedding presents go with the territory of getting married,' Cristo fielded smoothly, a lean hand settling to the base of her spine to steer her back in the direction of the villa.

'But not between us, not in *our* sort of marriage,' she parried with spirit.

'I promised to treat you as my wife and that is what I am trying to do.'

'So…' Belle murmured tightly in the echoing hall. 'This present…?'

'It's waiting for you in the ballroom,' Cristo informed her, nodding to Umberto to open the double doors.

Belle crossed the hall slowly, peering into the vast room to focus in astonishment on the catwalk now dissecting it. 'My goodness, what the heck—?' she began in confusion.

'Every woman wants a new wardrobe. I arranged to have a selection flown in along with the models to show the clothing off. All you have to do is choose what you want to wear.'

Every woman wants a new wardrobe? Most social climbing, gold-digging women would certainly fall into that category, Belle reflected with a helpless little moue of distaste that he should have assumed that she was that sort of a woman. But he hadn't given her a choice. This was what Cristo thought she wanted and, it seemed, he was happy to deliver on that score and it would be needlessly confrontational for her to deny him the opportunity. One step into the ballroom she was introduced to Olivia, who whisked a tape measure over her with startling speed and efficiency and announced that any garments she selected would be delivered sized to fit by lunchtime the next day.

Funky music kicked off in the background as Olivia took one of three comfortable seats awaiting them while urging Belle to define what Olivia described as 'her personal style'. Belle had to hinge her jaw closed at the question because she had no idea how to answer it. In any case Olivia had already embarked on a commentary on the first outfit while a brunette model wearing something floaty, purple and weirdly shaped like a lampshade strolled down the catwalk towards them. As a very tall blonde with a shock of almost-white chopped hair appeared in swimwear Olivia endeavoured to determine Belle's fashion preferences. But Belle had never had the budget to develop a taste for luxury. As a student, she had worn jeans in winter and shorts in summer with only the occasional cheap skirt or dress purchased for nights out. Money had always been in short supply in her life, clothing generally purchased from her part-time earnings as a bartender, and she had only ever shopped in chain stores.

'Don't you like any of it?' Cristo prompted, shooting his bride a questioning glance from his brooding dark eyes when she remained awkwardly silent.

As she connected with his stunning eyes her heart flipped inside her chest and turned a somersault. 'It's a bit overwhelming…all this,' she admitted breathlessly.

'Then I'll choose for you.'

And *what* Cristo chose was highly informative and Belle almost burst out laughing, for without fail every short skirt, backless gown and low neckline received Cristo's unqualified and enthusiastic vote of approval. On that score he was very predictable, very male and reassuringly human. Amused by the very basic male he was revealing beneath the sophisticated façade, Belle began to regain her confidence and started to quietly voice opinions, shying away from the more spectacular garments in favour of the plainer ones, insisting that she couldn't possibly wear shocking pink with her hair.

'I like pink,' Cristo argued without hesitation. Though as Olivia took up the conversation he sud-

denly remembered his feelings of horror at the many
shades of pink spun throughout the small home back
in Ireland. But his *wife* in pink…that was a different matter.

'There are only certain shades of pink which you
should avoid,' Olivia, ever the highly accomplished
saleswoman, assured her.

At that point the blonde appeared in a ravishing
set of ruffled turquoise lingerie and Cristo sprang upright and actually approached the catwalk. 'I want
that,' he spelt out without an ounce of discomfiture
in his bearing.

Belle's cheeks flamed while she noted the manner
in which the very leggy blonde was posing for Cristo
like a stripper, loving the attention as her breasts jig-
gled in the bra with her little dance movements, and
she spun round to display her almost bare bottom taut
in panties that were little more than a thong. Cristo
seemed mesmerised by the spectacle, his dark golden
eyes veiled, his sinfully seductive bronzed features
taut as if he was struggling to conceal his thoughts.

He was attracted to the blonde, Belle decided with
a sinking sick sensation in the pit of her stomach, and
he couldn't hide the fact.

'Thank you, Sofia,' the saleswoman said loudly as
she stood up and the music stopped mid-note, leaving a sudden uncomfortable silence in its wake. Olivia
said her goodbyes and took her leave through the rear
door of the ballroom.

'Well, wasn't that educational?' Belle remarked freez-
ingly when Cristo finally wandered back to her side.

His winged ebony brows drew together in bewilderment. 'How so?'

Her generous mouth compressed. 'You fancied the blonde,' she told him bluntly.

Cristo frowned.

'Oh, don't bother denying it. I saw you,' Belle told him thinly. 'You couldn't take your eyes off her!'

Cristo moved steadily closer in a slow stalking movement that was quite ridiculously sensual. Belle looked up at him, fearless in her condemnation, and collided with smouldering golden eyes so intense in focus that she was rocked back on her heels. All the oxygen in the atmosphere seemed to have dried up and she parted her lips to snatch in air.

'I have only one point to make. It wasn't her I was seeing...it was *you*,' he spelt out hoarsely, his brilliant eyes pinned to her with mesmerising force. 'It was *you* I was picturing in that get-up.'

Disbelief assailed Belle and she flicked him a scornful upward glance of dismissal. 'Like I'm going to believe that with a half-naked beauty cavorting in front of you!' she derided.

'*Believe*...' Cristo urged in a roughened undertone that vibrated with assurance in the stillness. 'When I've got a real woman like you, why would I want one with fewer curves than a coat hanger?'

Her mouth fell wide at that less than flattering description of the beautiful model. 'Not your type?'

'You're my type,' Cristo confided huskily. 'The erotic image of you bountifully filling those little blue scraps of nothing turns me on fast and hard.'

A *real* woman? Belle almost laughed out loud at that label. After all, the rigorous dieting she had tried in her teen years had failed to hone an inch off the solid bone structure that gave her defiantly curvaceous hips and voluptuous breasts. Back then she would have given her right arm to be one of the more fashionable 'skinny-minnies' at school. But she was not fool enough as an adult to instantly dismiss the idea that some men actually preferred curves to more slender proportions. It simply hadn't entered her head before that Cristo might be one of those men.

He brushed a straying curl from her cheek and tucked it behind her ear with a casual intimacy that unnerved her. It said that he had the right to touch her, a right she had already denied him. An alarm bell shrieked in her brain, warning her to back off and enforce her boundaries yet again. But he was close, *so* temptingly close that she could smell the evocative scent of cologne and masculine musk that he emanated. He smelt so unbelievably good to her that her senses swam and she felt light-headed. Her knees wobbled beneath her while warmth snaked down from the breasts straining below her camisole to the very core of her, leaving her feeling hot and achy and dissatisfied. Even staying still in that condition was a challenge.

He touched her face, a long tanned forefinger gently tracing the line of her jaw to the cupid's bow above her upper lip while a thumb stroked the soft fullness of her lower lip. Belle trembled, scarcely able to breathe for the rush of excitement that had come out of nowhere at her. Her body raced up the scale in reaction, temperature rising, heart pounding, pulse hammering. Her lashes lowered to a languorous half-mast as she gazed up at him in helpless silence, for she had no words to describe what he was doing to her. He was so beautiful, so devastatingly beautiful that she hadn't even blamed the models for concentrating their attention on him while they displayed their wares. Not only was he the buyer, but also a male so handsome that he made women stare while they struggled to comprehend what it was about those lean, darkly dazzling features that exercised such sinful power and magnetism over their sex. Belle didn't know; she only knew that the minute she stopped looking at him, she *needed* to look again. It was a compulsion she couldn't fight.

'You can put on that blue set just for me,' Cristo murmured hungrily, stunning dark eyes flaring wicked gold at that prospect.

'In your dreams,' Belle warned him without hesitation, thinking he would wait a very long time if he hoped to see her tricked out in provocative underwear for his benefit. Playing the temptress wasn't her style and in her opinion he didn't need the encouragement. That conviction in mind, she walked into the drawing room, where at least their conversation would be unheard by the staff.

'Don't tell me that you don't have the same dream,' Cristo chided, shifting in front of her to clamp his lean hands possessively to her hips.

Belle was about to hit him, push him away, stamp on his foot, loudly lodge a protest to physical contact of any kind. She really was going to do at least one of those things and then his mouth plunged down hungrily on hers and her hands spread against the hard, warm contours of his chest and slowly fisted into the fabric of his shirt as she fought herself and fought the craving he induced.

In that split second between her thinking and acting, his tongue snaked into her mouth to taste her and

she was lost while he nipped and teased at her lips and
delved deep. The hot, throbbing sensation between her
legs rose in intensity until she was rocking her hips
against his, wanting more, *needing* more with an urgency that unnerved her. She could feel the long, hard
ridge of his arousal against her belly and their clothes
were an obstruction she couldn't bear, overwhelming
physical hunger surging through her quivering body
with a force she couldn't withstand.

Cristo lifted his handsome head, eyes hot and bright
with sexual heat, black hair tousled by the fingers she
had dug into the luxuriant strands, an edge of colour
accentuating his hard cheekbones. 'Shall we take this
upstairs?' he murmured thickly.

No was on Belle's lips but yes was in her heart because her body was drenched with treacherous longing for his. She took in a slow steadying breath and
struggled to clear her head, fighting the wanting clawing at her with all her strength.

'I want you…you want me, *cara,*' Cristo said drily.
'What's the problem? Are you still suspicious about
that model? Do you really think I'd be that crass?'

'No,' Belle conceded reluctantly, for she would have
used that as an excuse had she been able to do so. Unfortunately, her brain was in free fall. He had spoken
the truth: the attraction between them was explosive.
Furthermore, had he not been strongly attracted to
her in the first place, he probably wouldn't have offered her marriage. Even so the bond that was being
created between them solely on a physical level was
too superficial for her to accept and she wanted more.

Cristo elevated a sleek black brow. '*Then?* Are you
still judging me as if I'm my late father?' he demanded

impatiently. 'Or is it something in your own past which makes you so suspicious of men?'

Belle stiffened. 'I don't know what you're talking about—'

'I think you do. You watched Gaetano run rings round your mother and hated him for it,' Cristo contended. 'But I'm *not* him.'

Belle bridled and gritted her teeth. 'I know that and I didn't say you were.'

'Why else would you accuse me of coming on to that model right in front of you?' Cristo slung back, tension etched along the hard line of his cheekbones and the angle of his strong jawline. 'What sort of a man would behave like that?'

'I overreacted. I'm sorry.' Belle turned her vibrant head away, guilt and mortification piercing her. There was a certain amount of truth to his condemnation. She did distrust men but not *all* men. During her years at university she had been hurt by boyfriends who were offended by her refusal to get straight into bed with them before she even got to know them. The same boys had deceived her with other girls and let her down but no more so than any of her friends, who had suffered similar wake-up calls from young men who wanted nothing more lasting from a woman than physical release.

'If you want this marriage to work, this isn't the way to go about it,' Cristo delivered in a measured undertone.

'You said honesty was the best policy,' Belle reminded him, walking away a few steps and then turning back to face him, her lovely face flushed and tense. 'Then I'll *be* honest. For this to work for me, I want something more than just sex with you. I want us to get to know each other. You can't build a relationship purely on sex.'

'I've never known anything else,' Cristo growled.

'Do you have any female friends?'

When he nodded with a faint frown, Belle smiled. 'Well, then, you have known something else.'

'Why didn't you make these demands *before* you married me?' Cristo derided.

'I didn't think it through until now,' Belle confided truthfully. 'I was desperate to make the children secure and marrying you was the price. I didn't think beyond that. I didn't think about how I would *feel…*'

Marrying you was the price. Not a statement he had expected to hear from Belle, not one he was even sure he could believe, Cristo mused grimly, dark eyes shielded by his lush lashes. She wanted more. Why did women always want more than was on offer? Were they programmed to want more at birth? All this and five children too, he reflected heavily—had he really thought about what he was doing either?

The forbidding look tensing his lean, dark features stirred Belle's conscience. 'I realise this is coming out of nowhere at you and you have a right to be irritated.'

'That's not quite the word I would've chosen,' Cristo countered curtly.

Belle steeled herself to be more honest than she really wanted to be. 'I *did* have thoughts I shouldn't have had when I agreed to marry you,' she admitted gruffly, her pale skin suddenly blossoming with mortified colour. 'But none of those thoughts related to personal enrichment or social advancement.' Feeling more uncomfortable than ever, she hesitated. 'Although I wouldn't go as far as to say that I had thoughts of getting revenge for what Gaetano put my family through over the years, I certainly had an inappropriate sense of satisfaction when you offered to marry me and I quite deliberately wore my mother's wedding dress to get married in. I'm ashamed of those feelings now. After all, it was very unfair that you should have to pay in any way for your father's mistakes. But then we're both doing that now,' she completed ruefully.

Cristo was violently disconcerted by her complete honesty. He hadn't expected that, hadn't been prepared for her to admit any reactions that might reflect badly on her motivation in marrying him. Getting a rich and powerful Ravelli to the altar had briefly thrilled her but she had owned up to it and that impressed a male who was rarely impressed by the women he met.

'*La via dell'inferno è lastricata di buone intenzione*…the road to hell is paved with good intentions,' Cristo translated sibilantly. 'Do you ever do anything for the sheer hell of it?'

'No.' Belle stiffened as she made that admission. 'And it doesn't have to be hell,' she pointed out uncomfortably. 'We can make the best of the situation. You said you wanted to treat me like a proper wife, wanted to show me respect…'

The reminder hung there like a dark cloud between them, with Cristo finally registering that his partiality for that lingerie set had evidently caused offence. Last night he had become her first lover and she had been *amazing*, he recalled, arousal slivering through him at even the memory. He was expecting too much too soon and he gritted his perfect white teeth together. 'I'll try harder,' he told her in a driven undertone.

'I'll try too,' Belle responded with a tentative smile.

But it was too late because Cristo had already turned away and could not have seen her smile, which had combined both regret at her inability to be the purely sexual object he so clearly wanted her to be and her hope for a better understanding between them in the future. Spirits low, she went upstairs to find her little brother and give Teresa a break. Franco's warm affection and trusting acceptance that he would be loved back were wonderfully soothing to her troubled state of mind. She played hide and seek with the little boy and the upper floor rang with laughter and thudding feet.

Umberto paused in Cristo's office doorway to say warmly, 'It is a joy to hear a child playing here again.'

'There's another four of them—a boy and a girl of eight and a pair of teenagers,' Cristo confided, for he had known the kindly manservant since he was a child.

'Your late father's children?' Umberto prompted.

Cristo's brows drew together. 'How did you know?'

'I heard rumours over the years. My cousin flew Mr Gaetano's helicopter right up until his retirement,' the older man reminded him gently.

'Let's hope the rumours stay buried,' Cristo commented wryly.

'No one in my family will gossip,' the older man assured him with pride. 'But Mr Gaetano had other staff who may not be so discreet.'

A current of uneasiness assailed Cristo, who had ensured that his father's surviving employees were paid off with adequate remuneration for their years of service. Was it possible he had got married for no good reason? And inexplicably, at that point, he thought of

Franco, who demonstrated such a desperate need for male attention. Franco definitely needed a father figure, Cristo reflected, his stern mouth softening as the toddler's gales of laughter echoed down from above.

'No…no…*no*, Franco!' Belle gasped in dismay when she found her little brother picking in delight through the collection of items lying on the dressing table in Cristo's bedroom. 'Don't touch those.'

Jingling the car keys still in his hand, Franco dropped the wallet he had been investigating and it fell to the floor. Belle knelt down to gather up the banknotes that Franco had crumpled, smoothing them out before returning them to the wallet along with credit cards, a couple of business cards and…a tiny photograph. Belle lifted the photo and stared down at it in surprise, recognising Nik Christakis's estranged wife, Betsy. She was a little blonde sprite of a beauty with delicate features and big blue eyes. Her brow furrowed. Had the photo fallen out of the wallet or had it just been lying there forgotten on the floor? The rug beneath her knees, however, bore the ruffled evidence of recent vacuuming. So, assuming the photo *had* been inside Cristo's wallet, why was her husband carrying round a photo of his brother's wife?

And was she even going to ask him why? Belle came out in a cold sweat at the very prospect of so embarrassing a conversation. After her misjudgement of his behaviour with the model, he would never believe that she had accidentally seen the photograph. He would think she had been snooping in his wallet and he would naturally assume that she was one of those madly jealous, distrustful women, who would always be scheming to check his cell-phone messages and his pockets for evidence of infidelity. Cringing at that likelihood, Belle slotted the photo back into his wallet and returned it circumspectly to the dressing table. No, she wasn't about to ask him any more awkward questions.

Matters were tense enough between them. And yet so many important things hinged on the success of their marriage, she thought wretchedly. If she and Cristo couldn't make a go of it, what would happen to her siblings? She had made promises, not least those in the chapel, which she had to, at least, *try* to keep. Unless she was prepared to let Cristo go free, she had to make more of an effort.

But please, no, she prayed, let not the only avenue to success demand the sporting of saucy underwear....

CHAPTER EIGHT

BELLE SAT ALONE at the breakfast table out on the terrace, which overlooked the glorious gardens and, beyond them, the beautiful panorama of the idyllic Umbrian landscape, and decided that nobody would ever credit how miserable and insecure she was. Here she was, all dressed up in gorgeous surroundings, married to an even more gorgeous man and already she had made a mess of things! Although, to be fair, expecting her to be willing to put on provocative lingerie for his benefit had scarcely been calculated to soothe her misgivings.

Do you ever do anything for the sheer hell of it? Cristo had asked. And the truthful answer would have been, no, *never*. So, how on earth had she managed to leap into marrying Cristo without fully considering what she was doing? She still couldn't answer that question to her own satisfaction. Had her treacherous attraction to him destroyed every single one of her brain cells? Why hadn't she listened to her grandmother's warnings? After all, nobody knew better than Belle that relationships between men and women were often difficult and prone to unhappiness.

Her mother's over-hasty marriage at a young age to

Belle's drunken father followed by Mary's long affair
with Gaetano Ravelli had taught Belle to be very cautious and sensible and to carefully reason out every
move she made in advance with men, *except* when
it came to the opportunity to marry Cristo when she
had—inexplicably to her—jumped right in with both
feet. And her current wary attitude to intimacy was
creating friction with Cristo. Could she blame him
for his outlook?

What, after all, had Cristo *gained* from their marriage? Her silence, no court case and five pretty needy
children he had promised to adopt into the Ravelli
family. Her tense mouth down-curved on the discour-
aging suspicion that he had sacrificed much more than
she had and that few people would feel sorry for her
having given up her freedom to work and instead live
in the lap of luxury with her fancy designer wardrobe.
That thought made her eyes sting fiercely with tears
because she had very little interest in the luxury and
the vast selection of new clothes that had been delivered in garment bags to her room before she even got
out of bed. In fact, she had only donned one of the out-
fits, a silky top and skirt, because she hadn't wanted
Cristo to think that she was ungrateful for the gesture
he had made.

But unfortunately, Cristo wasn't even around to notice what she was wearing. That was the problem of
separate bedrooms in a massive house and two people
who didn't know each other's habits very well, Belle
reflected wretchedly. Cristo had been absent at dinner
the night before and now he was absent again. Was
he avoiding her? Fed up with her immature outlook?
It seemed pretty obvious to her that she was getting

absolutely everything in their marriage wrong, and to achieve that at such an early stage suggested that she had cherished completely unreasonable expectations of what being married to Cristo would entail. He had assumed she was a gold-digger and, having brooded over that accusation, she wasn't sure she could blame him for his cynicism. After all, he didn't know her and possibly connecting on a physical level was the only way Cristo knew *how* to get to know a woman, so her coming over all prudish and standoffish because he had hurt her feelings wasn't helping the situation...

And worst of all, Belle knew she couldn't even phone her grandmother. Isa Kelly's sensible advice would have been very welcome even though Belle could not have brought herself to mention the bedroom side of things to the older woman. Indeed even the sound of Isa's voice and those of her siblings would have been a comfort. Belle was horribly homesick and missed the family dog, Tag, almost as much. But Belle knew that if she phoned home within days of the wedding her grandmother would be astute enough to suspect that things weren't working out and it would be very, very selfish to lay yet another worry on her grandmother's already overburdened shoulders.

Disgusted at her self-pitying mood and lack of activity, Belle suddenly pushed her chair back and stood up. Sitting here feeling sorry for herself and agonising over her possible mistakes wasn't *fixing* anything, was it? It was time to go and find Cristo.

Questioned, Umberto smiled and indicated a door at the foot of a short corridor off the main hall. 'Mr Cristo has been working round the clock in his office since news of the banking crisis broke...'

What banking crisis? Belle had not seen a television or a newspaper since the morning of her wedding. She had noticed that the nanny, Teresa, had a TV in her room but had drawn a blank when she looked for access to one for her own benefit. Perspiration breaking on her brow, she knocked on the door of Cristo's office and then opened it.

Dark eyes flying up from his laptop screen, Cristo swung round in his chair. Belle's appearance shocked him on two levels. *Dio mio,* he had a wife and he had forgotten about her, and then his next thought was that forgetting about her should have been impossible when she was such a beauty, standing in the doorway, a slender, wonderfully leggy figure taut with uncertainty in a peach-coloured top and skirt that toned in perfectly with her torrent of vibrant spiral curls. Wide grass-green eyes assailed his

'I wondered where you were,' she said awkwardly, transfixed as she always was at first glimpse of his tousled dark head, perfect bronze profile and striking eyes. The fact he hadn't shaved merely added a raw-edged masculinity to his charismatic appeal and she could feel her face warming up, her tummy flipping, her heart rate skipping upbeat: all standard reactions to Cristo. 'Then Umberto mentioned a banking crisis of some kind. I'm afraid I haven't seen a newspaper since I arrived and I didn't know about it. Do you need any help?'

'Help?' Cristo queried, ebony brows rising in surprise. 'How could you help?'

'I have a first-class degree in business and economics and I worked as an intern for a year in a Dublin bank as part of the course,' Belle confided hesitantly.

A line of colour flared across Cristo's cheekbones as it crossed his mind that he should've known such elementary facts about the woman he had married, and rare discomfiture sliced through him. 'I had no idea.'

Her eyes sparkling with genuine amusement, an involuntary grin slanted Belle's wide and generous mouth. 'So, you just assumed you were marrying an uneducated Irish peasant, did you?'

'If you're willing to help, I'd be grateful, *bella mia,*' Cristo admitted, smoothly, gratefully ducking that issue entirely. 'I'm trying to work with my London staff remotely and it's complicated but this is supposed to be our honeymoon.'

'I've got nothing else to do,' Belle pointed out gently, convinced that a couple of their ilk scarcely qualified for the itinerary or the behaviour of a normal honeymoon couple.

Cristo immediately recognised yet another screaming indictment of his behaviour as a new husband and hurriedly sidestepped that awareness by offering Belle the laptop beside his own and springing upright to ask Umberto to go and find another chair. His conscience reacted as though someone had given it a good hard kick. Marriage, he was learning by slow and painful steps, would demand much more of him than he had imagined and would entail considering Belle's needs as well as his own.

For the first time, he appreciated that he had had absolutely no right to judge his brother, Nik, for the mess he had made of his marriage to Betsy. After all, he only knew *one* side of that story and tiny, fragile Betsy weeping out her heartbreak on Cristo's chest had definitely cornered the sympathy vote as far as

appearances went. His lip curled as he skimmed a
glance across Belle's composed and lovely face and
he almost smiled in relief. There was nothing helpless
about Belle and at least she wasn't crying hysterically,
complaining, condemning…

'Yes, she's amazing,' Cristo agreed in Italian with his
chief finance officer in the London branch of his investment bank. 'If I wasn't married to her, I'd hire
her!'

Cristo studied his wife with an involuntary sense
of pride. Belle was curled up in a chair with a laptop,
long incredible legs in shorts on display, auburn hair
spiralling down round her shoulders, enhancing porcelain-pale freckled skin while her fingers flew over
the keyboard. It was the pivotal moment when he realised that he had struck literal gold and had seriously
underestimated her worth when he married her. For
a woman of her beauty to have retained qualities of
such natural likeability and unpretentiousness was extraordinary. She was also intelligent, resourceful and
hardworking. Not once had she complained over the
past three days about the very long hours they were
putting in and she had kept pace with him every step
of the way. He winced when he recalled the lingerie
episode at the fashion show.

Belle stood up to stretch and set the laptop down.
The banking crisis was over and she was almost disappointed by that reality since it had acted as a bril-
liantly positive antidote to the friction between them.
They could work together now, talk to each other. He
had stopped treating her like some sort of glorified
sex doll expected to offer him entertainment and she

had learned to her own satisfaction that Cristo was as smart as a whip while being as stubborn and impatient as she was.

Her clear gaze wandered over him while he sprawled back against the edge of the desk, long powerful thighs sheathed in denim splayed, a crisp lemon shirt open at his strong tanned throat. She looked at his wide, sensual lips and recalled the passionate intoxication of his kiss and momentarily felt dizzy. Her mouth ran dry, hunger stirring at the core of her as it had so often in recent days when her body reacted to the presence of his. She leant slightly forward, willing him to make a move to hold her, touch her, kiss her...*anything*!

'Put on something fancy. I'm taking you out to dinner, *bella mia*,' Cristo volunteered, glancing up to transfix her with spectacular dark golden eyes heavily fringed with lush black lashes.

Belle flushed to her hairline, mortified by her thoughts and drawn up short by the unexpected invitation. 'Only if you want to.'

'*Dio mio!* Of course I want to,' Cristo countered with a frown.

'You don't need to thank me for helping out,' Belle told him stubbornly.

Cristo expelled his breath in a slow hiss. 'Is it so hard for you to accept that I might want to take my beautiful wife out and show her off?'

Belle laughed at the idea. 'Not when you put it that way, you smoothie!' she teased.

Cristo winced. 'Don't call me that...it makes me think of Gaetano.'

Belle wrinkled her nose in agreement. 'You don't remind me of him in any way.'

'*Grazie a Dio*...thank God,' Cristo retorted with visible relief.

Belle collided with Franco on the way into the office. Her little brother pushed past her to throw himself at Cristo with a shout of satisfaction. Although they had been incredibly busy in recent days, Cristo never turned Franco away and she appreciated that, glancing back as Cristo tickled Franco and engaged in the kind of rough, noisy, masculine play that the toddler adored. While she hovered, Cristo answered the buzz of his cell phone.

At supersonic speed she registered that something bad had happened and she moved back into the office because Cristo's lean, strong face had clenched into rigid lines, his eyes darkening, his mouth compressing as he finished the call in clipped Italian. He released Franco and the little boy scampered off into the hall, already in search of fresh amusement.

Cristo settled dark eyes now flaming accusing gold on Belle and asked harshly, 'Have you been talking to the press?'

Astonishment furrowed her brow. 'No, of course not! What on earth are you talking about?' she parried, instantly cast on the defensive.

'A friend who's a journalist in London just called me to warn me that the story of Gaetano, your mother and the kids will be appearing in print some time soon in a British tabloid!' Cristo bit out furiously.

Belle paled at that news but rallied fast because her own conscience was clear. 'Well, that's very unfortunate.'

Cristo sprang upright, six feet plus inches of enraged, darkly powerful masculinity. '*Unfortunate?* Is that all you think this is?'

Infuriated by his attitude and wounded by the speed with which he had leapt to distrust, Belle squared her slight shoulders against the wall, her lovely face flushed and taut with strain. 'Keep this in proportion, Cristo, and try to be reasonable.'

'*Reasonable?*' he growled as if he didn't recognise the word. 'I married you to keep that sleazy story out of the newspapers!'

And just then, Belle could have done without the reminder of that fact.

'I always thought it was unlikely that you could prevent that story from *ever* coming out,' she admitted reluctantly. 'My mum was with your father for almost twenty years and everyone for miles around, who enjoyed a bit of gossip, knew about their relationship and the children. All it would have taken was for *one* person to talk to the wrong person, who saw some chance of profit in the information and the secret would have emerged.'

Lean tanned hands clenching into fists by his side, Cristo jerked his arrogant dark head in grudging acknowledgement of that possibility, his innate intelligence warring with his equally natural aggressive instincts to persuade him that she was talking sense.

Belle prowled forward like a stalking tigress and flicked his shirtfront with an angry finger. 'But how dare you even *think* that it might have been me who leaked the story to the press?' she launched at him, green eyes bright with indignation. 'I wouldn't do that to my brothers and sisters. They've already paid a high enough price for the sins of their parents and the very last thing I would ever want to do is upset them more!'

'I didn't accuse you.'

'You *asked* me if I had been talking to the press. What sort of a question was that to ask your wife? What reason would I have to expose all of us to that kind of unpleasant public attention?' Belle demanded.

'Revenge? Gaetano may be dead but you hate his guts and never got the chance to tell him so. In fact I suspect you distrust and dislike anyone called Ravelli!' Cristo slammed back at her in condemnation.

'I've changed.' Yet Belle wanted so badly to slap him that her palm tingled. Only the knowledge that *before* she met him she had had that attitude burned her deep with shame, for one thing she had learned to appreciate since then was that Gaetano's hedonistic lifestyle had damaged almost every life he touched, not least those of the children he had fathered without parenting. 'Well, then I'd have a real problem with my identity, wouldn't I?' she fired back with ringing disdain. 'Considering that now I'm a Ravelli too.'

'*Sì,* and my wife, *cara mia.*' Cristo found himself suddenly savouring that reality as he looked at her, aggression switching into another similarly testosterone-driven reaction, his attention surging from her beautiful defiant face down to her heaving breasts shimmying below the light tee she wore, arousal roaring through him like an engine revving up.

'But not so happy to be your wife right now!' Belle hissed a split second before Cristo cornered her by the wall, closing an ensnaring hand into her tumbling curls to tip up her mouth and then silencing any objection she might have made with the heat of his own.

Belle pushed against his chest but it was, at most, a half-hearted protest because, as fired up by emotion as she was, she couldn't fight the overwhelming rush of sexual hunger that assailed her the instant Cristo touched her. His kisses were ravenous, both of his hands fisted in her hair, his lean, powerful body pinning her to the wall while his tongue teased and delved inside her mouth with ravishing force. A moan was wrenched from her lips as he squeezed the straining bud of one tender nipple through her clothing and the sensation ran like dynamite to the aching heart of her. She felt frantic, possessed, needy way beyond anything she had ever experienced before.

Belle wrenched at his shirt, struggling with the buttons and then finally yanking in frustration at the barrier between them, so that the buttons flew and the shirt parted and he drew back for an instant. She was shocked by what she had done, her colour high but, regardless, she succumbed to the overpowering desire to mould her palms to the hard planes of his hair-roughened chest and feel the wild heat and strength of his very masculine body.

'I've never wanted any woman as much as I want you,' Cristo bit out, taking a long stride away from her to slam the door shut, turn the lock and stalk back to her with clear devastating intent in his devouring gaze.

And Belle had never known what hunger felt like until she met him and, even though she was shaken by her own primitive urges, her passionate desire was stoked higher by the boldly visible erection he sported below his chinos. 'Take off the shirt,' she told him.

'Getting bossy now?' Cristo quipped as he dropped it on the floor.

'Oh, you have no idea,' she murmured, relishing the sight of his powerfully muscled chest and impressive abs, helpless anticipation lancing through her as she curled her fingers into his belt and hauled him back to her.

At that point, Cristo flung back his handsome dark head and laughed, lowering his head to kiss her again in the midst of lifting her silk top up and up and finally, somewhat clumsily for a man of his sophistication, off over her head. She was not wearing a bra and he shaped the firm full globes he had revealed with reverent hands, thumbs and fingers stroking over the swollen tips. 'I *love* your curves,' he confided with husky emphasis, skating his palms down admiringly over the sloping softness of her hips before his hand slid below the skirt and ran unerringly up the hot skin of her inner thigh. Lost in the grip of urgent need, she angled away from the wall towards him, wanting, inviting, and truly *needing* his touch.

Her eyes slid shut as he teased the swollen hot flesh already damp with desire at the heart of her and, with a little sound of impatience, he knelt down to dispose of her panties and lingered to appreciate that most tender part of her with his tongue and his sensually skilled mouth.

'Cristo!' Belle gasped.

'For the last three nights while you went to your bed and I went to mine, I've been dreaming about doing this,' Cristo confessed with carnal boldness, the low growl of his roughened intonation vibrating down her spine.

He tasted her and savoured her as though she were the finest wine and intoxicating waves of sensation engulfed Belle until she was trembling and only the wall and his arm at her hips were keeping her upright against that seductive onslaught. Only when she literally couldn't take any more of the taunting, delirious pleasure that he wouldn't allow to progress to its natural conclusion did he sweep her up in his arms and sit her down on the edge of the desk. Once she was in position, he stepped between her spread thighs and crushed her reddened mouth below his again with a primal insistence that consumed her like an adrenalin shot injected straight into her veins.

'I didn't see us doing this…*here*,' Belle muttered shakily.

'I don't know how I kept my hands off you the last few days, *bellezza mia*,' Cristo confided hoarsely, nuzzling his cheek down the extended length of her throat with a deeply expressive masculine groan of agreement. 'I didn't want to rock the boat.'

'Rock it!' Belle urged him on breathlessly as he began to push inside her, her inner walls initially protesting the unflinching demand of his entrance and then slowly stretching around him with a delicious sensation of fullness that made her moan in elated response.

His hands firm on her hips, Cristo tipped her back and then he drove home to the hilt with a power and immediacy that was even more thrilling for her highly aroused body. He pulled back and then slammed home again, jolting her with an excitement that ran like a river of fire through every erogenous zone she possessed. Her heart was racing, her entire body straining and pleading for the ultimate climax while he increased the speed of his strokes, driving faster, deeper while the frenzy of her need and exhilaration combined into a wild roller-coaster ride of ever-increasing pleasure. Her body clenched and she convulsed, crying out and quivering as the pleasure burst like shooting fireworks inside her, sending surge after surge of breathtaking ecstasy travelling through her trembling body.

Cristo wasn't quite sure he could stay upright as his own climax engulfed him and he held her close, groaning out loud as he spilled his seed inside her, and the very newness of that sensation sent him back on full alert. '*Che diavolo!*' he exclaimed in consternation, immediately imagining the worst possible scenario. 'I didn't use a condom!'

Taken aback by the sudden admission, Belle blinked uncertainly as he wrapped both arms round her and steadied them both. 'Oh...' she framed against his chest, his heart thundering against her cheek, the musky male scent of his skin wonderfully familiar and extraordinarily soothing to her now.

'I've never ever *not* used one before,' Cristo assured her in a driven undertone. 'You got me so worked up.'

'It's all right,' she mumbled, hiding a smile of satisfaction at the awareness that she could be responsible for exciting him to the extent that he failed to exercise his usual self-discipline. 'I started taking the pill before the wedding, so there shouldn't be any consequences.'

Cristo pictured Franco purely in terms of a consequence and was quite astounded to recognise the tiniest pang of disappointment when she reassured him that there was no risk of such a development. He shook his handsome dark head as if to clear it of such an insane thought, seriously rattled by it and where it might have come from. He had no desire for a child, had never had a desire for one and yet there was something about Franco...

'You're incredible, *bellezza mia*,' he husked, blanking out those unsettling weird reflections in favour of kissing her brow, the tip of her nose and finally her luscious mouth. 'You have a passion and an ability to excite me that most men can only dream about finding with one woman.'

Slowly, carefully he lowered her back down to the floor before helpfully lifting her top to slide over her head and back over her torso. Dazed, she leant back against the desk again, cheeks as hot as coals, eyes screened by her lashes as she absorbed that last statement with pleasure but also because she was shockingly disconcerted by the wildness they had shared and the sheer screaming intimacy of the experience.

A couple of hours later and groomed to within an inch of her life, those tumultuous emotions and sensations carefully tamped down, Belle scrutinised her reflection with a sharply critical gaze. It was a beautiful dress and her youngest sister would have told her that she looked like a princess in it because Lucia, in common with their late mother, adored feminine frills. Pale pink and full length, the gown was bare at the shoulder and moulded to her figure at breast and hip. Did she look just a little *too* busty? She hitched the bodice and then almost laughed, pretty much convinced when she thought about it that Cristo would enjoy the view.

Betsy rang Cristo as he emerged from the shower in his own room next door. He listened as he always did but he felt strangely detached from his sister-in-law and her problems. It occurred to him that he had never lusted after Nik's wife the way he did after his own and he marvelled at that reality, wondering if some internal censor button had somehow prevented it or whether indeed she didn't appeal to him quite that much on that more basic level, which struck him as an extraordinary possibility.

He was *still* listening to Betsy recount the latest hostile moves his brother had made in the divorce battle when Belle came downstairs and his mind went totally blank because Belle looked fantastic and he couldn't think of anything else. He ended the call with an apologetic mutter.

'Who were you talking to?' Belle asked, her attention locked to the unusually distracted expression on his lean dark features.

'Betsy.'

'Nik's wife?'

Cristo struggled not to sound defensive. 'We're friends.'

'That must be awkward,' Belle remarked. 'Were you friends before they got married?'

Cristo tensed, a muscle pulling taut at the corner of his shapely mouth. 'No. It happened because of the way they broke up.'

Like a bloodhound on the trail, Belle was in no mood to settle for less than she wanted to know. 'And why *did* they break up?'

'For very private reasons. But something I let slip when I should have kept quiet and minded my own business contributed to it.' Cristo framed that admission of guilt in a harsh undertone. 'I'm sorry I can't

tell you more but I caused a lot of trouble by once carelessly revealing a secret which Nik had shared with
me and…I definitely have lived to regret it.'

Belle wanted to drag the whole truth out of him
there and then because all her suspicious antennae
were now waking up to full alert. Exactly what did
his 'friendship' with Betsy Ravelli entail?

Outside the limousine awaited them. 'Where are we
going?' she asked to fill the strained silence, which
confirmed for her that there had to be a very good reason why Cristo was quite so wary and uncomfortable
when it came to discussing his brother's estranged
wife. Was she being fanciful in being so suspicious?
Was his reaction simply the result of his guilty conviction that he might have contributed to the breakdown of the couple's marriage? But if that was true,
why did he carry a photo of Betsy in his wallet? That
lent an all too personal dimension to the relationship
that could only make Belle feel troubled.

'We're going to Assisi. There's a very special
restaurant there,' Cristo imparted, relieved she had
dropped the touchy subject of Nik's marriage breakdown.

'Assisi…as in the birthplace of St Francis?'

Cristo gave her a droll look. 'There is only one.'

'To be actually going there just feels so weird. It
was my mother's lifelong dream to visit Assisi. She
was a great believer in the power of St Francis,' Belle
explained, a certain amount of embarrassment at that
unsophisticated admission mingling with the very real
sadness that claimed her when something touched on
her many memories of the older woman.

'And Gaetano never brought Mary to Italy?' Cristo prompted in surprise.

'Are you kidding? He never took Mum anywhere,' Belle countered between compressed lips of grim recollection. 'Their relationship only existed behind closed doors.'

'And your mother didn't object to that?'

'No and what's more she *still* thought the sun rose and fell on him. Gaetano didn't take her money, knock her around or get drunk, so in her opinion he was perfection. She wasn't very bright or well educated,' Belle proffered in a guilty undertone because she felt disloyal making that statement about the parent she had loved. 'But she was a very loving, loyal and kind person.'

'She must also have been very tolerant and forgiving. That's probably why their affair lasted so long,' Cristo commented with a wry twist of his mouth.

Belle's throat thickened with tears and she swallowed with difficulty. 'Sometimes I miss her so much it *hurts*,' she admitted quietly.

Cristo tensed when he noticed the glimmer of moisture on her cheeks. He breathed in slow and deep, unfroze his big powerful body with difficulty and pushed himself to close a hand over her tightly clenched fingers where they rested on her lap. 'I can't even say that I can imagine how you feel because it would be a lie,' he conceded ruefully. 'I'm not particularly close to my mother and I had no relationship with Gaetano to mourn when he died. You're fortunate to be a part of such a close family.'

In silence, Belle nestled her fingers beneath the warmth of his and marvelled at that unexpectedly thoughtful gesture of comfort and the sentiment from his corner.

They dined at a table set for two on a massive terrace surrounded by amazing views of the picturesque hillside town. The streets they had driven through had been a geranium-hung blaze of flowering colour and she had caught glimpses of medieval back lanes and piazzas adorned with ancient fountains.

'Where are all the other customers?' Belle asked, surveying the empty tables around them.

'Tonight, we're the *only* customers and one of Italy's most famous chefs is cooking solely for us, *bella mia*.'

'And you arranged it that way?' Belle prompted in amazement.

'This is the very first time I've taken you anywhere,' Cristo pointed out bluntly. 'And we've been married a week, which basically tells me that I owe you a decent night out. I also owe you for all the work you put in for me without complaint.'

'I like working. I like feeling useful,' Belle confessed truthfully, green eyes sparkling, generous mouth warming into an unrestrained smile because simply sitting there in her beautiful dress with her even more beautiful husband opposite made her feel ridiculously spoilt and contented.

Hungry desire flaming through him afresh and coalescing in an ache of raw need so eager to stir at his groin, Cristo studied his wife, marvelling at the explosive effect she had on his libido. Although he didn't consider himself to be either an emotional or sentimental man, he found her natural warmth and liveliness amazingly attractive.

The waiter brought the menu and the chef came out

to greet them and offer recommendations. By then dusk was falling and the candles were lit. Belle cradled her wine and sipped, rejoicing in the fact that she could at last relax in Cristo's company.

'You still haven't explained why Bruno and Donetta were sent to boarding school,' Cristo drawled lazily.

Her fingers tightened round the glass in her hand. 'Bruno was never an athletic boy and he finally admitted to Gaetano that he was only interested in art. Your father asked him if he was gay…he was only thirteen at the time,' she completed in a tone of disgust.

Cristo swore under his breath.

'Then Gaetano decided to make that a running joke and whenever he saw Bruno after that he called him "gay boy". Eventually someone else overheard and talked and Bruno started getting bullied at school but he didn't tell us what was happening,' Belle explained heavily, having to pause to breathe in deep before she could continue to tell the distressing truth. 'Bruno tried to kill himself but, very fortunately for us and him, we found him in time and he recovered.'

Cristo was honestly appalled by the confession while he recalled that skinny-wristed boy with the anxious eyes who had cornered him on the day of the wedding. 'I was remarkably lucky, it seems, to escape Gaetano's concept of how to be a good father.'

'Well, after that Donetta finally picked up the courage to tell us what had been going on at school and that's why they both went into boarding,' Belle advanced. 'Bruno's experience with Gaetano is the main reason why I hated your father. And my brother, by the way, is *not* gay.'

'It wouldn't have made any difference to me if he

was,' Cristo remarked as the first course was defer-
entially laid before them. 'The poor kid.'

'He's a very talented artist and the change of environment was exactly what he needed, even if it does
mean he and Donetta are separated from the family.'

'When they move to London, they won't be separated any longer,' Cristo reminded her. 'They can attend a day school or even board and come home at
weekends—whichever they would prefer... It's up to
them.'

'I know. I wanted us all to be together again,'
she confided ruefully. 'But you might find it a little
crowded with all of us around.'

Cristo dealt her a wicked look teeming with all the
passion that simmered so close to the surface of his
apparently controlled exterior. 'I think I will enjoy
being crowded by you.'

CHAPTER NINE

WITH A GROWING sense of awe, Belle studied the laptop pictures of the latest London property details sent for their perusal by the consultant hired by Cristo. Cristo had told Belle simply to pick a house, as his penthouse apartment was too small to house her family. He had very little interest in what his new home would be like, having merely specified a room to house an office and sufficient space in which to entertain. Belle was staggered, not only by the sheer meteoric cost and superb appointments of the elite properties tendered to them, but also by the level of responsibility Cristo had entrusted her with.

At the same time, she would have been the first to admit that during the past weeks in Italy their relationship had changed out of all recognition. Most mornings she helped Cristo catch up in the office. After that they would spend the rest of the day exploring, eating out, swimming, generally just relaxing and often with Franco in tow. And equally often they would sit out until very late talking over guttering candles on the terrace where they usually dined. A dreamy expression clouded Belle's eyes in tune with the increasing sense of security that she was feeling in her new life.

Nothing seemed that daunting with Cristo by her side. No, not even his mother, Princess Giulia, who had arrived with his stepfather, Henri Montaldo, with very little warning only the day before. Belle's mother-in-law had literally shrieked in infuriated horror once she finally grasped the identity of the woman whom her one and only child had married.

'What are the children of this unscrupulous Irish woman to do with you?' the princess, an imperious, ageless little brunette dressed in the latest fashion, had demanded in outrage of her son.

'They are my family,' Cristo had responded quietly and Belle's chest had swelled with pride, for she knew what an achievement it was that he had now moved beyond his original feelings to regard her siblings in that just and unselfish light.

And the battle between mother and son had then switched to incomprehensible volleys of furious Italian while Belle offered Cristo's stepfather, Henri, a mild-mannered man, coffee and tried to pretend that she wasn't aware that his wife was undoubtedly engaged in attacking Belle's late parent, Mary, for the reckless choices she had made in life.

'Gaetano is Giulia's one blind spot,' Henri had remarked ruefully under cover of the argument raging back and forth between mother and son. 'He was the love of her life.'

'Yet you've been together...?' Belle had begun awkwardly.

'Since Cristo was a toddler,' Henri had confirmed in the same even, accepting manner. 'Don't worry about this. Cristo will settle it. He knows how to handle his mother.'

By the time the coffee was being served, the argument had become a much less tense discussion laced with Henri's soothing comments, and Belle swiftly recognised that Cristo both liked and respected his stepfather. Indeed by the time the volatile princess had departed, the older woman had recovered her mood to the extent of ruffling Franco's black curly hair, remarking what a very handsome little boy he was and kissing Belle on both cheeks and welcoming her to the family. The threat of lingering bad feelings that Belle had feared might result from such an encounter had been successfully averted.

'So, as you witnessed this afternoon, everybody gets embarrassed when it comes to family members,' Cristo had remarked in bed the night before while she still lay boneless and weak with drowning contentment in the circle of his arms. 'My mother has a very short fuse. She loses her head and throws scenes.'

'But she calms back down again and she doesn't hold spite,' Belle pointed out lightly. 'That's a plus.'

'I didn't want her to upset you, *bellezza mia*,' Cristo admitted. 'It's more than a quarter of a century since she divorced Gaetano and, let's face it, what he did after that and who he did it with is none of her business.'

'But at one time she obviously cared a lot for him,' Belle mused, drowsily settling her head down on his smooth bronzed shoulder, breathing in the scent of him in a state of sublime relaxation. 'And his infidelity and his lies must have hurt her enormously. A woman would've needed to be hard as a rock or wilfully blind like my mother to handle Gaetano without getting chewed up into little pieces.'

'I'll always be honest with you,' Cristo declared, long tanned fingers skimming her tousled curls back from her brow as he looked down at her, dark eyes sexy gold below the stunning black of his luxuriant lashes. 'I can promise you that much.'

That was a big promise and an even bigger temptation, Belle reflected sleepily. She knew she ought to ask him about the photo in his wallet but just at that moment when she felt deliciously happy and comfortable felt like the wrong moment and she kicked the idea back out of her head with relief. No man had ever made her feel secure the way Cristo did, she conceded blissfully. She would ask him some time soon and would no doubt quickly learn that she had been agonising over nothing. Perhaps he had had the photo for some reason and had simply forgotten he still had it...

Recalling that thought, Belle drifted back to the present to find Cristo on the pool terrace regarding her where she reclined in the shade with an abandoned book, his amusement unhidden. 'You were a thousand miles away.'

'So, I daydream sometimes,' Belle parried, studying him with helpless appreciation: a lithe sun-bronzed god of a male, lean, powerful frame garbed in black jeans and a white tee. His breathtaking good looks still enthralled her but then *she* wasn't the only one looking, she recognised with pleasure as Cristo's gaze whipped with flattering appreciation over her bikini-clad curves. 'Were you looking for me?'

'*Sì.*' Cristo hesitated. 'I'm flying the rest of your family here this afternoon.'

Brow furrowed in surprise, Belle sat up. 'What are you talking about?'

'I've been warned that the story about Gaetano and his children by your mother will be published tomorrow, so I'm taking your grandmother and the children out of harm's way and over here where no one will bother them.'

Thrown off balance by that terse explanation, Belle exclaimed, 'When did you decide to do that? My gran as well? They won't want to come at such short notice, for goodness' sake.'

'Bruno's bored stiff at home over the summer and counting the hours. I Skyped him and he believes he will like the Umbrian landscape,' Cristo supplied with a decided hint of one-upmanship.

'You *Skyped* him?' Belle gasped in complete disconcertion.

'I alerted your grandmother to the situation last week. She's now only awaiting your call to reassure her that they won't be intruding on us,' Cristo completed.

'But she never said a word when I last spoke to her...' Belle's voice trailed away, for she could scarcely recall what she had discussed with the older woman during that call and would have been the first to admit that her concentration hadn't been what it was of late. More and more her entire world seemed to be defined by the closed little world she inhabited with Cristo, where nothing else seemed to matter very much.

'She didn't want to worry you, so will you ring her and assure her they're all welcome and that we have plenty of space for them?' Cristo prompted. 'The experience of having the paparazzi on the doorstep would be traumatic for the children.'

Pale and dismayed at the threat of her family being

exposed to that kind of rude and humiliating attention, Belle was propelled straight off the lounger and back indoors.

When she phoned her grandmother, Isa was her usual calm and logical self. 'Whatever happens we'll weather it the way we've weathered everything else. You don't *have* to bring us to Italy,' she declared staunchly.

'I'm dying to see you all again. I know it's only been a few weeks but it feels more like months,' Belle confided truthfully. 'And Franco keeps on asking for you all.'

'Newly married couples need privacy and five children and a granny are going to put quite a dent in that,' Isa forecast ruefully.

'You're family—that's different,' Belle protested. 'And I've missed you all so much.'

And that was true, regardless of her contentment with Cristo, she acknowledged. In fact her time away from the family had already taught her how much she had taken their presence for granted before her marriage and how much she had since missed the warm hurly-burly of their home and her grandmother's soothing support.

With her family's coming visit confirmed, Belle went off to consult Umberto about where everyone was to sleep and discovered that Cristo had already spoken to him on the subject the week before. Isa suffered from arthritic knees and sometimes found stairs a challenge and Belle was further disconcerted to learn that a room downstairs that opened out on a seating area on the terrace had already been set up for the older woman's occupation.

'When did you organise the room for Isa?' Belle asked Cristo curiously as she came to a halt in the doorway of his office.

'As soon as I knew she was coming, *bellezza mia*. My grandmother also preferred ground-floor accommodation,' Cristo told her quietly.

Belle collided with his spectacular dark heavily fringed eyes and her heart hammered behind her breastbone. 'Is your grandmother still alive?'

'No. She died the summer after I graduated but she was very much a part of my life when I was younger,' Cristo admitted.

'How does your brother Zarif feel about the news article that's about to be published?' Belle asked worriedly. 'I know how worried you were about the effect it might have on him.'

'Zarif never panics and he believes that such a juicy story was always going to escape into the public domain. He says he'll ride it out.'

In receipt of that assurance, Belle felt a little of her tension evaporate. She wanted to ask Cristo if he now felt that he had married her for nothing. After all, he had married her to bury that story and the safeguard hadn't worked. 'That's good.'

Cristo sprang upright, his attention pinned to Belle's pensive face, the sparkle in her eyes and the ripe curve of her mouth. 'You're happy your family's coming to stay, aren't you?'

Belle cast off her insecurities and a grin relaxed her mouth. 'Yes. I've missed them a lot.'

'I really didn't appreciate how close you all were. Growing up, I was strictly an only child. I first met my half-brothers when I was a teenager and only then because my stepfather argued in favour of it.'

Within hours, Cristo received an emailed copy of the article that was to be published in a leading tabloid newspaper the following day.

'You've been immortalised in print!' Cristo growled from the doorway of the bedroom where Belle was putting a pile of fashion magazines in place for her younger sister, Lucia. A dark flush had overlaid his hard cheekbones and his eyes were bright with anger.

Belle whirled round to study him the instant she glimpsed the papers that he was angrily burnishing. 'I beg your pardon?'

Her heart in her mouth, she stared down at the email he'd printed out, spread flat on the table beside her. The headline *'Ravelli's Secret Irish Family'* spelt out the facts and shock reverberated through Belle when she saw the number of photos in the spread, not least the one of her clad in her wedding gown, which looked rather as though it might have been taken by a camera phone outside the chapel on the day. The main picture, however, was of her pregnant mother and her siblings taken at a local fair shortly before Franco's birth. There was even a small snap of her grandmother.

'So, the story really is going to be printed… I'm so sorry. I know how you felt about this,' Belle breathed heavily.

'But how *dare* they publish a photo of you?' Cristo demanded in a raw undertone, stabbing the offending item with a blunt forefinger. 'Smearing you with

Gaetano's sleaze as if *you* had anything to do with your mother's choices!'

Disconcerted by the focus of his rage, Belle swallowed hard. 'Who was it who talked to the press?'

'Gaetano's former driver.'

Belle was hurriedly reading the article, noting with relief that her grandmother was referred to as 'well-respected' and that she was merely mentioned as Mary's 'recently married' daughter. 'Luckily nobody seems to have made the connection that I got married to a Ravelli,' she remarked in astonishment. 'In fact there's no reference to you at all—'

'Isn't there?' Frowning in surprise at that news, Cristo bent to scan the blurred newsprint. 'Well, that's something at least.'

'And it doesn't say anything that isn't true. I mean, Gaetano was married throughout most of their affair and my mother wasn't the only woman in his life at the time.' Belle breathed in deep, colliding head-on with his burnished gaze and feeling her tummy flip in response. 'You know, I think the article could have been a lot nastier in tone than this is.'

'I just don't like you being soiled with Gaetano's sleaze,' Cristo admitted in a roughened undertone while he ran an admiring finger along the softened line of her generous mouth. 'But I suppose you're right and if Zarif can handle the fallout, we certainly can.'

Almost of their own volition her lips parted and she laved his fingertip with the tip of her tongue. His lashes lowered, his semi-screened eyes flashing burning gold and scorchingly light against his bronzed skin as he hauled her into his arms and covered her mouth hungrily with his own. Excitement flared through Belle's slender body like a storm warning and the instant surge of desire stirred a sharp ache between her thighs.

'I want you,' Cristo ground out against her swollen lips, arching her into him with an imprisoning hand splayed across her hips, ensuring that she was fully aware of his arousal.

Belle lifted an unsteady hand to his lean dark face and her fingertips traced a hard masculine cheekbone in a helpless caress. 'Well, I'm not doing anything else...' she whispered teasingly, hot as an inferno inside her own skin and literally weak with longing.

He took that invitation with a thoroughness she could only appreciate. Lifting her in his arms, he took her back to their bedroom. Her heated bare skin revelled in the brush of the cool, crisp linen on the bed when he tossed the sheets back. She was excited by the crushing weight of her lover and his forcefulness as he stretched her arms above her head, her wrists gripped between the fingers of one strong hand, and ravished her mouth erotically with his own. Between the sheets, Cristo was dominant and she rejoiced in that aspect of him. Her heart thundered in her ears as he stroked and teased the tender tissue between her thighs, her slender spine arching in helpless delight as he took advantage of the welcome offered by the honeyed dampness of her sensitive flesh.

When Cristo flipped her over onto her knees, a sound of surprise was wrenched from her and then, before she could say or do anything, he was driving into her hard and fast, stretching her with shocking fullness, every entry and withdrawal perfectly timed to deliver the maximum possible pleasure. Insane excitement roared through Belle like a hungry fire, burning up every thought in the heat of the flames. She was out of control, lost in sensation, a slave to the delight. Her body raced to the climax it craved and she cried out in pure ecstasy, hearing his answering groan. Afterwards she collapsed in a heap on the bed, her muscles like jelly, her breath still hissing in and out of her gasping throat as she struggled to reason and speak again.

'Did I ever tell you how fantastic you are in bed, *bella mia*?' Cristo husked, pulling her back against his hard, damp body, his broad chest still heaving from the exertion of their encounter.

'Maybe you've mentioned it once or twice.' A smile as old as Eve curved Belle's reddened mouth because it made her feel good that he could think that even in the light of his much greater sexual experience.

Black hair wildly tousled, Cristo rubbed a stubbled jaw across a slim, smooth shoulder and murmured earthily, 'I can't keep my hands off you…you're killing me.'

Belle laughed softly and curved round him, every possessive urge in her body thrumming on full charge. She was happy, so happy that the horrible newspaper article hadn't rocked their relationship as she'd once feared, but still a sense of unease niggled in the back of her mind. The moment she looked for it, that tiny little seed of doubt about Cristo and Betsy refused to stay buried any longer. She wanted, no, she *needed* to know the truth, which she was convinced would be entirely non-threatening in reality.

'Why do you carry a photo of your brother's wife in your wallet?' Belle lifted her head to ask, the question as bold and instinctive on her lips as it was in her mind.

CHAPTER TEN

CRISTO'S BIG, POWERFUL frame froze and, that fast, Belle knew she had made a fatal mistake in assuming that she had nothing to worry about.

Dark blood rose in a revealing banner across Cristo's cheekbones. His spectacular bone structure had hardened into taut angles and hollows overlaid with the rigidity of fierce self-control while his dark golden eyes remained carefully shielded. 'What are you talking about?'

No longer warm and relaxed in the intimate circle of his arms, Belle rolled away and sat up against the tumbled pillows, tugging the sheet up to cover her breasts with hands that now felt clumsy. 'Franco got hold of your wallet one day and the photo fell out of it. I wasn't snooping, I *swear* I wasn't, but naturally I wondered why you had it.'

'Franco,' Cristo groaned, raking the long fingers of one tanned hand through his black hair and sitting up while he played for time and considered his options. That blasted photo, which he had forgotten he still had! He could lie, of course he could lie to her, but the memory of Gaetano's frequent lies and deceptions had left his son with an ineradicable desire never to follow in the older man's footsteps. Besides, lying was not only a weakness but also an act of deceit. Belle was his wife and she was entitled to the truth, he reasoned grimly, even if it was a truth he was in no hurry to share or recall. But where there was honesty, he believed there would be no future misunderstandings or grey areas.

He breathed in deep and slow and then released his breath again in an impatient hiss, his handsome mouth compressing. 'Betsy turned to me for support after her marriage to Nik broke down...for a while I thought I'd fallen in love with her...'

Belle was already in the grip of mental turmoil because his visible reaction to her question had immediately betrayed that she had stumbled onto a sensitive issue. Her head ached with the ferocity of her tension and her conflicting thoughts and incipient panic made her a poor listener. *I fell in love with her* was all Belle took from that fractured speech and his confession had the same impact on her as the announcement of a sudden death. *I fell for her.* Her mouth ran dry, her heartbeat accelerated and her tummy performed a sick somersault. *I fell for her.* She could feel the blood draining from her face, the clawing clench of her fingertips on the edge of the sheet and the resulting ache in her knuckle bones. For a truly dreadful moment she was scared she might throw up where she sat, and then mercifully the tide of sickness receded while her brain kicked feverishly back into action.

Cristo had fallen in love with little fairy-like Betsy, who was so tiny and exquisite that Belle was convinced that she herself would look like a comic-book character standing beside her. Belle was taller, cur-

vier, and physically larger in every way, her hair rau-
cous red to Betsy's pale, subtle blonde. No two women
could have been more diametrically opposed in the
looks department. Did he try to fantasise that she was
Betsy in bed? That cruel suspicion pierced Belle like
a knife in her chest, shock still winging through her
in blinding waves while her mind leapt on to make
even more offensive connections. Cristo had actually
dared to marry her when he was in love with another
woman! Appalled at this knowledge that sucked out
every atom of her former happiness and contentment
in her role, Belle slid out of bed and swept up her wrap.
She folded herself into it in a jerky motion because her
limbs still felt oddly detached from her body.

'Why on earth did you marry *me*?' Anger was roaring through Belle in a giant floodtide that drowned
every rational thought and controlled every response.
'I mean, you were in love with another woman, so why
the heck would you ask me to marry you?'

Taken aback by her behaviour, his incomprehension
growing at her overreaction to what he now saw as a
comparatively insignificant mistake on his own part
that had caused no one any harm, Cristo frowned in
bewilderment. 'Why should it bother you?'

'It doesn't bother me. I'm not one bit bothered!'
Belle proclaimed in furious vehement denial, her pride
answering for her. 'But obviously I don't like what it
says about *you*. What sort of man gets involved with
his brother's wife?'

Understanding crossed Cristo's sleek dark face,
swiftly followed by an unmistakeable expression of
distaste. 'I wasn't sexually involved with Betsy. I didn't

make a single move that crossed the boundaries of friendship with her.'

'Are you trying to tell me that you *haven't* had an affair with her?' Belle demanded incredulously. 'Do I look that stupid?'

Honesty, it suddenly struck Cristo for the first time, could be a poisoned chalice. His gift of honesty, offered with the best of intentions, had simply stirred up more serious suspicions. He sprang out of bed and reached for his jeans, pulling them on commando style in a fluid motion. Stunning dark eyes met unflinchingly with Belle's accusing stare.

'There was never any question of an affair. For a start, I never told Betsy how I felt, and naturally there was no physical intimacy. *Dio mio*, she's my brother's wife. I couldn't possibly cross that line.'

'But they're getting a divorce!' Belle cut in furiously.

'Nik will always be my brother. I could still *never* go there and from the outset I accepted that there was no future in my feelings for her.'

'Yet you married me even though you *loved* her!' Belle reminded him painfully, scarcely able to frame the words through her chattering teeth. She felt cold and clammy and nauseous. She had never felt so hurt and rejected in her entire life and it was as though a great well of anguish deep inside her was threatening to drag her down and swallow her alive. Suddenly the world looked dark, her future empty and full of threat.

'Why shouldn't I have married you? How I believed I felt about Betsy is pretty much irrelevant now. There was no way I was ever going to have anything but a friendship with her, and let's not forget that you and I agreed to a marriage purely based on practicality.'

That reminder was brutally unwelcome. Belle's nails bit painfully into the flesh of her hands as she knotted them together. A *practical* marriage. When had she contrived to forget that revealing description of his expectations and her own agreement on that basis? When had she developed expectations of something a great deal more emotionally satisfying than a detached marriage of convenience? And whatever the answer to those questions was it didn't really matter at a moment when she was in so much pain that she could barely bring herself to look at him. Just then she was too worked up to argue with Cristo and she was desperate to make an escape lest she embarrass herself by saying something she shouldn't.

'Excuse me,' Belle breathed curtly, sidestepping Cristo to stalk into the bathroom.

The door closed, the lock turning with a fast and audible click.

In frustration, Cristo swore under his breath. Why was she so angry? Why the hell was she so angry with him? Blasted relationships, he reflected with brooding resentment. He was no good at them, and never had been. He had always settled for sex and got out before anything more complex was required. But he couldn't walk away from Belle and their marriage any more easily than he could escape the fallout from what appeared to be a disastrous error of judgement on his part. He pictured Belle's face when he had truthfully answered her question. She had turned pale as snow, her eyes blank while immediate constraint tightened her features. One minute she had been in his arms, smiling and happy and affectionate, the next angry and distant and...*hurt*. His wide sensual mouth compressed grimly at that awareness. Every natural instinct told him he should have lied in his teeth and made up an excuse for still having that photo in his wallet. But although he had told her about Betsy, it had decidedly not been the moment to tell her the rest of that story because she would never have believed him in the mood she was in, he reasoned bitterly.

Trembling with reaction, Belle splashed her face with cold water. Tears were running from her eyes and she washed them away with punitive splashes of more cold water, finally burying her chilled face with a shudder in a soft warm towel. Cristo was in love with Betsy and nothing had ever hurt Belle so much as that discovery. Why was that? she asked herself wretchedly; why was she taking the news so badly, so...*personally*?

They had married for convenience and her main motivation before the wedding had been the welfare of her brothers and sisters. That goal had been achieved most successfully for Cristo was already accepting that her siblings were also his and therefore family to them both. He wasn't going to turn round and suddenly desert the children, he was too honourable for that, she reflected heavily. To date he had also kept his promises to her. To say the very least, he treated her with warmth and respect.

Had she hoped he felt more than that where she was concerned? Belle nibbled at her lower lip, afraid to meet her own eyes in the mirror because, on her terms, their relationship had very quickly become intensely personal both in and out of bed. The limits of practicality had been bypassed and forgotten by her within days of the wedding. She had learned to care for Cristo, to enjoy his company, his sense of humour, his kindness to Franco, his thoughtfulness whenever it came to a question of what made her happy. In short she had travelled all the way from initial admiration and appreciation to falling madly in love with her husband, which was why hearing that he loved someone else had caused her such pain. Stupid, *stupid* man—why on earth had he told her? And, even worse, why had he looked at her as though she was insane when she reacted with furious condemnation? Didn't he understand *anything* about women? About her? Maybe she should have framed the experience in terms he would have understood...

'*Cristo!*' Belle bawled across the bedroom on her noisy return, the bathroom door still shuddering behind her from her aggressive exit.

Cristo emerged from the dressing room in the act of buttoning a shirt and fixed enquiring dark eyes on her with exaggerated politeness. 'You called, *bella mia*?'

Belle reddened fiercely. 'All right, I shouted. I'm sorry. It's just you don't seem to understand how I feel, so I thought I should give you an example.'

A winged ebony brow elevated. 'An example?'

'Try to imagine how you would feel if I was to tell you right now that I was in love with Mark Petrie,' she urged.

Before her very eyes, Cristo froze into an icy bronzed statue. '*Are* you?'

'You see, the boot's very much on the other foot now, isn't it?' she fired back. 'No, of course I'm not in love with Mark, but you don't like the idea, do you?'

'Of course, I don't—you're my wife.' Dawning comprehension slivered through Cristo and his shrewd gaze veiled but he remained stubbornly silent, wary as he was of setting her temper off again.

'No wife would want to hear that her husband *ever* loved another woman,' Belle pointed out with dignity. 'It's not personal, it's simply a matter of what's… what's…acceptable. You're my husband. I'm possessive about you. I can't help that.'

'We're both possessive by nature, *bella mia,*' Cristo husked, relieved that the storm had been weathered and she appeared to be calming down.

But Belle was simply putting on an act to save face. She had her pride. She didn't want him to know how she felt about him. Determined to act normally, she shone a light smile of acceptance in his direction before returning to her own room where her clothes were still kept. While she dressed for lunch, she concentrated her rushing thoughts on the knowledge that her family were arriving within hours. Family, that was what *really* mattered. There was absolutely no point in tearing herself apart over what went on in Cristo's dark, complex head because she couldn't change that.

No doubt, though, he had Betsy on a pedestal. Betsy would always be the unattainable perfect woman in his eyes while Belle would have to settle for being the much more convenient, accessible and real-world wife, who would dutifully help him raise their orphaned brothers and sisters. Well, she could live with that unromantic reality, couldn't she? Of course she could, she told herself urgently, while in the back of her mind furious objections flared. It wasn't a matter of being second-best, she told herself. That was a degrading label and she would go insane if she started picturing herself as some kind of martyr.

Keep it simple, she urged herself sternly. She loved her husband. How had that happened? She had once been so afraid of falling in love and getting hurt, yet miraculously those concerns had been overwhelmed by the powerful emotions Cristo drummed up inside her. He was very generous, very attentive and absolutely breathtaking in bed. What's not to like, she asked herself accusingly. To want or expect more than she was already getting was downright greedy. He couldn't help what he felt. She should respect his privacy, she reasoned in an even more frantic loop of planning; she shouldn't concern herself with his emotions. And telling him that he was never to see or even speak to Betsy again would not be a winning move... *would it?*

Cristo watched Belle across the lunch table, utterly distrusting her demure expression as she fed Franco from her own plate, breaking her own rules and using the child as a distraction every time Cristo spoke. Franco, of course, lapped up the extra attention and would throw a merry tantrum the next time he was refused a selection from someone else's plate. Cristo was torn between a strong desire to shake Belle and an even stronger desire to drag her back to bed and stamp her as *his* again. Suspecting that he might strike out in that field, he decided to throw in the towel. Belle was in a mood and she would get over it but he was exasperated by the way she was behaving and the wedge she was driving between them. His chair scraped across the terrace tiles as he pushed it back and plunged upright.

'I have a couple of calls to make. I'll see you later,' he said drily.

Targeted by shrewd dark-as-night eyes, Belle went pink and then parted her lips. 'I was planning to sleep in my own room tonight. If the article is to be published tomorrow, I want to be really rested so that I can be with my family,' she muttered uncomfortably.

Cristo gritted his perfect white teeth. It wasn't as if he kept her up *all* night *every* night! Was he a little too demanding in the bedroom? Wouldn't she have complained before now? Belle was no human sacrifice and indeed had a whole repertoire of delightful approaches calculated to wake him up hot and hard at dawn. It was an unfortunate recollection when every basic instinct he possessed craved a renewal of the very physical connection they shared. Handsome mouth set in a steely stubborn line, Cristo strode away.

'Now Cristo's annoyed with me,' Belle mumbled into Franco's tousled hair as he sat on her lap. 'He never says anything. He just gives me this sardonic look and it makes me cross and it makes me sad and for some peculiar reason it makes me want to run after him and say sorry.'

'*Kiss-do*,' Franco slotted with emphasis into that confused flood of confidence and the little boy began wriggling off her lap, suddenly keen to be free.

Belle watched her brother race after Cristo and her mouth down-curved; it promised to be a long and lonely afternoon.

In the echoing hall of the palazzo, Tag leapt straight out of his travel box and flung himself in a passionate welcome at Belle, pink tongue lolling, ragged tail wagging like mad, his little white and black body wriggling frantically. No sooner had he achieved that reunion and more than a few hugs of reciprocal affection, he glanced at Cristo and growled long and low in his throat.

'*No*, Tag!' Bruno stepped forward to say forcefully, casting his older sister a look of reproach as he scooped up the little dog and walked to the door with him to let him out to run off his over-excitement. Pietro and Lucia, the eight-year-olds too wound up to stay still after hours of travelling confinement, hurtled back outside in the dog's wake. 'You have to be very firm with him, Belle. He doesn't understand anything else.'

'She's the same with Franco,' Cristo remarked wryly. 'Lets him get away with murder.'

'Well, thank you both for that vote of confidence,' Belle countered as her grandmother laughed and folded her into a warm hug. 'How have you been, Gran?'

'I missed you,' Isa confided, her shrewd gaze searching her granddaughter's pale face and shadowed eyes with a frown. 'Missed that little scamp, Franco, as well. We all did.'

'Bruno says there's no shops near here.' Donetta sighed, her pretty face troubled and self-pitying. 'And I've got nothing to wear in this heat.'

'We'll go shopping,' Cristo promised.

'Well, don't expect me to come, especially not if Lucia is going as well.' Bruno winced and shot Cristo a rueful look. 'Lucia only likes the colour pink and won't wear anything else. Getting her into a school uniform will be a nightmare.'

'It's only a phase. She'll get over it,' Belle told him soothingly.

'Mum never did,' Bruno reminded her wryly, his mobile face shadowing with a sudden stark grief that he couldn't hide and which made him hurriedly study the floor with fixed attention.

Belle tensed and tried and failed to think of something comforting to say. Isa grabbed her hand to draw her attention back to her. 'You can start the official tour by showing me to my room,' she suggested. 'And a cup of tea would be even more welcome.'

Isa was tireless in the questions she asked about the Palazzo Maddalena and astonished to be told that Cristo's aristocratic mother didn't care for her former family home.

'The princess grew up here and much prefers life in the city,' Belle explained. 'Cristo only comes here for the occasional holiday so the place does need updating, but I don't like to wade in and start talking about changes when we're only just married.'

'You sounded so happy when you phoned me ,' Isa remarked thoughtfully as she sank with an appreciative sigh into a comfortable wicker armchair on the terrace and reached for the tea Umberto had brought. 'What's happened since then?'

Belle forced a smile. 'Nothing,' she swore with determination. 'I am very happy with Cristo.'

'A man and a woman can find it a challenge to live together at first,' Isa commented gently. 'Being part of a couple entails compromise.'

'Cristo is really, really good to me,' Belle muttered in a rush, keen to settle any concerns her grandmother might be cherishing. 'I really do have nothing to complain about.'

'Then why aren't you happy?' Isa prompted bluntly. 'I can see something's not right.'

'But it's not something I can discuss… It's something I need to talk about with Cristo,' Belle declared, recognising in that moment that she had actually spoken the truth. Much as she would like to, she could not avoid the subject of Betsy. That had to be discussed and she had to come to terms with it, she registered unhappily. The worst possible stance she could take would be to hold Cristo's feelings against him and poison every other part of their relationship with her bitterness. But it was so very hard to suppress the resentment, jealousy and hurt bubbling up inside her every time she looked at him.

'That sounds sensible,' her grandmother commented with approval and deftly changed the subject to bring Belle up to date on what had been happening in her family since her wedding.

Dinner was served out on the terrace at a big table Umberto had retrieved from a storeroom. The meal was an uproarious affair with all the children talking together, exchanging insults, pulling faces at Franco's table manners, and Belle could see that Cristo was disconcerted by the sheer liveliness of their over-excited siblings. Pietro and Lucia could barely spare the time to eat before they, with Tag in hot pursuit, chased off to explore the gardens again, with Franco trying desperately to keep up with them and breaking down into floods of tears when he was left behind. Cristo went to retrieve the toddler left sobbing at the top of the steps.

'Time for bed, I think,' he murmured quietly. 'I'll call Teresa.'

'No, I'll take him up,' Belle interposed, holding out her arms to take her little brother. 'A bath will soothe him.'

'I'll carry him,' Cristo countered flatly, stunning dark eyes hard and challenging as he studied her set face. 'I'll be back down in—'

'Oh, don't worry about us,' Isa cut in hastily, glancing at Bruno and Donetta. 'The three of us have a date with the television Umberto has most kindly set up for our use.'

Belle stomped upstairs in Cristo's wake, wondering what was wrong with him, her face still burning from that hard, impatient look he had angled at her.

Teresa greeted them on the landing and lifted Franco from her employer's arms. 'Poor little pet… he's exhausted. I'll put him straight in the bath,' she announced.

Belle turned on her heel but a strong tanned hand closed round her forearm to prevent her hurrying back downstairs. 'I'd like a word in private,' Cristo breathed.

Temper sparking fast in the strained mood she was in, Belle rounded on him, her green eyes flashing a fiery warning. 'What on earth is the matter with you?' she hissed.

'You've been avoiding me and ignoring me since this morning,' Cristo pointed out.

Belle's face flamed. 'I'm only trying to keep things polite for the family's benefit.'

'Then you can't act worth a damn,' Cristo told her succinctly, his hand on her forearm sliding down to engulf her fingers instead in a firm grip as he dragged her down the corridor with him. 'And we need to clear the air.'

'I don't want to talk…I'm not ready yet,' Belle exclaimed with more honesty than she had intended, because she had not yet reached the desirable stage where she could consider his feelings for Betsy without raging resentment infiltrating her every thought and reaction.

'Too bad. I'm ready now,' Cristo decreed, shoving wide the door of his bedroom and urging her in ahead of him.

'Is that why you're suddenly acting like a cave man?' Belle demanded furiously.

'No, that's entirely your fault,' Cristo fielded without hesitation. 'If you want to argue with me, argue with me, don't go all passive-aggressive and do it from behind a fake smile.'

'That is not what I've been doing!' Belle protested angrily.

'That's exactly what you've been doing and I've had enough of it. I made the mistake of admitting that at one stage I thought that I had fallen for Betsy—'

'No, you said you *had* fallen for her!' Belle contradicted.

'You mustn't have been listening,' Cristo told her severely. 'For a while before I met you I did believe I'd fallen for her, but once I met you I soon realised that I'd misconstrued my response to her.'

Belle abandoned her angry pacing round the room and fell still. *'Misunderstood?'* she questioned sharply, turning her head back to look at his darkly handsome face.

His lean, strong features taut, Cristo expelled his breath in a rueful hiss. 'You have to understand how I felt at the time Nik and Betsy's marriage broke down. I felt unbearably guilty and accountable because—'

'You told some secret of Nik's to Zarif and he talked when he shouldn't have and let the cat out of the bag,' Belle interposed impatiently. 'Yes, I remember—'

'And Betsy was devastated and she turned to me as Nik's brother, believing that I might know or understand why Nik had done what he had done. That was why she came to me. Unfortunately I didn't know or understand, and I couldn't help, but I felt extremely sorry for her. For whatever reasons, Nik had treated her badly. I felt very protective towards her and angry with Nik and I honestly assumed that those feelings were love.'

While she listened to what Cristo had to say, Belle was slowly breaking out in a cold sweat of relief because she was finally recognising that somehow in her hot-headed emotional response she had got the wrong end of the stick. Cristo had misinterpreted his feelings for Betsy and then recognised his mistake. Belle could understand how confused Cristo must've felt at the time, torn between guilt and responsibility for his brother's marriage breakdown while feeling both disloyal to his brother and strongly sympathetic towards Betsy's plight.

'I can understand that. You felt responsible so you tried to be helpful and provide a supportive shoulder.'

'I did still think I loved her when I asked you to marry me even though I'd never been attracted to Betsy the way I was to you,' Cristo admitted with a twist of his mouth. 'That sounds ludicrously naïve, doesn't it?'

Belle was frowning in surprise. 'You *weren't* attracted to her?'

'No. I assumed that was because I still thought of her as my brother's wife but I think it was more because she wasn't my type and didn't appeal to me on that level.'

'But…I've seen photos of her and she's incredibly pretty!' Belle fired back at him in ridiculous challenge.

'I've discovered that tall, curvy redheads are much more my style, *amata mia*,' Cristo quipped. 'Particularly ones who can give as good as they get in a row and can function as my intellectual equal.'

Belle dragged in a steadying breath before she could ask uncertainly, 'Are you talking about me?'

'Who else?' Dark golden eyes locked to her bemused face and lingered. 'After all, it was only because I fell in love with you that I learned to appreciate that I'd *never* been in love with Betsy.'

Mouth running dry, eyes wide, Belle was suddenly feeling very short of breath and even slightly dizzy, as if the floor below her feet were rocking. And indeed it might as well have been because it seemed that most of her pessimistic assumptions had been glaringly wrong. 'You fell in love with me?'

'And it was almost love at first sight,' Cristo teased with a charismatic smile. 'Before you decided to try and convince me that you were your mother and a forty-odd-year-old woman, I saw you crossing the lawn, wearing a pair of shorts, and you have curves and legs to die for,' Cristo told her with a wicked grin.

'You're so superficial,' Belle mumbled in a pained

tone of amusement. So superficial but *mine*, she was thinking lovingly.

'Not at all. I love your legs but I love your brain and your ready tongue more,' Cristo confided without hesitation. 'In fact there's a whole host of things I like about you that have nothing to do with your very sexy appearance.'

'Like...?' Belle pressed shamelessly.

'Your loyalty and love for your family, your kindness, your lack of greed,' Cristo enumerated, moving closer step by step while Belle continued to survey him with wonder. He loved her, not Betsy, and her brain was struggling to process that alien conviction. She was not second-best; she was his *first* choice and he genuinely cared about her. The first heady spur of joy surged through her like a rejuvenating drug.

'I like lots of things about you too,' Belle burbled. 'But I fell in love with you without knowing I was doing it. It was only when I thought you loved Betsy that I realised how I felt about you.'

'Great minds think alike,' Cristo purred, stroking the side of her face with a gentle forefinger. 'You love me, I love you. We're a perfect match.'

'No, we're imperfect but that's okay...we're only human,' Belle mumbled unsteadily, her heart leaping behind her breastbone as Cristo drew her into his arms and eased her wonderfully, reassuringly close to his lean, powerful frame. 'Oh, I can't believe this...I was *so* miserable today!'

'I would've told you how I felt about you then if you hadn't been so angry I was afraid that you wouldn't believe me,' Cristo confessed. 'Let's face it, neither of us was looking for or expecting love in this marriage, but you turned out to be the best thing that's ever happened to me and I think the family we already have will be the icing on the cake.'

Belle dealt him an anxious upward glance, afraid he was being too optimistic in his outlook. 'But you can get lots of little problems too with family.'

'And together we'll deal with them,' Cristo asserted huskily as he brushed his mouth very tenderly over hers, lifting his handsome dark head to stare down at her with tender love and appreciation softening his stunning gaze. 'You're mine, my love, my wife, my future…'

'I like the sound of that very much,' Belle admitted, snuggling into his broad chest with a happy sigh. 'But you know when you said that it wouldn't be worth my while learning Italian, I assumed you only saw me as a short-term prospect.'

'*Ma no*…certainly not,' Cristo chided huskily. 'I only meant that these days I don't spend a lot of time in Italy.'

'I'd still like to learn.'

'I love you,' he told her in Italian and she repeated the words faithfully back with a little giggle as he backed her down on the bed with a clear agenda in mind.

Belle greeted her family with a shining smile the following morning. Isa beamed and said nothing. Franco was scolded for trying to steal off Cristo's plate and Tag for snarling at Cristo's ankles. Pietro and Lucia squabbled as usual. Donetta wanted to know when they were going shopping and Bruno was making rapturous comments about the quality of the light.

Below the level of the table, Cristo gripped Belle's hand in his and breathed, 'Family is what it's all about, *amata mia*. My father missed out on so much.'

EPILOGUE

FOUR YEARS LATER, Belle stood at a cheval mirror and pulled her stretchy dress away from the very small bump she sported.

'You're pregnant. You're supposed to be that shape,' her grandmother told her reprovingly.

'I'm putting on a lot of weight though,' Belle groused, checking the generous curve of her bust and hips in the mirror as she turned round and pulled a face.

'Not too much,' Isa contradicted. 'You're very active and naturally you need to eat. At least you're not as sick as your mother was when she was expecting.'

'There is that,' Belle conceded reluctantly. 'Now, are you sure you're going to be all right while we're away?'

'Belle, you and Cristo will only be away for five days, of course we'll be all right,' the older woman declared lightly. 'Stop fussing.'

Cristo and Belle were celebrating their fourth wedding anniversary in Venice where they would be visiting the princess and Henri in their palazzo on the Grand Canal but staying in a small intimate hotel that Cristo had carefully selected for them. Belle could barely credit that so much time had passed since their wedding and that soon she would be a mother in her own right.

Cristo had bought a fabulous house for them in Holland Park. Bruno was now studying art at college and Donetta was planning to do fashion design. Pietro and Lucia were both in secondary school and fought a little less often now that they were so conscious of being almost teenagers. Franco was a sturdy six-year-old in primary school, who insisted on having his curls cropped the minute they became visible and who modelled his every masculine move on Cristo, whom in common with the twins he called, 'Dad.'

Although they had started out with a ready-made family, who had been officially adopted by Cristo and Belle within months of their first wedding, Cristo had never overlooked their personal relationship or taken it for granted. They had, after all and at his insistence, had their marriage blessed in an Italian church service shortly before the first Christmas they had shared, both of them feeling the need to exchange their vows with rather more sincerity and emotion than had figured when they had initially married. They also enjoyed regular weekend breaks and holidays as a couple.

It had been during their last romantic break that Cristo had admitted that he would love her to have his child. That development had taken place far sooner than either of them had expected because Belle had fallen pregnant within a month of that decision. She smiled, hand splaying across her tummy as she thought of the little girl on the way to joining the Ravelli family. She could hardly wait and her brothers and sisters were equally excited at the new addition in the offing.

Indeed, Belle was happier than she had ever dreamt of being with Cristo and her family. And she had never been so busy. The palazzo, where they usually spent their summers on a family holiday, had been modernised. The whole family circle had drawn closer. Cristo's brother, Nik Christakis, still intimidated Belle but his life had taken some surprising turns since their first meeting and he had definitely warmed up from the driven workaholic he had once been.

Zarif's life was still a story under development and Belle loved visiting Vashir with its colourful vibrant culture and fabulous history. Cristo's younger brother had weathered the storms over the scandal of his father's secret double life because the rumours about Gaetano's misbehaviour had once been so wild that the truth was no more shocking to the populace, who could only marvel that Zarif was such a conservative male in comparison.

Belle clambered into the limo that was to whisk her to the airport to meet Cristo and smiled, looking forward to the promise of having her husband's undivided attention for a few days. An hour and half later, she boarded the private jet, her attention switching straight to Cristo's tall, well-built figure as he pushed aside his laptop and sprang upright to greet her in the aisle.

'You look beautiful, *amata mia*,' he told her huskily.

Belle slid self-mocking hands down over her bust and hips and quipped, 'Well, you are getting a more generous portion of me with every month that goes past...'

'And I *love* it,' Cristo growled, bending down to

kiss her ripe peach-tinted mouth with hungry appreciation. 'I think you look incredibly sexy.'

'Tell me more,' she urged as he settled her down in a comfortable seat beside his and fastened her belt for take-off.

'Later. Right now it's time for this…' Cristo slowly slid an emerald ring onto her wedding finger. 'It's the same colour as your eyes and it is to signify my gratitude and appreciation for four very happy years of marriage.'

'Thank you, it's absolutely gorgeous. Unfortunately my gift is unavailable right at this moment, so you'll have to wait.'

'What is it?' Cristo asked curiously.

'Well, it might be turquoise and frilly and exactly the sort of thing you like but you'll just have to wait and see,' she warned him with an irreverent grin. 'It has to be love, Cristo. It really has to be love I feel for you.'

'I adore you, *amata mia*,' Cristo murmured, holding her hand in his. 'And if you're talking about what I think you are, I can hardly wait.'

Belle rolled her green eyes teasingly and her colour heightened. 'You don't have to wait. I'm wearing it. Have you ever heard of the Mile High Club?'

* * * * *

Cesar was losing it. He knew he was losing it. But he couldn't take his mouth off Lexie's. He'd never tasted anything so sweet. Or so wicked. The way that lush mouth softened under his, the feel of that body under his hands...

Dios.

Cesar finally pulled back, heart hammering. He did not ravish women in the back of his cars. He was cool, calm, controlled. Right now he felt anything but. He could hardly see straight. His body was on fire.

Lexie was looking at him with huge eyes. She thought he'd done that on purpose. And he had—but not for the reasons she obviously suspected. He wanted to make sure there was no ambiguity about how he felt about her.

He cupped that delicate jaw. Her mouth was pink, swollen. He couldn't help running his thumb across that pouting lower lip, feeling its fleshy softness.

'Make no mistake, Lexie, I want you...and not just to distract the crowds. You know the truth of what I said earlier. We will be lovers for real.'

BLOOD BROTHERS

Power and passion run in their veins

Rafaele and Alexio have learned that to feel emotion is to be weak. Calculated ruthlessness brings them immense success in the boardroom and in the bedroom. But a storm is coming with the sudden appearance of a long-lost half-brother, Cesar, and three women who will change their lives for ever…

*Read **Rafaele Falcone's** story in:*
WHEN FALCONE'S WORLD STOPS TURNING
February 2014

*Read **Alexio Christakos's** story in:*
WHEN CHRISTAKOS MEETS HIS MATCH
April 2014

*And read **Cesar Da Silva's** story in:*
WHEN DA SILVA BREAKS THE RULES
June 2014

WHEN DA SILVA
BREAKS THE RULES

BY
ABBY GREEN

Published in Great Britain 2014
by Mills & Boon, an imprint of Harlequin (UK) Limited,
Eton House, 18-24 Paradise Road, Richmond, Surrey, TW9 1SR

© 2014 Abby Green

ISBN: 978 0 263 24646 9

Printed and bound in Spain
by Blackprint CPI, Barcelona

PROLOGUE

CESAR DA SILVA hated to admit that coming here had had any effect on him, but his gut was heavy and tight as he stood on the path near the grave. He asked himself again why he'd even come and reflexively his fingers closed around the small velvet pouch with its heavy weight in his hand. He'd almost forgotten about it.

He smiled cynically. Who would have thought that at the age of thirty-seven he'd be obeying urges and compulsions? Usually he was the king of logic and reason.

People drifted away from the open grave a short distance across the hilly green space. Ornate mini-mausoleum-style headstones dotted the cemetery in the hills of Athens, its grass no doubt kept generously watered in the Greek heat.

Finally there were only two men left by the grave. Both tall, of similar height, with dark hair. One had slightly darker and shorter hair than the other. They were broad, as Cesar was, with powerful builds.

It was no wonder they were all similar. He was their half-brother. And they had no idea he even existed. He saw one put his hand on the shoulder of the other. They were Rafaele Falcone and Alexio Christakos. They all shared the same mother, but had different fathers.

Cesar waited for icy rage to surge upwards upon seeing this evidence of the family he'd always been denied, but instead he felt a kind of aching emptiness. They came towards him then, talking in quiet voices. Cesar caught his youngest half-brother's words on the slight breeze—something like, *'Couldn't even clean up for the funeral...?'*

Falcone replied indistinctly, with a quirk to his mouth, and Christakos riposted, smiling too.

The emptiness receded and anger rose up within Cesar. But it was a different kind of anger. These men were joking, joshing, just feet away from their mother's grave. And since when did Cesar feel protective of the woman who had taught him from the age of three that he could depend on no one?

Galvanised by that very unwelcome revelation, Cesar moved forward and Falcone looked up, words dying on his lips, smile fading. Falcone's gaze was enquiring at first and then, as Cesar drilled holes into him with his stare, it became something else. Cold.

With a quick flick of a glance to the younger man by his half-brother's side, Cesar noted that they'd also all inherited varying shades of their beautiful but treacherous mother's green eyes.

'May we help you?' Falcone asked coolly.

Cesar glanced over them both again and then at the open grave in the distance. He asked, with a derisive curl to his lip, 'Are there any more of us?'

Falcone looked at Christakos, who was frowning, and said, *'Us?* What are you talking about?'

Cesar pushed down the spreading blackness within him and said with ominous quiet, 'You don't remember, do you?'

But he could see from the dawning shock that his half-brother did, and Cesar didn't like the way something inside him tightened at that recognition. Those light green eyes widened imperceptibly. He paled.

Cesar's voice was rough in the still, quiet air. 'She brought you to my home—you must have been nearly three, and I was almost seven. She wanted to take me with her then, but I wouldn't leave. Not after she'd abandoned me.'

In a slightly hoarse voice Falcone asked, 'Who *are* you?'

Cesar smiled, but it didn't meet his eyes. 'I'm your older brother—*half-brother*. My name is Cesar Da Silva. I came today to pay my respects to the woman who gave me life…not that she deserved it. I was curious to see if any more would crawl out of the woodwork, but it looks like it's just us.'

Christakos erupted. 'What the *hell*—?'

Cesar cast him a cold glance. Somewhere deep down he felt a twinge of conscience for imparting the news like this, on this day. But then he recalled the long, aching years of dark loneliness, knowing that these two men had *not* been abandoned, and crushed it ruthlessly.

Falcone still looked slightly shell-shocked. He gestured to his half-brother. 'This is Alexio Christakos…our younger brother.'

Cesar knew exactly who he was—who they both were. He'd always known. Because his grandparents had made sure he'd known every single little thing about them. He bit out, 'Three brothers by three fathers…and yet she didn't abandon either of *you* to the wolves.'

He stepped forward then, and Alexio stepped forward too. The two men stood almost nose to nose, Cesar topping his youngest brother in height only by an inch.

He gritted out, 'I didn't come here to fight you, brother. I have no issue with either of you.' *Liar*, a small voice chided.

Alexio's mouth thinned, 'Only with our dead mother, *if* what you say is true.'

Cesar smiled, but it was bitter. 'Oh, it's true all right—more's the pity.' He stepped around Alexio then, before either man could see the rise of an emotion he couldn't name, and walked to the open grave.

He took the velvet pouch out of his pocket and dropped it down into the dark space, where it fell onto the coffin with a hollow thud. In the pouch was a very old silver medallion featuring the patron saint of bullfighters: San Pedro Regalado.

Even now the bitter memory was vivid. His mother was in a black suit, hair drawn back, Her features as exquisitely beautiful as any he'd ever seen. Eyes raw from crying. She'd taken the medallion from where it hung around her neck on a piece of worn rope and had put it around his neck. She had tucked it under his shirt and said, *'He will protect you, Cesar. Because I can't at the moment. Don't ever take it off. And I promise I will come back for you soon.'*

But she hadn't come back. Not for a long time. And when she finally had it had been too late. Something had withered and died inside him. *Hope.*

Cesar had taken off the medallion the night he'd let that hope die. He'd been six years old. He'd known then that nothing could protect him except himself. She deserved to have the medallion back now—he'd had no need of it for a long time.

Eventually Cesar turned and walked back to where his half-brothers were still standing, faces inscrutable. He might have smiled, if he'd been able, to recognise this familiar trait. An ache gripped him in the region of his chest where he knew his heart should be. But as he knew well, and as he'd been told numerous times by angry lovers, he had no heart.

After a taut silence Cesar knew he had nothing to say to these men. These strangers. He didn't even feel envy any more. He felt empty.

He turned and got into the back of his car and curtly instructed his driver to go. It was done. He'd said goodbye to his mother, which was more than she'd ever deserved, and if there was one tiny piece of his soul that hadn't shrivelled up by now then maybe it could be saved.

CHAPTER ONE

Castillo Da Silva, near Salamanca

CESAR WAS HOT, sweaty, grimy and thoroughly disgruntled. All he wanted was a cold shower and a stiff drink. A punishing ride around his vast estate on his favourite stallion had failed to put a dent in the dark cloud that had clung to him since his return that afternoon from his half-brother Alexio's wedding in Paris. Those scenes of chirpy happiness still grated on his soul.

It also irritated him intensely that he'd given in to the rogue compulsion to go.

As he neared the stables his black mood increased on seeing the evidence of a serious breach of his privacy. A film was due to start shooting on his estate after the weekend, for the next four weeks. If that wasn't bad enough, the stars, director and producers were all staying *in* the *castillo*.

He wasn't unaware of his complicated relationship to his home. It was both prison and sanctuary. But one thing was sure: Cesar hated his privacy being invaded like this.

Huge equipment trucks lined his driveway. People were wandering about holding clipboards, speaking into walkie talkies. A massive marquee had been set up, where locals from the nearby town were being decked out as extras in nineteenth-century garb.

All that was missing was a circus tent with flags flying and a clown outside saying, *Roll up! Roll up!*

One of his biggest stable yards had been cleared out so that they could use it as the unit base. The unit base, as a film assistant had explained earnestly to Cesar, was where the actors got ready every day and where the crew would eat. As if he cared!

But he'd feigned interest for the benefit of his friend Juan Cortez, who was the Lord Mayor of Villaporto, the local town, and the reason why Cesar had given this idea even half a second's consideration. They'd been friends since the age of ten, when they'd both had to admit defeat during a fist fight or remain fighting till dawn and lose all their teeth. And they would have—both were stubborn enough.

As his friend had pointed out, 'Nearly everyone has been employed in some capacity—accommodation, catering, locations, the art department. Even my mother is involved in making clothes for the extras and putting up some of the crew. I haven't seen her so excited in years.'

Cesar couldn't fail to acknowledge the morale and economic boost the film had already brought to the locale. He was known in the press for his ruthless dealings with people and businesses—one journalist had likened his methods to those of the cold, dead-eyed shark before it ate you whole. But Cesar wasn't completely heartless—especially if it involved his own local community.

More than one person caught a glimpse of his glowering features and looked away hurriedly, but Cesar was oblivious, already figuring out how he could rearrange his schedule to make sure he was away for as much of the next four weeks as possible.

To his relief, his own private stable yard, which was strictly off-limits to the crew, was empty when he returned. He wasn't in the mood to deal with anyone—not even a groom. After unsaddling his horse and hosing him down, Cesar led him back to his stall and made sure he was secure, patting his still quivering flesh after their exertion.

It was only when he was turning to leave again that Cesar spotted a movement out of the corner of his eye and turned to look.

And stopped breathing, and thinking.

In the other corner of the quiet stable stood a woman. Cesar felt slightly dizzy for a moment and wondered if he was seeing an apparition.

She was wearing a white corset that cinched in her waist to almost impossible proportions while provocatively pushing up the abundant swells of her breasts. Long wavy golden hair was pulled back from an ethereally beautiful face and left to tumble down her back. Very feminine hips curved out from that tiny waist and a long, voluminous skirt almost touched the ground.

She was stunning…exquisite. She was Venus incarnate. She couldn't be real. Nothing so perfect existed in reality.

Almost without realising that he was moving, Cesar closed the distance between them. She didn't move. Just stared at him, looking as transfixed as he felt. Imbuing the moment with an even headier other-worldly feeling.

Her eyes were huge and blue…piercing. She was tiny, and it seemed to call to some deep, primal part of him. Evoking an alien urge to protect.

Her face was small and heart-shaped, but with an inherent strength that elevated it out of the merely beautiful to the extraordinary. High cheekbones. Elegant straight nose. A full, lush mouth made for sin and sinners. Skin like alabaster.

There was a beauty spot close to the edge of her upper lip. She exuded an earthy and very feminine sexual allure. She couldn't be real. Yet every single ounce of his masculinity was humming and throbbing in reaction to her luminosity.

As if to check that he wasn't losing it completely, Cesar reached out a hand, noting with almost dispassionate surprise that it trembled slightly. He cupped his hand near her cheek and jaw, without actually touching her, almost afraid that she might disappear if he did…

And then he touched her…and she didn't disappear. She was *real*. Warm. Skin as soft as silk.

A movement made his eyes drop and he saw her chest moving up and down rapidly with her breaths.

'*Dios,*' he said faintly, almost to himself, 'you are real.'

Her mouth opened. Cesar saw small, even white teeth. Her tongue-tip pink. She said, 'I…' and then stopped.

Just that one tiny word had been uttered in a husky voice, making Cesar's whole body tighten with a need that was unprecedented.

Sliding his fingers further around her jaw to the back of her neck, silky hair tickling his hand, Cesar tugged her into him and after a minute hesitation she came, stumbling ever so slightly. All he knew, once he felt the barest whisper of a touch of her body to his, was that he couldn't hold back now even if a thousand men tried to stop him.

He lowered his head and his mouth touched hers, and all that sweet, soft voluptuousness pierced him right to the centre of his being, and threw him into the pit of a fire of lust so strong it obliterated everything he knew, or thought he knew.

Cesar felt her hands clutching at him, grabbing his shirt. Any resistance vanished when her mouth opened under his, and his arms tightened around her as his hungry tongue thrust into that hot, moist cavern.

However sweet that first initial taste had been, it turned to pure sin. Decadent and rich. Her tongue was sharp and smooth, teasing. Stoking his levels of arousal so that every bit of blood seemed to be rushing to the centre of his body, making that shaft of flesh lengthen and stiffen painfully.

Moving his hands to her waist, encircling it, Cesar almost groaned aloud when he felt his fingers meet. That evidence of her intense femininity pushed his body over the edge, made it betray him as if he were an over-sexed teenager.

He could feel her chest, struggling with constricted breath, moving up and down rapidly. Blood surging anew, Cesar lifted a hand and dragged it up between their bodies, itching to touch that smooth pale skin.

When he came into contact with the swell of one breast his body pulsed with a need that shocked him. He broke the contact of their mouths for a moment, resting his forehead against hers, overwhelmed at the strength of his desire.

'Please...'

Her voice sounded even huskier...needy. The way he felt. He needed this woman *now*. Needed to free himself and lift up her skirts and plunge right into the centre of that taut, smooth body. To feel her legs wrap around him.

On some very dim and distant level Cesar was aware that he had become animalistic. Reduced to the cravings and needs of a base animal in an effort to achieve a kind of satisfaction he'd never anticipated before.

But that still couldn't stop him. Not after that husky *please* had filled the space between them.

Branding her mouth with his again, the kiss was open-mouthed and carnal. Electrifying.

In the act of lifting up her skirts, almost desperate now, Cesar jerked and flinched when a flash of light seemed to illuminate the world for a second. Like the crack of a whip. Shattering the heady moment.

Lifting his head from where their mouths were welded together, Cesar could only see two huge pools of blue,

ringed by long black lashes. That plump mouth was pink.
He could feel her chest moving against his.

Then there was another flash, and a rapid jarring, click-
ing sound. He flinched again. Some vague notion of reality and sanity returned from a long distance. He turned
his head, but it was the hardest thing to do—to look away
from that face. Those eyes.

He saw a man standing at the entrance of the stables
holding a camera up to his face. It was the equivalent of
having a bucket of cold water thrown over him. Suddenly
reality was back.

Cesar straightened up. Instinctively he pushed the
woman behind him as he snarled at the man who was
backing away, still shooting, 'Get out of here. *Now.*' One
of Cesar's grooms appeared near the door and he rapped
out at him, 'Get Security now—and get that man's camera.'

But the photographer had disappeared, and even though
Cesar's groom darted away after him Cesar had the sinking
feeling it would be too late. He'd reacted too late himself.

Becoming aware of rapid harsh breathing behind him,
Cesar turned around.

And almost fell into the pit again when he saw those
huge blue eyes staring up at him and that body which
made him ache.

But reality had intruded. This woman was no apparition
or ghost. She was flesh and blood, and he had just lost his
legendary control spectacularly. *Dios*, had he gone mad?

Accusingly, Cesar asked, 'Who the hell *are* you?'

Lexie Anderson was barely aware of the sharp accusation
in the deep, deliciously accented voice. She couldn't seem
to get enough breath into her challenged lungs to speak. All
she could ask herself was: *what the hell had just happened?*

She remembered wandering away from the camera tests

while they set up the lights and finding these quiet stables. She loved horses, so she had come in to investigate.

Then the peace had been shattered when this man had appeared in the courtyard on a huge black stallion. He'd swung down off the horse's back and from that moment on everything had got a little hazy.

Lexie had been mesmerised by his powerful physique and the play of muscles under his close-fitting polo top and jodhpurs as he'd tended to the horse. And that had been before she'd seen his face properly. When he'd heard her and turned around.

He was stunning. Beautiful. But with a masculine edge that made 'beautiful' sound too…pretty. He was hard. Edgy. Dark. Messy dark blond hair. A sensually sculpted mouth surrounded by stubble shadowing a very masculine jaw.

But it was his eyes that rendered Lexie a bit stupid and mute even now, as he waited for her reply. They were green—unusual and stark against dark olive skin. Not hazel, or golden, or light green. Something between all three. Unnerving. Mesmerising.

And he smelled of *man*. Sweat and musk and heat. Along with something tangy. Woodsy.

Lexie shook her head, as if that might make all this disappear. Maybe she was having some bizarre dream. Because she knew that what had just happened was unprecedented. She did not react to complete strangers by letting them kiss her, or by feeling as if she'd die if they didn't *keep* kissing her.

She remembered his big hands around her waist, then reaching under her skirts to pull them up, and how she'd burned between her legs for him to touch her there.

Now was most definitely *not* the time to be assimilating that cataclysmic information.

'I'm…' She stopped, her tongue feeling heavy in her

mouth. She tried again. 'I'm Lexie Anderson. I'm with the film.'

Lexie's face burned when she realised exactly how she was dressed, and how this man's eyes had widened when he'd seen her. Belatedly self-conscious, she went to cross her arms but realised the corset only made things worse—especially when those green eyes dropped to her heaving flesh again.

Feeling trapped now—literally backed into a corner—and not liking it, Lexie forced her legs to move, wobbly as they were, and stepped cautiously around him.

He turned to face her. Eyes cool, unreadable. Hands clenched into fists by his sides. 'You're Lexie Anderson... the lead actress?'

She nodded.

He looked at her, his eyes no longer unreadable now. Angry. 'And how did you get in here?'

She blinked, not understanding for a moment. 'I didn't see any sign or a gate...I just saw the horses—'

'It's off-limits here. You should leave—now.'

Anger gripped Lexie. She'd just behaved in a way that was completely out of character. The last thing she needed was to feel the lash of *his* censure. Stiffly, she replied, 'I didn't realise this was off-limits. If you can tell me how to get back to the unit base, I'll happily leave.'

His voice was harsh, curt. 'Turn left. It's at the end of the lane and to your right.'

Seething inwardly now, because she had been over-come by the first rush of physical desire she'd ever felt, and it had been for some anonymous person who worked at the castle and not even someone she *knew* or who was particularly charming, Lexie stalked off, tense as a board.

Then she heard the man curse and he commanded, 'Wait. Stop.'

Lexie stopped, breathing hard, and turned reluctantly again, rigid with tension.

He walked towards her, his movements powerfully agile, and she stepped back. His eyes flashed but she just tipped up her chin. What was wrong with her judgement? There wasn't anything remotely forgiving or alluring about this man. He was all hard edges and brooding energy.

He looked grim. 'That was a paparazzo. He got our picture.'

She'd forgotten. Her brain was refusing to work properly. Lexie could feel her blood draining south. The man must have feared she was about to faint or something, because he took her arm and none too gently drew her over to a haystack by the entrance, where he all but pushed her down onto it.

She ripped her arm free and glared up at him, hating the betraying quiver in her belly at his touch. 'There's no need to manhandle me. I'm perfectly fine.'

As if to confirm her worst suspicions, the young groom came running back, his face red.

'Well?' barked the man.

Lexie felt like standing up and telling him to go and take out his aggression on someone his own size, but she was disgusted to feel that her legs might not hold her up.

'Señor Da Silva…'

The groom spoke quickly after that, in incomprehensible Spanish, but Lexie was now gaping at the tall, angry man who was answering equally gutturally and quickly, making the groom turn puce and rush off again.

Lexie was too shocked to care for the groom's welfare any more. He turned back to her and she said faintly, 'You're Cesar Da Silva…?'

'Yes.'

He didn't seem to be too thrilled she'd made the connection. She'd thought he was a worker! Lexie hadn't recognised him as the owner of this entire estate because he was famously reclusive. Also, she'd never expected *the* Cesar Da Silva to be so young and gorgeous.

She had to will down her mortification when she thought of how she'd been all but crawling all over him like a hungry little kitten only minutes before. Begging. *'Please.'*

Oh, God.

She stood up. She had to get out of here. This was not her. She'd been invaded by some kind of body-snatcher.

'Where do you think you're going?'

Lexie looked at him. Anger flashed up again—at him and herself. She put her hands on her hips. 'You just told me to leave, didn't you? So I'm leaving.'

She moved around him again, towards the entrance, relieved that her legs were working.

'Wait.'

Lexie stopped and sighed heavily, turned around. She arched a brow, hiding how damn intimidating she thought he was. 'What now?'

He couldn't have looked more stern. 'That photographer got away. My groom saw him get into a car before any of the security guards could be alerted. I would imagine that right about now he's emailing pictures of us to any number of agencies around the world.'

Lexie felt sick. She felt even sicker to think that she was potentially going to be splashed across the tabloids *again*. And with Cesar Da Silva, one of the most reclusive billionaires in the world. It would be a sensation and it was the last thing she needed—*more* intense media interest.

She bit her lip. 'This isn't good.'

'No,' Da Silva agreed, 'it's not. I have no desire to become the centre of some grubby little tabloid sensation.'

Lexie glared at him, incensed. 'Well, neither do I.' She pointed a finger at him. 'And *you* kissed *me*.'

'You didn't stop me,' he shot back. 'And what were you doing in here anyway?'

Lexie burned. No, she hadn't stopped him. Anything but. She'd been caught up in a dreamlike state of…hot insanity.

'I told you.' Her voice was stiff, with the full ramifications of what had happened sinking in. 'I saw the stables, I wanted to see the horses… We're doing camera tests with Make-up and Wardrobe, and while they were setting up the lighting…'

She tensed as realisation hit.

'The camera tests! I have to go back—they'll be looking for me.'

Lexie went to rush off, but her arm was caught by a big hand. She turned and gritted her jaw. Those green eyes were like burning gems in his spectacular face. His hand on her arm was hot.

'This isn't over—'

Just then a PA rushed into the yard, breathless. 'Lexie, *there* you are. We've been looking all over for you. They're ready to shoot again.'

Lexie pulled free of Cesar Da Silva's grip. She could see his irritation at the interruption but she was glad, needing to get away from his disturbing presence and so she could try to assimilate what had just happened.

Lexie tore her gaze from his and hurried after the officious PA, who was speaking into the walkie-talkie microphone that came out of her sleeve near her wrist. Lexie heard her saying, 'Found her…coming now…one minute…'

Her head was reeling. She felt as if in the space of just that last…fifteen minutes?…her entire world had been altered in some very fundamental way.

She'd let that man…who had been a complete stranger… walk up to her and kiss her. Without a second's hesitation. And not just kiss her…*devour* her. And she'd kissed him back.

She could still feel that dizzying, rushing sweep of desire like a wave through her body. Impossible to ignore or deny. Immediate. All-consuming.

It was crazy, but she'd felt protected by his much larger bulk when he'd put her behind him as soon as he'd seen the paparazzo. Lexie wasn't used to feeling tiny, or in need of protection, even though she *was* physically small at five foot two. She'd been standing up for herself for so long now that she wasn't usually taken unawares in a situation like that. It sent a shiver of unease through her.

The photographer.

She felt sick again. Memories of lurid headlines and pictures rose up. Before she could dwell on it though, they'd entered the yard where the camera tests were taking place and everyone snapped to attention as soon as she appeared.

The cameraman beckoned her over. 'Right, Lexie, we need you over here on your mark, please.'

Cesar paced back and forth in his office, behind his desk. If it were at all possible his black mood had just become even blacker. Like a living, seething thing crackling around him. He had a file open on his desk and there were clippings and pictures strewn across it.

It was a file on Lexie Anderson. And it was not pretty.

One of the film assistants had furnished Cesar's office with files on everyone involved in the film. As much for security purposes as for a little general knowledge about the cast and crew. He hadn't even looked at them before now, because he hadn't been interested.

The files generally just held people's CVs. Except for Lexie's file. Her file was fat, not only with her CV, covering work which consisted mainly of TV and some indie movies before she'd shot to stardom via some vacuous-looking action movies, but also with numerous clippings from papers and magazines.

There were pictures of her, scantily clad, for a lads' magazine some years previously. One image showed her posing as some sort of half-dressed cheerleader, in nothing but thigh-high socks, knickers and a cardigan, teasingly open just enough to show off the voluptuous swells of her breasts and the sensual curve of her tiny waist. Her hair was down and tumbling sexily over her shoulders.

It was exactly the kind of image that Cesar found a complete turn-off, but right now he was having to battle with his own body to stop it responding as helplessly as if he were an over-sexed teenager all over again.

Cesar cursed and picked up the picture, throwing it aside. It fluttered to the floor. She was an actress. That was what she did.

But much worse than that were the more recent pictures and headlines: *Luscious Lexie—Homewrecker!* The tabloids had indulged in a feeding frenzy because she had been involved with a married actor who had subsequently left his heartbroken wife and children. He and Lexie weren't together now, though. According to the salacious copy, once he'd left his wife, heartless Lexie hadn't been interested any more.

Cesar knew that he couldn't have cared less what any lead actress got up to in her spare time, or with whom. But he'd kissed this woman in a moment of extreme madness only a short time before.

The imprint of that petite lush body against his was still branded into his memory. No woman had *ever* got him so hot that he'd lost control like that. He'd been moments away from backing her into a wall and thrusting up into her slick body if they hadn't been interrupted by the paparazzo when they had.

Cesar cursed. And then his phone rang. He answered it abruptly.

His solicitor's voice came down the line, 'Cesar, I've got some news you're not going to like.'

If his solicitor could have seen Cesar's expression right then he probably would have put the phone down and run. But he couldn't, so he went on, oblivious.

'You were photographed at Alexio Christakos's wedding this morning in Paris.'

'So?' Cesar offered curtly, his mind still full of lurid images of Lexie Anderson and her effect on his body.

His solicitor in Madrid sighed heavily. 'Well, it would appear that some very industrious reporter decided to do a quick search, to see if there was any connection between you and Christakos. They came up with the fact that the recently deceased Esperanza Christakos was briefly married to one Joaquin Da Silva, years before she became a renowned model.'

For a second Cesar saw only blackness. He sat down. 'How did they find this?'

'It's not a secret who your mother was, Cesar,' his solicitor pointed out carefully. 'It's just never been discovered before...the connection...'

Cesar knew this. His mother had left so long ago that no one had ever seemed to have the inclination to go digging. He came from the Da Silva dynasty and that was all people cared out.

Until now.

Cesar managed to give an instruction to his solicitor to monitor the media attention closely and put his phone down.

The press would have a field day. He was the estranged half-brother of two of the most renowned entrepreneurs in the world. It would be open season on prying into their lives. For speculating on why nobody had ever spotted the connection before now. And so on, and so on.

He was well aware that this was hardly big news—people discovered half-siblings all the time. What he wasn't prepared for was the prospect of ignominious media intrusion into an area of his life that had always been shut away. Not acknowledged.

The only time the reality of his brothers had been acknowledged, it had been used to taunt him. To drive home the fact that he was not the chosen one. That he could trust no one. Ever. As much as he hated to admit it, the scar was still deep. He only had to think back to earlier that day to remember how it had felt to be so black and bitter next to their happiness and ease with the world. A world that had taught them they could trust. That mothers didn't leave you behind.

Cesar cursed the maudlin direction of his thinking. Cursed himself again for having gone to Christakos's wedding.

With this film on his estate his privacy was already being well and truly eroded. Now this.

And then another picture of Lexie caught Cesar's eye and a headache started to throb behind his right temple. He feared that the reclusive life he'd lived for so long was about to slip out of his grasp unless he could do some serious damage limitation.

CHAPTER TWO

'MISS ANDERSON? MR DA SILVA would like to see you in his office, if you could spare a few minutes?'

Lexie knew it wasn't really a question. It was an order, and she chafed at the autocracy, already imagining his dark, forbidding expression. He'd been a complete stranger to her less than a couple of hours ago, known only by his reputation and name, yet now his saturnine image was branded like a searing tattoo on her brain. *His taste...*

Hiding her reaction, Lexie just shrugged her shoulders lightly and smiled. 'Sure.'

She followed the smartly dressed young woman down a long hallway. She'd just arrived back at the *castillo* from the camera tests and was dressed in her own clothes again. Worn jeans and sneakers. A dusky pink long-sleeved cashmere top, which suddenly felt way too clingy.

The make-up artist had scrubbed her face clean and she'd left her hair down, so now she had no armour at all. She hated the impulse she had to check her reflection.

Lexie hadn't had much time yet to look around the *castillo* as she'd been busy since they'd arrived, doing rehearsals and fittings. It was massive, and very gothic. The overall impression was dark and forbidding. Oppressive. Not unlike its owner. Lexie smiled to herself but it was tight.

A stern housekeeper had shown her to her room when

she'd arrived: dressed in black, hair pulled back in a tight, unforgiving bun. She might have stepped straight out of an oil masterpiece depicting the Spanish Inquisition era.

Lexie's bedroom was part of an opulent suite of rooms complete with an elaborate four-poster bed. Reds and golds. Antique furniture. A chaise longue. While it wasn't her style, she had to admit that it was helping her get into character for the film. She was playing a courtesan from the nineteenth century, who was torn between leaving her profession for her illegitimate son and a villainous lover who didn't want to let her go.

It was a dark, tragic tale, and the director was acclaimed. This film was very important to her—and not just for professional and economic reasons. One scene in particular had compelled Lexie to say yes, as she had known it would be her own personal catharsis to act it out. But she didn't want to think of that now.

After a series of soulless but financially beneficial action movies, this was Lexie's first chance to remind people that she could actually act. And hopefully move away from that hideous *Luscious Lexie* image the tabloids had branded her with. Not entirely unjustly, she hated to admit.

The young woman stopped outside a massive door and knocked. Lexie's mind emptied. Her heart went *thump* and her throat felt dry.

She heard the deep and curt *'Si?'* And then the woman was opening the door. Lexie felt as if she was nine again, being hauled up in front of the head nun at her school for some transgression.

But then Cesar Da Silva was standing in the doorway, filling it. The woman melted away. He'd changed. Washed. Lexie could smell his scent—that distinctive woodsy smell. But without the earthy musk of earlier. It was no less heady, though.

Wearing a white shirt and dark trousers should have

made him appear more urbane. It didn't. The material of his shirt was fine enough to see the darkness of his skin underneath. He stood back and held out an arm, stretching his shirt across his chest. Lexie saw defined hard muscles. Heat flooded between her legs.

'Come in.'

Lexie straightened her spine and walked past him into a massive office.

She was momentarily distracted by its sheer grandeur as he closed the door behind them. It was shaped like an oval, with a parquet floor, and it had an ante-room that looked like a library, with floor-to-ceiling shelves of books upon books.

Something very private and poignant gripped her inside.

'Please, take a seat.'

Da Silva had moved behind his desk, hands resting lightly on top, but not disguising his obvious tension. The desk was huge, awe-inspiring. A very serious affair, holding all sorts of computers and machines and phones.

And yet less than two hours ago she and this man had mutually combusted and she had been oblivious to who he was.

Feeling uncharacteristically awkward, she started, 'Look, Mr Da Silva—'

'I think we've gone beyond that, don't you?' His face was mirthless and hard.

Lexie wondered for a crazy moment what he would look like if he smiled. Genuinely smiled.

She burned inwardly at that rogue little thought, and in rejection of his autocratic tone. 'I…well, yes.'

Her big slouchy handbag was slung over her shoulder. She let it slip down now, and held it in front of her like a shield. Something was telling her this wouldn't be a quick meeting.

A bright colour caught her eye then, and she glanced

down to see a photo of herself on the ground. Frowning, she bent to pick it up. When she registered the image, her insides roiled. She'd been twenty-one. Completely naive. Cringing inside with embarrassment. Not that you'd know it from the picture. She'd been hiding behind a well-developed wall of confidence and nonchalance that hadn't come easily.

She held the picture between thumb and forefinger and looked at Cesar across the desk. He was totally unrepentant. Something hard settled into her gut. The awareness she had of his sheer masculine physicality made her feel like a fool. And very vulnerable—which she did not welcome. It had been a long time since she'd allowed anyone to make her feel that way.

Then she saw the open file and all the other cuttings and clippings and pictures. She didn't have to read the lurid headlines to know what the characters said even from here, upside down. *Luscious Lexie.*

She went icy. Her bag slipped to the floor unnoticed.

'What is this?'

'This,' Cesar da Silva offered tautly, 'is your life, I believe.'

Lexie looked at Cesar and right at that moment despised him. She'd barely exchanged more than twenty sentences with the man, and he'd displayed not an ounce of charm, yet she'd blithely allowed him to be more intimate with her than any other man had ever been.

Her conscience mocked her. That wasn't technically true, of course. But the other experience in her life hadn't been consensually intimate. It had been a horrifically brutal parody of intimacy.

Lexie forced her mind away from that and raged inwardly at the injustice of his evident blind belief in the lies spread before him. She hated that a part of her wanted to curl up and cringe at how all this *evidence* was laid out so starkly across his desk. Ugly.

She forced her voice to be light, to hide the raging tumult. 'And do you believe everything you read in the papers, Mr Da Silva?'

He gritted out, 'Call me Cesar.'

Lexie smiled prettily, hiding her ire, 'Well, when you ask so nicely... *Cesar.*'

'I don't care enough to give the time to believe or disbelieve. I couldn't really care less about your tawdry sex life with married men.'

Lexie saw red. She literally saw a flash of red. She forced air into her lungs. Clenching her jaw so tight it hurt, she bit out, 'Well, then, perhaps you'd be so kind as to let me know what you want to discuss so that I can get on with my *tawdry* life.'

Cesar had to force back the urge to smile for a second. She'd surprised him. Standing up to him so fiercely. Like a tiny virago. Or a pocket Venus.

It took an immense physical effort not to let his gaze drop and linger on the swell of her breasts under the clinging soft material of her top. Or to investigate just how snugly those worn jeans fitted her bottom.

When she'd walked in he'd taken in the slim, shapely legs. The very feminine swell of her hips. She was the perfect hourglass, all wrapped up in a petite, intoxicating package. Her hair was loose and wavy over her shoulders. Bright against the dark wood of his office. *Against the darkness of the castillo.* Something lanced him in a place that was buried, deep and secret. He didn't welcome it.

He didn't like that he'd also noticed her beauty spot was gone. The artifice of make-up. It mocked him for believing himself to have been in some sort of a dream earlier.

For thinking she was some sort of goddess siren straight out of a Greek myth.

But she was no less alluring now in modern clothes than she had been in a corset and petticoats. In fact, now that Cesar knew the flesh her clothes concealed, it was almost worse.

And he'd just been ruder to this woman than he'd ever been to another in his life.

He could actually be urbane. Charming. But as soon as he'd laid eyes on her again he'd felt animalistic. Feral. Even now his blood thundered, roared. For her. And she wasn't even remotely his type.

He ran a hand through his hair impatiently. His conscience demanded of him that he say, 'Look, maybe we can start again. Take a seat.'

Lexie oozed tension and quivering insult. And he couldn't blame her. Even if her less than pristine life *was* spread all over his desk.

'I'm fine standing, thank you. And where, might I ask, did you get your hands on what appears to be a veritable scrapbook of my finest moments?'

Her voice could have cut through steel it was so icy. Cesar almost winced.

'Someone working on the film compiled information on the cast and crew.' His eye caught another lurid shot of Lexie pouting over the bonnet of a car. His body tightened. He willed himself to cling on to some control. 'It would appear that person was a little over-zealous with the back catalogue of your work.'

Lexie flushed, her cheeks filling with dark colour, and Cesar felt his conscience twinge again. As if *he* was in the wrong. When this woman was standing there with her chin tilted up, defiant in the face of her less than stellar reputation.

She came forward and Cesar's gaze couldn't help but

drop to where her breasts swayed gently under her top. She stopped at the other side of the desk and put her hands on it and glared at him, her huge blue eyes sending out daggers of ice.

She plucked out the image of her on the car and held it up accusingly. '*This* is not a back catalogue of work. *This* is a naive young girl, trying to get on in a ruthless cut-throat business—a girl who didn't have the confidence or economic security to say no to bullying agents and photographers.'

She spat out the words.

'You might consider that the next time you find it so easy to judge someone you were only too happy to kiss without even knowing who she was.'

Before Cesar could respond to her spiky defence, not liking the rush of a very alien emotion within him, she'd gathered up all the cuttings and pictures, her CV and head-shots, and marched over to a nearby bin, dumping the lot.

She turned around, her hair shimmering as it moved over her shoulder. She crossed her arms. 'Now, what was it you wanted to discuss?'

Lexie hated that her body was humming with awareness for this man. Who was blissfully immune to the angry emotions he was arousing.

What a judgmental, supercilious, arrogant, small-minded—

'I owe you an apology,' he said tightly.

Lexie blinked. The anger inside her suffered a body-blow. 'Yes, you do.'

His mouth was a grim line. 'I had no right to judge you on the basis of those pictures.'

'No, you didn't,' Lexie snapped, but then she flushed again when she thought of another similar shoot she'd done relatively recently—albeit for a much more up-market publication and with a world-famous photographer. But still, she couldn't exactly claim the moral high ground either... 'It's fine,' she dismissed airily, 'let's forget about it.'

He sighed heavily then, and opened up the laptop that was on the desk in front of him. 'You should see this.'

Trepidation skittered over her skin. Warily Lexic walked around the desk until she could see the laptop, acutely conscious of her proximity to him. When she saw the images, though, her belly swooped alarmingly.

It was her, and him, locked in a clinch that looked positively X-rated. Both his hands were under her skirt, pulling it up, baring her legs. Her breasts seemed about to explode from her corset, crushed against his chest. Their mouths were locked together in a passionate kiss, their eyes closed. Lexie's hands gripped his shirt so tightly that her knuckles were white. And just like that it all came back in a rush: the desperation, the craving, the *aching*. The need.

Lexie could feel heat from behind her. She swallowed. There could be no mistaking that whatever had happened between them had consumed them both. It was not a comfort.

'Where is this?' she asked hoarsely, unable to stop looking away from the image with some kind of sick fascination.

'It's on a well-known internet gossip website. It's only a matter of time before it hits the papers.'

Lexie backed away from the laptop as if it might explode...retreating around the desk, feeling marginally safer once something solid was between them.

Cesar's eyes were glittering. His disdain was palpable. He might have just apologised, and surprised her by doing so, but there was no mistaking his disapproval of the entire situation.

Stung, Lexie said defensively, 'There were two of us there.'

He was grim. 'I'm aware of that, believe me.'

'So...' She swallowed painfully, thinking of the inevitable re-igniting of press interest and the weariness and fear of exposure that would provoke. 'What now?'

Cesar looked at her for a long moment and crossed his arms. 'We contain it.'

Lexie frowned. 'What do you mean...contain it?'

'We don't give it air to breathe. You're here in the *castillo* for the next four weeks. There should be no reason why it won't die a death if they have nothing to work with.'

Something icy touched Lexie's spine. 'What are you talking about exactly?'

A muscle pulsed in Cesar's jaw. 'What I'm talking about is that you don't leave this estate.'

Fire doused the ice. Lexie pointed at herself. '*I* don't leave the estate? What about you?'

Cesar shrugged minutely, arrogant. 'Well, of course I will have to leave. I have business to attend to.'

Lexie emitted a laugh that sounded far too close to panic for her liking. 'After a passionate embrace is plastered all over the world's press, you appear in public with me nowhere to be seen...do you know how that'll look?' She answered herself before he could. 'It'll look as if you're rejecting me and the press will be all over it like a rash.'

Cesar's jaw pulsed again. Clearly he was not used to having anyone question his motives. 'You will be protected in here from the press.'

'Oh, really?' asked Lexie. 'That paparazzo managed to get in, and I assume even a reclusive fossil like you has heard of camera phones?'

She was so angry right then at Cesar's preposterous plan that she barely noticed that he'd moved around the desk, or that his eyes flashed dangerously at her childish insult.

'What's to stop some enterprising crew member from snapping pictures of *poor jilted Lexie* on the set of her new film…?' Lexie was on a roll now, pacing back and forth. 'The press will love documenting *your* exploits while I'm the rejected fool, locked in the castle.'

Lexie stopped and rounded on Cesar, who was at the other side of the desk now and far too close and tall and dark. She took a step back.

She shook her head. 'No way. I'm not going to be incarcerated in this grim fortress just to make life easier for *you*. I'd planned to visit Lisbon, Salamanca…*Madrid!*' That last came out with more than a little desperation.

Lexie had dark memories of being all but locked up once before, and it wasn't going to happen again in her lifetime—not even on an estate as palatial as this one.

Cesar looked at Lexie and was momentarily distracted by her sheer vibrancy and beauty. Her cheeks were pink with indignation, her eyes huge and glittering. Her chest was heaving. As she'd paced back and forth energy had crackled around her like electricity.

Her words hit him then: *I'm not going to be incarcerated in this grim fortress…* He felt like cracking a bleak smile. He knew only too well what that was like. And he could sympathise with her rejection of the idea.

He rested back against his desk and crossed his arms, because right now they itched to reach out and grab her and pull her into him. So close to her like this he could smell her scent, all but feel those provocative curves pressed against him.

His body tightened, blood rushed south. He cursed silently.

'So…what would be *your* suggestion, then?'

Lexie blinked. Cesar marvelled that her every thought was mirrored on that expressive face and in those huge eyes. He'd never seen anything like it. He was used to women putting on a front, trying hard to be mysterious.

She bit her lip and that was even worse. *He* wanted to bite that lip.

She looked at him. 'We go public.'

Cesar's eyes snapped up from her mouth to her eyes. His crossed arms dropped. 'We go *what*?'

'We go public,' she repeated.

'As in...?'

Her eyes flashed brilliant blue, like fire. 'As in we are seen together. As in we go out in public. As in we let people think that we are having an affair.'

Cesar tensed for the inevitable rush of rejection at that proposition. He didn't *do* high publicity—especially not with women like Lexie, whose second home was among the tabloids. Whose life was laid out in a series of lurid pictures amid salacious headlines.

But it didn't come. The rejection. What did come was an intense spiking of anticipation in his already hot blood. His brain clicked and whirred at the thought of this audacious plan. The news of his half-brothers would be hitting the newsstands possibly as soon as tomorrow...

'Well?'

Lexie's voice cut through the snarl of thoughts in Cesar's head. Somehow, without analysing it fully right now, he knew that a news story featuring *them* would inevitably be more colourful and interesting than one about his family connections. That would be diminished in favour of a far more scandalous story: *Reclusive billionaire beds homewrecking Luscious Lexie.*

'I think,' Cesar said slowly, letting his eyes fill with Lexie again, 'that your idea has some merit.'

Some of the tension left her shoulders even as she crossed her arms, which pushed the swells of her breasts up. *Dios*, Cesar cursed again silently. Suddenly all rational thoughts of distracting the press via a story about him and Lexie fled, to be replaced with the very *real* urge to touch the woman in front of him.

'Good,' she said now. 'Because I really do think that's the best solution. And the fairest.' Her mouth firmed. 'I know the press, and sometimes you have to play them at their own game rather than fight them.'

She lifted her chin then, and something about the move was so endearingly spiky that Cesar had to stop himself from reaching out to trail his fingers across her jaw. Out of nowhere came a surge of something that felt almost like *protectiveness*.

His hands curled around the edge of his desk beside his hips. He forced his mind back to the conversation. 'I have a charity auction to attend in Salamanca next weekend. We can go to that.' The devil inside him compelled him to continue. 'And we'll have to be convincing, Lexie.'

Those big blue eyes narrowed. 'Convincing?'

Cesar smiled, the anticipation inside him tightening now. 'Convincing…as lovers.'

Lexie's arms tightened, pushing those firm swells up even more. 'Oh…well, yes. I mean, that's obvious…but that'll be easy enough… I mean…I'm an actress after all.'

Suddenly the confident woman of only a few moments ago was not at all sure of herself. Cesar was more intrigued than he liked to admit. He shifted on the desk, crossing one ankle over the other, and noted how Lexie's eyes dropped to his mid-section for a second before skittering away again.

But then the suggestion that she'd have to *act* with Cesar hit home and made something hot and dark pierce him inside. He tensed. 'So what happened earlier, Lexie? Were you just practising your *acting* skills on the nearest stable hand you could find?'

She looked at him. 'No. It wasn't like that.'

Cesar felt more exposed than he liked to. 'So what *was* it like?'

For a second he fancied that the turmoil he could see in those blue depths mirrored the part of him that still couldn't make sense of what had happened. But the very suggestion that it had been in any way within *her* control and not his made something snap inside him.

He straightened up and did what his hands had been itching to do ever since she'd walked into his study. He reached for her and pulled her into him, and something treacherous in his mind quietened as soon as those soft curves fell against him.

Her hands were pressed against his chest and a soft *oof* escaped her mouth: a sigh of shock. She looked up. 'What are you doing?'

Cesar's body was already hardening against hers. An automatic and helpless reaction to her proximity and touch. He hated this feeling of being out of control — it had been a long day of that very unwelcome sensation. He gritted out, 'I'm seeing how good you are at improvisation.'

And then he bent his head to hers, and her mouth was as firm and yet as soft as he remembered, and those lush contours sent his brain into a tailspin all over again.

Lexie was drowning. Her hands looked for purchase anywhere she could find it to try and cling on. Cesar's mouth was searing and hot. Hard. His arms were welded tight around her. She was off-balance and plastered against him, breasts crushed against rock-hard contours. One of his hands moved up to her head, angling it Their mouths were open, tongues touching and tasting. Stroking, sucking.

Lexie wanted to wrap her arms around his neck and rub herself up and down his hard length, seeking to assuage the stinging in her nipples and the ache growing inside her.

She could feel a hard ridge against her belly and it caused a spasm of damp desire between her legs.

And then the haze lifted ever so slightly, when he took his mouth away for a moment and she remembered his grim look and what he'd said, *'I'm seeing how good you are at improvisation.'*

As if a cold bucket of water had been thrown over her Lexie jerked backwards, almost stumbling in an effort to right herself. She was shaky all over, breathing heavily. Cesar was resting on the edge of the desk, barely a hair out of place, even if his cheeks were flushed and eyes were glittering brightly.

Lexie wasn't ready for this onslaught of physical sensations and feelings. Barely able to get her head around articulating much, she asked, a little redundantly, 'What was that in aid of?'

'Proving that it will be no hardship to *act* out being lovers. In fact it's almost inevitable that we will *become* lovers.'

Lexie rebelled at that arrogant tone even as her body betrayed her spectacularly. 'Don't flatter yourself, Mr Da Silva.'

He smiled. 'It's Cesar, please.'

Lexie felt dizzy at how quickly this man was dismantling the bricks and mortar that had protected her for years. She couldn't analyse it now, but she knew that he must have connected with her on some very deep level for her to have allowed him to kiss her—not once, but twice. Without even putting up a fight.

Panic galvanised her and she reached down and picked up her bag, slung it over her shoulder. She forced herself to look at Cesar but it was hard. The air between them was saturated with electricity and tension and something else far more disturbing and new to Lexie: *Desire.*

She hated to admit that she was also stung to think

that he believed she was the kind of person who would just widen her eyes and say yes to such an autocratic announcement.

She bit out, 'I am *not* an easy lay, Cesar. Evidently you believe what you read in the papers, but I can assure you that I am perfectly capable of controlling myself. I am interested in putting forward a united front in order to get the press off our backs…that is all.'

Cesar stared at her for a long moment and then shrugged. He folded his arms across that wide chest, making the muscles of his arms bunch against the silk of his shirt.

'We'll see,' he said carelessly. As if he truly didn't care if she tumbled into his bed one way or the other. As if he knew that she would be helpless to resist him when the time came.

Curbing the urge to take her bag and swing it at his head, Lexie backed away to the door, her blood boiling—and not just from his words and that arrogance. She turned around and was reaching for the doorknob, relishing the prospect of removing herself from his orbit, when he called her name softly.

With the utmost reluctance Lexie gritted her jaw and turned around, keeping her hand on the door. He was still sitting there, eyes hooded, watching her.

'Don't forget…next weekend…Salamanca. That's if you still want us to proceed with *your* suggestion.'

For a second Lexie contemplated the alternative and saw herself pacing up and down the dark *castillo* corridors or in the grounds. Trapped. With the press digging her life up again. Speculating. She went cold at that prospect. There was no choice.

She managed to say icily, 'I won't forget.' And then she pulled the door open and left, with her dignity feeling badly battered.

CHAPTER THREE

WHEN LEXIE GOT to her room she paced. Full of pent-up energy. Hot and then cold at the same time when she re-considered the equally disturbing prospects of appearing in public *with* Cesar and *not*. And the ramifications of the press's interest in her if that was the case.

There was no doubt about it: appearing with Cesar would be the better scenario. It was only in the last few weeks that the tabloids' interest in *'Luscious Lexie the homewrecker'* had let up. If she was going to become press fodder again so soon, then she would *not* be the victim.

Cesar was unmarried. A bachelor. An affair with him would be old news very fast. And, she realised with some cynicism, it couldn't hurt the film to be linked to this kind of publicity.

What she hadn't counted on was the attraction she felt for Cesar. She'd just kissed him back again, as passionately as she had earlier, with no qualms. No hesitation! It was as if as soon as he touched her some ever-vigilant switch in her brain turned to *off* and she became mute. Acquiescent.

She held out her hands and noted that even now they were trembling slightly. Disgusted, she shoved them under her arms and then spied her electronic tablet. She marched over and opened it up.

She hated herself for it, but she found herself search-ing for Cesar Da Silva Girlfriend. Predictably not much came up except a few photos of him at events with beautiful women. They were all tall, brunette. Sleek. Classy. One was a UN diplomat. The next an attaché to a world leader. Another was a human rights lawyer.

There were also pictures of Cesar with world leaders at economic summits.

Lexie put a hand to her mouth to stem a slight surge of hysteria. She was seriously out of her depth with this man, and she didn't like her feeling of insecurity when she was faced with the evidence of his previous lovers' undoubted intellectual accomplishments. The plan for them to appear as lovers mocked her now. Who would ever believe he'd choose *her*?

Feeling like a stalker, she looked up his background. To her surprise, a new news article popped up. And a picture of him from earlier that very day, taken at a wedding in Paris. Lexie frowned for a second, wondering how he could have come from Paris back to the *castillo* in such a short space of time—and then she recalled hearing a helicopter earlier. Of course—to a man like Cesar Da Silva travel between European bases was far removed from most people's more tedious, lengthy experiences.

She focused on the short piece again. It had been the wedding of Alexio Christakos and his very pretty bride— someone called Sidonie. The article seemed to be implying that a familial relationship existed between Alexio Christakos and Cesar Da Silva. And also another man: Rafaele Falcone.

Lexie frowned. She knew Christakos and Falcone were half-brothers. They'd been notoriously eligible bachelors before settling down. So…what? Cesar was related to these men? Lexie kept searching and found a very brief reference to his father. Joaquin Da Silva had been famously disinherited from his family after leaving to train as a bullfighter.

He'd achieved some fame early on, before dying tragically in a goring by a bull.

There wasn't much else apart from Cesar's current accomplishments, of which there seemed to be many. He was listed as one of the world's leading philanthropists.

The picture of Cesar at the wedding caught her eye again. She looked more closely. There was a definite resemblance between the two men. And Rafaele Falcone. She couldn't be sure, but it looked as if they all shared varying shades of green eyes. Unusual. *Too* unusual.

A suspicion slid into place inside Lexie. He'd agreed so quickly to appearing in public with her, when all the evidence pointed to a man who would find that kind of exposure anathema. *He wants me.* Lexie shivered at the thought. Was he prepared to court the press's attention just to get her into bed? That idea was both intoxicating and terrifying.

But perhaps Cesar had his own reasons for wanting to divert the press? If something was about to break about his family? She didn't like it, but a feeling of empathy gripped her. And curiosity...

Just then a knock sounded on her door. Lexie's heart jumped. She put the cover over her tablet's screen and went to the door, steeling herself. But when she opened it, it was Tom—the producer. An acute dart of disappointment made her want to scowl.

She forced a smile. 'Tom?'

He held up his own tablet to reveal the same picture of the kiss that Cesar had shown her just a short while before. Her insides tightened again at seeing herself in such an alien and lurid pose.

'Ah...' she said.

'Ah...' the older man echoed. 'I didn't realise you had history with Da Silva. You never mentioned anything...'

'I don't really want to discuss it, Tom, if that's all right.'

'Look,' he said quickly, mollifying her, 'I'm not complaining, Lexie—far from it. This is PR gold dust for the film. *If* you two are…together.'

Tom was obviously concerned that an affair between her and Cesar Da Silva might jeopardise filming if it wasn't all that it seemed. He could throw them off his estate at any moment if he so wished.

Lexie's jaw was tight. She imagined the press furore after they appeared in public next week. 'Yes…' she said reluctantly, as if not even wanting to give the words oxygen. 'We are…together.'

The relief that crossed the producer's face was almost comical. 'Okay, that's good. I mean, like I said, it's gold dust for the film. We could never have generated this much press just by—'

'Tom?' Lexie cut him off, forcing another smile. 'I'd appreciate an early night. I've a lot of prep to do this weekend before we start shooting on Monday.'

He backed away, putting a hand up. 'Of course. I'll leave you to it. Night, Lexie.'

When he was gone she sagged back against the door with relief. Out of the past, the words of her counsellor came back to her: *'Lexie, one day you'll meet someone and you'll feel desire. And you'll feel safe enough to explore it…and heal.'*

Lexie stifled a semi-hysterical giggle. She'd felt it today, all right, but she didn't feel safe right now. She felt in mortal danger. Especially when she thought of those distinctive green eyes and that hard-boned face…and that powerful body. That dark, brooding energy…

She felt anything but safe.

She thought again of Cesar's nonchalant assertion that they would become lovers. A dart of anger gripped her insides. He was obviously used to women falling at his feet if he could make such a declaration. He had no idea of the scars that scored her insides like tattoos. Not visible to the naked eye, but she felt them every day. Scars she'd fought hard to overcome so she could function and live and work.

She resented Cesar Da Silva right then for inserting himself so solidly and irrevocably into her life. And yet she had no one to blame but herself.

Sighing volubly, Lexie pushed off the door and vowed to do whatever it took to focus on the most important thing in her life right now: the job she had to fulfil for the next four weeks. Her *real* acting job, as opposed to the acting she'd be doing in a week's time. Although that filled her with a lot more trepidation because she was afraid that she wouldn't have to act at all.

Midway through the following week Lexie was pacing back and forth on the set while they set up the cameras for a new shot. She was listening to the script on her mp3 player and repeating her lines to herself.

They were shooting not far from the *castillo*, in a walled garden. Inevitably, though, her thoughts deviated yet again to the person who had dominated almost every waking and sleeping moment since she'd met him, in spite of her best efforts.

He'd appeared to watch the filming at various intervals, effortlessly unsettling Lexie in the process. If he was around she became acutely self-conscious. And being dressed in cleavage-revealing nineteenth-century garb didn't help.

Right then, just as she was sighing with relief that he *hadn't* appeared today, he did appear—as if conjured up from her overheated imagination—striding towards her on the narrow path. She had nowhere to go. Trapped. All of the crew were busy working, oblivious to the seismic physical reaction inside Lexie as Cesar bore down on her in a secluded part of the garden.

Her heart sped up. She went hot all over. Pinpricks of sensation moved across her skin. Nipples tightened against her bodice. The corset became even more constrictive. She pulled the long coat she wore to keep warm more closely around her, to try and hide some of her far too buxom cleavage. She took the earphones out of her ears and fought the urge to take several steps back.

Cesar came to a stop in front of her. It didn't help that he was dressed in much the same way as when she'd seen him for the first time, in a close-fitting polo shirt and jodhpurs. Hair mussed. Jaw stubbled. He'd obviously just been riding.

For a bizarre second Lexie actually couldn't speak. His eyes were hypnotic. When *he* spoke, it jarred her out of the daze she was in.

'I've arranged for my assistant to have some clothes delivered to you from a boutique in Salamanca.'

Lexie looked at him blankly. 'Clothes?'

'For the weekend...for future events.'

Suddenly Lexie realised what he meant, and immediately chafed at the implication that he had to buy clothes for her because she wasn't as classy or elegant as his other lovers. And she hated that she'd thought that.

Stiffly she said, 'You really don't need to do that.' Lexie knew she was out of his league; she didn't need a reminder.

Cesar was obdurate. 'Well, it's too late. They've been delivered to your suite.'

Lexie opened her mouth again, but Cesar put up a hand.

'If you don't want to use them, that's fine. See what's there and decide. It's no big deal.'

No, thought Lexie churlishly, because all it had taken was a mere snap of his fingers. She looked at him suspiciously. 'How did you know what size I was?' She immediately regretted asking the question when his gaze swept up and down her body. What he could see of it…

'I asked the costume designer, just to be safe, but my own estimation wasn't far off.'

Lexie burned with indignation and something much hotter to imagine Cesar guessing her vital statistics.

Just then a PA came close and hovered. When Lexie looked at her she made a signal that she was required. Lexie looked back at Cesar and said, with evident relief, 'I have to go. They're ready to shoot again.'

But he didn't get out of the way. And Lexie knew she wasn't supposed to step onto the manicured lawn.

She was about to open her mouth when he moved closer and put a hand around the back of her bare neck, exposed because her hair was up in a complicated chignon. He bent down and pressed a fleeting but hot kiss to her mouth, and then pulled back, letting her go.

Lexie tingled all over. Her head felt fuzzy. 'What was that for?'

Cesar smiled, but it didn't reach his eyes, and Lexie felt something tug inside her, wondering again what he'd look like if he *really* smiled.

'As you so memorably pointed out, there are camera phones around. I'm just being vigilant.'

Lexie flushed to recall what she'd said to him. There was nothing remotely fossil-like about this man. He was all bristling, virile energy.

Faintly she said, 'Celeste will have to retouch my lipstick.'

He smirked. 'Well, you'd better run along and let Celeste do that.'

For a second Lexie blinked at him. There was a tantalising glimmer of something lighter between them. But then he was turning and striding back the way he'd come, and as Lexie walked over to the main hub of the set she couldn't be unaware of several appreciative female *and* male glances that lingered in his direction and then on her with undisguised envy.

Cesar was waiting for Lexie in the main *castillo* drawing room three days later. Looking back on the last tumultuous week, he did not relish the twisting and turning of events since he'd taken one look at that woman and his brains had migrated to his pants.

Cesar was renowned for lots of things: his inestimable wealth; philanthropy; scarily incisive business acumen; a zealous desire for privacy; success. And control. Above all control over his emotions. He'd become a master of controlling them from a young age. Too young.

His usual choice of woman was tall and brunette. Elegant. Classic. Not blonde, petite and curvy, with blue eyes big enough to drown in. And with a dubious reputation splashed across the tabloids.

On some level he'd always sought to stay away from prying eyes, as if somehow they might see something in him that he couldn't articulate himself. A darkness that had clung to him for a long time. The stench of abandonment. The cruelty of neglect and a lack of care. It had been like an invisible stain on his skin.

Yet for someone who had spent his life largely on the periphery of the media glare, largely due to his very *non*-scandalous social life, the prospect of suddenly being thrust front and centre was not having the effect he might have expected.

Of course he didn't relish the idea. But at the same time it didn't fill him with repugnance.

Cesar poured himself a drink and smiled grimly. Right now though, all those concerns were receding and being replaced by something else. Some*one* else. Lexie Anderson. Cesar had been due to go to North Africa that week, to attend a meeting about aid, but had cancelled it on the flimsy pretext of wanting to make sure that the first week of filming went smoothly.

Cesar would be the first to admit that he had dismissed the film industry as flaky and narcissistic, but just one week had proved him wrong. The crew were tireless and worked twelve- and thirteen-hour days—if not longer. He was also surprised by how quickly and well they worked as a cohesive unit.

The producer had explained that most of them had worked together before, but there were lots of inexperienced locals in the mix and Cesar had witnessed more than one incident of a more experienced crew member patiently showing someone the ropes.

Lexie was one of the most tireless. Standing for long minutes on a mark while the lighting crew and cameraman worked around her. Her co-star would invariably go back to his trailer. Cesar had found out that she could have insisted they use a stand-in but had wanted to be there herself. He had to admit that he hadn't really expected her work ethic to be that strong.

She was popular. Especially with the male members of the crew. Cesar was more aware of that than he liked to admit. He'd never been jealous because of a woman before and he didn't welcome jealousy's appearance.

He heard a sound then, and with something whispering over his skin like a warning Cesar took a breath and turned around.

Bombshell. That was the only word that seemed to compute in his head when he saw the woman standing in the doorway. Her effect on him was like a bomb too—exploding out to every extremity and making his flesh surge as blood pumped south.

He took in details, as if he couldn't handle the full reality. Glossy blonde hair, trailing over one shoulder in classic screen siren waves. Pale skin. Slim bare arms. A sleeveless gold lamé dress that fell to the floor in a swirl of glamorous luxury.

She was poured into it, and the material highlighted her curves to almost indecent proportions. The deep, plunging vee of the neckline drew his eye to that abundant cleavage.

She was every inch the glittering movie star. And the most provocatively beautiful woman Cesar had ever seen in his life. He knew that if they hadn't already kissed, if he hadn't already seen her up close, he might have seen her like this and dismissed her as too garish. But right now he could no more dismiss her than recall his own name.

His hands clenched so tightly that he heard a crack, and he looked down stupidly to see his heavy Waterford crystal glass about to break in his hand.

He put it down on the sideboard with a clatter that jarred his ragged and sensitised nerve-endings.

She moved into the room, and the sinuous sway of her hips nearly undid him. Normally he had finesse. He could utter platitudes to women like *You look beautiful*. But right now all he could do was say gruffly, 'My driver is waiting outside—we should go.'

Lexie fought down a betraying quiver of insecurity as she preceded Cesar out of the room, and cursed herself for wanting his reassurance that she looked okay and not too over the top. Her dresses were normally fine—fairly standard designer fare, given to her after photo shoots or premieres—but when she'd compared them to the finery he'd ordered there had been no competition. She'd had to choose one of his.

She had not been prepared for his impact on her in a classic black tuxedo. It was obviously a bespoke suit, moulded to his powerful body in a way that most men's weren't. It should have made him appear civilised. Just like trousers and a shirt should make him look civilised. But the structured clothes only made him seem more raw. Untamed.

His hair was always on the slightly messy side, and Lexie didn't like the way that small detail already felt familiar. But his jaw was clean-shaven, and somehow it gave him a more youthful air.

He took her arm with one big hand and Lexie had to curb her response not to jump. She could feel slightly rough calluses. It made her think of how he'd looked swinging lithely from that huge horse the first time she'd seen him... muscles bunching and quivering. He was no mere soft-palmed money man. The very heart of her feminine core grew hot and damp.

She tried to pull her arm free but his hand was firm. She sent him a sharp glance, irritated at his effect on her, which quickly turned to something else when she saw him gazing at her intently. His hand slid down her arm and took her hand. It was a relatively chaste gesture, and yet it had an almost embarrassing effect on Lexie.

She let herself be led to the exclusive black car and Cesar let her go so she could slide into the back, with the driver holding the door open solicitously.

When he got in on the other side he sent her a look that made Lexie feel utterly exposed. As if he'd been toying with her, taking her hand like that.

Feeling unbearably prickly, Lexie stared out of the window. Anything to escape that dark green mocking gaze.

His voice was cool. 'This was your suggestion, you know. You don't have to look as if you're about to go to the gallows.'

Lexie tensed and felt angry. She turned back to Cesar. 'I don't regret my suggestion for a second. It's still the best option.'

The tinted windows gave the back of the car a disturbingly cocoon-like atmosphere. And since when had the privacy window gone up? Lexie's skin prickled. She could have sworn it had been down when they'd got in. And was it her or had the temperature in the back of the car just shot up by about a thousand degrees?

Cesar was lounging on the other side of the car like a pasha surveying his concubine. She almost wished he was glowering at her, as he had done that first day. She could handle that. She couldn't handle this far more ambiguous energy swirling between them.

Feeling a kind of desperation rising up, she said, 'What happened before…the kissing…it won't happen again.' *So why can't you stop thinking about what it would be like to be kissed again…and more?*

Something in Cesar's eyes flashed, but he said easily, 'We can't stand ten feet apart, Lexie. We'll have to… touch…display moments of affection. Surely it shouldn't be so hard for you to feign besotted devotion?'

That prickliness was lodging in Lexie's gut, and it made her say waspishly, 'Yes, well, I'm not the only one who has to be convincing.'

Before she could react, Cesar had reached for her hand and taken it in a firm grip. Lexie gasped as he brought it to his mouth and kissed her sensitive inner palm. It felt shockingly intimate, and a shard of pure sensation pulled at her belly and groin.

He took his mouth away, eyes glittering fiercely. 'Is that convincing enough for you?'

Lexie knew her eyes were wide, her breathing choppy. He'd just kissed her hand and she was a puddle. *Her hand!* She yanked it away before he could make a complete fool of her.

Cesar saw how Lexie shrank back and everything in him rejected that even as he saw the signs of mutual attraction: the hectic pulse at the base of her neck, flushed cheeks.

Almost accusingly she said, 'You don't look like the type of guy who relishes PDA.'

Cesar bit back the urge to clamp his hands around that tiny waist and haul her into him to show her *exactly* what he thought of PDA. Every time she moved her breasts moved with her, deepening that enticing line of cleavage. But a warning bell went off in his head. She was right, and it irked him that she'd read him so easily.

He *didn't* like public displays of affection *at all*. In fact he really wasn't a tactile person. He usually discouraged his lovers from touching him, preferring to keep their contact confined to the bedroom.

Human touch had been non-existent when he was growing up in the *castillo*. When it had come it had been rough, perfunctory. *Unloving*. A minute shove. A clip around the ear for some transgression. Worse after he'd been caught rolling around in the dirt with Juan Cortez, swinging punches at each other.

If a lover slipped her hand into his, or wound her arm through his, his first instinct was to flinch away. Except right now all he could do was see the wide chasm of distance between him and Lexie in the back of the car and resent it.

Salamanca wasn't far. And it was for *that* reason, Cesar told himself, that he said softly, 'Come closer.'

'*You* come closer,' Lexie responded spikily.

Unbidden, Cesar felt a burgeoning…lightness within him. He even felt a rare smile tip the corners of his mouth. 'I asked first.'

Lexie's expression turned mutinous and had a direct effect on Cesar's already raging blood. Arrowing directly to his groin.

'Lexie,' he growled, 'if you can't bring yourself to move

closer in the back of a car, with no one watching, how do you expect us to convince a wall of paparazzi?'

With palpable reluctance Lexie huffed a sigh and moved across the seat, still keeping a healthy few inches of space between them. Cesar was intrigued. She was spiky, confident. And yet she showed these tantalising glimpses of another side altogether...one less sure of herself.

Her faintly floral scent tickled his nostrils. He fought not to just grab her and haul her onto his lap.

'So, tell me something about yourself...'

'Like what?' Lexie's voice was almost sharp.

Even more intriguing. She was seriously unsettled.

'How did you get started as an actress?'

Lexie glanced at Cesar. The sensation that he was seeing a part of her that no one else cared to observe was acute and uncomfortable. Once again all of her deepest secrets and vulnerabilities felt very close to the surface, as if he might just peel a section of her skin back and see them all laid bare.

Right now, facing a barrage of photographers and pretending to be this man's lover would be infinitely preferable to this intimate cocoon in the back of the car. Then she remembered the awful, excoriating feeling of seeing her life spread across his desk in a series of lurid pictures and she said with faux sweetness, 'You mean you skipped the part about the casting couch in that extensive research file?'

That earned her a twitching muscle in his jaw that distracted Lexie momentarily. His jaw was so hard, so resolute. As if hewn from a lifetime of clenching it.

His voice was equally hard. Clearly he did not welcome her sarcasm. 'I'd like to know how you really got started.'

Lexie's belly dipped ominously and she looked at him suspiciously. He seemed to be genuinely interested. But that reminded her uncomfortably of how she'd once believed someone else had been *genuinely interested*. That experience had left her splashed all over the tabloids, with her reputation ground into the muck. Mocking her for how quickly she'd trusted the first person who had appeared to want to know the real her. After she'd lived a lifetime protecting herself.

The reminder was not welcome now.

In a desperate bid to avoid this, Lexie racked her brain for a pithy and superficial answer. But his gaze was too direct. Too...unforgiving.

'Well,' she started reluctantly, 'I was in a shop one day... I'd just moved to London from Ireland. I was sixteen.'

He frowned. 'You're Irish?'

She nodded, hiding the dart of pain. 'Originally, yes.' When he said nothing more, she continued. 'I was in this shop...and a young kid was in front of me. Suddenly, out of nowhere, the owner accused him of shoplifting—which he hadn't done. So I stepped in and defended him.'

Lexie shuddered slightly when she recalled the oily owner's eyes devouring her overly buxom curves. She'd developed early—another unwelcome reminder right now.

'The next thing I knew,' Lexie went on, eager not to think of that time, 'I was shouting at him. I told the kid to run...and then a woman arrived.' Lexie looked at Cesar, but he was just watching her. She felt silly. 'Look, this is a really boring story...'

'I want to hear it. Go on.'

Lexie glanced away and then looked back after a moment. His gaze was intent. She took a breath. 'The woman had heard me shouting and came to investigate. She stepped in and defused the situation. Afterwards she took me for a coffee. She told me she was a casting director and asked if I'd like to audition for a part in a short film.'

Lexie recalled how bleak those days in London had

been. How alone she'd felt. How impoverished. Vulnerable, but trying to be strong...optimistic...

'So I said yes...and I got a leading role in the film. It was shown in the fringe category at the Cannes Film Festival the following year, and it won an award.' She shrugged one slim shoulder, self-conscious all of a sudden, but determined not to let him see how easily he seemed to be able to unsettle her. 'That's it. That's how I got started. But it was a rocky road... I had an unscrupulous agent for a while... It takes time to realise who has your best interests at heart.'

For a long moment Cesar was silent, and then he said, 'I'd imagine if anyone had tried to lure you onto a casting couch you would have subjected them to the same treatment as that shop owner.'

A dart of unexpected warmth pierced Lexie—and then she thought of the lurid photo shoots she'd done and the warmth fizzled out. 'Unfortunately I wasn't always so sure of what to say no to...'

Something in the air shifted between them. Lexie couldn't look away from Cesar's gaze. It was hypnotic. He seemed a lot closer. For an awful churning moment she wondered if she had moved closer to him without even realising?

'You didn't say no when I kissed you in the stable.' His voice was deep, rough.

Breath was suddenly in very short supply to Lexie's lungs. 'Proof that my track record doesn't appear to be improving with age.'

Her brain was short-circuiting. Was it only a week since she'd first kissed this man? It felt as if aeons had passed. Cesar slid an arm around her waist, pulling her into him. She gasped, filled with a fatal but delicious hot lethargy that urged her not to think. Just to feel. He was going to kiss her, and all Lexie felt was intense anticipation. Her blood was sizzling.

His mouth touched hers. Soft, coaxing. Taking Lexie by surprise. Dismantling any feeble defences she had. His other arm pulled her in even closer and lust exploded deep in her solar plexus.

His mouth was firmer now—insisting, demanding that she respond. As the last shred of trepidation melted away Lexie's mouth opened, and Cesar's attack was brutally sensual and complete. His tongue was stroking hers, sucking it, forcing her to respond.

Without even being aware of it, Lexie touched his jaw, her fingers spreading, threading through his hair, gripping it. Learning the shape of his skull.

One of his hands cupped the weight of her breast and it sent no flares of danger into her brain. Only a desire for *more*. She arched into that hand and heard a low, feral growl of approval.

When his hand left her breast and his mouth left hers she let out a husky breath of disappointment. She opened heavy eyes to see two dark glittering pools of green and black, swirling with depths that reached inside her and tugged hard.

Cesar's fingers slid under the strap of her dress, dislodging it. Her heart-rate accelerated. The first tendrils of panic pierced the haze of heat.

'Cesar… I…'

'Shh…' he said, and that hand was busy peeling down the strap of her dress.

As if knowing just how to subdue those faint tendrils of panic, he kissed her again, pulling her under even more. Making her hot, making her *need*. Making something tight coil inside her until she had to move to try and alleviate it.

When air whistled over the bare slope of her breast Lexie tore her mouth away, breathing hard. Cesar was breathing harshly too. He was looking down, and she followed his gaze to see her breast, its nipple pink and tight and pouting. His hand seemed huge and dark against her pale skin.

'*Dios*…you are truly exquisite.'

His thumb moved back and forth over her nipple, making it pucker, grow harder. She bit her lip to stop from crying out at the exquisite feeling. The tightening sensation deep in her belly was sharper. She could feel wetness between her legs, against her panties.

She couldn't think…couldn't rationalise. She wanted to know how his mouth would feel on her. Tasting her… His tongue… But something was trying to break through. Sense, sanity…self-preservation?

Cesar pulled away from her abruptly, adjusting her dress at the same time, covering her up, and then Lexie heard it: the insistent knocking on the privacy window. A cold wind whistled over her skin.

She felt completely dazed, and could only watch as Cesar, who looked as if nothing had happened, pressed a button and said a few words in Spanish. He turned back to her, but already shame and embarrassment were clawing up inside Lexie.

An insidious image of his usual lovers inserted itself into her brain. She would bet that he didn't subject *those* cool beauties to such sensual attacks in the back of his car.

She pulled the strap of her dress up fully, covering her sensitised breast. Through the window behind Cesar's head she could see people milling, see the flashing pops of cameras. See security people waiting for them to emerge.

Realisation sank into her belly like a cold stone. Of *course* he didn't normally do this. He'd engineered that kiss purely because he'd known exactly how close to Salamanca they were. He'd known they were about to emerge from the car and had wanted to make things look as *authentic* as possible.

She couldn't meet his gaze, and tried to pull away

when his fingers caught her chin. 'What?' she spat out, livid with herself for the dart of hurt that she shouldn't be feeling. 'Do I not appear sufficiently dishevelled to make the paparazzi believe we've been making out like teenagers?'

He flushed angrily. His accent was stronger. 'That was not premeditated, Lexie. But now that you mention it...'

Eyes sparking, Cesar covered her lips with his mouth again and Lexie fought him, closing her mouth. But with expert precision and ruthless intent Cesar proceeded to show her just how pathetic her little outburst had been. Within seconds her mouth was open under his and he was bending her head back with the force of his kiss. And she was matching him, her anger heightening the tension between them.

Cesar was losing it. He knew he was losing it. But he couldn't take his mouth off Lexie's. He'd never tasted anything so sweet. Or so wicked. The way her lush mouth softened under his...the feel of that body under his hands. Her breast...that hard peak under his thumb... He'd wanted to taste it.

Dios.

Cesar finally pulled back, heart hammering. He did *not* ravish women in the back of his car. He was cool, calm, controlled.

Right now he felt anything but. He could hardly see straight. His body was on fire.

Lexie was looking at him with huge bruised eyes. She thought he'd done that on purpose. And he had—but not for the reasons she obviously suspected. He'd wanted to make sure there was no ambiguity about how he felt about her.

He cupped that delicate jaw, a little aghast that his hand shook minutely. Her mouth was pink, swollen. He couldn't help running his thumb across that pouting lower lip, feeling its fleshy softness.

'Make no mistake, Lexie, I want you…and not just to distract the crowds. You know the truth of what I said earlier. We will be lovers for real.'

CHAPTER FOUR

WE WILL BE lovers for real.

Lexie's hand was held tight in Cesar's. She hadn't had time to respond because the driver had opened the car door. And, as much as she wanted to pull free, right now she needed the support. They'd just run the gauntlet of the press outside. Lexie had felt so raw after those kisses that she'd probably looked as green as an *ingenue* at her first premiere.

Cesar had seemed as cool as a cucumber. He'd even rustled up a smile. It was galling. Shouldn't he be the one flinching and snarling?

Lexie finally managed to pull her hand free, once they were in the marble lobby of the very exclusive hotel that was hosting the event.

Cesar frowned. 'Are you all right?'

Lexie wanted to scream. She felt wild, dishevelled. Not herself. 'Not really,' she ground out. 'I need to freshen up before we go in.'

She spotted the powder room and made a beeline for it. Once inside she found it was mercifully empty and she let out a great shuddering sigh of relief. When she looked in the mirror she nearly lost the ability to breathe again.

Her hair was mussed. Cheeks bright pink, mouth swollen. Eyes huge and glittering far too brightly. Lexie pulled tissues out of the box and started to repair the damage.

Damn him. She cursed him roundly. Once again she was floored by how instantaneous his effect on her was and how her body betrayed her every time, jumping gleefully into the fire without any hesitation.

When Lexie was done she surveyed herself again and caught her own eyes in the reflection. There were shadows and secrets in their depths that only she could see. Someone like Cesar could never guess at them. She might be stronger now, but once she'd been utterly broken and had never thought she'd be whole again.

But when Cesar touched her it made her feel whole. It made her forget everything. Forget what had happened to her. There was none of the reflexive instinctive fear that had come when other men had kissed her—even if that had been in the safe environment of a film set.

We will be lovers.

Lexie couldn't seem to stem the tiny flicker of hope inside her. As inconceivable as it seemed…as unsuitable as Cesar Da Silva was…perhaps he was the one who could repair something in her that she had believed destroyed a long time ago? Just allowing that thought to enter her head made Lexie sway on her feet as a giddy mix of excitement and terror rushed up inside her.

There was a knock at the door, and then, 'Lexie, are you okay?'

Lexie's breath jammed in her throat. Her recent thoughts were too nebulous, too scary. She called out threadily, 'I'm fine. I'll be out in a second.'

When she did emerge she didn't like the spurt of emotion at seeing him leaning nonchalantly against a pillar, nor the way his gaze raked her face. He straightened up and just like that her mind started becoming fuzzy again.

She reined herself in with an effort. More people were milling around now, but to Lexie's relief he didn't take her hand again. He put it to her lower back instead, to guide her into the main ballroom where the dinner was being held. His touch burned like a brand through the back of her dress.

Lexie didn't like how aware she was of other women staring at Cesar, of the flurry of whispers that would stop as they grew close only to start up again after they'd passed. It reminded her uncomfortably of what it had been like to walk into a crowded room after the story had broken about her and Jonathan Saunders.

Cesar guided her to a seat and once she was sitting took his own, beside her. He stretched his arm out behind her, and his thumb was rubbing back and forth across the top of her bare back. Lexie almost closed her eyes as her body responded violently: nipples peaking, belly softening, warmth pooling and spreading.

His voice came close to her ear. Too close. 'Relax. You look as if you're about to shatter into pieces.'

Lexie opened her eyes and turned her head, and Cesar's face was so close she could see the darker flecks of green in his eyes. Green on green—an ocean. She had the bizarre urge to reach up and touch his face, and had to curl her hand into a fist to stop herself.

The line of his cheek was a blade, giving his features that edgy saturnine impression. Something came over her—perhaps the knowledge that she could touch him in public as it would be expected. She lifted her hand and touched his jaw. She felt it clench under her hand and looked at him. His eyes had darkened and something hard shone through their depths. Cynicism.

It made her snatch her hand back. But not before he caught it with lightning swiftness and captured it, pressing an open-mouthed kiss to the skin just as he had in the car. It was no less devastating this time.

'You are quite the actress...'

Before Lexie could respond with some acid retort that

might deflect from the fact that a scary poignancy had gripped her on seeing that cynicism, a menu was being handed to her by a waiter and she had to accept it. There was no room for poignancy; she didn't care if Cesar was cynical.

Lexie stared at the menu blankly for a moment as she regained her composure. Damn the man. *Again*.

But of course the menu still remained largely incomprehensible to her. Another kind of dismay filled her— especially when she was so keyed up. She didn't need this particular vulnerability right now.

'It helps if you turn the menu the right way up.'

His voice was low and gently mocking. Lexie's hands tightened on the thick vellum as embarrassment washed through her in waves, making her hot. She sent a glare to Cesar, who had that tantalising smile playing around his mouth again.

She turned the menu around but of course that made no difference. She could see the waiters taking orders now and started to panic. With the utmost reluctance she said to Cesar, in a low voice, 'What would you recommend?'

He glanced at her for a moment and then perused his own menu and said, 'Personally I'd recommend the quail starter—'

'Quail?' Lexie asked, feeling ill at the thought.

Cesar looked at her. 'Well, there's a brie starter too.'

'I'll have that,' Lexie said with relief.

Cesar glanced back at the menu. 'Then there's a choice of salmon risotto, beef carpaccio...'

'The beef,' Lexie said, too ashamed to look at Cesar. Especially when she thought of his multi-lingual lovers who would be well used to these situations.

He said from beside her, 'Not everyone is used to menus in French—it's nothing to be embarrassed about.'

Lexie's own mortification made her lash out. 'Don't patronise me, Cesar. I'm not stupid, I'm just—'

But before she could finish a waiter had arrived and Cesar was ordering for both of them. Lexie clamped her mouth shut. Did she *have* to let every tiny detail of her life out whenever she opened her mouth?

When the waiter moved on Cesar's attention was taken by someone sitting to his left, and Lexie was facing a table full of people looking at her with varying degrees of curiosity.

To her immediate right was an older woman who leaned into Lexie and said in an American accent, 'My dear, you've quite set the cat among the pigeons, arriving with one of the most eligible bachelors in the world.'

Lexie smiled weakly. To her relief, she discovered that the woman was as charming as she was obviously eccentric and rich, and she regaled Lexie with stories of her expat life in Spain.

Relieved to have an excuse to avoid that green-eyed scrutiny, Lexie conversed enthusiastically with the woman.

Cesar willed himself to relax for the umpteenth time. The food had been served and eaten. Lexie had managed to spend most if not all that time ignoring him. It was unprecedented. He'd never had this experience with a woman before. And certainly not with one he'd kissed.

When he'd noticed her struggling with the menu, and that she'd had it upside down, a lurch of emotion had tightened his gut. He remembered her story about how she'd got started in the industry, leaving home so young, and presumably leaving school. She hadn't gone to university. She obviously wasn't as sophisticated as the women he was used to. And yet there was something refreshing about that.

Just before they'd been interrupted she'd said angrily, *'I'm not stupid.'* But that was one thing that had never come into his mind. Lexie Anderson had more intelligence sparking out of those blue eyes than he'd ever seen in his life.

With some of his previous lovers Cesar had found himself calling things off purely because of mental exhaustion. It was as if they felt they had to prove to him what worthy candidates they were by conversing in three languages at once, about complicated political systems that he had no interest in. And in the bedroom more than one had been keen to initiate kinky scenarios that had felt anything but sexy.

But with Lexie…every time he looked at her he felt kinky. He wanted to tie her down to some flat soft surface and ravish her.

Perhaps it was due to the fact that when they'd stepped out of the car earlier, to face the press, his body had still been humming with an overload of sexual frustration, but the experience hadn't been half as painful as he'd imagined. Having Lexie by his side had seemed to mitigate his usual excoriating feeling that the lenses of the paparazzi had some kind of X-ray vision.

When he saw her dining companion get up to leave the table he felt a rush of satisfaction. Now she would have to turn back to *him*. Cesar wasn't unaware of the looks she'd been drawing all evening in that provocative dress. She outshone every other woman. Literally. Cesar couldn't even recall seeing another woman. It was as if she'd blinded him. *With lust.*

He didn't like the hot spokes of anger that lanced him every time he caught some man's gaze sliding to her abundant curves.

Lexie could sense Cesar beside her. Waiting… Mrs Carmichael had gone to the bathroom and she was ready for his gaze to be censorious for having avoided him so obviously.

Taking a breath, she turned back—and just like that a jolt of pure electricity shot through her belly. Cesar had his hand on the back of her chair again, far too close for comfort. He'd taken off his jacket and his shirt was pulled taut across his chest, doing little to hide that stunning musculature.

He spoke. 'What I said earlier...before you turned your back on me so comprehensively...'

Lexie flushed and was about to remonstrate, but she knew she couldn't. She felt like a child.

'Mrs Carmichael was interesting,' she supplied a touch defensively.

'I know Mrs Carmichael very well and she *is* interesting.' His lip curled slightly. 'About the most interesting person here.'

Lexie glanced around at the very important-looking men and women. 'But aren't these your friends?'

Cesar all but snorted, surprising Lexie.

'They pretend to be my friends because I come and bid an obscene amount of money at their auction and then go. The only reason I do it is because I believe in this particular charity and because the money goes directly to the source, rather than via a dozen government agencies.'

'Oh,' Lexie answered, a little taken aback at Cesar's words.

She'd have put him in the same category as many rich people who contributed to charity for far too cynical reasons. But this *was* a worthy charity; it was aimed at combatting sex trafficking—a cause close to Lexie's own heart. She knew it was not one that was especially 'trendy' in the media, so the fact that Cesar was endorsing it had to help.

'Mrs Carmichael told me about it.'

Cesar picked up a card with his free hand and held it out to her. 'Here's a list of items to be auctioned—see if anything takes your fancy.'

His insouciance and his air of almost bored expectation that she would expect to be indulged made Lexie feel bizarrely disappointed. Then the fact that she couldn't *read* the card sent a spurt of anger up her spine. Something bitter gripped her.

She whispered angrily, 'I might not be as intellectual as your usual lovers, Cesar, but you really don't have to treat me like some kind of bimbo just because I'm blonde and—'

'That's enough.' Cesar straightened up, his hand tensing across the back of her chair, his fingers touching her neck in a very light but subtle admonishment.

She tensed against her inevitable reaction and could have laughed. To all the world they must look besotted. Close together, staring at each other, intent...

She could see in his face that he was surprised at her response. She moved, dislodging his hand slightly. 'I'm sorry. I overreacted.'

Cesar grimaced faintly. 'I didn't mean for it to sound so dismissive or flippant.'

Lexie was once again taken aback by his ability to apologise. Slightly mollified, she said, 'Maybe I'll want to bid on something myself?'

To give Cesar his due, he didn't laugh before he said, 'Do you know how much the cheapest item is marked at?'

Lexie shook her head. He glanced down and then looked back up, naming a price. She paled and said faintly, 'I guess I won't be bidding, then.'

Cesar handed her the card and Lexie took it. She should really tell him—especially if he was going to have her so on edge that even reading a menu would be a challenge for her.

'About the menu earlier...I should explain—'

'No.' He shook his head. 'I didn't mean to imply for a second that you're stupid.'

Now Lexie shook her head, regretting her defensive response. 'The reason I wasn't reading the menu very well was because I'm severely dyslexic.'

Lexie could feel her insides contracting, as if she were waiting for a look of disdain in Cesar's eyes. She'd seen it before.

But that didn't happen. He just said, 'And...?'

Lexie blanched. 'And...I can read perfectly well, but if I'm stressed...or under pressure...it becomes nearly impossible. I just need time.'

Cesar moved closer, his fingers whispering over her skin, under her hair. Lexie repressed a shiver of sensation.

'And are you?' he asked. 'Stressed? Under pressure?'

She wondered how it would be if she told him about the severe pressure and stress she felt under right now, with her body sparking and firing on levels she'd never even been aware of before.

Instead she said dryly, 'A little.'

He moved back slightly. 'You should have told me. A good friend of mine is dyslexic and he uses special software to help him. I'm sure I don't need to tell you of the renowned geniuses who had dyslexia but didn't let it hold them back.'

'Of course you don't,' Lexie said, almost feeling cross that Cesar was the one defending dyslexia and not her! 'I go to some of my local schools in London and talk to the kids about it—help them see that it won't limit them.'

He frowned, 'How do you manage with the scripts for your films?'

Lexie fiddled with her napkin self-consciously. 'I usually get an actor friend of mine to read them out. I record them, then I transfer them to my mp3 player...'

Someone sounded a gavel just then, and Lexie looked away with an effort. She was so engrossed in *him*. But people were sitting down again and she was glad of the interruption.

Not that long ago another man had duped her into thinking he was interested in her and she'd almost fallen for it. Now Cesar was coming perilously close to making her believe that *he* was interested but she knew that it was just lust. The spike of excitement in her gut was shameful, but she couldn't ignore it.

Cesar's attention had turned to the front. And then Lexie found herself distracted as with admirable nonchalance he made bids on the most expensive lots, only to get an assurance from the auctioneer that the lots he'd bought would be raffled for free at the charity for its workers.

When it was over, and Cesar had spent more money than Lexie had ever heard of, he turned to her and said brusquely, 'Are you ready to go?'

She nodded, too intimidated by what she'd seen to say a word. Lexie could see all the sycophants vying for his attention as they left, but he didn't stop for anyone, his hand on her back again.

His car and driver were waiting outside, as if psychically informed of his departure, but Lexie knew it must have been a series of frantic Chinese whispers from the staff, who had been watching his every move like a hawk.

Once they were in the back of the car, the darkness closed around them like a blanket, cutting out sounds, cutting out reality. It made Lexie exceedingly nervous and she scooted right over to her side of the car. The thought of Cesar kissing her again in this seductive gloom was far too scary to contemplate, even if the thought of his words *we will be lovers* tantalised her more than she cared to admit.

Through the tinted windows Lexie could see the lights of Salamanca glittering. It distracted her. She said on an awed breath, 'It's so beautiful...'

After a moment Lexie head Cesar say something to his driver in the front and then the car was turning around.

She looked at Cesar. 'Wait...what are you doing?'

A little gruffly he said, 'You should see the Plaza Mayor at night when it's lit up.'

After watching how generous he'd been to the charity, Lexie was mortified to think that he might feel the need to act as tour guide. 'It's fine,' she protested. 'I can come back again some evening.'

He ignored that and asked, 'Are you hungry for something sweet?'

Lexie blinked in the gloom. She hadn't had dessert. How did the man know she had a sweet tooth?

'A little…maybe…but really we don't—'

He cut her off. 'I know a place. We'll go there.'

The car parked on a street where couples strolled arm in arm. Cesar got out, and by the time Lexie had her door open he was standing waiting, holding out a hand for her to take. Muttering her thanks, she let him help her.

The early autumn air had a slight nip, and before Lexie could say anything she felt Cesar's dinner jacket being settled around her shoulders. His warmth and scent surrounded her like an intoxicating cloak.

When he took her hand Lexie had to battle the urge to pull it free again. The truth was she liked the way it felt to have her hand in his. She glanced up at Cesar and saw that his bow-tie was gone and the top button of his shirt was open. It made him appear rakish.

Lexie was attracting attention in her long gold dress. 'Do you think the photographers will be around here?'

Cesar looked down at her. 'They could be—they saw us leave.'

They rounded a corner then, and Lexie's mind blanked at the beauty before them. Salamanca's famous Plaza Mayor was lit up in golden lights. They spilled from everywhere and illuminated the huge ancient buildings. It was like the inside of a magical golden ornament. Lexie had known the old part of the city was a UNESCO heritage protected site and now she knew why. The square was huge…awe-inspiring.

Cesar led her across the airy space and she felt tiny in the midst of the baroque grandeur. When she was able to stop looking up and gaping at the beautifully ornate buildings, she saw that they'd stopped outside one of the cafés which was still open.

A small old man came rushing out, welcoming Cesar effusively and offering them a table under one of the massive arches that lined the square. They sat down. Lexie was relieved and disappointed in equal measure to get her hand back.

Cesar asked, 'What kind of dessert do you like?'

Feeling very bemused at being here with him, Lexie said, 'Anything…cakes…pastries.'

He arched a brow. 'Coffee?'

She nodded. 'Yes, please.'

Cesar said a few words to the proprietor, who looked as if he was about to burst with pride at having such an esteemed guest—clearly he knew who Cesar was.

A few people lingered over coffee, glasses of wine. Cesar's jacket swam on Lexie, but his warmth still tantalised her skin. It was incredibly seductive.

The owner bustled back out, with another young man following him. They set down coffee and a tray of different desserts. Lexie's mouth watered. When they'd left, Cesar explained what they were. There was an almond sponge cake, candied almonds, small fritters filled with cream, sweet puff pastry, small chocolate cakes…

Lexie groaned after she'd tasted some of the delicious pastry. 'If only I didn't have to worry about getting back into that corset in a couple of days.'

Cesar paused in the act of drinking his coffee and looked at her. Lexie looked back. The air between them sizzled. That moment in the back of the car earlier invaded her head like a lurid B movie.

He put his cup down. 'When I saw you for the first time I thought you were some kind of an apparition. That you weren't real.'

Lexie swallowed her dessert with difficulty. She remembered the transfixed expression on his face that day. She'd never forget it. While she hadn't thought he was an apparition, she'd felt something similar.

'I knew you were real...' she admitted. 'But I know what you mean. I wasn't meant to be there.'

Cesar grimaced. 'I was harsh on you.'

Lexie glanced down at her coffee and shrugged. 'Your privacy had been comprehensively invaded by hundreds of strangers...'

'I'd also just returned from my half-brother's wedding in Paris.'

He sounded so grim that Lexie looked up again. She recalled seeing the pictures on the internet of that wedding, the speculation.

Her curiosity piqued, she asked, 'So you *are* related, then?'

He frowned. 'Why do you ask?'

Lexie flushed, feeling like a stalker. 'I saw something on the internet when I went looking to see if there were any more pictures...of us.' It wasn't entirely untrue, she reassured herself.

Cesar's face was hard. 'Yes, it's true. He and Rafaele Falcone are my half-brothers.'

Lexie had the sense she was entering into a minefield. 'But this wasn't common knowledge?'

Cesar took a swift sip of his coffee and shook his head, putting the cup back down with a clatter. He was so tense all of a sudden that Lexie half expected him to jump up and stride away. But he didn't. Although for the first time his gaze was avoiding hers.

'We had the same mother but different fathers.'

'You didn't know them growing up?'

He shook his head and then speared her with a look that she couldn't read.

'No. I just knew of them. My mother was more interested in a life of opulence and luxury to think about cosy reunions, or to worry about the fact that she'd abandoned her eldest son.'

A multitude of questions hit Lexie. Why had his mother left him? But then that very first niggle of suspicion she'd had came back. 'Does that have anything to do with… *this*?' she asked carefully.

Cesar frowned. 'What do you mean?'

Lexie wasn't even sure herself. She only knew that she was feeling increasingly exposed on a level she didn't welcome.

'I mean, does the fact that it's come out about your brothers have anything to do with the fact that you were happy to agree for us to be seen together in public?'

His mouth tightened. 'I will admit that I saw an advantage in allowing another story to take precedence.'

Lexie had suspected that this might be a possibility. So why was a feeling of hurt blooming deep inside? A snide voice answered her—because she'd been seduced by his touch and his words into thinking his desire for her was his only motivation.

Of course someone like Cesar Da Silva would normally prefer to keep her tucked away out of sight, so that he could make it look as if that first kiss had been some crazy brief aberration. It had been his initial reaction.

Why hadn't she even questioned it properly at the time? His ready compliance? Because he'd turned her brain to mush exactly at the same time as he'd turned her insides molten.

She thought of the bathroom earlier—when she'd entertained the notion of their becoming lovers for a moment. The dizzying rush of exhilaration that had gripped her. *God*, she'd been so easily caught.

Lexie looked away from him and blindly picked up her cup again, not even noticing when some coffee sloshed over the rim to fall on her dress. Suddenly she couldn't stand it—being under his cool assessing scrutiny.

Almost knocking the small table over with her jerkiness, she stood up, any inherent ability to act deserting her. 'Would you mind if we left now? I'm quite tired…it's been a long week.'

She whirled away from the table and started to walk. Agitation was rising up from her gullet and also a kind of panic. Panic that she'd not thought more clearly that *obviously* he'd have an ulterior motive for wanting to be seen in public with her. He'd just been toying with her, while she'd been perilously close to proving how easily duped she could be—*again*.

She vaguely heard a muttered curse and some change being thrown on the table and just when she'd reached the middle of the golden square which by now was almost empty, her arm was caught in a big hand. She was spun around to face a familiar glowering expression. She welcomed it.

'What the hell was that about, Lexie?'

She wrenched her arm out of Cesar's grip, dislodging his coat from her shoulders. It fell to the ground, unnoticed by either of them. Words trembled on her lips, but if she uttered them she only risked exposing herself even more.

His lip curled. 'You find the fact that I have my own reasons to avoid the press digging into my life unpalatable?

That I was left behind like some unwanted luggage, with half-siblings who never even knew I existed?'

'What?' Lexie said, his words shocking her out of her own turmoil for a moment. 'No! Of course not… I didn't even know anything about your family.'

Cesar's mouth was tight. 'My mother hoped to get a good deal by bringing me back to the family home, but she hadn't banked on my grandparents giving her an ultimatum: just me or neither of us. So she left me behind.'

Lexie's agitation drained away. She put out a hand, 'Cesar…I had no idea.'

He stepped back. The huge magnificent square seemed to frame him in a leonine glow, making his masculinity even more impressive.

'That's what is about to hit the papers any day now. The full lurid story of Esperanza Christakos—née Falcone, née Da Silva—her rise from poverty to incalculable wealth and fame. And the gory details of the son she abandoned.'

Even as his words touched a painful nerve within Lexie she let out a tiny gasp of recognition at the name. She'd never put two and two together and realised that the world-famous beauty had been related to his brothers—*or him*.

She shook her head. 'I didn't know anything about her.'

Cesar, clearly angry at himself for letting all that spill out, said curtly, 'Well, *what*, then? If not that?'

Lexie's equilibrium was all over the place again. How could she articulate the fact that she was hurt because he evidently hadn't been motivated to appear with her in public simply out of sheer desire? When all along she'd protested vehemently at his arrogant assertion that they'd become lovers even as she'd pathetically melted whenever he touched her. And yet now that he clearly had another motivation it only highlighted her inner confusion and the tumultuous desires he evoked within her.

She searched his face for any hint of softness. But found

none. She realised then just how truly hard he was, and couldn't stop the tug of emotion at imagining a small child being left in that huge grim *castillo* without his mother.

Racking her brain for a way not to betray herself, she avoided his question and said weakly, 'We don't have to do this…if you don't want to.'

Right now even the prospect of staying in the *castillo* to avoid the press was more appealing than the thought of exposing herself like this again.

Cesar moved closer. His face wasn't so hard now. There was an explicit gleam in his eye that had a direct effect on Lexie's blood.

She spoke quickly, to hide her frayed nerves. 'Maybe this isn't such a good idea. If we stop now we can make it look like it was just a brief…fling.'

Cesar shook his head and said in that deep voice, 'We've gone too far to turn back now.'

Lexie's heart thumped hard. Her mouth dried. Treacherously, she didn't feel inclined to argue.

He said then, 'We both have our reasons for doing this, Lexie…and we're adults. This happened in the first place because we took one look at each other and couldn't keep our hands off each other.'

She thought of what he'd told her about his half-brothers. About his desire to avoid press intrusion around what was obviously a tender subject. Even though she didn't know the full story it resonated within her. She too had secrets to keep—dark ones. She found herself feeling a dangerous kinship with him. They were in this together.

He was sliding his hands and arms around her waist now, tugging her unresisting her body into his. All Lexie could feel was steel. Warmth and steel.

She put her hands on his chest. The moment felt slightly unreal. They were surrounded by the golden shimmering lights of the square.

Lexie's recent feelings of exposure and vulnerability were nowhere to be felt when Cesar's mouth touched hers. And they were certainly nowhere to be found in the almost shameless way she responded so quickly—opening her mouth, inviting him in, arching closer, demanding more.

There was a flash from nearby and it made her jerk in Cesar's arms. He pulled back, cursing. A photographer was feet away, snapping them. She felt Cesar tense but he made no move to stop the photographer, who was already walking away, checking his digital images.

Cesar turned back to Lexie and there was a distinctly satisfied gleam in his eyes. 'There goes any chance to protest that this was just a brief fling.' The satisfied gleam became something else—*hotter*. 'Whatever our reasons were, it's about *us* now. I want you. And you want me. It's that simple.'

CHAPTER FIVE

ABOUT AN HOUR later Lexie lay in bed with his words reverberating in her head. After that moment in the middle of that beautiful square Cesar had said nothing else. He'd just taken her by the hand and led her back to the car.

They'd remained in silence for the journey, as if both contemplating what lay ahead. Lexie's mind had been slightly numb, though. Too full to be able to tease out the different strands.

When they'd returned to the *castillo* the dour housekeeper had met them and told Cesar that he had some phone calls he must return. Lexie had welcomed the chance to escape, pleading tiredness, but she hadn't missed the intensity of Cesar's expression as he'd bade her goodnight. It had set a fire alight deep in her belly.

She could feel it now. As if she'd been awoken on some deep level. This hadn't happened with Jonathan Saunders, her *alleged* married lover... He'd appealed to an altogether less visceral side of her. Perhaps he'd appealed to the part of her that had finally been ready to trust again and she'd just chosen unwisely.

Suddenly that revelation made her heart beat fast. Perhaps she hadn't lost it completely. Perhaps she was still in control. This was totally different from what had happened before. There was no hint of scandal.

Cesar had not touched her innermost feelings and secrets. *He hadn't,* she told herself fiercely in the dark. He'd kissed her and she'd come alive. That was all. It was *physical.* And if anyone was long overdue their awakening it was her. She'd just got a little confused for a moment. Confused lust with feelings. Cesar was offering her a chance to explore this sexual attraction. And she realised with an almost desperate feeling that she wanted to. With *this* man.

What he'd revealed about his brothers and mother struck her again. That feeling of empathy. She knew exactly what it was like to want to avoid scrutiny of your most private self.

Cesar was a cynical being. It oozed from every part of him. Cynical and dark… She could appreciate why now. Lexie was cynical too—it had been branded onto her at an early age when she'd come face to face with the harshest side of life.

She'd prided herself on cultivating a sense of optimism over the years, but she knew that cynical shell hadn't really worn away completely. She could be as cynical as him now. More so. She had infinitely more to gain from this than he could ever realise.

And when the time came to walk away Cesar could go back to his classically coiffed intellectual lovers and Lexie would have achieved a personal emancipation she'd only ever dreamed about.

It was that simple.

'Thanks for a great day, everyone, that's a wrap.'

Lexie let out a sigh of relief. They'd finished shooting their scenes in the walled garden and would be moving further into the *castillo* estate for the rest of the week.

Cesar had been absent from the set all day, and Lexie had been glad of the space to try and get her bearings and remember that she was here to work. But her assertion to herself that she'd been glad of the space mocked her.

She hadn't seen Cesar since Saturday night, when he'd left her hot and bothered with that look. She'd felt so antsy on Sunday that she'd gone out for a long walk around the estate—and still no sign of Cesar.

After coming to the momentous personal decision that she would embark on an affair with him, she felt suddenly deflated now he'd disappeared into thin air. Without his unerring ability to distract her, and hypnotise her with his charisma and intensity, Lexie felt vulnerable.

She cursed herself for those weak feelings as she scrubbed her face clean in the empty make-up truck. It took her so long to get out of her costume that the base was usually quiet when she left. Only the wardrobe crew were still there, and the facility men who looked after the trailers. And the second assistant director, whose job it was to make sure Lexie was everywhere she needed to be and on time.

Lexie called goodnight and made her way back to the *castillo*. She didn't like the frisson of loneliness that assailed her and scowled at herself.

She was still scowling when she entered the *castillo* and ran straight into a wall. Except this wall was warm and it had hands that came around her arms, steadying her.

The singing rush of warmth and excitement made her scowl even more as she looked up into the elusive Cesar Da Silva's face. Damn him.

'I was just coming to find you.'

'Well, as you can see I'm here,' Lexie said testily, irritated at being irritated.

Cesar whistled softly. 'Bad day at the office, dear?'

His unexpected dry humour sparked something inside Lexie, but she pulled free of his hands before he could see it. She didn't want him to be flirty or endearing.

'I'm sorry,' she blurted out, avoiding his eye. 'It has been a long day.' *Liar,* her conscience mocked her.

She felt self-conscious in comfy leggings and a loose shirt. Face clean, hair pulled back into a messy knot. For all she knew he might have been wining and dining some dark beauty last night…

Cesar cut through her feverish thoughts.

'Those phone calls the other night…one of them resulted in me having to attend an urgent meeting in Paris early this morning, so I left yesterday.'

Lexie fought to repress the crazy lurch of relief. She shrugged a shoulder minutely and said airily, 'Really? I didn't notice.'

Cesar came close and tipped Lexie's jaw up so she had to look at him. She hated being small right now. If she'd been taller she could have eyeballed Cesar.

'Liar,' he said softly. 'Because I was aware of every minute I was away from this place.'

His words made air whoosh out of Lexie's lungs. An instantaneous bubble of lightness infused her blood. She couldn't help a rueful smile. 'Well, your meeting can't have been very exciting.'

Cesar shook his head. 'It was deadly dull.'

The air sizzled between them. And just like that all of Lexie's doubts and fears melted away again. His effect on her was ridiculous. But she couldn't resist.

He took his hand away. 'We hit the papers today…I thought you'd want to see.'

Lexie fought not to let him see how much he affected her. 'Of course.'

He stepped back. 'We can go to my apartment—it's more private.'

Lexie looked at him as he started to walk away, 'Your apartment?'

She walked quickly to keep up with him. He glanced at her and then took her hand, setting off a million butterflies.

'I have my own apartment here within the *castillo*.'

Curious as to what it might be like, in such a mausoleum of a castle, Lexie followed him down a warren of corridors, passing the study where she'd had that first cataclysmic conversation with him.

He stopped outside a door that had a keypad lock and entered a code. The door swung open. As he walked in and Lexie followed, her hand still in his, her jaw dropped. It was like stepping into another world.

The apartment was huge, cavernous. Like stepping into Narnia from behind the coats in the wardrobe. One side was dominated by a massive wall of windows. On the other side was a modern state-of-the-art kitchen. Steel and chrome with industrial lights.

The floor was wooden—parquet, like his office—and strewn with huge oriental rugs, softening it. One corner of the room was filled with three old battered leather couches and a low coffee table. A TV and music system. Along that wall was nothing but shelves and books—rows and rows of books.

Lexie felt that pang again. She loved books and reading, but for her it was a torturous process. Remembering how Cesar had responded to her dyslexia made her melt a little more.

'I have an office through here.'

As Lexie followed Cesar she saw another door, and glanced in as they passed to see a huge bedroom with a massive bed, sheets tangled on top. The image was incendiary and unbelievably intimate. She felt herself blushing. Would she be in that bed with him soon? Limbs entwined?

Her face was burning when he let her hand go inside the office. She was glad the lighting was dim and looked around. This was obviously a private study. Not as imposing as his other one, but somewhere he obviously spent a lot of time. Books were strewn around...papers. It was lived in. Comfortable. Messier than she would have imagined for someone who seemed so controlled.

He had some newspapers on the desk and turned one around to face her. Carefully keeping her expression neutral, she read the headline.

Hot! Hot! Hot! Luscious Lexie bags the world's most reclusive bachelor and richest man!

It was more or less what she had expected, but still a blow to her gut. She couldn't take her eyes off the pictures. One was of them arriving at the function the other night, her hand in his. She was practically welded to his body. She hadn't even realised that she'd been stuck to him like that. Her eyes were huge. Like a deer in headlights. Pathetic.

Another showed his head bending to hers. She couldn't remember what he'd said—something about going inside after another minute. But it looked as if he was whispering a sweet nothing. Her face was turned to his.

And one last one was a shot from inside the hotel; it must have been taken by a guest or a waiter on a camera phone. They were at the table, his arm around the back of her chair, heads close together.

Lexie felt horribly exposed, even though she was used to seeing her picture in the papers by now. But not like this. These showed just how enticing and fascinating she found this dark and difficult man. She was relieved that there didn't seem to be any pictures from the square. Even now those moments felt raw.

Cesar was perched on the edge of his desk, one powerful thigh in her eyeline, distracting her.

His voice sounding far too smug, he said, 'They look convincing…although you'd be more used to this sort of thing than me.'

Feeling prickly at his tone—obviously the experience

had been far more cataclysmic for her—and hating that he evidently believed in her guilt, Lexie stepped back and blurted out, 'I had nothing to do with ending up in the tabloids with that man.'

Cesar frowned. 'What do you mean?'

Lexie started to pace, agitated. Dammit, she didn't have to explain herself to this man. But...treacherously...she wanted to. Even if Cesar wasn't really interested.

She stopped pacing and faced him, crossing her arms in a classic defence pose. 'I didn't have an affair with that man.'

His eyes narrowed on her. 'So how did it come about?'

'Jonathan Saunders...' Lexie stopped for a moment. Even saying his name made her angry. 'We'd just done a small West End play together for a few weeks. I'd worked with him years before on my very first short film. He'd been nice to me at the time—kind of like a mentor. I considered us friends... During the play he made a point of hanging out with me. Making sure I got home okay. Stuff like that.'

Lexie felt queasy to think that his easy affection and hands-off attention had sneaked under her skin so that she'd believed she could trust him. And even though she hadn't really felt anything for him physically, she'd believed him to be a genuine friend. She'd been susceptible enough to consider that if he made a physical move she'd give him a chance. The thought made her skin crawl now.

'After we'd finished the play he called around one day and he was in a state, saying he needed somewhere to stay. He had some story about being chucked out of his house because he couldn't afford to pay the rent. I knew he wasn't that successful as an actor—it seemed believable. I had a spare room so I offered it to him and he moved in for about a week.'

'Did you sleep with him?'

Cesar's voice was sharp and Lexie glared at him, annoyed with herself for even bringing it up. It was only exposing her even more.

'I told you I didn't have an affair with him.'

'So what happened?'

'He left early one morning, and I only found out because there was banging on the door. I'd been asleep. I figured it was him—that he'd left something behind—he'd started rehearsals for a new play. I was half asleep, and when I opened the door the street was full of photographers.'

Lexie's face burned.

'I was dressed in night clothes...barely awake... I discovered later that Jonathan was actually married and had had a huge row with his wife because she'd found out he was having an affair and that his girlfriend was pregnant.'

Her mouth went tight.

'He'd known it was coming, because he'd been tipped off by his lover that the press suspected something, so he cultivated me. Made friends. Got me to trust him so that he could use me to be the fall guy when he wanted to protect his *real* girlfriend. He was terrified they'd track her down.'

Lexie sighed.

'His lover was the wife of a prominent Conservative cabinet minister; she wanted to avoid scandal at all costs. He figured *I* was a better prospect to throw to the ravenous press and he set me up well—living with me for a week, letting them believe we'd moved in together.'

Lexie looked at Cesar.

'I hadn't even known he was married. He'd said nothing at all about his wife. Or kids.'

'Why didn't you defend yourself once you knew the truth?'

Because she hadn't wanted to give the press any excuse to look into her background in case of what they might find.

A feeling of *déja vu* struck her. Here she was again, feeling the urge to *trust*, to believe. But if the last few minutes of rehashing the events of that unfortunate period told her anything it was that she couldn't trust. Not really. So she shrugged minutely. 'I didn't want to add fuel to the fire…attract even more attention. And I felt sorry for his wife and kids.'

She avoided his gaze. At least that was part of the truth.

There was something achingly vulnerable about Lexie as she stood in front of Cesar with her arms crossed so tight. He might have told himself before that he couldn't care less what she'd done, but right now he did care. And the fact that she hadn't slept with that guy made a tightness ease in him. Even as he wanted to find him and punch him. And that surprised him. Women didn't arouse feelings of protectiveness within him, a desire to avenge them. He shouldn't care.

A second too late Cesar saw that her eye had caught one of the other newspapers that had been delivered. A different headline: *Cesar Da Silva's long-lost family!*

Before he could stop her she'd reached out to pull the paper free. On the cover were recent photographs of all three men: Cesar, Rafaele and Alexio. And another of their beautiful mother. Shining out from all four photos was the undeniable genetic link of their green eyes.

Cesar stood up. Tense.

Lexie said slowly, 'That's where your green eyes come from. She was very beautiful, your mother.'

'Yes, she was,' Cesar said tightly, his skin prickling at having Lexie looking at the blatant evidence of his mother's lack of love for him. It made him feel raw again when he thought of the other night—how Lexie had all but run from the table in the square. When his irrational feeling had been that she'd seen the darkness in his soul and was repulsed by it.

Lexie gazed at him now and all he could see were those blue eyes. Something in him tightened when he saw the compassion in their depths, but it didn't make him want to run.

'Well,' she said a little awkwardly, dropping the paper down, 'I should go. I have an early start again tomorrow.'

When she turned to leave Cesar rejected it with every fibre of his being. 'Wait.'

He reached out and put his hands on her elbows, pulled her into him until their bodies were flush. The palms of her hands landed on his chest and his entire body thrummed with need.

His eyes roved over her face, as if learning every tiny detail.

'*Dios,*' he muttered. 'You are so beautiful.'

Lexie tried to duck her face. 'I'm not.'

'You are.' Cesar's ferocity made her look up. '...stunning. And I want you more than I've ever wanted anyone.'

Lexie felt the excitement in her blood obliterating the scary empathy that had come as soon as she'd seen the picture of Cesar and his half-brothers and mother. She'd *felt* the tension in his body.

Cesar's head dipped and his mouth found hers unerringly. She fell headlong into the flaming pit of the kiss. It burnt her up from the inside out, from the depths of her being.

This was *right*. She felt it in her bones. She trusted this, whether she liked to admit it or not. Her hands gripped his biceps in order to stay standing, and she came up on tiptoe, straining even closer.

Cesar undid her hair and she could feel it fall loose behind her shoulders. He was backing her towards something, and when she felt something solid behind her she realised dimly it must be his desk.

Still their mouths were clinging to one another, their

tongues tangling in a heady dance. Cesar lifted Lexie effortlessly until she was sitting on the desk. Instinctively she hooked a leg around one of his and heard his growl of approval as it brought his body into contact with hers.

The hard press of his arousal against her belly only set off another spasm of lust deep in her body. And between her legs. This was infinitely preferable to trying to rationalise her thoughts and feelings.

His hand was between them, unbuttoning her shirt. Lexie felt hot. Yearned for air, a breeze. His touch. When it fell open he pushed it off one shoulder, taking her bra strap with it, tugging it down her arm.

She wanted only one thing: *more*. When Cesar took his mouth from hers they were both breathing harshly. Somewhere she heard the ring of a phone—a mobile. She tensed.

He said gutturally, 'It doesn't matter.'

Lexie felt dazed, despite the intrusion of the phone. 'I want to see you.'

Standing up straight for a moment, Cesar undid his buttons and opened his shirt. Lexie closed her eyes when the intoxicating scent of man and musk hit her nostrils. Like when she'd first seen him.

When she opened them again they widened. He was magnificent. Broad and hard muscled. Dark blond hair dusted his chest, drawing her eye down to where it bisected the ridges of his abdomen muscles in a line and then disappeared into his pants.

And just like that Lexie became aware of being out of her depth. Overwhelmed. She knew that if they didn't stop now this would end in bed, and as much as she thought she wanted that she wasn't sure if she was really ready. And she realised a small part of her needed to know that he would stop.

She put a hand on his chest and felt him tense. It almost made her forget her intention.

'Wait...' Her voice felt rough, breathy. 'This is moving so fast...'

She looked up at him, wishing she could read what was in those green depths. Decipher that inscrutable expression.

Cesar stepped back and Lexie let her hand drop. It felt as if a chasm had opened between them. With a shaky hand she pulled her shirt and bra strap back up. She couldn't really think straight when Cesar was half clothed in front of her, and cringed as she realised it was only seconds ago that she'd been begging to *see* him.

Humiliation scored her insides. She was damaged. She couldn't just throw caution to the wind and do this. That was the problem.

She slid off the table, her legs unsteady. Between them she throbbed lightly. Mockingly.

Expecting Cesar to be irritated, put out, she caught her breath when she looked up at him and he smiled. Lexie nearly had to put her hands behind her to catch the desk. *Lord.* When he smiled something inside her ached because she hadn't really seen him smile before now.

He moved close again and rubbed his thumb across her bottom lip. His smile faded. 'We want each other.'

Lexie's heart thumped. Hard. 'Yes...' How could she deny it? God. She felt as gauche as a sixteen-year-old contemplating her first make-out session. But then she'd never had that experience.

'Next weekend there's a function in Madrid. You said you wanted to see the city?'

Her head felt fuzzy. Had she?

But Cesar didn't even bother to wait for her agreement, he just said, 'We'll go together. I have an apartment there so we can stay overnight.'

Lexie's heart nearly pounded out of her chest at the

thought but she managed to nod. 'It'll be good for us to be seen together. It'll be good for the press.'

'Yes,' Cesar agreed equably. 'But it's not just about that, Lexie. It's for *us*.'

When Lexie had left Cesar had to wait another few minutes for his body to cool down. He'd been ready to lift her up and carry her into his bedroom. His conscience mocked him—as if he could have held back from taking her right there on his desk.

When she'd pulled back, put her hand on his chest, everything within him had screamed with rejection. And then he'd come to his senses and realised just how close to the edge he was. So he'd welcomed a little space...sanity.

He was a civilised man, even though the last time he could remember feeling remotely civilised was over a week ago—just before he'd laid eyes on Lexie Anderson for the first time.

Cesar went to the window that looked out over a private section of the *castillo* gardens, tucking one arm under the other across his chest.

Something skated over his skin...a very old memory. A feeling. Vulnerability. He didn't like it. It harked back to a time before he'd made sure he was immune to such weaknesses.

He wanted Lexie, but she was dangerous. Because when he was near her he seemed to forget himself. His mouth tightened.

Everything in him had always urged him to trust nothing—and especially not women. After all, his mother and grandmother had taught him that lesson very well.

A memory came back, blindsiding him: his grandmother, dragging him painfully up to a first-floor window. Forcing him to sit down on the window seat. Every day, for hours on end. Before and after his lessons. Because she'd found him there one day. Watching…waiting.

'If you like it here so much then you'll do it every day. Watch, Cesar. *Watch*. See how she does not return for you. And when you tell me that you believe me we can stop playing this game.'

Cesar could remember glaring at his grandmother's thin, bitter face mulishly before she'd taken his ear painfully and pulled his face back to the window. Tears of pain had sprung into his eyes but he'd blinked them back. Loath to show her any emotion. Because even at that tender age of five he'd already known better.

And so he'd looked out of the window—fiercely—for hours on end, willing the figure of his mother to appear. Sometimes he'd thought he'd seen something, but it had only been a mirage. It had taken another full year before he'd finally told his grandmother what she wanted to hear.

His grandmother had made sure that he would see pictures of his mother enjoying her life in Paris. Becoming successful. Famous. A model. Having another son. His half-brother. Forgetting about *him*.

His mother *had* come back, with his younger brother, another year after that. The shattering pain of seeing his brother's hand in hers had been unbearable. He'd hated her—hated them both so much that he'd rejected her right back.

He'd lost his father before he'd even really known him. Then his mother had left him behind like a piece of unwanted luggage. Cesar's grandmother and grandfather had shown nothing but disdain and faint tolerance for their grandson. Their only motivation in making him heir had been their own greed and fanatical obsession with the family name.

The past finally receded from Cesar's head. He castigated himself for letting a woman, no matter how alluring, have this effect on him, for making him think about those things again. He *wanted* Lexie—pure and simple.

He was impervious to anything above and beyond sating himself with her. He would never want anything more with a woman than momentary satisfaction. And Lexie was no different.

CHAPTER SIX

Towards the end of that second week Lexie's nerves were jagged and fraying. It was almost certainly because of the constant presence of Cesar on the set. She felt his gaze on her like a physical touch sometimes.

She wasn't used to this. This excruciating build-up of sexual awareness and frustration. She hated Cesar for having done this to her, having this hold over her, while in the same breath she wished he would just stride across the set and take her in his arms and kiss her to make her head stop spinning.

But it wasn't just the physical sensations. He seemed to have snuck deeper. And she couldn't believe she was in danger of being gullible all over again even though this was infinitely different from what had happened with Jonathan Saunders.

Madrid and the weekend loomed large. The irony was not lost on Lexie—she was playing the part of a jaded sexual libertine and yet she had no idea of the reality of what that should feel like. She felt like a fraud, and gave thanks that no one seemed to have called her on it yet.

But after this weekend, a sly voice pointed out, *you'll know exactly what it feels like.*

When they finally called a wrap that day, and Lexie saw that it was Cesar waiting for her with a golf buggy to get her back to the unit base instead of one of the PAs, she snapped and said caustically, 'Don't you have a world leader to meet or something equally important to do?'

Cesar just looked incredibly sanguine and stepped out of the buggy to help her in, saying *sotto voce*, 'I'm your besotted lover, remember?'

Lexie stifled a snort and pulled the coat she wore to keep warm around her, hiding her voluptuous curves in the elaborate dress.

And then she felt churlish. She glanced at Cesar's patrician profile. He was even more gorgeous dressed down in faded jeans and a long-sleeved top. Workmanlike boots. He looked younger like this, less intimidating. Less a titan of industry.

As much as his presence on the set unnerved her, she'd come to expect it now. Two days ago she'd been waiting for the camera to be set up and had wandered behind one of the equipment trucks to find Cesar deep in conversation with one of the oldest members of the crew. A veteran who had worked on some of the biggest films ever made.

Cesar had been listening intently and asking him about his career. The effect this had had on Lexie was nothing short of pathetic. It had been akin to seeing Cesar cradle a small puppy. Inducing warmth, tenderness. *Danger*.

When they reached the base Cesar helped her from the buggy and opened the door of her trailer for her. Before she could go in, though, he caught her hand.

She looked at him warily.

'I have to go to London tomorrow morning for twenty-four hours. But I'll be back to take you to Madrid on Saturday. We'll leave after lunch.'

He let her hand go to cup the back of her neck, drawing her to him. Even though Lexie had a split second of realisation that he was going to kiss her the touch of his mouth to hers was still like an electric shock, infusing her blood with energy and heat. It was a chaste kiss, and he drew back almost as soon as it had started. But Lexie wanted more.

'Till then.' He let her go, stepped back.

Lexie's heart was beating fast. This was the moment. She could say something now— back out, not go through with it. *Stay safe.*

She opened her mouth. Cesar's green gaze was almost black. And, treacherously, she shut her mouth without saying anything. A recklessness within her was urging her to seize the moment.

Lexie saw other crew members arriving back from the set. Her dresser hurrying to help her out of her costume.

She took a breath. 'Fine, I'll be ready.'

Cesar smiled and it was distinctly predatory. 'I look forward to it. Don't miss me too much, will you?'

Lexie wanted to make a face but he was already turning to go. She really didn't like the impulse she felt to run after him and beg him to take her with him.

On Saturday Lexie was dressed casually, in a stripy long-sleeved top, a long, loose, gypsy-style skirt and soft boots. She had a weekend bag and was waiting for Cesar in the imposing reception hall of the *castillo*, trying not to think about the butterflies fluttering around in her belly at the prospect of seeing him again, or to think too much about what the weekend would bring.

So she thought of the difference between his private apartment and its soaring modern space and the rest of the *castillo*. So different. It made her wonder what it must have been like to grow up here…and why his mother had left him behind.

Something caught Lexie's eye through a doorway and she put down her bags for a moment to walk into a long formal room. It was filled with portraits and she shivered a little as she looked at them. They were all so stern and forbidding—much like the dour *castillo* housekeeper.

She walked around them and came to the most recent ones. Lexie figured they had to be of Cesar's grandparents. They appeared sterner than all the rest put together and she shivered again.

'Cold?'

Lexie jumped and put a hand to her heart, looking around to see Cesar lounging against the door frame, watching her. She took him in. He was wearing dark trousers and an open-necked shirt. He looked smart, yet casual. Gorgeous.

'You startled me.'

He straightened up and came in, hands in his pockets, which made her feel minutely safer. Her skin was hot. And an ache she'd not even been aware of noticing eased. *She'd missed him.* For one day.

Dragging her eyes away from him, she regarded the portraits again. 'Are these your grandparents?'

He stood beside her and a frisson of electricity shot straight to her groin.

He sounded grim. 'Yes, that's them.'

Lexie was curious. 'What were they like?'

He was clipped. 'Cold, cruel, snobbish. Obsessed with the family legacy.'

She looked at him and almost gasped at how hard his face had become. Stark. Pained.

'What did they do to you?'

He smiled, but it was hard. 'What *didn't* they do? My grandmother's particular favourite hobby was getting me to compile scrapbooks of newspaper cuttings featuring my mother and half-brothers, further driving home the message that they wanted nothing to do with me.'

Lexie stared at Cesar, too shocked to say anything for a moment. No wonder there was such tension in him when he mentioned his family. And yet he'd gone to that wedding... He glanced at her and she could see it in his eyes: *Not up for further discussion.* What surprised Lexie was the wave of rage she felt welling inside her at the horrific cruelty he'd endured.

'What happened to your father? Is it true that he was a bullfighter?'

Cesar looked away again and Lexie thought he would ignore her, but then he said, 'He rebelled. He wanted out and wanted nothing to do with his inheritance. So he did what he could to ensure that his family would disown him: he became a bullfighter. It was the worst insult to his parents he could think of. And they duly disinherited him.'

'Your mother...?'

Cesar kept his eyes on the portraits.

'My mother was from a small town down south, where my father went to train as a bullfighter. She was poor. He fell in love and they got married, had me.'

'Did she know who he was? Where he'd come from?'

Now Cesar looked at Lexie, and she almost took a step back at the cynicism etched on his face. He seemed older in that moment.

'Of course she did. That's why she targeted him. If he hadn't died she probably would have persuaded him to return home—especially once they'd had me.'

Lexie tried to hide her dismay at seeing this side of him. He seemed utterly unapproachable at that moment.

'You don't know that for sure, though...' she said, almost hopefully.

'Of course I know,' he dismissed coldly. 'As soon as my father died she brought me here, but my grandparents wanted nothing to do with her. Only me. They realised that their legacy would be secure with an heir. Once she knew there was nothing she could gain, she left.'

Lexie put a hand to her belly in a reflexive action as

the old pain flared inside her hearing his words. To think of the awful wrench it must have been for his mother to give him up. No matter what he said, she couldn't have been that cruel.

'But she came back…? You said that she came back some years later.'

A bleak look flashed across Cesar's face, but it was so fleeting that Lexie wasn't even sure she'd seen it.

'Yes, she did. Maybe she thought she could benefit then. But it was too late.'

'How old were you?'

'Almost seven.'

Lexie gasped. 'But that's so young…you were still so young. Why didn't you go with her?'

Even as she realised that Cesar wasn't going to answer her she had a moment of intuition. He'd been left here when he was so tiny, yet he had been old enough to remember. Remember his mother walking away. Lexie couldn't even begin to imagine what had broken inside him in those years after his mother had left him. Broken so badly that he'd let her walk away from him again.

Cesar stepped back and said, 'We should go. The plane is ready.'

After a short trip in a sleek Land Rover to a local airstrip, Lexie knew she shouldn't have been surprised to see a small private plane waiting for them—reminding her, as if she needed it, just who she was dealing with.

Except the man she was dealing with had just shown her a side of himself that was raw and bleak, and she couldn't stop her chest from aching. Even though she knew that he wouldn't thank her for it. He hadn't had to say a word for her to know that he would scorn the slightest hint of pity.

Cesar parked the car and swung out of the driver's seat

with lithe grace. He'd come around to help Lexie out before she could object, taking her hand in his firm grip.

An assistant took their bags to the plane. The pilot was waiting to greet them, and then they were stepping into the plush, luxurious world of the super-rich. Although Lexie was still a bit too shaken up by what Cesar had revealed to truly enjoy this novel experience.

A steward showed her to her seat solicitously, and Cesar took the seat opposite. There was no waiting for other people to arrive, to sit down. Once they were in they buckled up and the plane was moving.

In a bid to try and shake some of the residual melancholy she felt at hearing about Cesar's less than happy-sounding childhood, Lexie asked, 'So what's the function this evening?'

Cesar stretched out his long legs across the aisle. 'It's a dinner and Spanish music event at the Italian Ambassador's residence.'

Lexie felt her stomach plummet. 'Seriously? But I've never met an ambassador in my life...I won't know what to say—'

He leaned across and took one of her hands out of her lap and held it to his mouth, kissing it. Effectively shutting her up. The air in the cabin seemed to get hot and sultry.

'You don't have to worry about saying anything. They're not going to present you with an IQ questionnaire before dinner to see if you qualify.'

Lexie hated this insecurity that stemmed not only from her dyslexia but from having left school early. 'But they'll be talking about politics and the EU and economics...'

'And,' Cesar replied without hesitation, 'if they do I can't imagine that you wouldn't know just as much if not more than them. These are *people*, Lexie, they're not intellectual giants.'

'Well, you are...' She was being distracted by the hypnotic stroke of Cesar's thumb on the underside of her wrist. His thumb stopped and he frowned at her.

'Where on earth do you get that from?'

Lexie shrugged, feeling exposed again for having researched him in the beginning.

'You're one of the most successful men in the world… you go to economic forums…all those books in your study and apartment…'

Cesar's mouth twisted. 'All those books in my study belong to my family. The only reason I haven't ever got rid of them is in case I need them for reference and for reasons of pure vanity—because they look good.' Then he said, 'Me, though? The books I like reading are popular crime thrillers—nothing more intellectual than that, I assure you.'

Something shifted inside Lexie. An ominous feeling of tenderness welled up.

'And as for school…I was not a natural A student—far from it. I had to work for every one of my grades. Once my grandparents realised this they recruited the local swot—Juan Cortez, who is now the Mayor of Villaporto, the local town—to come and help me.'

The tenderness swelled. 'Are you still friends?'

Cesar smiled. Another rare, proper smile. Lexie had to stop herself from gripping his hand tighter.

'Yes, but only because we nearly killed each other when we were ten.'

Lexie asked impulsively, 'What happened?'

He looked rueful. 'I had issues with someone being smarter than me.' And then he said, 'I'm a hustler, Lexie. I go to these forums and meetings because I have inherited and manage a vast legacy. For a long time I thought I wanted to do what my father had done and turn my back on it, but then I realised that if I did and the fortune got carved up I'd be cutting off my nose to spite my face. I realised that I enjoyed being an entrepreneur—I was good at it. And once my grandparents died I could finally put the family's vast wealth to some good use.'

'How old were you when they died?'

Cesar's easiness vanished. 'Fifteen when my grandfather died and then eighteen when my grandmother died.'

Lexie squeezed his hand but said nothing. She could see the lack of grief for them in his eyes—it was almost defiant. Her own silly heart ached to think of him taking on all that responsibility at such a young age. And as a boy growing up with no love. The thing was, she knew what that felt like—albeit on a different level.

The lack of affection in her own family had come after shattering events and had never been repaired.

The steward appeared then, to offer them some refreshments, and Cesar let her hand go. To Lexie's relief the conversation turned to more neutral topics after that.

It felt like no time at all before they were descending into Madrid, and Lexie looked out of the window eagerly to catch her first glimpse of the capital city.

When they emerged from the plane after landing it was pleasantly warm with a hint of autumnal freshness. A car was waiting for them.

Cesar said in the back of the car, 'We'll go to the apartment and then I'm taking you out on a tour.'

'Okay,' Lexie answered. An incredibly light feeling was bubbling up inside her, and she was determined not to analyse it too carefully.

When Cesar put out his hand for her to come closer she didn't hesitate, sliding along the back seat until she was right beside him. His arm went around her, his fingers splaying provocatively just under Lexie's breast, making her toes curl in her shoes.

His apartment building was on a very grand, wide, tree-lined street. It was an old building, and his apartment was at the top. When he opened the door to let her in Lexie wasn't surprised to see that the same kind of modern design as was in his *castillo* apartment ran through this space too. The old building was the shell, but classic furniture and abstract paintings gave it a very contemporary and slightly eclectic Art Deco aesthetic. It oozed class and luxury. Good taste.

Lexie asked, as he led her down a corridor, 'Did you design this and your other apartment at the *castillo*?'

'Yes. A friend who is an architect helped me. Luc Sanchis. He oversaw the structural work and his team did the interiors.'

'Wow,' Lexie said, awed. Even she'd heard of the famous constructive architect.

Cesar stopped at a door. 'We've also come up with a plan to completely remodel the interior of the *castillo* but it's undergoing a lengthy planning permission process. As you can imagine it's protected because it's so old, and we have to incorporate that integrity with the new design.'

Lexie wrinkled her nose. 'I think it would be great... It's an amazing building, but...'

'Completely stuck in the Middle Ages and not in a good way?'

She smiled. 'If you say so. I couldn't possibly be so rude.'

He reached out and rubbed his thumb along her lower lip. Lexie's blood sizzled. And then, as if he had to make a physical effort to stop touching her, he gritted his jaw and let his hand drop.

He pushed open the door and let her precede him. It was a bedroom, with a massive en-suite bathroom and dressing room. The same Art Deco stamp on the furnishings. She loved it.

'This is your bedroom.'

She turned around, her heart speeding up. He was putting her bags at the bottom of the bed and turning around.

'I'm not even going to say it, Lexie… You know I want you. But this is your space.'

Beyond touched, and reassured in a very deep place that *needed* reassurance, Lexie got out a husky 'Thank you…'

A few hours later Cesar stood at the window in the reception room. He was waiting for Lexie, his hands stuck deep in the pockets of his black trousers. His hands had never itched so much in his life. The previous few hours had been both heaven and hell. Torture.

When he'd asked her how she'd like to see the city and she'd professed an interest in an open-top bus tour that was what they'd done.

He'd never done one of these tours in his life—it was completely alien to anything he'd normally do—but he had noticed them in various cities and always envied the kind of people who went on them.

Lexie had been like a child, her face lighting up to see the beautiful city. And Cesar had ended up inadvertently doing a better job of being tour guide than the actual tour guide. A small crowd had gathered around them on the top of the bus so they could hear his take on the various sites. It had helped that he spoke multiple languages.

Lexie had been laughing when they disembarked, because some of the American tourists had insisted on tipping him—one of the wealthiest men in the world!

In that moment, when Lexie had been laughing, Cesar had felt a dizzying rush of something that was also completely alien to him…it was only now that he could recognise it with a sort of incredulity. *Happiness*.

For a moment he'd felt pure, unadulterated ease. Joy. The blackness that seemed to be his constant companion had dissipated. And it had lasted even as Lexie had asked if they could walk back to the apartment because it wasn't far.

They'd stopped and had coffee and cakes on the way.

Cesar had never, ever spent such an enjoyable couple of hours with anyone.

The threads of that happiness lingered now, like a seductive caress. But Cesar was aware of something very strong inside him that refused to believe it. It was urging him to be vigilant, not to trust in this ephemeral feeling.

Anything that had felt vaguely like this had been ripped away from him at such an early age that now it seemed too...*easy.*

He heard a sound then, and turned around, and when he saw Lexie it was like a punch to his gut—it was that physical.

He couldn't have analysed what she was wearing in any kind of detail. All he knew was that it was black and seemed to cling to every curve she had with a precariousness that made Cesar's body stiffen in wanton reaction. Her shoulders were bare. Her hair was pulled back, revealing her long delicate neck.

She was a goddess.

Cesar walked over to her before he could melt into a pool of unrestrained lust and lock them both in this apartment until she finally gave in to him. He was actually afraid to touch her—afraid that if he did he'd turn into some feral being.

'My car is waiting outside.'

Lexie smiled, but Cesar could see a slight nervousness in her eyes. The thought of dinner? Was she feeling insecure? It made unwelcome protectiveness rise up, but lust was also rising, too, high and fast for him to be able to focus on it or let it bother him.

He let her precede him, her scent light and fresh. Floral. Her long dress swung around her hips and legs, and Cesar all but closed his eyes and sent a prayer up to the God he hadn't consulted in a long time for the ability to show some restraint.

* * *

Lexie was finally relaxing. Although she knew it probably had as much to do with the second glass of wine she was on as the fact that the dinner was proving to be far less scary than she'd thought.

But the location was beyond intimidating in its grandeur. It was a very old palace in the centre of Madrid that had been turned into the Ambassador's residence. If everyone hadn't been in modern clothes it would have been hard to ascertain where the past ended and the present began under the soft, seductive lighting of hundreds of candles.

She'd imagined that people would be talking about complicated fiscal policies and the merits of a single currency, but they were actually far more interested in talking to her about the famous people she'd met and what they were really like.

She felt a large hand on her thigh and her lower body spasmed in pure need. She put her hand over his to remove it, but instead her fingers wound their way through his. Holding him there. Her body and her mind were in two different places...

She smiled brightly at the man beside her and took advantage of the lull in the conversation to turn and face Cesar on her other side.

He looked at her. 'Okay?'

She smiled wryly. 'I've been telling the esteemed Secretary to the Greek Ambassador exactly which celebrity tour he should take his kids on when they go to LA next month.'

Cesar smiled and leant forward to kiss her on the mouth. Lexie found herself wanting to cling to him, her fingers tightening on his on her thigh. *She was ready.* Her heart sped up at the thought even as old tendrils of fear made her trepidatious.

He drew back and his eyes were glowing dark green.

'There's a dance showpiece after dinner. We don't have to stay if you don't want to.'

Lexie shook her head, giving in to that fear like a coward, delaying the moment of inevitability. 'No, it's fine. I'd like to see it.'

As the dinner ended and they moved into the room where the showpiece was taking place Lexie seemed to be existing in a haze of shimmering heat. She was acutely aware of Cesar's every move.

Their afternoon on the bus had been delicious torture. Cesar had been dressed down, in jeans and a casual top and jacket. He'd pressed so close against her that she had barely taken in a word he'd said about any of the stunning monuments and squares they'd seen, all too aware of him.

He'd been so gracious and patient when the other tourists had wanted to listen to his explanations and she'd seen another side of him completely. He wasn't as misanthropic as first impressions would have led Lexie to believe—far from it. But she wondered if he even realised that himself.

They had front row seats for the dance performance— by a flamenco dancer. When the lights went down a hush went around the crowd and then a lone guitar started playing the most hauntingly beautiful Spanish music.

Lexie glanced at Cesar to find him staring at her with an intensity that made her insides liquefy. Only with extreme effort could she look away.

A spotlight lit up the small stage and a beautiful dark-haired woman with the lithe body of a dancer walked into the middle. She wore a long red dress, very plain and simple, red shoes, and a red flower in her hair.

She made the most exquisite shapes with her hands and body—typical flamenco postures. Then the hard soles and heels of her shoes started hitting the boards of the stage as the rhythm of the guitar picked up pace. Tiny hairs stood up on the back of Lexie's neck.

It was mesmerising. There was something so elemental and beautiful about this woman and the power in her body. It made a ball of emotion lodge in Lexie's chest and throat. She was acutely aware of the man beside her, of his sheer overwhelming masculinity. Something seemed to be flowing between them through the beat of the music, even though their thighs and arms were barely touching. It was carnal and earthy. Sexual.

The beat and power of the dancer's feet seemed to resonate with Lexie's heartbeat. Cesar had unlocked something powerful within her—something that she was finally connecting with herself after such a long time.

The beat of her own sexuality.

It was something she'd feared lost for ever, stolen from her too long ago ever to claim it back. Lexie wanted to look at Cesar again, but she was afraid that if she did, and he was looking at her, he'd see how raw her desire for him was.

She could see the sheen of exertion on the dancer's skin. The music and the dance were building and building. Lexie fancied she must have a similar sheen to *her* skin…she felt so hot. The expression on the woman's beautiful face was intense as her feet beat out the relentless passionate rhythm. Lexie felt it rise up through her body too.

As the music and the dance reached a crescendo, and as if he could sense how affected she was, Cesar's hand closed around Lexie's, his fingers twining through hers with an unmistakably possessive touch.

Her nipples pricked painfully. She was breathing harshly, every part of her body tingling with desire for the man beside her, as the music exploded and the woman came to a dead stop with her arms high in a proud and beautiful pose, her chest heaving with exertion. People started to clap rapturously. But still Lexie was almost afraid to look at Cesar.

'Lexie?'

She finally turned her head towards him and her world coalesced down to this moment and this man. She wanted him with a fierce drumbeat of need.

Another performer was coming on and she said impulsively, 'Would you mind if we left now?'

Cesar shook his head, a frankly explicit look coming into his eyes as if he could read what was on her mind, feel her desire. 'No—let's go before the next act starts.'

By the time they were walking out Lexie had taken deep breaths and regained some control. But she still trembled all over. Never had anything impacted her in such a deeply physical and visceral way as it had sitting beside this man and wanting him so badly that their very surroundings seemed to echo with it.

They were at the front of the residence now and Cesar's car was pulling up. The driver opened the door for her and Cesar got in on the other side. He reached for her almost immediately and Lexie went willingly.

Their mouths met and their kiss was hungry and desperate. Lexie's blood thundered and roared. She was still borne aloft on the sheer exhilaration of the dance. She drowned in the kiss, in the rough stroke of Cesar's tongue against hers and the feel of his arms around her.

By the time they reached the apartment she was half sitting on his lap, arms around his neck, mouth swollen, breathing fast.

Gently he took her arms down and opened his door before stepping out. He reached in and Lexie had one crazy moment of thinking she could just shut the door, instruct the driver to drive all the way back to the *castillo* and shut out the clamours of her body.

But she didn't. She'd already proved to herself that she was strong enough to withstand the worst things that could happen to a woman. She was certainly strong enough to withstand reclaiming her body and her right to sensual pleasure.

Lexie put her hand in Cesar's and let him pull her out. Keeping a tight grip on her hand, as if he was aware that a rogue part of her still wanted to escape, he greeted the concierge and led her to the lift. Once inside they didn't speak. But the air hummed with awareness and expectation. It was heavy.

When they entered his apartment and the door closed behind them the silence swirled around them. Lexie's heart was beating so hard she thought it had to be audible.

Cesar shrugged off his jacket and threw it over a chair haphazardly. Looking at Lexie, he pulled at his bow tie, undoing it. She was clutching her bag tightly, her eyes glued to his mouth, wanting it on hers again.

He reached down and took her bag, threw it aside to join his jacket. Then he put his hands on her arms.

'You're sure?'

After a moment Lexie nodded and said, 'I've never been more sure of anything in my life. Make love to me, Cesar.'

CHAPTER SEVEN

FOR A MOMENT Cesar did nothing, and a wave of cold clammy horror gripped Lexie as she imagined being rejected. But then he dipped, and she let out a little squeal when he lifted her into his arms against his chest.

He strode down the corridor, past her bedroom to another door on the opposite side. Lexie took in no details of the room he walked into beyond the fact that it was dark, palatial and had a massive bed.

He walked right over to it and let Lexie down, before reaching for a light and switching it on to put out a pool of golden light.

Light, Lexie thought. *Light is good*. The enormity of what she was doing was sinking in.

Reverently Cesar put his hands on Lexie's shoulders. She tried to calm her thundering pulse. Then he turned her around and it went haywire again.

He pulled the pins from her hair until it fell down. Then he brushed it aside over one shoulder. Lexie shivered when she felt him come close behind her, wrapping an arm around her midriff and pressing a kiss to her bare shoulder.

His fingers were on her zip at the back of her dress. Slowly, so slowly, he started to pull it down. The dress loosened around her chest and she curled her hands into

fists to stop herself from impeding its progress as it fell
forward and down.

Now she was bare from the waist up except for a strap-
less lace bra.

Cesar's hand had drawn the zip all the way to the top
of her buttocks, where it ended. Then with both hands he
pushed it over her hips so that it fell to the floor. She was
aware of a rough indrawn breath, and then his hand was
cupping her bottom in her silk French knickers, smoothing over her hip.

Her legs were losing their ability to hold her upright.

When he put his hands on her shoulders again, to turn
her around, Lexie looked down. She felt hot, excited and
scared. All at once. Cesar's hands were on her waist, pulling her into him.

'Lexie…look at me.'

She bit her lip, but looked up. His face was flushed,
eyes glittering like dark jewels. His gaze dropped to her
mouth, and then lower. Her skin went on fire.

He lifted a hand and cupped one breast. Her nipples
were hard and stinging. Pushing against the lace of her bra.
He brushed his thumb across one nipple, making Lexie
gasp. Making her want more. *His mouth*.

Cesar sank back onto the bed and pulled her into him.
Lexie nearly stumbled in her shoes and she kicked them
off jerkily, steadying herself on his shoulders.

His hands closed around her waist again, and with her
breasts at easy reaching distance for his mouth he explored
her through the lace, his tongue laving the lace-covered
tips, first one and then the other.

Lexie's hands were like claws gripping his shoulders. It
was torture. The stinging chafing of the lace against those
throbbing moist peaks. She almost sobbed with relief when
he reached around to undo her bra and then cupped one

breast before he encircled that aching naked tip with his wicked, hot mouth. It was exquisite.

Her hands moved to Cesar's head, fingers threading through silky strands of hair. When he tried to draw back she had to release him. She looked down, dazed, drunk. Instinctively she reached for his shirt, undoing his buttons, her breasts swaying with her movement.

He took over, emitting a soft growl of impatience when a button got caught, ripping it apart and off. Then his chest was bare. And gorgeous. Lexie had to sink down onto one thigh, unable to stand any more.

Cesar caught her to him with a strong arm, his other hand finding her chin and angling it so that he could plunder her mouth in a scorching hot kiss. He let that hand trail down to cup and massage her breast again, fingers pinching her stiff nipple.

Lexie squirmed. Between her legs she was stinging. Moist. Sensing her need even before she acknowledged it, Cesar moved his hand down over her waist. He pushed her legs open, his mouth still on hers, distracting her, until she felt those fingers exploring the delicate skin of her inner thigh. She held her breath as they trailed over her sex, hidden under the silk of her panties.

Lexie broke the kiss. Cesar's eyes were half lidded, hot with need. She was clinging to him and his hand was *there*, right where she felt swollen and needy. He was pressing against her flesh, moving rhythmically.

In a fast-moving world that had been reduced to all things physical Lexie tried to cling onto reality and the feeling that she could trust Cesar.

She put her hand on his wrist, stopping his movements, and said threadily, 'I don't want you to hurt me.'

He could never know the wealth of history behind that plea.

He frowned and removed his hand, bringing it up to touch her jaw again.

'I would never hurt you. We'll take this slow, okay?'

Lexie nodded. Relief flooded her. In a smooth move, Cesar lifted her from his lap and onto the bed. She sank back and looked up, watching him undo his trousers and push them down.

Her eyes widened on the bulge in his boxers, and they widened even more when he'd dispensed with the rest of his clothes and put his hands to the edges of those boxers. He pushed them down and his erection was freed.

Lexie waited for rejection, revulsion, fear…but it didn't come. She only felt intense excitement. And need. Euphoria bubbled up inside her. Lightness. When Cesar bent down and put his hands to her panties she lifted her hips to let him pull them down.

His body was awe-inspiring. He was a very masculine man in his prime. Broad through the chest and shoulders, slimming to lean hips, and down to powerful buttocks and thighs.

He came down on the bed beside her, on one arm, and looked at her. His gaze left scorching hot trails where it rested on her curves. 'You're more beautiful than anything I've ever seen.' He ran his hand up and down her body, barely skimming, teasing her.

Lexie touched his jaw reverently, feeling the tough line under her fingers, following the line of his cheek down to his mouth, tracing that sensual shape.

Her belly contracted when he caught her hand and sucked one finger deep. Then he took her finger out of his mouth and, not taking his eyes off her, trailed his hand down over her breasts to the curls protecting her sex.

Gently, he encouraged her to open her legs. Lexie held her breath. Keeping the heel of his hand against her, he explored her with his finger, seeking the seam of her body and parting it, releasing her desire to smooth his passage.

She was breathing again, but it was laboured as Cesar moved his fingers over her and pressed his palm against her. Without her even knowing it Lexie's body was moving, hips twitching, circling, seeking more.

He bent his head and took her mouth, and she almost sobbed into it when she felt him thrust one finger inside her. Her hands had to hold onto something and she found his arms, fingers digging into hard muscles. Cesar shifted and she could feel his erection against her hip.

She was too shy to reach out and touch it, but she wanted to. Wanted to explore what all that power would feel like encased in silken skin.

But right now his finger was moving in and out of her body and causing sensations such as Lexie had never experienced before. There was a delicious tightening feeling, building and building. An urgency. A desire for more.

When one finger became two, and Cesar's tongue thrust deep into her mouth, her hands tightened on him.

He broke away. '*Dios*…you're so responsive…I don't know how slow I can go…you're killing me.'

Lexie blinked. Cesar looked like a dark golden lion in the dim light. She whispered throatily, 'Don't go slow.'

He gazed at her, his breath coming sharp and fast. He was on the edges of his control…she could sense it. Right then Lexie felt invincible. Strong. In control.

Cesar disappeared for a moment and Lexie heard a drawer open and shut, then the sound of foil ripping. He came back and she saw him smoothing protection onto his erection.

A spurt of jealousy that he was touching himself so intimately caught her unawares, making her want to giggle with the sheer joy of discovering her own body again. Of being here and feeling *safe*.

Cesar came over her, careful not to crush her, but the weight of his naked body over hers was something Lexie craved. She reached for his body, clasping him, urging him down.

He cursed. 'I don't want to hurt you.'

'You won't,' she said, and meant it, feeling emotional.

Lexie felt him push her legs apart further with his hips, stretching her. Poised above her, he nearly undid her when he pushed some hair back off her hot cheek and pressed a kiss to her mouth. As if somehow…he *knew*.

And then she felt him—hard, forceful, pushing into her, seeking her acceptance. Her body resisted and Lexie sucked in a breath. She willed herself not to let the darkness of her past reach out to poison this moment. She willed her body to relax, to *trust*.

After several heart-stopping moments, punctuated only by their harsh breathing, she felt a shift and Cesar's body slid in a little more. Filling her.

'You're so small…so tight.'

She moved her hips experimentally and earned herself a long, low growl from Cesar that sounded feral.

She could see the cost of his restraint showing on his face, in his tense shoulders. He reached down a hand and moved it under her thigh, encouraging her to lift her leg around his waist.

The movement brought him deeper into her body, and now Lexie groaned as excitement built, a restless, surging yearning for a deeper connection between their bodies.

She lifted her other leg and Cesar pulled out before sliding back in, his body huge and powerful. He angled his body so that he was thrusting as deep as possible. He put a hand between them and found the cluster of cells at the juncture of her thighs. Lexie gasped out loud as that building excitement shot right through her core.

Her whole body was alive with a deep mystical energy, coiling and binding her to this man with an invisible weave. Cesar's chest touched hers, hair a delicious friction against her breasts. Lexie arched her back to ask mindlessly for *more*.

Cesar's movements were becoming more urgent, stronger. Faster. Her heels were digging into his muscular buttocks, driving his body deeper into hers, holding him to her.

She could feel wave after wave of ecstasy washing through her until they gathered such force that she begged Cesar to release her from the torture and let her fly. But she wasn't coherent.

He bent his head and kissed her. 'It's okay, *querida*, I'll catch you.'

Those words unlocked the tension and Lexie soared on a blissful plateau of pleasure so intense that it was almost painful. And as she fell, feeling the powerful contractions of her body around Cesar's, she bit his shoulder to stop herself from screaming out loud. His own body tensed powerfully before he let out a guttural shout, and he fell just behind her.

Cesar's brain was in meltdown. Even now he could still feel the ripples of Lexie's orgasm keeping his body hard, not letting him come down completely from the most intense climax he'd ever experienced.

It was the most difficult thing in the world to break the connection between their bodies, but Cesar gritted his jaw and moved, releasing them both. Lexie winced minutely. Her eyes were wide, cheeks flushed, hair in disarray around her head.

He moved so that he didn't crush her and came onto his side, pulling her into him so that they were face to face. Normally when Cesar made love to a woman he felt the overwhelming need to get away. Right now it was the last thing on his mind. She fitted him. One leg was still looped over his thigh. The centre of her body was still flush with his, doing little to help his arousal subside.

He could only look at her. The expression on her face was as stunned as he felt. A lock of hair was across one hot cheek, damp with her sweat. He raised a hand, noted vaguely that it was trembling, and tucked her hair behind her ear.

As his normal faculties returned Cesar was aware of feeling more and more vulnerable. But still he couldn't seem to move, to be able to unweld his arms from around her.

Then he saw a brightness in her gaze in the dim light. Her mouth wobbling even as she bit into her lower lip to disguise it. Cesar's belly dropped as if from a great height as something very cold lanced him. He'd just assumed... been so focused on how intense it had been for him... Even though he'd believed it had been the same for her, but she was so small...

He could feel tremors in Lexie's body now—as if she was experiencing a delayed reaction. Cesar moved and came up on one arm, cold terror trickling through him. 'Did I hurt you?'

Rapidly she shook her head and Cesar saw her eyes fill in earnest now, felt the tremors in her body getting stronger. Her cheeks paled. Was she going into some kind of shock?

Her body, which had felt so warm and languorous seconds before, now felt cold. Galvanised by increasing panic, Cesar gathered Lexie into his arms and stood up from the bed, taking her with him. She curled up against his chest, making something like bile fill him at the thought that he'd hurt her. She said nothing.

He walked into the bathroom and straight into the shower, where he turned on the powerful spray of hot water and stood them both under it. He felt Lexie gasp, her body curl even tighter into him, and he also felt those tremors increase as she started crying in earnest.

Her face was buried in his chest and her slim back was heaving with the force of her sobs as her hands pressed against him.

Cesar felt as if his chest was being ripped apart by bare hands. 'Lexie...*Dios*...please tell me...did I hurt you?'

She shook her head against him. The slimmest sliver of relief went through him. Cesar rested his back against the wall and wasn't even sure how long he stayed like that, under the powerful spray, while Lexie sobbed in his arms. He could still feel the power of the emotion running through her slim body.

Eventually the storm passed and she became still. They were surrounded in hot steam. She started to move, and then he heard a husky, rough-sounding, 'You can put me down. I'm okay.'

Reluctantly, even though his arms were stiff, Cesar let her down until she stood. She wouldn't look at him and he had to tip her chin up. When he saw those huge bruised eyes and her swollen mouth he had to curb his almost instantaneous reaction. *Again*. Already...

'Lexie...what...?'

She shook her head, came close, put her hands on his chest. 'You didn't hurt me...' Her voice sounded raw. 'The opposite. I promise.'

Cesar frowned as water ran in rivulets down their bodies, plastering their hair to their skulls. 'But...why?'

Lexie ducked her head, resting her forehead against him for a moment and making something incredibly alien flood through Cesar. Then she looked up again, 'I just... It's never been like that. That's all.'

Cesar had the distinct feeling that that *wasn't* all, but

something held him back from forcing her to explain. He hadn't hurt her. The relief was almost overwhelming.

'Come on,' he said gruffly. 'Let's get out.'

He turned off the water and stepped out, reaching back for Lexie. She emerged from the steam, taking his hand, and he couldn't stop his gaze from devouring those naked curves greedily. She was looking at him too, and Cesar had to stop himself from pressing her up against the shower wall and taking her there and then.

Instead he wrapped a towel around her and her hair. She stood as mute as a child and let him dry her off, and after he'd dried himself roughly he took her back into the bedroom.

He dropped his towel and gently took hers off and led her back to the bed. Her hair was damp but she didn't look inclined to dry it. He could see her eyes heavy with the need to sleep. Heavy after the outpouring of emotion that had left tentacles of panic inside him at the thought that he'd hurt her.

She crawled into the bed and lay down, and Cesar looked at her before getting in beside her. This was anathema to him—sharing a bed after lovemaking. But it was something he wasn't in a position to question right now.

Lexie burrowed straight into his arms, wrapping her legs around him, resting her head on his chest. Those soft abundant curves melted into him. His heart thudding unevenly, it was only when he could feel her body relax into sleep and her hold on him loosen that he was able to relax himself.

When Lexie woke up she opened her eyes and blinked at the dawn light coming in through long grand windows. She felt completely disorientated. Her body felt...different. Heavy. Lethargic. *Sated*. Hers...

She became aware of something moving steadily under

her cheek. *Cesar's chest.* She lifted her head and looked up to see him asleep. Dark stubble lined his jaw. And then her eye caught something else and she let out a small gasp of dismay.

A neat row of small teeth marks scored the flesh of his shoulder. And suddenly Lexie was back in that moment of such extreme pleasure that she'd had to bite him to keep from screaming.

She ducked her head again quickly, face burning. It all came back…every scorching moment. Taking him into her body had been far more momentous and emotional than she would ever have imagined it might be.

She'd cried like a baby.

Lexie cringed to think of how she'd curled up into his chest and sobbed. How he'd asked if he'd hurt her. Far from it. She felt almost guilty—as if she'd misled him by not telling him about herself. As if she'd taken something she only had half a right to. This man would never know the precious gift he'd unwittingly given her.

A sense of liberation from the dark past rushed up in a giddying sweep of emotion so physically acute that Lexie had to move or risk waking him. And she wasn't ready for that assessing gaze to land on her just yet.

Moving stealthily, she managed to extricate herself and climb out of the bed without disturbing Cesar, who lay in a louche, sexy sprawl. She couldn't help stopping for a moment and looking at him covetously. He was so beautiful…his skin a deep olive, his chest broad and powerful, and lower… Her face burned even hotter at the thought of how he'd felt moving inside her. So gentle but so powerful.

Emotion tightened like a fist around her heart. On first acquaintance with this man, she never could have imagined he'd have so many hidden depths, or have the capacity to be so…*considerate.*

Lexie immediately dismissed the direction of her

thoughts when a kind of panic seized her guts. She had to lock off her emotions. This was purely physical. She'd gone into this with eyes wide open. It was an affair. And when the time came she would walk away with her head held high.

Lexie grabbed up her things and crept out of the room. Once she was in her own room she had a shower, before donning faded comfy jeans and a V-necked cashmere top. She pulled her hair back into a ponytail and went to find the kitchen.

Lexie had found a radio station playing classical Spanish music and was blissfully unaware of the tall man resting his shoulder against the door, arms crossed, as she made breakfast.

It was only when she turned around to find some salt and pepper that she saw him and nearly jumped out of her skin.

He straightened. 'Sorry, I didn't mean to startle you.'

Lexie flushed, still not ready to see him. Already a hum was starting in her blood. 'You didn't…' She flushed some more. 'I mean, you did—but it's okay.'

He was bare-chested and wearing jeans with the top button open. Lexie nearly melted. Her body was unaccustomed to this overload of sensations and desires.

He came into the kitchen, right up to her, and growled softly, 'I woke up alone.'

'I just…I woke up and you were asleep,' Lexie stammered. 'I didn't want to disturb you.'

A look she couldn't identify came into his eyes and he said, 'You didn't.'

He bent then, and pressed his mouth to hers. In an instant she was on fire, her mouth opening under his, seeking more. When he pulled back she was breathing fast.

She was out of her depth. This whole morning-after thing was totally alien to her.

In a bid to try and disguise her discomfiture Lexie turned back to where she was frying some eggs and bacon, glancing over her shoulder. 'I hope you don't mind… I found some food in the fridge. Are you hungry?'

She was babbling now.

Cesar just leant back against the island in the kitchen and said huskily, 'I'm starving.'

But the look he sent up and down Lexie's body told her he didn't mean for food. She bit her lip and tried to ignore her body's reaction. Was this even normal?

Somehow she managed to make something resembling breakfast and coffee, and to serve it up without it ending up all over the floor.

The state-of-the-art kitchen in Cesar's apartment led into a large open-plan dining/living space. She sat down at the table there and noticed that there were Sunday papers, and—thankfully—that Cesar had put a top on.

He saw her glance at the papers and explained, 'The concierge drops them in if I'm here.'

Lexie spotted something that piqued her interest and pulled one of the more tabloid-looking papers out of the pile—only to realise that the press had managed to catch her and Cesar on their open-top bus tour.

There were also pictures of them walking hand in hand back to the apartment.

Something about that sent acute disappointment to her gut. It had been a spontaneous moment. This tainted the memory. She said faintly, 'I never imagined they could have known that we'd be doing that.'

Cesar took a sip of coffee and said, almost absent-mindedly, 'I called my assistant—told her to tip them off anonymously.'

Something cold slithered into Lexie's gut. She put down

her fork and looked at Cesar and brought up a dim recollection of him on his phone briefly at one stage on the bus.

'But....' Lexie was about to ask him *why* when she stopped herself. Of *course* he'd wanted to tip them off. They were meant to be courting the press—for both their benefits. Why waste an opportunity to document it?

'But...?' he asked.

She hated to think it, even to acknowledge it, but she felt betrayed. And she shouldn't be feeling that. Because if she did then it meant that Cesar had attained a significance for her that she had no control over.

She forced a smile and shook her head. 'But nothing. Of course you should have tipped them off. It was a good opportunity to let them see us.'

Cesar watched Lexie continuing to eat her breakfast and something twisted inside him. She looked so young, so innocent.

When he'd woken up alone in the bed his immediate reaction had been irritation that she'd left. He'd been about to go and find her when he'd remembered her tears, that incredible outpouring of emotion, and like a coward he'd stopped. Not sure if he was ready to face that searing blue gaze in the morning light.

The look in her eyes just now, though, made him feel like a heel. His own conscience mocked him. Making that call to his assistant yesterday had come out of a gut reaction to how Lexie's lit-up face and smile had made him feel. A gut reaction to doing something so out of his comfort zone. Cesar didn't *do* quirky, fun sightseeing tours with lovers. He didn't engage with the public. But he had—and moreover he'd found himself enjoying it.

He was dark and brooding, and most people ran a mile when they saw him. But not when he was with Lexie.

And that, frankly, had terrified him. So he'd called Mercedes and once he'd instructed her to alert the press he'd felt that he *hadn't* lost his mind completely.

Now, absurdly, he felt guilty.

Lexie was taking a sip of coffee, wiping her mouth, avoiding his eyes. Cesar reached out and took her hand. He saw her tense and that guilt intensified. *Damn her.*

Warily she looked at him.

Carefully Cesar said, 'Our becoming lovers was inevitable. Diverting the media is a beneficial consequence for both of us.'

Lexie blinked. Cesar saw how her expression became inscrutable, hidden.

'Of course. I know that. Don't worry, Cesar, I'm not some soft-hearted teenager who is weaving fantasies around a happy-ever-after scenario. I know that doesn't exist. Believe me.'

Something about the harshness of her tone caught at Cesar's chest, making it ache even as everything within him urged him to agree with her, to feel relieved.

She stood up to take their plates and Cesar caught her wrist, said gruffly, 'Leave it. My housekeeper will attend to it later, when we're gone.'

He tugged her towards him until she put down the plates and fell, resisting, into his lap.

She huffed out, 'What are you doing?'

The feel of her soft, lithe body against his made a lie of every one of Cesar's last words. All he could think about was how much he wanted this woman. But Lexie was stiff in his arms and that made him feel slightly desperate.

His hand was on her waist and he could feel a sliver of silky skin under her top. He explored underneath, over the indent of her naked waist and higher. Already he could feel the effect, the softening and relaxing of her body into his.

'Lexie…'

Slowly she turned her head to his, and for a moment

there was something unguarded in the depths of her eyes. Something very raw and pained. But it didn't make Cesar want to run.

His exploring hand came into contact with the bare swell of her breast. *No bra.* And just like that lust surged between them, red-hot and powerful. Their mouths connected, their kiss deepened, Lexie groaned softly and Cesar cupped the full weight of that breast in his hand.

Weakly he drowned out the clamouring voices in his head that told him he was deluding himself if he believed that he was half as in control of this as he would have Lexie believe.

CHAPTER EIGHT

'*LET'S GO AGAIN,* folks.'

Lexie clenched her jaw. This was the thirteenth take, and if she fluffed her lines one more time more than one crew member would want to wring her neck. Including herself. The director called *action* and by some miracle Lexie managed to get through the dialogue with no mishaps.

There was an audible sigh of relief around the set. Everyone was tired. It was the end of the third week and fatigue was setting in. The prospect of another week here and then two weeks in London stretched like a never-ending horizon line.

As they called that scene complete and started to set up for the next one Lexie was whisked back to the unit base for a costume-change. She relished the time to try and gather her scattered and fragmented thoughts.

Since the previous cataclysmic weekend, and their return to the *castillo* from Madrid on Sunday, Lexie had been avoiding Cesar at every opportunity. It didn't help that he was almost constantly on set—hence her fluffed lines and general state of being flustered. But today he hadn't shown up, and that had nearly been worse.

Lexie was terrified that she'd gone and fallen for the first man who had come along and kissed her whole body awake—much like Sleeping Beauty in the fairy tale.

That was why she'd been avoiding Cesar all week. She

felt as if she wasn't in control of these new and overwhelming desires. It was like having a car and not really knowing how to drive it—being afraid that if she got behind the wheel it would careen off the road and cause mayhem and destruction.

She felt feverish, excited. Exactly like the soft-hearted teenager she'd mocked only days ago.

That weekend he'd only had to pull her onto his lap and kiss her before she'd been reduced to a puddle of lust, letting him take her back to bed and make love to her again and again. Showing her the heights her body could attain with just the barest sweep of his clever fingers against her body's core.

He had no idea who he was dealing with. The dark secrets Lexie harboured. But every time Cesar touched her she felt more and more exposed—as if sooner or later she wouldn't be able to stop it all tumbling out. Baring her soul to him.

So she'd been avoiding him. Like a coward. Even though all she could think about and dream about and yearn for was him.

It was affecting her work. And it didn't help that one scene in particular was due to be shot at the beginning of the following week and Lexie was dreading it, but unable to say anything to anyone about it.

After her dresser had left Lexie waited for the call to go back to set, pacing up and down her trailer, repeating her lines, trying to force all other thoughts out of her head.

When a knock came on her trailer door she said distractedly, 'I'll be out in a minute,' assuming that it was the call for set. But then the door opened and Lexie whirled around, copious amounts of silken layers rustling as she did so, only to see Cesar coming up the steps and entering.

Immediately the relatively big space was tiny. He closed the door behind him. He looked dark, gorgeous. Intent.

Lexie was breathless, and it only had a little to do with her costume. 'You shouldn't be here—they'll be calling for me in a minute.'

Cesar crossed his arms. '*Here* seems to be the only place I can find you without you avoiding me or hiding in your room.'

Lexie flushed, her whole body tingling just to be near him. She couldn't deny the sheer excitement that gripped her, the anticipation at the look in Cesar's eye. Especially when his gaze dropped to the swells of her breasts, made even more provocative than usual in the dress.

Lord, she wanted him right now. *Here*. Like some lurid parody of the stories she'd heard of actors and actresses behaving badly while shooting on location.

Cesar came towards her and Lexie had nowhere to escape to. He wrapped an arm around her waist and pulled her into him. Her body sang and, bizarrely, something inside her calmed. She felt more centred.

'Why have you been avoiding me all week?' he growled.

'Work…I need to concentrate on my work,' Lexie blurted out weakly.

His eyes flashed. 'Well, you're singularly to blame for *me* not being able to concentrate on a single thing.'

'Really?' Inordinate pleasure snaked through Lexie to hear that. To imagine this stern, unflappable man being distracted because of her. She felt like smiling.

'I don't play games, Lexie.'

She blanched. 'You think…you think I'm playing some *game*?'

His jaw was set, stern. Her belly swooped.

'Cesar…I'm not playing a game… I was avoiding you because last weekend… It's just been a long time for me.' *Try for ever,* said a small voice, but she blocked it out. 'I'm not used to this—I don't have *affairs*.'

Flustered, she ducked her head. Cesar put a finger to her chin to tip her face back up.

His gaze dropped to her cleavage and his voice was rough. '*Dios*...do you know what it does to me to see you in these dresses?' His eyes met hers again and his arm tightened around her. 'Come to my apartment this evening.'

Resistance was futile. Lexie felt herself dissolving, aching to say *yes*, let him take control so she didn't have to think or analyse. Just *be*.

'Okay.' She smiled, unable to keep it in.

Cesar was about to kiss her when a knock came on the door and a PA called out, 'Lexie, they're ready for you.'

Cesar stopped and Lexie almost groaned. 'Okay, thanks,' she called back.

Then he smiled, and it was wicked. 'I'll cook dinner. Come by when you've wrapped. Bring a weekend bag.'

Lexie almost rolled her eyes, 'My room is in the *castillo*. If I need anything surely I can just ?'

Cesar cut her off. 'Just...do it.'

'Okay,' Lexie said again, her smile turning wry at his autocratic tone.

She let Cesar lead her out to where her driver was waiting in the car to take her back to the set.

The following day Lexie grumbled good-naturedly, '*Why* can't you tell me where we're going?'

Cesar stopped abruptly and Lexie almost careened into him. He caught her hands and held them. The breeze had mussed up his hair. He looked vital, and so gorgeous that she sighed with pure appreciation. He looked darker too, all dressed in black.

He was mock stern. 'Just do as you're told.'

Lexie saw a staff member carrying their bags to a waiting helicopter. It was sitting on a landing pad at the back of the *castillo*.

Cesar had woken her early that morning and she'd stretched like a satisfied cat amongst his very tousled sheets before she'd even really realised the enormity of where she was.

In Cesar's bed, in his private apartment. After a night of lovemaking that had almost brought her to tears again. She'd only held them back with gritted teeth, determined not to let him see her get so emotional again.

But she couldn't help it. With every touch, every kiss, this man was rebuilding the very fabric of her soul. A fabric that had been torn apart brutally years before.

As instructed, she'd packed some things the previous evening and had gone to his apartment after work to find him waiting for her, busy in his kitchen making dinner. The sight had been so incongruous and so...*sexy* that Lexie had struggled to affect a nonchalance she hadn't felt.

Before she could say anything else Cesar took her by the hand and led her to the helicopter, bundling her inside. Lexie gave up trying to figure out where they were going and did as she was told, putting on earphones and buckling up.

Cesar leant over from his seat to help her just as the rotor blades started up outside, and adrenalin and excitement kicked in her belly.

He grinned at her. 'Don't worry—you'll like it, I promise.' And then he pressed a swift kiss to her mouth and sat back.

Lexie scowled at him, hating that his grin made her heart clench and that he could so easily affect her. But then her mind emptied as the chopper rose smoothly into the air and she saw the *castillo* drop away underneath them.

Cesar had obviously asked the pilot to take a tour of the estate, and he pointed out vineyards and more land than she had ever realised belonged to him. It was truly mind-boggling. And sobering to realise the extent of his responsibilities.

Then they were banking and heading away from where the sun had risen only a short while before. Lexie was transfixed by the changing landscape underneath them as they passed over low mountains and rivers.

Eventually she could see that the sparse countryside was making way for more built-up areas. Cesar took her hand and pointed out of the main window of the helicopter. She could make out a smudge of blue...*the sea*?

She glanced at him and he smiled. One of those rare smiles that made her want to smile back like a loon. She could see that they were flying over what had to be a city. The rooftops were terra-cotta, glinting in the sun. She saw a very majestic-looking castle on a hill.

They seemed, impossibly, to be heading right for the city centre. Lexie could see a bridge spanning a huge river, and the way the city was spread out on hills. It didn't look especially modern. There were trams and beautiful old crumbling buildings covered in coloured tiles.

She gasped and turned to Cesar and shouted over the noise, 'Lisbon?'

He nodded. So that's why he'd told her to pack her passport. A rush of incredible emotion and gratitude filled Lexie. She remembered standing in his study that day and exclaiming with a feeling of panic that she wanted to visit Madrid, Salamanca and Lisbon.

So far he'd taken her to all of them.

The helicopter set down on the rooftop of a building and Cesar helped her out. Lexie realised it was a hotel when the staff greeted them and led them inside where solicitous customs officials were waiting for them to check their passports. Cesar took her hand once they were done and she sent him a quick, dry look. 'No queues for you?'

Cesar smiled. 'My name, Da Silva, isn't strictly Spanish in origin. It comes from a very distant Portuguese ancestor. So I'm allowed…certain liberties…'

Lexie all but rolled her eyes as one of the staff got Cesar's attention. She'd just bet he was allowed untold liberties for the promise of his favour and business opportunities. The fact that he was obviously a regular visitor to Lisbon told her that he didn't take advantage of their respect and that made her feel soft inside.

They went one floor down and were shown into the most sumptuous suite of rooms Lexie had ever seen.

She explored on her own and found a terrace outside the bedroom's French doors. She went out. The view was astounding. She could see the huge imposing castle up on a nearby hill, lots of steep streets with distinctive yellow trams. And then what had to be the River Tagus, spanned by a massive bridge.

She felt a presence behind her and then arms came around her, hands resting by hers on the rail. Lexie shut her eyes for a second at the way her body wanted to melt, and when Cesar pressed close behind her she *did* melt into him, blocking out the voices screaming *Danger! Danger!*

One of his hands disappeared and she felt her hair being tugged back gently, so her neck was bared. Breath feathered there and then she felt his mouth, warm and firm. Lexie's hands tightened on the rail and the view became blurry.

She turned around to face him and looked up. His eyes were heavy-lidded, full of something dark and hot. A pulse throbbed between Lexie's legs.

'I have a whole agenda laid out for you today, Miss Anderson.'

Lexie arched a brow and tried to be cool. 'Oh, you do?'

Cesar nodded, and took some of her bright hair between two fingers. He tugged gently again and his eyes rose to hers.

'And right now I have something very specific in mind.'
Lexie was already breathless. 'You do…?'

'Yes.'

And then, with devastating precision, Cesar's mouth closed over hers and Lexie didn't care where she was in the world as long as she was right in this moment.

'A nightcap?'

Lexie looked at Cesar and nodded. 'That'd be nice, thanks.'

She watched as he turned and went to the drinks cabinet, her eyes devouring his tall, lean form sheathed in a dark trousers and a light shirt. He'd already shrugged off his jacket.

Lexie was reeling after the day. Not wanting Cesar to see how overwhelmed she was, she made her way out to the terrace that was accessible through the living room too. She heard the faint sound of a mobile and Cesar's deep tones as he answered.

A quiver of relief went through her—a moment alone, to try and assimilate everything. She sucked in the evening air, hoping it might cool her hot cheeks. They'd felt permanently hot since Cesar had made love to her that morning.

Afterwards, when she'd been sated and replete, he hadn't let her burrow back under the covers as she'd wanted to. He'd all but washed and dressed her, picking out a pretty shirt and jeans, sneakers.

They'd left the hotel and a car had taken them up to the impressive St George's castle, with its breathtaking views of the city. Peacocks had strutted on the paths, fanning their colourful tails much to the delight of the tourists

Then, as if reading Lexie's mind, he'd taken her on one of the old yellow trams down a steep hill. It had been so packed that Cesar had pulled her into his body in front of him, arms wrapped tight around her. By the time he'd pulled her out at another stop she had been thoroughly turned on.

She'd found herself being led though a dizzying labyrinth of ancient streets. Cesar had explained that it was the Alfama—the old Arabic quarter.

Beautiful murals decorated walls at the ends of alleyways, little children darted dark heads out of tiny windows and called, *'Bom dia!'* Washing hung on lines between houses.

They'd had lunch there, on a tiny terrace overlooking the river. Afterwards they'd wandered some more, Lexie's hand tightly in Cesar's. At one point she had tugged gently, and when he'd looked at her she'd asked, 'No paparazzi?'

Something had flashed across his face but he'd smiled and said, 'No. Not here.'

Something very dangerous had infused Lexie's blood to think that here they were truly anonymous. That Cesar hadn't automatically thought of the bigger agenda.

Dangerous.

The car had reappeared then, as if by magic, and had taken them to see the stunning sixteenth-century monastery where Vasco Da Gama was buried in Belem. Afterwards Cesar had pointed to a blue-canopied shop nearby, where a queue literally about a mile long waited patiently.

They'd joined the back of it. Lexie had looked at Cesar, but he'd said enigmatically, 'Wait and see. Then you'll understand why all these people are here.'

Eventually, when they'd reached the shop itself, Cesar had spoken in flawless Portuguese. He'd handed Lexie what looked like a small custard tart.

'Taste it,' Cesar had urged as they'd found stools in the heaving shop with its beautiful ornate interior.

Lexie had obediently bitten into the flaky pastry and the smooth warm custard had melted on her tongue. She'd groaned her appreciation, much as everyone else had.

When she'd been able to speak again she'd said, 'That was probably one of the best tarts I've ever tasted in my life.'

A smug Cesar had just said, 'See?'

And then they'd queued again for more.

After they'd taken a circuitous sightseeing route back to the hotel, instead of leading her up to the suite Cesar had taken Lexie down to the spa, where he'd consulted in Portuguese with the receptionist, who had gone bright pink and giggly. Lexie might almost have felt sorry for her if she hadn't been feeling a disturbing rise of something else. *Jealousy.*

Cesar had turned to her. 'See you in a couple of hours.' And after pressing a swift kiss to her mouth he'd left Lexie there, gaping at his retreating form.

Two women had emerged and Lexie had been taken in hand—literally. The full works of an all-over beauty treatment, followed by a full body massage.

Then, when she'd floated back to the suite, Cesar had been waiting with champagne, and once Lexie had changed into the dark pink off-the-shoulder dress she'd brought with her they'd gone to dinner.

And now...now...Lexie took in the sparkling view of one of the oldest cities in Europe and felt overwhelmed. No more in control of her emotions than she had been ever since they'd queued a second time for the glorious *pasteis de natas* in Belem. When Cesar had looked so carefree and years younger.

Conversely, it had reminded Lexie that she harboured dark secrets, and they were rising up within her now— because she was going to be coming face to face with a very personal old scar on set the following week. The thought of it terrified her, and she knew she was feeling more vulnerable about it because being with Cesar...being intimate for the first time…had ripped away some vital layer of protection.

'Sorry, I had to take that call.'

Lexie tensed at Cesar's deep voice. He came alongside her and handed her a small glass of port. She forced a smile and tipped it towards him after sniffing it appreciatively. 'Appropriate—given we're in the land where port is made.'

Cesar inclined his head. He looked absurdly suave and gorgeous this evening. Tall and imposing. Yet with that very definite edge of virile masculine energy.

Lexie took a quick sip of her drink. It was smooth and luxurious. Her feeling of vulnerability and the darkness on her soul made her want to avoid Cesar's far too incisive gaze. Even now he was regarding her speculatively. She felt raw after the day, and on some perverse level she almost felt angry with him—for charming her, for making her fall for him.

A rogue desire to crack that impenetrable façade he wore so well made her ask, 'So how come you're not married…?'

Lexie immediately wanted to claw the words back. Regretting the impulse.

Cesar's gaze narrowed predictably and Lexie squirmed, cursing herself. Thinking frantically of a way to save herself, she sought to mitigate it by saying lightly, 'You're a catch. I mean you have all your own teeth, your breath isn't bad. You own property…'

Somehow Lexie was afraid she hadn't fooled him. Her voice had sounded too breathy, slightly desperate. She took another sip of the port.

But when she looked back at him he was smiling wryly. 'No one's ever mentioned the boon of having my own teeth before.'

No, thought Lexie, she'd bet they hadn't. They'd probably looked at him and seen a walking, talking dollar sign.

Inexplicable anger rose up within her to think of women seeing him as a target, and then just as quickly dissolved. Cesar was so cynical that he would never be taken for that kind of a fool.

Suddenly loath to think that he might consider *her* a vulture like that, she said quietly, 'Thank you. Seriously, this day has been...amazing. I never expected it.'

Something painful gripped her inside. Their time was finite.

Not wanting to think about that, she figured she had nothing to lose so she dived in, telling herself she wasn't genuinely curious. 'Have you ever come close? To being married?'

Cesar tensed. His fingers tightened fractionally on his glass. Then the line of his mouth flattened. 'I was abandoned at an early age and then left in the hands of two people who were little better than uninterested caretakers. They resented the fact that my blood was not pure. That experience hardly left me with the qualifications to create a warm, inviting atmosphere conducive to family and such frivolous things.'

Lexie's insides clenched in rejection of that. Creating a family, a home, was not frivolous. Cesar's words, however, had been emphatic. She realised something about herself then, in a blinding flash of clarity: on some fundamental level she hadn't given up hope for herself. She hoped that some day she might have a second chance and her own rather dismal experience of what a family was could be proved to be the exception rather than the rule.

'Your half-brothers...' she offered huskily. 'They looked happy in the wedding pictures.'

Cesar's jaw tightened. 'They're different. They had a different upbringing, different perspectives.'

Lexie thought of his grandmother, cruelly making him

cut out and paste pictures of them growing up with their mother—*his* mother. Together.

'They had your mother... But I wonder if it was any easier or better for them just because she was there?'

'Perhaps—perhaps not,' Cesar said, but it rang hollow.

Lexie wanted to slide her arm around him but didn't. 'Are you going to see them again?'

He glanced at her and his face was hard. As it had been when he'd looked at the portraits of his grandparents.

'I have nothing in common with them. Especially not now.'

He turned to face her more fully and Lexie almost shivered at the frost in his eyes.

'I made a decision a long time ago never to marry and have children.'

'Why?' Lexie breathed, not liking how that declaration seemed to affect her physically. How it felt as if he was giving her a distinct message.

'Because I vowed that the *castillo* is no place for a child. The legacy of my family is tainted, built on obsessive greed. Snobbery. When I die the *castillo* will be left to the local town and they can do what they like with it. And all the money will go to various charities and trusts. That's what I'm building it up for now.'

'But...' Lexie searched wildly for a way to penetrate the cool shell that surrounded Cesar. 'You said yourself that you wanted to renovate the *castillo*, but...why bother? Why not just leave it behind now?'

Cesar looked at her then, and for a second Lexie saw bleakness in those green depths. A bleakness that resonated in her because she knew what it felt like herself.

'Because...' he was grim '...it's in my damn blood like some kind of poison.'

Lexie was stunned into silence. She didn't like the way she wanted to do something to comfort Cesar. Touch him.

And even though he was only inches away it felt as if a chasm yawned between them.

Huskily she said, 'I'm sorry. I shouldn't have said anything.'

His mouth tipped up but it was a parody of a smile, a million miles away from the smiles she'd seen earlier.

'What about you, Lexie? Do you wish for a cottage with a white picket fence and a gaggle of cherubic children?'

For a second Lexie felt nothing. The words seemed to hang suspended in the air between them. But then it was as if a roaring flood was approaching and gathering speed from a long way off. *Pain*. Incredible pain.

A kaleidoscope of images bombarded her—a tiny baby, crying lustily. Nurses with rough hands and judgemental looks. Officials. And then…nothing. Silence. More pain.

'Lexie?'

She blinked. Cesar was watching her, his eyes narrowing. Face stark. From somewhere she found a brittle smile and said through the ball of emotion growing in her chest, 'You forgot the dog…there's a dog there too.'

'Ah…yes, of course. No idyllic picture would be complete without a dog.'

Cesar put down his glass and took Lexie's from her too. He reached for her with both hands and pulled her into his body. Lexie felt cold, and she shivered lightly. She desperately wanted to drive away the chill and feel warm again. She desperately wanted to blank out the dark images she'd just seen.

Coming up on her tiptoes, Lexie reached up and brought her arms around Cesar's neck, pressing her whole body against his. She saw the flare in his eyes and felt herself start to thaw from the inside out.

'Kiss me, Cesar.'

Cesar smiled briefly before a look of almost feral intent crossed his face. He moved his hands up to Lexie's face.

The kiss was fierce and passionate, and before Lexie lost all ability to think clearly she knew that they were both running away from the demons nipping at their heels. This time, though, it didn't feel like kinship—it felt bleak.

Much later Cesar lay awake in the dark room. Traces of the constriction in his chest brought on by Lexie's questions were still there, faintly. Even though his body hummed with much more pleasurable sensations.

She was curled into him now, her naked curves keeping him at a level of near constant arousal. If it wasn't so damned intoxicating he could almost resent her for her effect on him.

Her breath was feathering softly across his chest, light and even, and her hair was soft and silky. One hand lay right over the centre of his chest, where he'd felt the constriction most keenly earlier.

'So how come you're not married?'

Other women had asked him that question with a definite look in their eyes. Lexie hadn't had that look. He never talked to anyone about his upbringing, but he seemed to be incapable of holding it in whenever those huge blue eyes were trained on him.

He'd told her...*everything*. He'd never even articulated his plans for the *castillo* to his friend Juan. He'd never told another soul. And when he'd told her something incredibly bleak had hit him. Bleak enough to drive him to taunt her, ask her if she pictured herself in that idyllic scenario.

And she'd looked for a moment as if he'd run a knife right through her belly. Pale. Stricken. Shocked. Clearly the thought was anathema to her, even though she'd joked about a dog.

Cesar went cold in the bed beside Lexie as something slid home inside him. The joke was on him, because for the first time in his life he was aware of a yearning sensation, a yearning for something he'd always believed to be utterly beyond his reach.

The following morning Lexie woke up alone in the bed. She sagged back against the pillows with not a little relief. Images from the night flooded her head and her cheeks reddened even as a tight knot of tension made her belly cramp.

She'd been able to drive away the demons for the night, but now they were back. The conversation with Cesar replayed in her head. The bleakness she'd felt when he'd spoken about the *castillo,* about leaving it behind so no child would have to endure what he had.

It shouldn't be affecting Lexie like this. If anything it should be inciting a sense of protection within her. A sense that as long as she could count on Cesar's obviously deeply rooted cynicism then she would be okay too.

But she couldn't keep fooling herself. That discussion with Cesar had told Lexie that she wasn't half as cynical as she'd always believed she was. It had told her that at a very deep core level she *did* harbour a fantasy. A fantasy of family and security and happiness. Fulfilment. It might not be dressed up in a vision of a cute cottage with a white picket fence and a dog and children, but it wasn't far off.

And it made Lexie feel physically ill, almost as if she'd betrayed herself, to realise that. She'd been betrayed in the worst way possible by the very people who should have loved and protected her. And she'd always vowed to herself that she'd never allow that to happen again.

She'd vowed it. But deep down she hadn't wanted to become that hard inside.

Lexie could see now that that was why she'd allowed herself to believe she could trust Jonathan Saunders, even briefly. Even then she'd been trying to prove to herself that she could trust again. That she could believe that she wouldn't be betrayed. But he *had* betrayed her. And that should have proved to her that she'd been right all along not to trust. It should have shored up her defences. Made her even stronger.

But it hadn't.

Because Lexie knew that any illusion of feeling in control of what was happening between her and Cesar Da Silva was exactly that. An illusion. And this man had the power to show her the true extent of how flimsy her defences had always been.

CHAPTER NINE

'WOULD YOU MIND if we returned to the *castillo* this morning? Something's come up that I have to attend to in the vineyards.'

Lexie was in the bedroom and had just finished dressing in the jeans she'd worn the day before and a stripy Breton top. For a second Cesar's words didn't even compute because she was just drinking him in, looking impossibly handsome in jeans and a light wool sweater.

Then the words registered and relief rocked through her. She'd been dreading facing Cesar so soon after her recent revelations.

'No,' she said quickly—too quickly. 'I don't mind at all. There's some heavy scenes next week so I'd appreciate some time to prepare...'

Anxiety at the prospect of what lay ahead for her gripped her again.

Cesar crossed his arms and lounged against the door. Instantly Lexie's skin prickled with awareness. She could feel her nipples drawing into tight buds. Even more reason why she would relish some space from this man

'You don't have to sound so eager.'

She blushed and glanced away for a second, feeling churlish. 'It's not that I want to leave...you've been so generous...'

Cesar closed the distance between them so fast her head spun. He looked stern. 'You don't have to thank me.'

Lexie said weakly, 'Yes, I do… It's polite.'

'I don't want your politeness,' Cesar growled softly. 'I want you.'

He cupped the back of her head and kissed her. Lexie clung to his arms to stop her legs from buckling.

When he drew back she opened her eyes. *Lord,* she could barely breathe.

'Maybe I can convince them they don't need me,' Cesar said roughly.

It took a second for his meaning to sink in and then, despite the lurch in her chest, Lexie said hurriedly, 'No, you should go back. And I *do* need to prepare for next week.'

'You're staying with me in my apartment, though.'

She opened her mouth to object and saw the glint of determination in Cesar's eyes. She sighed, feeling weak. 'Okay.'

Much later that night Cesar finally returned to his apartment in the *castillo*. He was irritated and frustrated. The problem in the vineyards had been more complicated than he'd thought, and then he'd been waylaid by his house manager and that had evolved into a long impromptu meeting about the renovations Cesar was embarking on. Renovations that were now taking on a new resonance—as if something had shifted inside him with regards to his long-term plans for the *castillo*.

But he didn't want to think of that. All he wanted *was to see Lexie*. His apartment was quiet. Empty. When he considered for a second that she might well have gone back to her own rooms the rise of an even deeper frustration made him clench his jaw.

But, no… He saw her sneakers, thrown off near the couch where a low light was burning. Cesar walked over

and his chest grew tight when he saw Lexie fast asleep.
Her top had risen up, revealing a sliver of pale soft belly.
One arm was flung over her head, the other was just below
her breasts.

He came closer and wasn't even really aware of the way
the irritation and frustration he'd been feeling moments
before had just dissolved away. To be replaced by a different kind of frustration. A hunger.

He spotted the earphones of her mp3 player in her ears,
the wires leading to the device. And that tightness was
more acute as he thought of her dyslexia and how hard it
must have been for her to overcome its challenges along
the way.

As if aware of his intense scrutiny, she opened those
huge blue eyes. It took a second for them to focus and then
Lexie scrambled up, her cheeks pink.

'Oh, my God, what time is it?'

Cesar came down on the edge of the couch and pinned
her with his arms. She lay back. She looked tousled and
delicious and sexy as hell.

'It's way past your bedtime.'

She smiled and an incredible lightness infused Cesar.
Addictive, seductive…

'Is it now? What are you going to do about it?'

Cesar said sternly, 'I'm going to make sure you go to
bed right now and tuck you in myself.'

He stood up and reached for Lexie, swinging her into
his arms, relishing the way she snuggled into his chest.
Relishing even more the way her mouth unerringly found
his neck and started pressing kisses there. Open-mouthed
kisses, so that he could feel the tip of that wicked tongue.

Lexie sank back onto the bed and Cesar loomed over
her, pulling off his top with one graceful move. She was
still in a delicious half-dream haze. She didn't even have
to be awake for him to have an effect on her.

But then, like a dream that became clearer on waking, the darkness of the material she'd been studying in the script came back to her. It made her mood change in an instant, dousing desire. She recalled too that just before she'd woken she'd been having disturbing dreams. Almost nightmares. And it was no wonder.

Cesar came down over her on his arms and just like that Lexie froze under him. In that instant she felt tainted, *damaged*. She could see now that the exhilaration of becoming more intimate with Cesar had helped her to forget for a moment who she really was. What had happened to her. The sheer extent of the dark secrets she harboured.

Right then it felt as if a chasm yawned between them. He wouldn't ever want to know who she really was. Why would he? This was just an affair. Fun. Lighthearted. Lexie felt anything *but* lighthearted. She felt acutely alone. As if she carried the weight of the world on her shoulders.

Cesar lifted a hand as if to touch her and Lexie flinched violently. Everything in her was screaming to get away *now*—before he could seduce her so much that she found herself spilling out all the awful ugliness that had no place here.

He stopped. 'Lexie…?'

Lexie scrambled out from under Cesar's arms and stood up by the bed, her whole body cold. Numb. Cesar was looking at her as if she'd grown two heads. Galvanised by panic, Lexie found her bag and started throwing things in.

'What are you doing?'

She shoved the blouse she'd worn the previous day into the bag, her belly swooping at the thought of that day. How perfect it had been. It felt as if it had happened to another person now. A person who *didn't* have the awful memories that were bombarding her right now.

'I'm going back to my own room.'

She picked up her bag but Cesar caught her arm. He was shaking his head, incredulous. 'What on earth is going on?'

She pulled her arm free and backed away, torn by the sense of increasing panic she felt and also by something much more disturbing: the desire to throw down the bag and launch herself into Cesar's arms, ask him just to hold her, to reassure her that she could feel safe with him. But that was not what he was interested in—Lexie being vulnerable. He'd run a mile.

Then he stopped looking incredulous. He folded his arms. 'I told you before that I don't play games, Lexie.'

Lexie felt sad. 'I'm not playing a game. I just can't do this right now. I need…some space.'

For a long second Cesar just regarded her, and then his face became unreadable. He stepped back and said coolly, 'By all means, Lexie, take all the space you need.'

Lexie gripped her bag and turned and walked out of the bedroom, and out of Cesar's apartment, adrenalin coursing through her system. When she got back to her own room it felt desolate. And then she realised with a sense of dread that *she* felt desolate.

The truth was that she was damaged and broken inside. For a brief moment in time she'd believed that she had somehow been miraculously cured. But she hadn't really. And this minor meltdown had just proved it to her.

'I need some space.' Cesar glowered so fiercely that his house manager saw him coming and scuttled out of sight. Those words had been eating away at him like poison for two days now.

One minute Lexie had been supine on his bed, flushed and sexy, huge eyes all but eating him up…and the next she'd become a different person. Cold. Stark. *Dios*, she'd flinched as if he might hurt her.

His skin prickled. He hadn't liked that feeling. And he

hadn't liked to acknowledge how feral she'd made him feel. When she'd said she needed space it had been like a punch to his gut.

The thought that she might have even glimpsed a tiny part of how ravenous she made him feel had made him go cold all over. He'd had to step back to stop himself from acting on the visceral impulse to prove her words to be a lie.

But even now he could remember the look in her eyes. It had been panicked. And he couldn't understand why.

The film unit was due to head back to London at the end of the week and Cesar was acutely aware of the fact— much to his chagrin. Especially when he'd set out at the very beginning to avoid getting involved at all costs.

For two days he'd deliberately avoided going near where they were shooting, in an old abandoned wing of the *castillo*. But today he found himself heading there even before he'd consciously taken the decision. The fact that he *needed* to see Lexie only put him into an even more foul humour.

Cesar saw the usual cluster of people as he got closer to the set—crew hanging around, waiting for someone to call for them urgently.

They nodded to him now. Said hello. He managed some civil responses. When he got closer he saw that the door to the set was closed. And there was a hushed air. He asked the third assistant director if they were shooting.

The young man shook his head and Cesar made to go onto the set, but the man stopped him. 'You can't go in there, Mr Da Silva.'

Cesar chafed at the obstruction. His need to see Lexie was like a burr under his skin now. 'Why not?' he demanded.

'It's a closed set. They're doing the rape scene. Essential crew only.'

The rape scene.

Cesar didn't know why, but he suddenly felt a chill in his blood. He looked around and saw the video assistant in the corner, with his wall of monitors which showed whatever the camera was seeing inside the room. Usually there would be a couple of producers or some crew watching the scenes, but today there was no one.

He went over and sat down. Just as he realised that he couldn't hear what they were saying the video assistant handed him some earphones. Cesar put them on and hunched forward.

They were about to shoot. The director was talking to Lexie and to Rogan, the male lead. Cesar's breath hitched when he saw her. Her hair was down, tousled, and she was wearing some kind of diaphanous white gown. It was open at the front, as if it had been ripped, and he could see the ripe curve of her breast.

And then the director disappeared, leaving Lexie and Rogan on the screen. The first assistant director called out the instructions to shoot and then the director called *action*.

Rogan grabbed Lexie by the arms and shook her, spittle flying from his mouth as he said crude, horrific things. She looked tiny and vulnerable. She was pleading with him. But he wouldn't listen. Then he brutally turned her and shoved her down on the bed, pulling her gown up over her thighs, undoing himself before he pressed himself into her, grunting like an animal.

The camera went close in on Lexie's face, pushed down onto the bed. Rogan's big hand was on the back of her head, holding her down. Her eyes were blank.

Cesar heard *cut*. But all he could really hear was the roaring of blood in his head. He wanted to move but he was paralysed.

On some rational level he knew it wasn't real. That it was just acting. He could see Rogan helping Lexie up. The actor looked faintly traumatised. Lexie looked impossibly pale, and sort of glassy-eyed. A shiver of foreboding went down Cesar's spine. He knew that it had obviously been a traumatic scene to shoot, but there was something else going on—he could feel it.

But then they were going again, and he heard the camera assistant say, 'Scene One Hundred, Take Twenty.'

Cesar pulled off the earphones and looked at the video guy incredulously. 'They've done this *nineteen* times?'

The man gulped. 'Yes, sir. We've been doing this scene all day from different angles. This is the last shot, but he's milking it.'

Cesar felt rage building inside him. The camera was close up on Lexie's face again and he saw a tear roll out of her eye and down one cheek. She hadn't cried last time.

Something rose up inside Cesar—something he couldn't even articulate. An overwhelming need to get to her. He surged to his feet, almost knocking over the wall of monitors. He stormed to the door of the set, swatting the protesting third AD aside.

He opened the door just as the camera assistant was saying, 'Scene One Hundred, Take Twenty-One.'

'Enough.' Cesar's voice cracked out like a whip.

Lexie turned her head and looked at Cesar. He saw only those huge bruised blue eyes, and something in their depths…a mute appeal. She wasn't acting any more. He knew it without even knowing how.

He walked straight over and scooped her up into his arms, and for the first time in two days he felt slightly sane again.

The director was standing up now, blustering. 'What the hell are you doing, Da Silva? You can't just barge in here like this.'

Cesar stopped in the act of turning around. Lexie was

far too slight a weight in his arms as he said coldly, 'You're on my property. I can do whatever the hell I want.'

'But we haven't got the shot yet.'

Even icier now, Cesar said, 'If you haven't managed to get it yet then perhaps you shouldn't be directing.'

He was barely aware of a suppressed snigger from one of the crew as he strode out of the room, Lexie curled into his chest, her head tucked down. It reminded him of how she'd curled into his chest after making love that first time. When she'd cried like a baby.

He carried her all the way to his apartment and took her into his bedroom. He sat down on the edge of the bed, still holding her. He was shaking from the adrenalin and anger coursing through his system.

After a long time, she moved in his arms. But she wouldn't look at him. She just said, in a quiet voice, 'I need to have a shower.'

Cesar got up and deposited her gently on the side of the bed, crouching down. Finally she met his gaze but her eyes were flat. As if she didn't see him. A shard of ice pierced him inside.

Reluctantly he left her to go and turn on the shower. When he came out she was standing, albeit shakily. 'Do you need help?' he asked.

She shook her head and went in, closing the door behind her. Cesar restrained himself from following her, making sure she was all right. The shower ran for long minutes.

Eventually it stopped. Lexie was so long coming out that Cesar was about to knock on the door when it opened. She was wrapped in his towelling robe. It swamped her. Her hair was damp and hung in long golden tendrils over her shoulders.

He handed her a glass of brandy. 'Here—you should drink some of this.'

Lexie wrinkled her nose, but she took it and sipped at it before handing it back. Cesar put it down on a nearby table. He felt unaccountably ill-equipped to know what to do. What to say.

'You shouldn't have done that.'

She was looking at him with her chin tilted up and Cesar arched a brow. 'Would you prefer to be back there doing Take Thirty right now?'

She paled so dramatically that Cesar reached out and put his hands on her arms.

'No,' he said grimly, leading her out to the living area and guiding her to sit down on the couch. 'I didn't think so.'

Lexie seemed impossibly tiny and fragile sitting on the big couch. Cesar stood over her and crossed his arms, because even now all he wanted to do was touch her. *I need space.* He cursed silently.

'So, are you going to tell me what's going on?'

Lexie glanced up at Cesar and then away again quickly. He was so…implacable. Determined. Stern. The numb shell that had surrounded her for the past two days was finally breaking apart.

When Cesar had burst onto the set and she'd seen him… He would never know the depth of the gratitude she'd felt. Because on some level she'd always needed to know that someone might have saved her.

She forced herself to look at him. 'Why did you do that?'

Cesar paced back and forth now, energy sparking off his tall, lean body. His mouth was tight. 'I don't know, to be honest. But when I saw you…I could tell something was wrong.' He shook his head, stopped pacing. 'You weren't acting, Lexie.'

Something huge inside her shifted to know that he'd

intuited something was wrong. 'No, I wasn't acting…not by the end.'

Cesar pulled a chair over to sit in front of her. Lexie gazed at him. Remembered how good it had felt when he'd swept her up into his arms. *Too good.* As if she'd been running for a long time and someone had finally allowed her to stop and rest.

She found that she wanted to tell him. She wanted to explain about the other night.

'Lexie…*what*?'

She took a breath and then said starkly, 'I was raped when I was fourteen.'

Cesar went white in an instant. His whole body tensed. 'What did you say?' His voice was hoarse.

Lexie bit her lip. She couldn't go back now.

'I was raped by my aunt's husband. One night my parents and my aunt had gone out—he said he'd babysit. He brought me into my parents' room when the others were in bed and raped me.'

'The others…?'

'My five younger brothers and sisters.'

'*Dios mio*… Lexie…that animal…' Cesar looked sick. 'You looked at me the other night like I was going to hurt you—you were scared…'

Lexie leant forward and touched his arm. 'No…'

But Cesar was almost recoiling now, and she could see the horror on his face that she might have thought for a second he was capable of something so heinous.

She shook her head, '*No*, Cesar. I wasn't afraid of you. I knew this scene was coming up… I was apprehensive about it… It's the first time I've ever had to do a scene like this and it was just too close to the bone.'

Cesar pulled free of her touch and stood up, pacing again. Lexie was tense, her hands forming fists in her lap.

He faced her, eyes flinty green. 'My God,' he said again—in English this time.

Suddenly a kind of hurt bloomed inside her. He was looking at her as if she was a stranger. A damaged stranger. The guilt that she had worked long and hard to believe wasn't hers reared its ugly head again. Her rapist's accusations were as clear today as they had been then. *'You were asking for it, you know. Always prancing around under my nose dressed in that uniform.'*

She felt cold and said tightly, 'I'm sorry. I shouldn't have told you.'

She stood up from the couch, hating that she'd been weak enough to confide in Cesar. Hating that she'd thought his intuition made her feel as if he deserved to know.

'Where are you going?'

She looked at him. 'Back to my room.'

She turned and headed for the bedroom, but Cesar caught her hand. This time when she looked at him his eyes were blazing. 'Dammit, Lexie, you're staying here.'

Hot tears pricked the back of her eyes, galling her. She hadn't even cried after she'd been raped—too shocked and traumatised—and yet with one touch, one look, this man could reduce her to tears and make her want to lean on him when she'd fended for herself for so long now…

'Damn *you*, Cesar.' She pulled her hand free and faced him. 'Just let me go.'

He shook his head. 'You shouldn't be alone right now.'

More hurt bloomed inside Lexie to think that he was acting out of a sense of duty. 'I've done my therapy, Cesar, years of it,' she sneered. 'You really don't have to act as my babysitter just because it turns out that your lover is damaged goods.'

Now Cesar was angry. He took her arms in his hands, gripping her. 'Don't you *dare* put words in my mouth. I don't think any such thing. And you are *not* damaged. You're perfect.'

Lexie's anger drained away, leaving her feeling shaky. 'I'm sorry. I just…I shouldn't have told you.'

'I'm glad you told me. It's just a lot to take in.'

He let go of her arms and stepped back, raking a hand through his hair. Lexie felt bereft.

'Look,' she offered, 'I'm fine —really, I always suspected this scene would be difficult. But it's one of the reasons I took the job in the first place. Initially I wanted to say no, but I knew I couldn't let it stop me. I dealt with what happened a long time ago, Cesar. But something like this would be difficult even under the best of circumstances.'

Cesar shook his head lightly. He came close again, touched Lexie's jaw.

'You shouldn't have had to face it alone.'

Lexie felt emotion building inside her. Terrified of it, she said simply, 'I've always been alone.'

Cesar looked at her with a burning intensity. Desire, pure and hot, sparked to life within her, mixing with the emotion to produce something volatile. She brought her hand up to cover his and saw his eyes widen slightly.

'Please…'

One word. She could see that he understood, and she trembled inwardly in case he might balk. He could never know the depth of how badly she needed him right now— for myriad reasons.

His voice was gruff. 'Lexie…are you sure? The other night…'

She nodded. 'I'm sure. The other night…it wasn't about you. It was about me.'

'I don't want to hurt you.'

'You won't…'

He didn't move, though. Frustration welled inside her. Maybe Cesar couldn't deal with the ugly truth of what had happened to her. She took her hand down, stepped back, dislodging his hand. She'd just exposed herself spectacularly.

'It's okay… If you don't want me any more because of—'

His hand shot out, caught her. She looked at him.

'Of *course* I want you.' He sounded fierce. 'I just have to look at you to want you.'

He came closer. Held her face with both hands. 'You're in my blood. I need you.'

Lexie's own blood sang. She needed him too. Her whole being came alive as he drew her close and lowered his mouth to hers. The kiss was so tender and gentle that she almost emitted a sob of emotion, but held it back.

When he drew back he took her by the hand and led her into his bedroom. There was no sense of hesitation within Lexie. No sense of that same panic that had gripped her the other evening. She knew now that that had been largely because of her apprehension of acting out being raped. And it was over.

Cesar stopped by the bed and she faced him. He said, 'If you want to stop…'

Something melted inside her. She shook her head, her hands going to the buttons on his shirt, her voice husky with need. 'I won't want to stop.'

Her hands were clumsy on his buttons and he gently took them away to undo them himself. Lexie sucked in a breath to see his chest revealed. She opened the knot on her robe.

Cesar looked down and she saw a dark flush slash across his cheekbones. He slid his hands under the shoulders of her robe and pushed it till it fell to the floor.

Lexie ran her hands over his pectorals, her nails grazing his nipples, making them stand up into hard little points. She reached forward and put her mouth there, swirling her tongue around one hard tip, feeling her core moisten with desire.

As she lavished kisses on his chest and nipples her hands were on his jeans, flipping open the buttons, feeling the hard ridge of his arousal brushing her fingers. She drew back and pushed his jeans down, taking his underwear with them, her breath disappearing when his erection was freed.

She wrapped a hand around him, awed by his sheer size and strength and the knowledge that he would never use it to hurt her. Cesar was kicking his feet free of his clothes and then he put his hands on Lexie's arms.

She looked up.

He sounded rough. 'I need you. I need to taste you.'

Her hand stalled on the thick column of flesh and gently Cesar removed it, pushing her down onto the bed. He came down beside her and his mouth was on hers, and Lexie moaned as she tasted him hungrily, sucked him deep. Wrapped her legs and arms around him as if she could bind him to her for ever.

Gently Cesar unbound her, spreading her arms out, his mouth leaving hers to explore over her jaw and neck. Over the tops of her heaving breasts. Taking each tight bud of her nipples into his mouth, making her moan even louder and her hips writhe against him.

But he kept moving down, over her belly. An arm came under her back, arching her into him, his other hand pushed her legs apart.

She felt dizzy. 'Cesar...'

His green gaze was blistering. 'Trust me.'

Trust me. Lexie sank back. She did trust him. She always had—from the moment she'd met him and let him kiss her. *Her*—with her history. The knowledge rushed through her. Wiping aside any trepidation or lingering hurt.

His mouth was moving down, kissing the top of her

thigh. Moving in. A big hand was splayed under her buttocks, tipping her towards his face. Lexie's breaths were coming so hard and fast she had to consciously slow down for fear of passing out.

And then his tongue touched her *there*. He licked her with explicit skill. All the way up the seam of her body, his tongue delving into her secret folds, opening her up to him, baring every part of her.

Lexie's hands gripped the sheet. Legs bent, back arched. Cesar licked and sucked and drove her more and more mindless. His tongue swirled with maddening strokes against her clitoris before leaving it to lavish attention elsewhere and then returning just when those cells were screaming for release.

When it came it was so huge...so all-encompassing...that Lexie thought she'd passed out. Because the next thing she was aware of was Cesar sliding into her, so deeply and thoroughly, and with such a fierce look of concentration on his face that it was all she could do to wrap her legs around him as far as they'd go and tilt her hips to take him even deeper.

They were locked in a dance that was as old as time and as profound. Lexie couldn't look away from Cesar even though she felt as though her soul was being turned inside out and he'd see it as clear as day. *She loved him.* And it went deeper than just loving him because he was the first man she'd allowed herself to be intimate with. He was the *only* man she could imagine being intimate with. The only man she *wanted* to be intimate with.

That revelation came just as bliss split her body in two, throwing her high into the air, where she seemed to hang suspended on the crest of a huge wave until it finally dropped her again. Cesar caught her in his arms and rolled them both so that she went limp across his heaving chest, their hearts thundering in unison, their skin slick with perspiration.

* * *

In the aftermath of her shattering climax and revelation Lexie felt as wobbly and vulnerable as a new foal trying to stand on spindly legs. So much had happened, and in the past couple of days since leaving Cesar's apartment she'd deliberately cut herself off from the people around her, dreading the upcoming rape scene.

It had reminded her of when she'd arrived in London for the first time, when she'd been completely alone and unsupported.

Cesar shifted now and she winced minutely as the connection between their bodies was broken.

He asked with obvious concern, 'Are you okay?'

Lexie nodded and looked at him. He was on one elbow, some hair flopping into his forehead, his face dark, eyes glowing like dark green gems. *She loved him.*

But even as she knew that she also knew, with a feeling of desolation, that he didn't feel anything for her other than desire…and maybe worst of all pity.

Cutting into her thoughts, Cesar asked, 'What happened to him?'

Lexie went cold inside. 'My uncle?'

Cesar nodded.

She braced herself for the pain that inevitably came whenever he was mentioned or she thought about him, but it wasn't as sharp. Lexie's mouth became bitter. 'Nothing. My parents didn't want to know when I told them. They were very religious—pillars of the community. My father was a salesman; he travelled a lot. The thought of the scandal was too much for them.'

Cesar was incredulous. 'You mean he just got away with it?'

She pulled the sheet around her and sat up against the pillows. 'He died in a car crash about a year after it happened. But, no, he never got prosecuted or punished.'

'How could they have done that to you? Just ignored it?'

Lexie glanced away from Cesar. There was an even darker stain on her soul than he could imagine. She suddenly felt jaded and weary. Knowing that she loved him, but that it would end when she left the *castillo* for London at the end of that week, she felt reckless. As if she had nothing more to lose.

'That wasn't all,' she said now in a quiet voice.

'What do you mean?' Cesar moved, sitting up too.

She looked at him. 'The rape resulted in me becoming pregnant.'

He frowned. 'Pregnant? You had a baby?'

Lexie nodded, suppressing the inevitable spasm of emotion. 'A baby boy. I named him Connor.'

Cesar shook his head, clearly finding this hard to digest. 'But…you don't… Where is he now?'

'I had just turned fifteen when I had him. My family sent me away to a distant relative down the country for the duration of the pregnancy, where I was pretty much kept a prisoner for nine months. He was adopted two days after the birth, and is growing up somewhere in the greater Dublin area—that's all I know. And that they kept Connor as his middle name.'

Lexie watched as Cesar, looking slightly stunned, blindly pushed back the covers and got out of the bed. A sinking feeling gripped her. This was it. Her ugly truth bared. She'd known on some deep level that it would be too much to take in. This relationship was about a flirty affair while they were filming—not about dark secrets.

She knew with a sick feeling that she had just ended it.

CHAPTER TEN

CESAR PULLED ON his jeans and then he faced Lexie again. She looked impossibly young against the sheets, eyes huge. He was literally speechless. Didn't know what to say. The knowledge of what she'd been through was…enormous. And it was making all of his own dark demons rear their ugly heads.

He felt tight inside. As if a hand was closing around his chest and heart and squeezing with remorseless pressure. He thought of her reaction when he'd first presented her with the option of staying in the *castillo* for the duration of the shoot. No wonder she'd looked panicked.

Lexie was a mother. She'd had to give up her baby. He knew rationally that she'd had no choice, but it impacted on him in a deeply raw place. He couldn't breathe.

'Why did you tell me this?'

Lexie's eyes widened. Her face paled. And then something in her features hardened, as if in response to Cesar's stoniness.

'I told you because I felt I could… But I can see I shouldn't have.'

Cesar watched as if slightly removed from his own body as Lexie reached for her robe and pulled it on, getting out of bed too. Belting the robe tightly around her.

So many different emotions were impacting on him that it was almost overwhelming. Among them was anger—

which he knew was directed at himself, for his less than coherent response, and at Lexie for bringing him face to face with things he didn't want to look at in himself.

'I don't know what you want me to say.'

Lexie stared at him, her hair tumbled around her shoulders. Right then she seemed like a tiny warrior queen. Majestic.

'You don't have to say anything, Cesar. I'm not looking for therapy. I had years of that. I told you…'

She stopped for a second and that tightening sensation in Cesar's chest grew stronger. He almost put a hand there, as if that could alleviate the pain.

'I told you because I've never been with another man.'

Cesar stepped back. Stunned. 'Since you were…?'

Lexie snapped. 'Since I was raped, yes. You were my first lover.'

Faintly, Cesar said, 'Why me?'

She crossed her arms. 'You were the first man I desired.'

Lexie had never regretted anything more than opening her mouth to Cesar. Self-disgust ripped her insides to shreds. She'd truly learnt nothing. For a long time she'd felt ashamed, dirty. That she was some kind of damaged goods. And then therapy had helped her make sense of what had happened and she'd begun the long process of healing and forgiving herself.

Healing. The physical process of that, which had started with Cesar's incendiary kiss in the stable, mocked her now. She'd confused physical intimacy with something deeper. Clearly it had never been about anything else for him.

Her own family had shunned her a long time ago, and she was damned if she was going to let that happen again.

Lexie stalked around the bed and into the bathroom, aware of Cesar's eyes on her. The fact that he was so silent, not making any attempt to touch her, said it all. She closed the door and with shaking hands that told her of the heightened emotion she was barely reining in, she took off the robe and put on the costume nightshirt she'd been wearing for the rape scene.

When she emerged Cesar had put on a top. He looked serious.

Lexie hated that even now she was acutely aware of her sensitised naked body under the voluminous robe.

She was brisk. 'I shouldn't have said anything.' From somewhere, Lexie even managed to force a smile—as if this *hadn't* just cost her everything.

'Lexie—'

She cut him off, dreading hearing some platitude, and a spurt of anger made her say, 'Cesar, we're wrapping here on Friday. It's not as if this was ever going to go further. The papers have already lost interest in us—we've done what we set out to do in the first place.'

'We have.' His voice was flat.

'Yes,' Lexie insisted, forcing herself to look at him even though it was hard. 'I wanted to salvage my reputation and avoid being dragged through the tabloids again as some kind of victim. You wanted to avoid unnecessary scrutiny into your family. It was a mutually beneficial affair—isn't that what you called it?'

Everything within Cesar rejected Lexie's terse words but something was holding him back. The feeling that the very walls around him were about to start crumbling—as if some sort of invisible earthquake was happening below ground.

Right at that moment the full impact of just how different Lexie was from any other lover he'd had hit him with the force of a blunt object. She'd turned him upside down and inside out.

'Yes,' he agreed, 'it was.'

Just then there was a knock on the main door of Cesar's

apartment. He cursed even as a very weak part of him welcomed the interruption. He strode through the main living space to get to the door, and opened it to see one of the film's PAs.

'Sorry to disturb you, Mr Da Silva, but the director is looking for Lexie.'

Cesar knew Lexie was behind him without turning around. His skin prickled. He felt disorientated, dizzy. Even now he had to battle an absurd urge to protect her and snarl at the young guy to leave.

Lexie was oblivious to the messy tumult in Cesar's gut. She stepped around him, didn't look at him, and spoke to the PA. 'Tell Richard I'll just change before I come to him.'

The PA hurried off, clearly relieved to have delivered his message. Cesar watched Lexie. She was avoiding his eye. He wanted to tip her chin up, force her to meet his gaze, but at the same time he didn't want to see what was in those blue depths.

'I should go and talk to Richard.' Lexie's voice was husky, her almost belligerent stance of moments ago less evident.

She looked at him then and Cesar tensed, but her eyes were clear. Unreadable. It irritated him—which irritated him even more.

'The next few days are heavily scheduled so that we get out of here on time. I think it's best if we just…let this be finished now.'

Cesar felt slightly numb. This was a novel situation: a woman who was ready to walk away before he was ready to let her go.

Humiliation scored at his insides. Lexie was right—this had only ever been about the short term. The thought of anything beyond this place was not an option. He did not chase women around the world. Whatever desire he felt would dissipate. He could not want her so badly that he was unable to let her go.

He was tight-lipped as he reached for the door and held it open. 'Goodbye, Lexie.'

Something flared in her eyes for a second, and then it disappeared. She didn't speak again, just turned and walked out, and as Cesar watched her go he thought numbly that she could be a ghost in the long white gown and in her bare feet.

He closed the door on her, on that evocative image, and pushed down the chilling sensation that she would haunt him for ever. Everything he'd been holding in since she'd told him about the rape, and then the baby, surged up in a tangled black mess of emotion.

He went to his drinks cabinet and took out a glass, poured himself a drink. Taking a swift gulp, he felt the liquid jolt him back to life. His hand tightened on the glass as he stared unseeingly at the wall in front of him.

His own mother had abandoned him and left him at the mercy of his grandparents. Lexie had given up her own son. For a moment pure unadulterated rage rose up within Cesar as he acknowledged what she'd done —but it was an old, reflexive anger that had more to do with his mother than with Lexie.

His rage dimmed when he thought of Lexie aged fifteen, a terrified and traumatised schoolgirl. What choice had she had? None.

For the first time in his life Cesar had to concede that by the time his mother had come back for him his grandparents had done such a number on him that he'd had no choice but to reject her.

And he had to concede too that perhaps there had been more to his mother's motives than pure greed and selfishness. Her distress when she'd said goodbye both times stung him now—hard. Like a slap across the face. This unwelcome revelation brought with it an even stronger feeling that everything he'd always counted on was falling apart at the seams.

Cesar pinched the bridge of his nose. All he could see was Lexie's face and those huge eyes.

Anger surged again. What had she wanted from him? Damn her! Had she expected him to take her in his arms and soothe her? Promise her that everything would be all right?

Cesar wasn't gentle. Or sensitive. Or kind. He was black all the way through, and he resented Lexie right then for making him see just how black he was. For showing him how little he could offer comfort. And for making him think of the bleak reality of his childhood, filled with a lifetime of resentment for his two half-brothers. How powerless he'd been under the influence of his bitter grandparents, intent on punishment and revenge.

Rage and a feeling of impotence wound up inside him so tightly that he exploded. He turned and raised the hand holding that heavy crystal glass and with an inarticulate roar of pain and rage flung it with all his might across the room at his stainless steel kitchen. He watched it shatter into a million pieces, amber liquid spraying everywhere.

An echo from a long time ago whispered across his soul, bringing a chill wind. It reminded him that no good came out of this dark, gothic place. And to have imagined otherwise, even for a second, was to have become weak.

Lexie Anderson would be gone in a few days, and right in that moment Cesar hoped he'd never set eyes on her again. Because she'd done the worst thing in the world: she'd made him forget who he really was.

Lexie was sitting in her chair on the set, waiting while they set up for a new camera shot. People milled around her, working, chatting. But she felt removed. She'd heard the helicopter leaving early that morning.

She'd known that Cesar had left the *castillo* even before she'd heard one of the producers say something about him having business to attend to in America.

She'd been awake for most of the night, alternating between seething resentment directed at Cesar for having awoken her body from a lifetime of numbness and anger at herself for being so stupid as to fall for him. She'd tried to tell herself that she hadn't fallen so hard...but the hurt was too real and too deep for feelings not to be involved.

She'd never forget the look on his face when she'd told him about her baby. He'd shut down. Lexie had only ever talked about her baby to her counsellor. No one else knew. It was one of the reasons she was paranoid about press intrusion—in case anyone ever dug deep enough to find out.

Her son would be thirteen now, and every day Lexie wondered about him—wondered how she would cope if he ever came looking for her, asking for information. Sometimes the thought was overwhelming. She went cold inside as something struck her. Had she, on some level, put Cesar in the role of confidante because she'd been so desperate for support?

Even as Lexie felt anger for being so weak she had to acknowledge that she could have asked for help before. She'd just been too stubborn. That had been borne out the previous evening, when she'd gone to find the director to try and explain to him why she'd reacted the way she had.

She'd told him about the rape, knowing instinctively that she could trust him.

He'd shaken his head and taken her hand, his eyes full of compassion. 'Lexie, you should have told me. If I'd had any idea of how huge that scene was for you I'd have approached it differently. We could even have got it out of the way in the first week...'

He'd humbled her, apologising for unwittingly causing her distress. It was as if another weight had lifted from her shoulders, and Lexie knew that if she hadn't already told Cesar there was no way she could have confided in anyone else.

That only made her angry with him all over again. He hadn't been able to get rid of her fast enough yesterday. His face had been hard. Clearly he'd rejected her unwelcome confidences. No doubt his other lovers didn't come with messy histories, or weep all over him after making love.

She was glad Cesar was gone because she knew all her bravado was very shaky and that if she saw him again her heart would splinter into a million pieces.

Over a week later Cesar returned to the *castillo*. It was as if there had never been a film unit on the estate. Apart from the flattened bit of grass where the extras' marquee had stood everything had been restored to its pristine state— and, perversely, it annoyed Cesar intensely.

For the past week he'd put in long days at board meetings he'd been neglecting. Because of a blonde-haired, blue-eyed temptress. Damn her. Those were his favourite words at the moment, and they beat a constant refrain in his head.

Damn her for coming into his life. Damn her for making him want her so badly that he seemed to have a constant ache in his gut. Damn her for being so light in spite of the horrific things she'd endured.

Just…*damn her*.

For making him think of things like his brother Alexio's wedding and how happy both his half-brothers had looked with their wives. And damn her for making him come to the uncomfortable realisation that he had to stop blaming his brothers for living their lives oblivious of his presence.

That realisation had hit him as he'd looked blearily into

the bottom of an empty bottle of whiskey in a dingy bar on the Lower East Side of Manhattan about two days ago.

Cesar stopped at the entrance of the *castillo*. It sat there, as forbidding and dark as it ever had been. But for the first time in his life it didn't feel quite so...oppressive.

It was quiet, though. And that quiet, which had never really bothered him before, seemed to reach around him and squeeze, bringing with it restlessness. Dissatisfaction.

Without even being aware of making the decision, Cesar found himself walking up the main staircase to the first-floor landing. He went and stood at the window where his grandmother had found him waiting, looking for his mother.

He felt the old pain like a bruise that would never fade. But it didn't bring with it that futile sense of anger. It only brought a sense of melancholy and a growing sense of something else. *Loss.* Acute, aching loss. Worse than anything he'd ever felt before—worse even the loss he could remember feeling as a child for his mother.

Cesar knew then that as much as his grandparents had all but imprisoned him in this *castillo* when he was a child, since he'd become an adult he'd happily inflicted the same punishment on himself, and self-disgust filled him.

Lexie's face and eyes filled his vision. How she'd looked that last time he'd seen her, in the ridiculous period night-gown. Pale. Yet strong. Defiant in the face of his frankly pathetic response to her pain and trauma.

Something had shut down inside him that day, as if to protect him from feeling the pain too acutely. But now that was breaking apart inside him as he stared out at a bleak view that was seared into his consciousness.

He was sick of bleak. He was sick of darkness. He was sick of himself.

Damn Lexie, indeed. Because she hadn't made him

forget who he was at all. She'd shown him *exactly* who he was and who he could be. If he was brave enough.

The street was stinking, narrow. Beggars lined it, calling out for mercy or money. Small children darted under people's feet. Lexie stepped out of the path of a horse and carriage only at the last moment and gasped as it whistled past. Her long skirts were splashed with mud. People jostled her. She was going against the tide. And all she could think about, even as the cameras were running, was *him*. Cesar.

She cursed him for about the hundredth time that day and hoped that her expression conveyed anger at her co-star, who followed her through the streets, tracking her like a hunted animal.

'Cut!'

Immediately Lexie stopped. All of the extras turned and went back to their first positions on the enormous set that had been built for the film on a back lot in the London studios. A swarm of crew moved in to rearrange things, fix focus marks, touch up hair and make-up.

Lexie felt removed, though. The director approached her and she smiled brightly.

He took her arm and said in a low voice, 'Lexie, are you all right? You just seem…not that focused.'

She grimaced inwardly, regretting having ever told him what had happened to her. He'd been overly solicitous ever since. 'Sorry, Richard… I'm fine. It's just—'

'*Oh, my God.*'

'Sir! *Sir!* You can't go onto the set without a pass!'

Richard frowned and looked past Lexie. 'What on earth is *he* doing here?' he said incredulously.

Lexie felt a prickling sensation and turned around to see a tall figure approaching them. But even now she couldn't really compute that it was *him*.

Cesar. Dressed in dark worn jeans. A jumper and a battered brown leather jacket. Dark golden hair glinting in the London sunshine. He was almost too gorgeous to be real.

She even heard one of the extras nearby say in an awe-struck voice, 'Who *is* that?' and Lexie could almost sympathise with the inevitable impact he would be having on some poor unsuspecting person's senses.

He looked as intense as she'd ever seen him. A security guard caught up with him and took his arm. Cesar shook him off and kept coming.

Her mouth had gone bone-dry. She wondered if she was seeing things. Damn this corset that constricted her breath…

Cesar stopped just feet away and the security guard came panting up behind him. 'Now, look here—'

Lexie put out a shaky hand. 'It's all right, we know him. I…know him.'

Then all the anger and pain that had been her constant companion for a week now came flooding up, boiling over. She hissed at Cesar, 'What are you doing here? We're in the middle of a scene.'

'So I see,' he remarked dryly, taking in all the gawping extras and the crew, who were loving the interruption. He looked back at Lexie, and then spoke as if they were continuing a conversation that had stopped only moments ago. 'The thing is I should never have agreed with you when you said we should end the affair.'

Lexie gulped and darted a look at the avid crowd. 'Cesar, do we really have to do this here?'

Just then Richard stepped forward. 'Now, listen, Da Silva—interrupting my set once was—'

Cesar took his eyes off Lexie to stare at the man, and Lexie shivered when she saw the familiar steel in his expression.

'How much will it cost to shut down production for the rest of the day?'

Lexie blinked. Richard spluttered. 'I'd have to ask the producer...'

'Well, why don't you find him and ask him, and whatever amount he gives you tell him I'll double it.'

A murmur started through the crew and the extras. Lexie could see the PAs galvanised into action at the thought of an early wrap and a day off. The set started to clear.

Cesar stepped right up to Lexie and she was rooted to the spot. Terrified of the flutters that had started in her belly. Her heart squeezed. She loved this man so much, but he'd hurt her, and if all he wanted was to continue their affair...

'Cesar, if you've come just because you're not ready to end the affair then I'm not interested.'

His gaze on hers became assessing. Lexie's body hummed with awareness. With hunger.

'So what *are* you interested in?'

She blinked, confused. Fear gripped her... *What had she just said?* 'I just told you—I'm not interested in an affair.'

A ghost of a smile touched Cesar's mouth and she realised very belatedly how dishevelled he was, with stubble lining his jaw.

'One thing I do know is that I am not ready to end the affair—and I don't think you are either.'

A ball of pain lodged in her gut. She didn't have it in her to keep seeing Cesar knowing that it would end. Even one night with this man would kill her, even though every cell in her body was crying out for his touch.

She stepped back, her movement slightly hampered by her long dress. 'Yes, I am. And you should go and tell Richard you were joking about shutting down the production before too many people leave. You've caused enough disruption in my life as it is.'

Lexie went to walk around him, cursing her costume when she couldn't move more freely.

Cesar caught her and whirled her around, eyes flashing. 'I've caused disruption in *your* life? What about the disruption you've caused *me*?' He pointed a finger at his chest and glared at her.

Lexie pulled free, her anger matching his, boiling over when she thought of how naive she'd been, baring her soul to him.

'I did nothing but warm your bed for a few weeks! I was a convenient lover who also handily deflected some heat from the press about your family issues, and you were quite happy to take advantage of that.'

'On the contrary—you weren't *convenient* at all! The fact is, Lexie Anderson, you have been the most singularly *in*convenient lover I've ever known.'

Cesar was practically roaring now, and Lexie's eyes stung with tears. She bit back the lump in her throat to hear Cesar declare so baldly just how much he resented his desire for her.

Her voice was thick. 'Well, then, what are you waiting for? Leave me be.'

She went to walk away before Cesar could see the extent of her distress, but he caught her again. She cursed out loud, but he had both hands on her arms now.

Lexie felt a tear slip down one cheek and cursed again, struggling against his hold. She stopped and looked up. 'Just…let me go, Cesar. Please. I can't do this.'

He paled under his dark skin. 'I didn't want to make you cry.' His hands tightened. 'The reason you were an inconvenient lover is because you made me face up to myself in a way no one ever has before. Or will again.'

Now Cesar looked almost angry, but something in Lexie went very still.

'I was doing just fine without anyone challenging my

emotionally barren life. And then *you* appeared, literally like some kind of vision, and from that moment on something broke inside me. Something that needed to be broken.'

Cesar moved his hands up to cup Lexie's jaw.

'The truth is that you were...you *are*...the most beautifully *necessary* inconvenience, because you've brought me back to life. I don't want to end the affair, Lexie—*ever*. I want it to last for the rest of our lives.'

Lexie tried to shake her head, as if that might improve her hearing. But Cesar's hands held her immobile. She had to put her hands out to touch him, barely able to breathe. 'What are you saying?'

The tendrils of something impossibly light and effervescent were scaring her, beckoning her to a place where surely she would face the most epic fall of all if she was dreaming this.

'What I'm saying is that I'm in love with you. I think I have been from the moment I saw you. And I want to spend the rest of my life with you. I want it all—the picket fence, children, even the damn dog. *Everything*.'

His mouth twisted.

'When you asked me about getting married I taunted you because I couldn't bear the fact that you'd put a seed of something incredibly fragile in my head. A hope for the future I'd never even allowed myself to think about or imagine.'

Emotion was blooming inside Lexie's chest, making it expand, making her dizzy. She wanted to laugh and cry at the same time. But then she remembered his stark non-reaction that day at the *castillo*. The way he'd let her go so easily.

One of her hands on Cesar's chest curled into a fist and she hit him ineffectually. Her voice was choked. 'You hurt me. I thought you didn't care.'

Cesar looked pained. 'I'm so sorry—my response was… pathetic. I cared so much I shut down. I literally didn't know what to do or say. You were telling me those things… and all I could feel was my own pain. I couldn't begin to understand the horror of what had happened to you. I wanted to go out and find that man and kill him with my bare hands.'

Lexie paled.

'For the last week I've kept imagining you as a young girl, alone and scared, going through pregnancy and birth without any support.' He shook his head, his eyes glittering a little too brightly. 'You're the bravest person I know. You humble me.'

'I thought…' Lexie was whispering now '…that you hated what I'd told you because it was too personal. And that you didn't understand why I had to do what I did. I thought afterwards that it must have reminded you of your mother.'

Cesar's thumb caressed her cheek. 'If anything it's helped me to understand her a little better, because it's not so black and white any more. She wouldn't have been human if she hadn't felt some pain on leaving me behind— and God knows what nefarious bargain my grandparents struck with her to make her stay away.'

Feeling absurdly shy, Lexie said, 'I thought you resented the fact that I'd told you those things because our relationship wasn't about anything but…sex.'

Cesar grimaced. 'At first I did. I was angry because you'd forced me to acknowledge that what I felt for you went a lot deeper than I'd admitted to myself.'

Lexie could see it on his face now—in his eyes. Love. Blasting her doubts and fears. But it was huge. She was scared.

As if he could tell, he moved even closer and said throatily, 'What is it?'

'I'm scared,' she whispered, baring herself in a way she'd never done with anyone before. 'I'm scared because my own family turned their backs on me. Betrayed me in the worst possible way. I couldn't survive that again.'

Lexie could feel the tension in Cesar's body, see the ferocity in his expression.

'I vow to you with every breath in my body that I will spend my life protecting you from hurt and harm. I love you, Lexie. You're as much a part of my soul as I am myself. A betrayal of you is a betrayal of me...and whatever the future brings I'm going to be right by your side to deal with it. Including Connor.'

Lexie's eyes filled with tears. The fact that he'd acknowledged her son dissolved the last of her defences.

Cesar was blurry in her vision as she came up on tiptoe and slid her arms around his neck. 'I love you, Cesar... so much.'

He groaned softly and covered her mouth with his. The kiss was searing and passionate.

Lexie broke free and looked up. 'Take me home, please?'

Cesar smiled and his thumbs wiped away the tracks of her tears on her cheeks. '*Espere querida*...wait... There's just one thing I have to do first.'

Suddenly Cesar disappeared, and Lexie gave a little surprised yelp to see him kneeling at her feet, her huge skirt between them. He was holding out a black box which he then opened. He looked up, his slightly nervous smile making Lexie's heart flip-flop.

'Lexie Anderson...will you marry me?'

More tears filled Lexie's eyes. Pure joy bubbled up inside her. Her heart was in her voice when she said simply, 'Yes!'

Cesar took her hand and slid a stunning antique gold and diamond ring on her finger. The fact that she'd barely looked at it didn't seem to bother either of them, because he stood up and swept her and her voluminous dress into his arms before kissing her senseless—much to the entertainment of the security guards, who were the only people left on the set.

A week later Cesar had arranged to have his private jet standing by at a nearby private airfield. As soon as Lexie was wrapped after her final scene later that day they were going back to Spain.

Cesar's mobile phone beeped with a message and he read it.

Congratulations on your engagement. Alexio and I would like to meet you, if you're ready. Call me any time. Rafaele.

Cesar showed the message to Lexie later, when they were on the plane, and she was sitting in his lap. She looked at him and he saw the way her eyes grew suspiciously bright.

She pressed a kiss to his cheek and said, 'I'm ready when you are.'

Incredible joy gripped him—there wasn't a hint of the old darkness and pain. Cesar grinned and threw his phone down, and then got busy showing his fiancée just how ready he was.

EPILOGUE

Eighteen months later

'I MEAN...THEY look so innocent, don't they?'

Cesar smiled at Alexio's almost incredulous tone. Rafaele sighed deeply on his other side. They'd been standing and talking and were now watching the three women who were sitting around a picnic table under a huge tree, a few yards away. They were on Cesar's lawn, at the back of the *castillo*, where a new outdoor pool twinkled invitingly through some small trees.

The *castillo* looked the same on the outside but it had been almost completely remodelled on the inside, so that very few vestiges of the past remained apart from the parts that had to be preserved. It was light and airy, with vast spaces, and decorated with a sumptuous yet understated luxury. Lexie had personally supervised the storage of the portraits of Cesar's grandparents in a special airtight room deep in the cellars.

'I know,' Rafaele said now. 'And yet in spite of that innocence they all—'

'Brought us down,' Cesar chipped in, sounding the happiest out of all of them.

Just then the three women's heads drew closer together: one dark, one bright blonde and the other reddish blonde. There came a very distinctive peal of laughter from Samantha Falcone, and then they were all guffawing inelegantly, heads thrown back.

Rafaele shifted uncomfortably. 'Why does that always make me nervous? As if they're talking—

'About us?' Alexio cut in.

'Because they probably are,' Cesar said equably, once again sounding like a Zen Buddha.

His younger half-brothers turned towards him and folded their arms, two versions of his own green eyes narrowed on him.

Alexio remarked dryly, 'I could take a photo of you right now and Tweet it and you'd lose your well-honed mystique in seconds.'

Cesar smiled and said ruefully, 'Be my guest. I think I lost that mystique somewhere around the first nappy-change, when my sense of smell got scarred for life.'

The tiny bundle wriggled against his chest and he looked down at the small downy head of his two-month-old daughter, Lucita, where she was burrowing into a more comfortable position. His hand supported her bottom in the baby sling protectively.

Just then a small toddler in a bright dress broke free of the women at the table and tottered towards the men with a determined expression on her face. A halo of strawberry-blond ringlets framed a heart-stoppingly cherubic face dominated by huge green eyes.

She'd already wrapped everyone within a ten-mile radius around her tiny finger—even Cesar's normally very taciturn housekeeper.

Cesar's chest grew tight as he imagined Lucita at that age. And growing older in a vastly different *castillo* from the one he'd experienced. One filled with light and love.

Alexio bent down and encouraged his daughter Belle the last few yards, until she fell into his arms with a squeal of excitement. Lifting her up, he settled her high against his chest, a distinctly soppy expression on his face as she rested her head between his neck and shoulder, thumb firmly in her mouth.

'How the mighty are fallen indeed,' Rafaele remarked wryly, observing this just as Milo, his almost five-year-old son, streaked by with his armbands on, ready to jump into the pool, followed swiftly by Juan Cortez's similarly aged son—Milo's new best friend.

Belle immediately straightened up to take her thumb from her mouth and pointed a clutching hand at where Milo was, exclaiming urgently in baby gibberish.

But Alexio's attention was fixated on his wife, Sidonie, who had followed her daughter and was sliding an arm around her husband's waist. She wore a long colourful kaftan over a bikini.

Cesar knew that they were sitting on the news that they were expecting again until Sidonie had passed three months. But Sid had already told Lexie, and Lexie had told Cesar, and he was pretty sure that Sam must know too—which meant Rafaele knew, which meant it was an open secret. But of course no one would acknowledge it till they did.

The look between Alexio and Sidonie was definitely carnal and very private.

She smiled as Belle wriggled to be put down. 'You know that now she's seen Milo she won't rest until she can play with him.'

Alexio scowled in Rafaele's direction and Rafaele raised a brow. 'What? It's not *my* fault she's hero-worshipping her cousin. She's displaying remarkably good taste in men already. That's a *good* thing!'

Sidonie just shook her head at the men's ribbing and took Belle's hand when Alexio let her down. She glanced fondly at where her new niece was cuddled against Cesar's chest. 'Lucita's due a feed, and Sam wants to take a nap, so I said I'd watch the kids. I'll take Belle to the pool.'

Alexio immediately declared, 'I'll come too,' and another hot, private look passed between them.

Samantha Falcone was walking towards them now, still graceful despite her seven months pregnant belly, evident under a stretchy dress. When she came near Rafaele drew her close and asked throatily, 'You're taking a nap?'

She looked up at him and nodded, and then said, far too innocently, 'You didn't sleep very well last night, did you? Maybe you should take a nap too?'

Cesar almost laughed out loud at the way Rafaele muttered something unintelligble and all but dragged his pregnant wife into the *castillo*. Rafaele had confided that this time was very poignant for him, because he'd missed Sam's pregnancy with Milo.

Alexio and Sidonie were now wandering off hand in hand, with Belle toddling in front of them, towards the pool.

Cesar looked over to where Lexie sat on the love seat beneath the tree, watching him. She smiled and crooked her finger. As if he needed any encouragement...

When he sat down beside her Lucita was already raising her head and mewling softly, clearly ready for her feed.

Deftly Cesar unhooked the sling and lifted his daughter out, holding her head securely as her huge blue eyes opened wide and she gazed back at him guilelessly. His heart clenched. Was it possible to fall even more deeply in love every time he looked at her? And then she smiled and the question became moot, because he fell fathoms deeper in a nanosecond.

'Look!' Cesar declared proudly, angling her for Lexie's inspection. 'She smiled at me.'

Lexie grinned and took their daughter from his safe

hands, settling her against the breast she'd bared, helping that seeking mouth to find her nipple.

As Lucita latched on, Lexie said wryly, 'I hate to burst your bubble but it's probably just wind.'

Cesar said nothing and when she peeked at him he was just smiling at her, a very private smile. He put his arm around her and said throatily, 'I could watch you nurse Lucita all day.'

Lexie rested her head back against him and smiled. 'Happy?'

Cesar looked down at her and felt his heart swell so much it might explode. Those huge blue eyes sucked him in as they had that very first time.

He shook his head and said quickly, '*Happy* doesn't even come close to how I'm feeling.'

He took Lexie's free hand—the hand on which she wore his rings. He brought it up and pressed his mouth there, over the rings that bound them together for ever.

He found himself admitting something he'd been too ashamed to admit before. 'Do you know…just before Lucita was born I was afraid…afraid that I couldn't possibly love any more than I already loved you?'

Lexie's eyes grew bright.

'But as soon as she was born I realised it's infinite. Love can't be bound to one person.'

'I know,' Lexie whispered. 'I felt it too.'

The pregnancy and birth had been incredibly emotional for them both, but especially poignant for Lexie, considering it had brought back everything she'd been through with her first baby. But Cesar had been with her every step of the way, and more supportive than she might have dared to imagine. With his encouragement she'd even been in touch with the adoption agency to leave word as to where she could be contacted should her son ever feel the desire.

A deep sense of peace and security pervaded her life now. And love.

Lexie huffed a small laugh then, even as emotional tears made her eyes glitter. 'You know, for someone who was deprived of love growing up you're remarkably good at it.'

Cesar smiled back and said, with not a little sadness, 'I can feel sorry for my grandparents now. They were so bitter and caught up in anger.'

Predictably, at the mention of his grandparents, Lexie's eyes flashed with emotion. But before it could rise Cesar pressed a kiss to Lexie's mouth, long and lingering, full of love.

When he drew back the fire of anger had gone out of Lexie's eyes to be replaced by another kind of fire, and she said, almost grumpily, 'That was blatant distraction.'

Lucita's mouth popped free and Lexie handed her back to Cesar while she prepared her other breast for feeding. When their daughter had emitted a gratifyingly robust burp Cesar handed her back. With Lucita settled again, Lexie looked at her husband. 'Are you ready for tomorrow?'

'Tomorrow?' he asked disingenuously, clearly much more interested in his wife and baby. 'Tell me what's happening tomorrow again?'

Lexie smiled. He knew exactly what was happening. Even so, she reminded him. 'Sidonie's aunt is arriving and it's her first time out of France, so we all have to be very mindful of her. Alexio is going to Paris to meet her and bring her here so she won't be nervous. Rafaele's father and his new wife Bridie are coming from Milan. And Juan Cortez and Maria are coming to pick up Miguel—although you know they'll probably end up spending the night because it'd be rude not to ask them to stay for the barbecue...'

'And,' added Cesar dryly, 'because Maria is as thick as thieves with you and Sid and Sam.'

Lexie smiled, but couldn't stem a niggle of anxiety for Cesar. This was their biggest family get-together yet. And it would getting bigger all the time—especially as Sam's new baby would be born soon and added to the mix. And then Sid's.

It had been easier for Lexie, knowing what it was to come from a sizeable family, in spite of their estrangement. And also because she and Sam and Sidonie had formed a solid and genuine friendship almost within the first ten minutes of meeting each other.

She knew that even though Cesar's relationship with his half-brothers had taken a quantum leap ever since that first meeting in Rome, when she'd gone with him to meet them properly for the first time, it was still a novel experience for him to play at happy families having come from the exact opposite experience.

But then, it had been healing for Cesar to hear how Rafaele and Alexio had suffered at the hands of their unhappy mother in their own lives. Happy families didn't come naturally to them either. Once he'd seen they could empathise with him he hadn't felt so alone in his experiences.

Lexie saw the glint of determination in Cesar's eyes and castigated herself for underestimating how he might deal with this. He pressed another lingering kiss to her mouth and then pulled back, saying with a grin that transformed him into someone infinitely younger and even more gorgeous, 'Am I ready? As long as you're with me I'm ready for anything.'

Lexie answered huskily, with her heart in her voice, 'Well, that's easy—because I'm not going anywhere.'

* * * * *

A sneaky peek at next month...

MODERN™

POWER, PASSION AND IRRESISTIBLE TEMPTATION

My wish list for next month's titles...

In stores from 20th June 2014:

☐ Christakis's Rebellious Wife — Lynne Graham

☐ Carrying the Sheikh's Heir — Lynn Raye Harris

☐ Dante's Unexpected Legacy — Catherine George

☐ The Ultimate Playboy — Maya Blake

In stores from 4th July 2014:

☐ At No Man's Command — Melanie Milburne

☐ Bound by the Italian's Contract — Janette Kenny

☐ A Deal with Demakis — Tara Pammi

☐ Wrong Man, Right Kiss — Red Garnier

Available at WHSmith, Tesco, Asda, Eason, Amazon and Apple

Just can't wait?

**Visit us
Online**

You can buy our books online a month before
they hit the shops! **www.millsandboon.co.uk**

0614/01

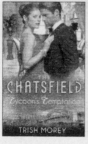

THE
CHATSFIELD®

Enter the intriguing online world of
The Chatsfield and discover secret
stories behind closed doors...

www.thechatsfield.com

Check in online now for your exclusive
welcome pack!

The World of Mills & Boon

There's a Mills & Boon® series that's perfect for you. There are ten different series to choose from and new titles every month, so whether you're looking for glamorous seduction, Regency rakes, homespun heroes or sizzling erotica, we'll give you plenty of inspiration for your next read.

By Request

Back by popular demand!
12 stories every month

Cherish™

Experience the ultimate rush of falling in love.
12 new stories every month

INTRIGUE...

A seductive combination of danger and desire...
7 new stories every month

Desire™

Passionate and dramatic love stories
6 new stories every month

nocturne™

An exhilarating underworld of dark desires
3 new stories every month

For exclusive member offers go to
millsandboon.co.uk/subscribe

Join the Mills & Boon Book Club

Want to read more **Modern**™ books?
We're offering you **2 more** absolutely **FREE!**

We'll also treat you to these fabulous extras:

- 🌹 Exclusive offers and much more!

- 🌹 FREE home delivery

- 🌹 FREE books and gifts with our special rewards scheme

Get your free books now!

visit **www.millsandboon.co.uk/bookclub**
or call Customer Relations on **020 8288 2888**